Martina Reilly, formerly writing as Tina Reilly, is the author of a number of bestselling novels, including the Impac-longlisted *Something Borrowed*. She is also the author of several award-winning teenage books. Martina has worked as a columnist for the *Irish Evening Herald* and does freelance columns for the *Irish Independent*. In her spare time she acts, teaches drama and writes plays.

For more information, please visit www.martinareilly.info

Praise for Martina Reilly

'Like Marian Keyes, Reilly takes a cracking story and adds sharp dialogue and buckets of originality' *Scottish Daily Record*

'Has all the elements of an excellent read: mystery, drama and romance' *Woman*

'A top holiday read' *Closer*

'Martina has the wonderful knack of combining sensitivity for a serious subject with a big dose of humour' *Irish Independent*

'Martina Reilly's characters are so well observed . . . a substantial read' *She*

'Hard to put down, laugh-out-loud funny . . . perfect holiday reading' *Woman's Way*

'Reilly is a star of the future' *Belfast Telegraph*

'[Will] have the most hard-hearted reader wiping tears – and not just of laughter – from their eyes' *Irish Evening Herald*

'Good, solid entertainment' *Irish Examiner*

'Reilly has a wonderful comic touch, both in the way she draws her characters and in her dialogue . . . a brilliant read' *U Magazine*

'Brilliant' *Liffey Champion*

Second Chances

MARTINA REILLY

Formerly writing as Tina Reilly

sphere

SPHERE

First published in Great Britain in 2008 by Sphere

ISBN 978-1-84744-090-7

Typeset in Baskerville MT by
Palimpsest Book Production Limited, Grangemouth, Stirlingshire
Printed and bound in Great Britain by Clays Ltd, St Ives plc

Papers used by Sphere are natural, renewable and recyclable products, made from wood grown in sustainable forests and certified in
accordance with the rules of the Forest Stewardship Council.

Mixed Sources
Product group from well-managed
forests and other controlled sources
www.fsc.org Cert no. SGS-COC-004081
© 1996 Forest Stewardship Council
FSC

Sphere
An imprint of
Little, Brown Book Group
100 Victoria Embankment
London EC4Y 0DY

An Hachette Livre UK Company
www.hachettelivre.co.uk

www.littlebrown.co.uk

For Colm with love.

Acknowledgements

Thanks to everyone who helped with the research for this book – especially to Keith Stafford, the editor of The Racing Pigeon website – www.racingpigeon.ie who provided me with lots of brilliant information and contacts.

Thanks also to Tom Fagan of the Celbridge pigeon racing club whose great ideas provided me with all the information I needed to write this book. Any mistakes in the writing of pigeons are mine.

Thanks to the staff in the Department of Transport who helped me out with some queries I had regarding legal issues. Lorraine McGurk and Helen Conway – thanks.

Thanks to the people at Sphere who have made writing such a pleasure for me. Thanks especially to the wonderful Margaret Daly – her talent and her company are two of the things I enjoy most when signing books.

Thanks to everyone who gave me publicity last time around – it means such a lot. And to the booksellers who are always so welcoming.

Prologue

THERE WAS SILENCE as the jury filed in. It had taken them two days to reach a verdict. Lizzie scanned their faces for some sort of a sign. Two days, she thought, when the case was cut and dried. Though not everyone seemed to think so. It was as if the town had been split in two. Her family and their 'supporters' lined one side of the courtroom, whilst Joe Jones and his lined the other. Joe's supporters included his parents, though his dad hadn't turned out to be the best character witness ever.

Lizzie felt a hand in hers and she squeezed her brother Billy's hand back in response. Billy was a shell of the guy he'd once been. His dancing brown eyes and quick grin had been altered for ever when the battered body of his twin sister had been found washed up on Grange Strand. He'd never drive a fast car again or laugh out loud at something ridiculous, Lizzie thought with a pang.

Her mother, once so fussy and bustling, was a hollowed-out shell of a woman, and her dad was broken. That was the only way Lizzie could describe him. He was so utterly sad. The sadness peeled off him like a fog and wrapped itself around anyone who stood too close. He'd given up fishing and sold his boat, swearing never to go on the sea again.

And her, what had happened to her? Besides the devastation, Lizzie had discovered how much she could hate someone. She stared once again across the courtroom at Joe and she wanted to tear his face off with her bare hands for what he'd done to her sister. He was twenty, the same age as Megan would have been. He'd come to their house once or twice and eaten meals with

1

them. Lizzie, at fourteen, had secretly fancied him: he was gorgeous with his tousled dirty blonde hair and brown outdoor-type face. But Joe had never given her a second glance. She hadn't blamed him; Megan had been a bright halogen light to her somewhat dimmer shine. Lizzie's hair was long, brown and uninteresting, her teeth were encased in steel braces and her pudgy face always had a spot or two. Megan's face had been perfect. Well, before she'd been in the sea for two days. Lizzie swallowed back a lump and Billy, sensing it, tightened his grip on her hand.

'Have the jury reached a decision?' the judge asked.

'We have, your honour.'

The foreman crossed to the judge and handed him a slip of paper. The judge glanced at it before asking the accused to stand.

Joe stood up and stared straight ahead.

Lizzie watched as Joe's impossibly glamorous mother clutched her husband. He wrapped an arm round her shoulders.

'How do you find the accused on the charge of murder in the first degree?' the judge asked the foreman.

'We find him guilty, your honour.'

Immediately there was commotion in the courtroom, with one side cheering and the other shouting out their objections. Joe stood, seemingly shell-shocked, staring at the man who had delivered the verdict.

'No!' Joe's mother cried. 'No—no, Joe wouldn't do that.'

She was pulled back, still crying, by her husband.

Lizzie, her mother, father and Billy clung to each other in relief. They were unable to cheer as Aileen, Megan's best friend, was doing. Tears at the decision coursed down their cheeks.

'Thank God,' her father said. 'Thank God.'

Lizzie watched as Joe, looking devastated, was handcuffed. He was shaking his head in disbelief. All through the trial he'd denied the charge, protesting his innocence every step of the way and making it very difficult for her parents as the murder of their daughter was laid out for them in graphic detail.

But, on the last couple of days of the trial, he'd been caught out on two major lies. Those had been the nails in his coffin.

Lizzie watched as Joe was led away, refusing to look at either of his parents. She hoped he rotted in hell.

Though even if he did, she thought numbly, it wouldn't bring Megs back.

1

Fourteen Years Later

THE MAN HANDED her a carved wooden box. It must once
have been pretty, but was now dusty and half rotten.

'Found that under the floorboards,' he said jovially. 'Lucky I
did or you might have lost it for ever.'

Unaware of how he'd shocked her, he left the house, the smell
of freshly varnished floorboards the only clue that he'd been there
at all.

Under the floor. This box. She had to sit down. She stared at
it for a bit before cautiously opening it. Inside, scattered, were
scraps of paper, old photos, a diary with scrawled writing, hand-
drawn pictures and, right at the bottom, a dried rose petal. A
whole selection of odds and ends.

She paused before touching the diary. Then, her eyes filling
with tears, she removed it from the box and began to read.

2

'SORRY I'M LATE.' Lizzie shoved open the door of the small dingy office and a blast of cold air hit Anna, her co-counsellor, in the face. 'Tom and I went out for coffee and we had a row in front of a whole café of people. Mortifying.'

Anna laughed. 'You and Tom had a row? I thought you never rowed.'

'There's a first time for everything.' Lizzie dumped her tasselled bag on the desk beside her phone and strode over to the electric heater to flick it on. It was freezing in the office.

'Not working,' Anna said glumly as Lizzie shook it. 'So, what's the story with Tom? I can't believe either of you'd fight. You're both so easy-going.'

'Oh, it was only a joke.' Lizzie sat down at her desk and pulled her coat around her to stay warm. 'You know the way he's in a play at the moment?'

'Uh-huh.'

'Well, I went to see him last night and he had one line.' To emphasise her point, Lizzie held one finger up. 'One line.'

Anna grinned.

'He was on stage for about . . . ,' Lizzie shrugged, 'two seconds at most. I mean, I sat through the most boring two hours of my life to see him for two seconds. So when he asked me over a ham sambo if I enjoyed the show, I just joked and asked him if he had found it hard to learn his line.'

'Aw, Lizzie, that was a bit insensitive.'

Lizzie squirmed. She knew that now.

'You are a counsellor,' Anna tapped the phone, 'and you go and say that to the love of your life?'

'I know. But honestly, Anna, one line. I was only teasing him. Anyway, he got all huffed and hurt and said that I obviously thought he was a joke. And I don't, Anna, I really don't.'

'I'm sure he'll forgive you. He's mad about you.'

'He's mad at me, more like,' Lizzie said glumly. 'And I'm starving now because I refused to eat the sandwich he bought me. I told him it'd help his ham acting.'

'You didn't!'

'I did.'

'That was mean.'

'I know.'

'Good line, though.'

Lizzie had to agree. She even thought that Tom had smiled before doing his offended act again. Aw well, she'd ring him in the morning when he'd calmed down.

Opening her drawer she took out her notepad – it was important to log all the calls she received. That way if someone rang more than once, the counsellors knew who they were dealing with. Most second-time callers liked to talk to the same person again. Lizzie had quite a few callers who spoke only to her.

She glanced across the office at the heater that wasn't working. 'I'll put an order through for one next week.'

'Aw well, I don't fancy your chances of screwing a new heater out of Mark,' Anna scoffed, referring to their boss. 'He's completely hyper about the fundraiser at the moment. What's the story with it?'

Lizzie was full time at Life, a free counselling service. Besides volunteering on the phones, she earned her living as a paid fundraiser for the charity.

'Well, the story is that it's ages away and he shouldn't be so hyper. But the big fundraiser this year is a parachute jump. We hope to raise enough to get a house for the charity and do face to face counselling.'

Anna whistled. 'Impressive if you can pull it off.'

Lizzie shrugged. 'Aw, it'll be fine. Just a question of money, really.' She wished she was like Anna and a genius at counselling, but fundraising did seem to be her forte. She could charm money from a dead man, Mark often said. 'Tea?' she asked Anna.

'Coffee, please.'

Anna's phone rang and she almost fell off the chair in her haste to answer it. 'Hello, Anna here at Life. Can I help you?'

Lizzie made the coffee and a tea for herself. She pulled a packet of biscuits from her bag and offered Anna one. Anna waved her away, she was busy taking notes, nodding and 'uh-huhing'. Lizzie could hear someone sobbing at the other end of the line. She hated when they cried. She remembered her first ever caller, who had cried for at least ten minutes before eventually sobbing out a story of how her husband had left her and wasn't paying any support. The woman was terrified that she'd lose her house. Listening to her, Lizzie had felt so powerless that she'd been tempted to send the woman on some cash. Anna had firmly talked her out of it. Becoming personally involved with a caller was strictly forbidden. And as Anna said, there were so many sad stories floating around the country that, if she helped one, where would she draw the line?

Placing her tea on her desk, Lizzie pulled a biscuit from the packet. Munching slowly on it, she wondered where the woman was now and how she was getting on. As far as Lizzie knew, she'd never rung again. It was something she'd found hard to get used to, but some stories didn't ever have an ending. They just vanished. There one day, gone the next. A bit like Megan.

Lizzie shook her head to clear it. Thinking about Megan was something she rarely indulged in nowadays. It still made her angry. And sad. She knew that her reasons for volunteering at Life in the first place were mainly due to Megan. It was her desire to try to finish other people's stories because her own would never have a satisfactory ending, but it didn't work like that. People had to sort themselves out – she couldn't do it for them. And that had been hard to accept. Was still hard to accept, if she were honest.

Instead she studied Anna, dark hair falling across her face. She'd known Anna for the last three years – they did volunteer counselling together on Thursday nights – but she didn't actually *know* Anna. Anna wore a wedding ring yet never talked of her husband; she had a little girl, Chloe, who was seven and she never mentioned Chloe's father at all. Lizzie often wondered if the man were dead, but if he was she felt sure Anna would talk about him. Instead, there was nothing. But then again, she had never told Anna about Megan. People rarely discussed painful things except to strangers, Lizzie had concluded.

They finished their shift at eleven-thirty. After bidding goodbye to Anna, Lizzie lit herself a cigarette and sauntered along a very quiet Grafton Street, enjoying the walk in the cold air and waiting to hear her favourite late night talk show on her MP3.

'Tanite on Dublen Live,' the DJ cut across an advert, his accent pure Dublin, 'we're talking childbirth.'

'I swear,' a caller said, 'the pain of labour was worse den being at some poncy theatre.'

Lizzie grinned, wondering if Tom was listening, though he was probably in the pub now with the cast of his play.

She turned up the volume and, just as she did so, a passing pedestrian caught her attention. Tall, shaved head, reasonably handsome, the man strode alongside her before passing her out. He was so intent on where he was going that he failed to notice her shocked expression as she stared after him.

No, she thought, it couldn't be.

It couldn't be.

Vaguely aware that people were looking at her because she had stopped walking, Lizzie forced herself to continue up the street. The noise of her programme receded as she stared numbly at the man striding in front of her. Still, most people looked the same from the back, she thought, her heart beginning a slow hammer. If she could just get one more glimpse of him . . . She quickened her pace. He was just ahead of her, bundled up in a big green parka jacket and thick brown boots. His hands were

9

shoved deep into his pockets and his head was bent against the cold. God, it looked so like him, but she was never going to catch up, her long legs no match for his longer ones.

Abruptly he paused and gazed into a shop window. A full-on profile and Lizzie gasped aloud, her mind beginning a slow free fall to the last time she'd seen him. In a suit and tie with the same look of horror she was probably wearing now.

She felt suddenly sick at seeing Joe Jones again.

Joe Jones. The name pounded in her head.

Joe Jones. Joe Jones.

He hadn't crossed her mind in a long time. In fact, she'd done everything in her power to forget about him and what he'd done. Even when her family had been informed that he was up for early release, Lizzie had clamped down her hate and her horror. Being distressed would only make her mother worse, and her mother had been close to a nervous breakdown at that time.

Seeing him now, though, made Lizzie realise that she hadn't forgotten about what he'd done at all. That she was still as affected now as she had been all those years ago.

Bastard! she wanted to shout out. *Murderer!*

She began to shake slightly. Tremble.

And then he began to move off again.

Rage and shock made her clench her hands into fists, before she started to walk as fast as she could after him. It wasn't a conscious decision at first. He was, after all, going in the same direction as she was – up Grafton Street. Little by little she started to gain on him, which wasn't surprising as while she was half running he seemed to have slowed down, stopping every now and then to peer into various shop windows. She didn't want to look at him, but she couldn't help it. It was like he was technicolour in a street of sepia. She noticed the slouching easy walk of him, the skin shaved smooth, the tight, close-cropped haircut, the curve of his jaw, the jut of cheekbones and the length of his legs. And she was furious.

When she had come within two feet of him, she spent minutes observing what she could see of his clothes in the semi-darkness.

He was dressed casually in jeans and a parka, and around his neck he wore a big red and orange scarf. She saw him glance at his watch before suddenly increasing his pace.

Shit!

Lizzie couldn't run and draw attention to herself, but she knew that if he continued to walk as quickly as that, she would lose him. The fact that she was wearing a big heavy oversized coat and thick boots didn't make speed walking exactly easy. Damn it, though, she wasn't going to lose sight of him. She often thought later that maybe it would have been better if she had, if he'd just vanished out of her life as suddenly as he'd reappeared. But that wasn't to be because, just as she'd given up hope of catching him, she saw, with mixed feelings, that he was striding towards the Luas tram – the same one she was catching herself. That was a stroke of luck. Now she could follow him wherever he got off and just hop back on another Luas when she was done. What she was hoping to achieve she hadn't got around to thinking about, but for now it would be enough to know where he lived.

She stood apart from him at the station, not daring to spend too much time looking in his direction in case she would attract attention to herself. In case he might recognise her. She didn't think he would. The last time they'd had contact she had been a chubby fourteen-year-old with mousey brown hair and braces. He had barely registered that she existed. Now she was taller, having spurted up suddenly at sixteen the way they did in her family; her hair, chopped short, was dyed a mishmash of various colours; and her braces had done the job and left her with nice straight teeth. Her skin had even cleared up and now she only got the odd spot.

Joe seemed to be concentrating on something and Lizzie saw that he, too, had an MP3 player.

As the Luas pulled up, Lizzie moved to just behind him in the crowd and followed him on to the third carriage. She sat down and watched as he graciously gave up his seat to a pregnant woman.

Huh, bit late to be nice now, she thought, her hands itching to slap his good-looking face.

He stood the rest of the journey, holding on to the strap as the Luas got going. Little by little, station by station, the tram began to fill. Lizzie kept her gaze firmly on him now as his back was to her. They arrived at Ranelagh and Lizzie groaned as he made to get off. Stupidly she'd thought he might get off at her stop. Still, nothing ventured, nothing gained. She decided to take a chance, she could always follow him and catch the next Luas. If there was one.

He was first off as the Luas came to a shuddering halt. Lizzie let a few people go in front before hopping after him on to the platform.

About ten minutes later, she saw him turn into a street full of old two-storey red-bricked houses. Lizzie watched him from the top of the road. He lived here, she was sure of it, he seemed to be taking keys out of his pocket. It was a nice street – quiet, even though Lizzie had the impression that many of the houses were converted into student flats. She watched as he eventually stopped outside an end-of-terrace house, the last in the street. He bounded up the steps to the front door and let himself in. The slam of the door echoed up to her.

Slowly, Lizzie walked towards his house. As she came abreast of it, she glanced up. Red door, slightly shabby, but the building didn't look rented. Lizzie memorised the number and location of the place.

She shivered suddenly, wondering why she'd followed him.

But it had seemed important. Somehow.

3

JOE LET HIMSELF into his hallway and winced at the cold in the house. Damn! He'd either forgotten to turn on the heating or he was out of oil. He kept his jacket on as he made his way into the small kitchen. Examining the heater switches, he groaned. He hadn't forgotten, so that meant he was out of oil. Great!

Flicking on the kettle, he made himself a cuppa and pulled out a few biscuits from the press.

Carrying his supper outside to his small back garden, he stood for a second inhaling the sharp air and listening to the soft sounds of his pigeons in their loft.

'Hiya, guys,' he half sang and the birds, recognising his voice, fluttered and cooed back.

Crossing to the pigeon coup, Joe smiled. God, he loved those birds. He had a full coup, eighty birds in all: breeders, young birds and old birds, which he raced every Saturday during the racing season, weather permitting The first race of the new season was this Saturday, all going well. He was quietly optimistic about his chances this year. These birds had saved his life, he reckoned. If he hadn't had them, he'd never have crawled back from the edge – he needed them far more than they needed him.

He drained his coffee before unlocking the loft. The birds, normally quiet when it was dark, fluttered as he entered. Prince, his favourite, the best racer he'd ever had, perched on his shoulder.

Joe stood for another while, enjoying the affection from his birds and showing them the same in return, before locking up the coup for the night and going back inside. He rinsed his cup under the tap before noticing that his answering machine was

13

blinking. Pressing it on, he groaned as he recognised his neighbour's voice:

'Joseph,' she said crossly. 'Joseph?' Then there was an expectant pause. 'Oh, it's not you, it's your answering machine. So you're really not there?' Another pause. 'OK, right. Well, it's Ellen from next door. Your birds did their business on my blouses again today. I can't get the stain out. I'd like if you'd call over tomorrow sometime. Thank you.'

Well, that wasn't true for starters, Joe thought, as the next message whirred and clicked on. He had let his pigeons out in the afternoon before heading to work that day and Ellen had taken all her washing in before then. He'd call and tell her that in the morning.

'Hi, Joe, it's Noel. Just reminding you that the first race of the season is on Saturday. Have your birds down at the club by six tomorrow. Looking forward to beating you.' Joe grinned.

Message three clicked on:

'Hello, Joseph. It's Dad. You might give—'

How had he found the number? Joe reached out and before he was aware of it he pressed 'delete', his heart hammering. His father hadn't contacted him in years. Or, rather, they hadn't contacted each other. And Joe didn't want to contact him ever again. He stood, staring at the machine that had brought his father's voice back into his life and gulped. Unplugging it, he wrapped the cord around it before dumping it in the bin. Some things hurt too much.

4

IT WAS AFTER twelve when Lizzie walked through the Royal Lawn estate where she lived with her brother and his partner, Aileen. When they'd bought the house, they'd asked Lizzie if she'd rent from them to help with the mortgage. Lizzie had agreed as her flat was costing her a fortune. Still, the estate looked anything but royal, she always thought: royal places didn't have bits of paper and tin cans thrown about the streets.

However, number 34 Royal Lawns had a very well tended garden and was kept clean and cosy, thanks to Aileen who was very house proud.

Lizzie let herself in and grinned when she saw that Billy, her brother, was still up. He was making coffee and asked if she wanted one.

'Yeah, please.'

'You're late,' he remarked as he flicked the kettle on again. 'I was beginning to get worried about you.'

He was always worrying about her, Lizzie thought. Well, they worried about each other. But in the last two years since becoming a home owner, Billy's worrying had got a lot worse. He was stick-thin now and had developed a nervous habit of scratching behind his ear whenever something bothered him.

Lizzie threw her bag across a chair and sat down. 'Is Aileen in bed?'

'Yeah, she's wrecked.' Billy handed Lizzie a coffee and sat down opposite her. 'She always seems to be tired lately. I told her to see a doctor but she says she's fine. All she needs is a good night out, she says.'

They laughed slightly. Aileen, while dying for a house of her own, had found her lack of funds a horrible side effect to having a mortgage.

'So, any mad callers tonight?' Billy asked, changing the subject with a small grin.

'Confidential,' Lizzie grinned back and tapped her nose. 'But nope. It was surprisingly quiet.' She paused, wondering how to broach the subject. She ran her finger around the rim of the coffee cup before venturing, 'But, eh, something a bit mad did happen tonight.'

'Yeah?' Billy looked mildly interested. 'What?'

'I saw a face from the past on the way home.'

'Yeah?'

'Yeah.' Lizzie deliberately got her voice under control before she added, 'Joe Jones.'

Billy's brown eyes widened. He placed his cup carefully on the table and repeated quietly, 'Joe Jones?'

'Uh-huh.' Lizzie nodded. She decided not to tell Billy that she'd followed him. It might sound a bit, well, weird. She could hardly believe she'd done it herself. And Billy would probably kill her. 'He was on the Luas. He got off in Ranelagh.'

'I heard he was in Dublin all right.' Billy whistled softly. 'Jesus. That's a bit of a shocker.'

Lizzie nodded. 'I thought so. He hadn't changed much, you'd know him if you saw him.' Pause. 'Bastard.'

Billy nodded. Now he, too, seemed to be on the verge of saying something.

'What?' Lizzie asked.

'He never admitted it, Lizzie.'

'So?' Her voice rose. 'What does that mean? Even his own dad said that he had argued with—'

'His father didn't have a choice.'

'I can't believe—'

'You can't believe what?' Aileen's six-foot, stripy-pyjama-clad frame swooped into the room, her gaze eager. She plonked into the chair beside Lizzie. 'God, Lizzie, I'm glad you're home. Billy's

16

bad enough when he's only got the mortgage to worry about. You'll set him over the edge altogether.'

Lizzie laughed as Billy made a face at his girlfriend.

'So what's the story? What can't Billy believe?'

'Lizzie saw,' Billy began, then paused, the words seeming to choke on his tongue. 'Well, Lizzie saw Joe Jones tonight.'

Aileen's smile faded. 'Joe?' She thrust her blonde tousled head towards Lizzie's darker one. 'No way!'

'Yep. On the Luas.'

'Did he see you?'

'No. I stayed out of his way.'

'And a good thing, too,' Aileen pronounced. 'Jesus.' She paused before slamming her fist on the table, making Lizzie jump slightly. 'The fecker. I wonder how long he's been up in Dublin.'

Lizzie shrugged.

'You must have got a shock.' She glanced at Lizzie's cup of coffee before saying to Billy, 'Make her something stronger, Bill. Will you have a hot whiskey, Lizzie?'

Lizzie waved her away. 'I'm fine, thanks.' She stood up. 'I'll head up to bed now. I've a busy day tomorrow.'

'You sure?' Aileen peered anxiously at her. 'You're OK?'

'I'm fine, honest,' Lizzie said. 'But I won't be if I don't get some sleep.'

Aileen nodded. 'Me too, I'm completely knackered.'

'We all have work tomorrow.' Billy placed the cups in the dishwasher. 'Let's all get to bed.' He turned back to Lizzie. 'If you see him again, you ring me and I'll collect you, OK?'

'I was hoping you'd say you'd thump him to a pulp.' Lizzie smiled a little.

'I wish I could,' Billy said softly, 'but what good would it do?'

Neither woman answered. Instead, Aileen slipped her hand into Billy's and kissed him softly on the cheek. He smiled a little sadly before nodding, 'Night, Sis.'

'Yeah, night, Bill. Night, Aileen.' Lizzie watched them leave, her thoughts turning back to Joe Jones. How could Billy not want to thump him up? She wished she was a man so she could.

17

But she knew where he lived now. At that, her heart gave a sudden, small skip. Excitement? Fear? She didn't know. But there had to be some way to make things right. No, she corrected herself, not right – things would never be right. But some way to make things even.

There had to be.

5

Friday, 25th June

My dad has found me a job. I can't believe it.
Despite the fact that I never even said I wanted a
job, my dad got me one. I had planned to have
a really cool summer, hanging out on the beach
with Aileen when she visits and going out with Billy
and maybe then looking for something. But oh no,
Dad has to be the one to tell me that he's found me a
job.

And is it a cool job like working in a clothes shop
and getting loads of discount clothes? Nope, it's in
Geoff Jones' newspaper offices. Selling ads.

I couldn't sell bibles to the Vatican, never mind ads
to complete strangers. Joe Jones, who sometimes works
with my dad on his boat, told him they were looking
for someone and my dad suggested me. Apparently Joe
jumped at it.

Dad said it was just a start until I found
something of my own. I know what he's up to, he's
hoping this job will be so rotten that I will get out there
and look for a proper one. Anyway, I'll give it a go
for a little while. Some money will be handy as I plan
on having a great time this last free summer of my
life.

Saturday, 26th June

Dad is determined to ruin my summer. Aside from finding me a job, he brought me, Lizzie and Billy out fishing today. The sea air is terrible for the complexion, I told him, but he laughed and told me to 'go away outta that'.

Billy and Lizzie love fishing and while I deliberately forgot my rod, they brought theirs. Dad was in his element. He loves having the three of us all together, but as I said, why can't he love having the three of us down in the pub together or at the pictures together? Being all together on a smelly old boat is not much fun, I don't think.

'Now,' Dad said, as he put some disgusting worms on the hooks, 'the most important thing is what?' He looked at me.

'The right bait,' I said, rolling my eyes but not able to stop grinning either. It has always been my question. I think he's afraid to ask me anything else in case I get it wrong.

'Exactly,' Dad smiled. 'Good girl.' He cast off. 'Find what they like and they won't be able to resist.'

Billy and Lizzie copied him. Then Dad gave his usual lecture about stillness and patience and silence. 'Easy and gently, no sudden jerks,' he said.

There was silence for ages. I wished I'd brought my *Hello!* with me. Then Lizzie got all red and excited and her line started to pull and Dad was up on his feet, helping her reel the fish in. 'If they don't think they're trapped, it's easy to reel them in,' he said. 'But when they start to struggle, that's the most dangerous part.'

'Dangerous?' Lizzie asked. Though she knew what he meant, she was just humouring him, the way we all do.

'In case he escapes,' Dad said. 'Reel him in rapidly

20

but with no stops and starts. You're committed to catching him now, you can't turn back.'

And ten minutes later an enormous fish was flopping about on the deck, gasping for breath.

The three of them clapped.

I almost got sick – I'd turn vegetarian only I hate vegetables.

6

LIZZIE RANG TOM first thing the next morning as she ate her breakfast. Billy and Aileen always left before she did. She wondered if Tom was up, he was a bit like her and liked to sleep in late. As she dialled his number her mind flitted back to the first time she'd met him.

It was eight months ago and she was out with Anna in the pub. She'd been queuing to buy a drink at the bar.

'Yo!' the barman nodded at her.

'A v—'

'A Bud and a Carlsberg,' a voice shouted from behind.

The barman ran off to serve the customer and Lizzie turned around to face a tall guy wearing a cool orange hat. 'You skipped the queue,' she said crossly.

Brown eyes glittered down at her. 'Queue?' His voice was nonchalant and mocking. But beautifully resonant. 'I don't see a queue.'

'The barman was talking to me.'

'Yeah, and I was talking to the barman.'

'I was here longer than you!'

The guy feigned a yawn.

When the barman arrived back, the Bud and the Carlsberg held aloft, the guy dug his hands into the pocket of a pair of tattered jeans, pulled out a few notes and took the pints. And then Lizzie did something that she'd normally never do. She banged into him and his drinks sloshed everywhere.

'Oh dear,' she said, wide-eyed, 'what have I done.' Then she turned away and called her order out to the waiting barman.

'Hey, you've ruined my shirt,' the guy said from behind.

'I didn't see you,' Lizzie said, 'just like you didn't see the queue.'

'You banged into me on purpose.' He sounded genuinely hurt.

'You skipped the queue on purpose.'

He looked suddenly shamefaced. 'Technically there wasn't a queue as such.'

'Technically I was in front of you. As such.'

'Technicalities, smechnicalities,' he said in a brilliant Woody Allen. A sudden wicked grin floored her. 'Guess you were the wrong girl to cross.'

Lizzie felt herself blush under the high voltage beam.

'Or maybe the right girl. How about I pay for your drinks to say sorry?'

'Yeah, OK,' Lizzie said. She turned back to the barman and shouted, 'Make them doubles!'

His face had fallen slightly. Then he'd recovered. 'OK. No problem.' And he'd bought them the drinks, bankrupting himself in the process and having to borrow three euro from Lizzie.

But they'd been seeing each other ever since.

Tom had turned out to be the best laugh she'd ever known. He was manic and permanently broke, ditching any job he had once he got a sniff of an acting part. Lizzie admired his attitude.

'Hello?' She was so lost remembering that his voice startled her and it took a second to realise that she was on the phone. His voice always made her heart skip a beat. It was pure sexy. Gravelly and distinct. A real actor's voice. This morning, though, it was groggy with sleep.

'Tom. Hi. It's Lizzie, your number one fan.'

She was rewarded with a semi-laugh. 'OK, number one fan, do you hate me so much that you have to wake me up early?' he kidded.

'No, I just want to say sorry about the awful joke I made yesterday.'

'Well,' Tom pretended to think. 'It did dent my ego but, hey, I guess I can see your point. You're not theatre savvy and you

23

wouldn't know that one line in this play is worth about a hundred in any other.'

'Sort of like the dollar and the euro,' Lizzie said.

'Eh, sort of.' He was smiling, she could tell. 'So, what's the plan for today, gorgeous?'

'Dunno yet. I can meet you for lunch.'

'Aw, no can do. I'm going for a casting for another play. How about Sunday?'

'I'm heading home.'

'Aw, pity. Well, I'll see you when you come back. Take care.'

'Yeah.'

'Kiss your parents for me.'

Her parents hadn't really 'got' Tom when they'd met. 'Will do.' She laughed as he hung up.

Two hours later, still yawning, Lizzie unlocked the door to the Life building and climbed up the stairs.

Life had three small rooms taken at the top of the building. The first room was Mark's office – he was the founder of Life and the boss. Forty years old, he was completely driven by the desire to make Life one of the best help centres in the country. The second office was the counselling office, with two phones and a computer. The volunteer in today was Barbara, a fifty-year-old mother of three, who had spare time on her hands and worked each Friday from eight until two.

'Hi, Barbs,' Lizzie called as she made her way past to her own office. She heard Barbara calling out a greeting in response.

Lizzie's office was cold and she shivered. She pulled her coat around her shoulders and began shifting through the post, which had arrived late the afternoon before. There was a lot of junk mail, which was surprising as she'd definitely told the post office that she didn't want this stuff any more. There was a card from a caller thanking them for some advice. Lizzie tacked it to the wall. Ripping open another envelope, she found a bank draft for five hundred euro with just 'Thanks' scrawled across a white page. Lizzie grinned. Mark would be pleased by that.

As if on cue, Mark came barging through the door. Dressed as if he'd just climbed out of bed, he looked impatient and flustered. One day he'd have a heart attack, Lizzie often thought. He never seemed to have the time to brush his hair or shave properly. Today his hair was tousled and stood out all over his head, while his chin sported more than a day's worth of stubble.

'I got a—' Lizzie attempted to show him the draft.

'What's the update on the parachute jump, Lizzie?' he said, interrupting her. 'Any more developments?'

'I'm fine, thanks for asking, Mark. And how are you?'

Mark rolled his eyes and made a dismissive gesture with his hand. 'When you're saving the world, Lizzie, you don't have time for niceties.'

'Oh, I thought saving the world was nice.'

He laughed. 'You give me any more cheek and I'll fire you.'

'Go ahead.' Lizzie grinned cheekily back at him.

'Oh, fuck off.' He crossed towards her and sat on the edge of her desk. 'Right. Jump. What are we up to?'

'I was going to type it out today and give it—'

'I don't have time to read things.'

'Why do I bother?' Lizzie joked, and then, becoming serious, she said, 'Well, we've about a hundred volunteers so far.'

'Good. So how much? Will we raise enough to buy a house at cost?'

Lizzie shrugged. 'Jim O'Brien of O'Brien's builders has promised to meet with me to see what he can do. If not, I'll scour the phone book. There is bound to be a builder out there who is willing to donate a house for the good publicity it'd give him.'

'Builders don't need publicity, they're making a fortune anyway. Greedy fuckers.'

'I wouldn't say that to Jim,' Lizzie said.

'Eh, I know.' Mark rolled his eyes. 'I'm not stupid. So, you think you can pull it off?'

'Who got the celebs to do the TV ad last year?' Lizzie reminded him.

'My genius charmer.' Mark stood up and grinned at her. 'If you pull this off, Lizzie, and we get a house, I'll give you a rise.'

'I'll see how it goes. Now get lost and let me make a few phone calls.'

'Going, boss.' Mark gave her a salute and left.

Lizzie spent the day emailing all her contacts and asking for support. It took ages as she typed up a personalised letter to each one. She also sent out press releases to radio shows looking for some air time. The jump was months and months away but Lizzie liked to concentrate her efforts on one major fundraiser a year. She started canvassing for it a long time in advance.

As she pressed 'send' on the final email of the day, she glanced at the clock. It was only five, an hour before clocking out. She opened up the Google screen on her computer and paused suddenly, her fingers poised over the keyboard. Should she or shouldn't she? It had been at the back of her mind all day. Still, she reasoned, it wasn't as if she was doing anything illegal or dangerous. She could stop when she wanted to. But the truth was, she didn't want to. She wanted to find out about the man who had made her mother half demented with grief, the man who had crushed her father's spark, who had turned Billy into a walking skeleton and had made it unbearable for her to see anyone she'd known from home. She had an urge to find out about the man who had left a hole inside her that nothing could fill. The man who had made her feel such fury last night by just existing.

'To hell with it,' she muttered as she typed 'Joe Jones' into the search engine.

Within seconds a list of eighty-five thousand results came up.

Shit. Joe Jones was obviously a very common name.

Joe Jones, Wexford. Just over one hundred entries. That was manageable. Eagerly she scanned through them, but none seemed to match. The only promising one was an article on a pigeon club site. There was a picture of a pigeon called Prince who had won some major race or other. Its trainer was a Joe Jones from

Ranelagh, originally a Wexford man. She wondered if it was him. And if it was, why on earth had they put a picture of the stupid pigeon instead of Joe on the site? Still, she vaguely recalled something about pigeon racing from years ago. Hadn't his grand-father been heavily involved in it? Lizzie looked at the pigeon for a while, as if the harder she looked the more information she would glean. But all it said was that its trainer was a Joe Jones from Ranelagh.

And then she had an idea.

She rang Billy, just to let him know that she'd be a little late home, and then she left the office.

Thirty minutes later, Lizzie got off the Luas in Ranelagh. What would be the harm in making sure that the Joe Jones she'd seen was the same one whose pigeon she had read about on the internet? And, if it was, maybe she could use it somehow.

It was beginning to drizzle as she made her way towards his house. She stood, a few doors up, and noticed that the house seemed deserted. All the lights were off. Slowly she walked towards it. The street was empty, except for a girl approaching from the opposite direction. They passed each other and, two steps later, Lizzie was going by the house. The curtains were not pulled in the front, she noted. What would be the harm in having a look in the window?

No harm at all.

She was only going to have a look.

Just to see what he had inside.

Trying to compose herself so she looked like a visitor and not some edgy woman spying on a man she barely knew, she climbed the concrete steps to the front door. There was no light at all inside the place so she felt confident ringing the bell, then, if anyone was observing her, they'd think she was a friend. The bell jangled somewhere inside the house and the door remained closed. Good. Lizzie peered inside. Nothing. The frosted glass in the hall door made it hard to see. She crossed to the sitting-room window and pressed her face against the pane. It was hard to judge because of the gloom, but it certainly didn't look like a rented room. It was fairly empty, she could make out a sofa, a TV and a stereo. Wooden floors. A light with no shade hanging from the ceiling. But all in all, fairly neat.

'Hello? Can I help you?'

Lizzie jumped.

'Oh, sorry, I didn't mean to startle you.'

Lizzie turned about, hoping her face wouldn't betray the guilt she felt rushing up through her. A woman was peering at her from the next garden.

'Oh, eh, hi,' she stammered out. 'I was, eh – well, looking for Joe.' It was weird saying his name like that, as if she actually liked the guy.

'He's gone out,' the woman said. She had to be in her seventies, Lizzie guessed. White hair, smiley face and very well dressed. 'He left about an hour ago.'

'Oh.' Lizzie nodded, as if disappointed. 'That's a pity.'

'I'll tell him you called.'

'Oh, there's no need, I'll ring him.'

'No, no,' the woman waved her hand, 'you tell me and I'll pass the message on.' She looked at Lizzie expectantly. 'Now, what's your name?'

'Eh,' Lizzie gulped. 'Just, eh, Mindy.' Mindy? Where had *that* come from?

'Mindy,' the woman nodded. 'And what's it in connection with? Are you a friend? Do you help him with his birds?'

'Birds?' Lizzie's heart leapt.

'Yes, his pigeons.'

'Oh, right. No. No, I don't have anything to do with his birds.' Bingo. She wanted to laugh out loud. It had been so easy.

'I don't blame you, those birds are a nuisance. Oh, I like Joseph, but his birds drive me mad, flapping and circling above the house the way they do. They've ruined about three of my blouses so far.'

'Terrible,' Lizzie nodded, wondering how on earth she could get away without appearing rude.

28

'Yes, it is. Joseph, well, he always pays me what they're worth. But it's not the same, is it?'

Lizzie shook her head. Maybe she could just say—

'At my age, I find it hard to get into the shops so money is no use. Joseph drives me sometimes, when he's free, he's good like that.'

Lizzie said nothing, reluctant to agree.

'But anyway, Mandy, Mindy,' she clicked her tongue, 'what was it again?'

'Mindy,' Lizzie said weakly.

'Mindy, that's right,' the woman nodded. 'I'll tell him you called and it's not about the birds, is it not?'

'No, not about the birds.'

'Right. Because he took a load of them away in a basket a little while ago.'

'Oh. Did he?'

'Yes, he did. And I hope they get lost on their way home. But of course I don't tell Joseph that. He's a little crazy about those birds. Told me this morning that they hadn't ruined my nicest blouse. Insisted that they hadn't been out at all yesterday morning. I believed him because he's a nice boy and he helps me with my shopping, but I won't the next time.'

'You'd do right not to.' The words were out before Lizzie could stop them and the woman's mouth made an 'oh' of surprise.

'Right,' she said after a little pause. 'Well,' she pulled her blue cardigan about her shoulders, 'that's not a kind thing to say about your friend. I've always found Joseph very nice.'

Lizzie gulped but found she couldn't unsay the words. Instead, she indicated the street. 'I, eh, have to go.'

'OK.' The woman was looking at her oddly and Lizzie, cursing herself for being so stupid, half ran down the steps.

'I'll tell him you called,' the woman shouted after her.

It was when she was clear of the house that Lizzie slowed to a walk. How could she have been so stupid? she thought.

But then again, she'd found out that he did have pigeons. And what's more, that he was a member of the Ranelagh pigeon club. It had all been so simple, almost as if she was meant to find out.

There had to be some way to use the information. But first, she would find out everything she could about this man and his life.

Her heart skipped a beat. She didn't know if it was in fear or excitement. They'd always felt pretty much the same to her anyway.

7

THE TRAFFIC WAS mental. Billy's car crawled along and, two hours later, they still hadn't reached Wexford. Lizzie was dying for a cigarette, but she couldn't ask her brother to stop: Billy hated stopping once he was on the road. And besides, he hated her smoking even more. Every time she lit up, Billy gave her a lecture. That was the problem with living with your older brother: he started to think he was a father figure.

Travelling with Billy and Aileen was not something that Lizzie had ever enjoyed – besides Billy's reluctance to stop, there was Aileen's obsession with Wham. Three hours of George Michael and Andrew Ridgeley was not Lizzie's idea of fun. Aileen insisted on singing along to all the songs in a woefully out of tune way.

'My friend had that song at her wedding,' she turned around to tell Lizzie as 'Wake Me Up Before You Go Go' came on. 'She knew the priest really well and she told him that she wanted this song played. Of course the priest didn't know it and my friend just told him it was about a guy who wanted his girlfriend to go everywhere with him. And when the day came she walked up the aisle to that.'

Lizzie giggled at the image.

'What song would you want played as you walked up the aisle, Lizzie?' Aileen asked then, stealing a glance at Billy, who seemed oblivious.

'Queen,' Lizzie grinned, '"I Want To Break Free".'

Aileen shook her head in disbelief. 'You and Billy,' she said mock sternly, 'you haven't a romantic bone in your bodies. Billy, what song would you like to see me walking up the aisle to?'

Billy flinched. 'I dunno. It's not something I think about too much.'

'So think about it now,' Aileen pressed. 'This is not a marriage proposal; I know we can't afford it.' She made beak shapes with her hands. 'Yadda, yadda, yadda.'

Billy sighed deeply. 'Aileen, you'd pick the music, not me, so it'd be up to you.'

'Oh.' Aileen looked impressed. 'Good answer.' She winked at Lizzie. 'OK, what would I like?' There was a few seconds' silence, punctuated only by George Michael saying he didn't want his freedom. 'I think I'd like something classy,' Aileen said slowly. 'Something that's gonna make everyone cry.' She thought some more. '"In a Country Churchyard", I think.'

'"In a Country Churchyard"?' both Billy and Lizzie said together.

'Yeah. That's what I'd like.'

'Maybe I'd better choose some music, too,' Billy said. 'I am not having my wedding full of Wham and Chris de Burgh.'

'Aw, so you're gonna marry me then?' Aileen teased.

'Only if you're lucky.'

Joe sat in his back garden. The day was gloomy but it wasn't raining, and he even imagined there was a hint of warmth in the air. If so, it was good. Prince liked good weather, he tended to fly better with the sun on his back. Noel, Joe's mate from the club, had rung to say that the birds had been released at nine o'clock. It was now ten-thirty and Joe's heart rattled every time he glanced skywards. No matter what flew overhead, he kept jumping up, hoping it was one of his pigeons.

'Are your birds out today?' Ellen McGrath poked her head accusingly over the wall dividing the two back gardens.

'I'm expecting them back any minute now.'

'I need to hang out my washing.'

Joe grinned. He didn't know how one old lady who lived alone could have so much washing.

'D'you know something,' he said, resting his arm on the wall, 'you're the best woman for washing I've ever met. I'd say if you had the power to wash away sins, you'd give Our Lord a run for his money. Would you agree?'

'You blasphemous man!' Ellen giggled in a surprisingly girlish way and flapped an arm at him. 'That'll end you up in hell, so it will.'

'Aw, I'm going there anyway.'

'Not at all.' She smiled at him. 'You're annoying but nice. Your birds will go to hell, though.'

'Thanks.' Joe looked up at the sky again and flinched. Was that one of his pigeons hovering around up there? He gave a long whistle but the bird didn't react. Disappointed, he figured that it was probably just a seagull or something.

'Oh, by the way,' Ellen shifted her washing basket to her other arm, 'you had a visitor last night. A girl. Young. Pretty. A bit cheeky, though. She was peering in your windows.'

'Yeah?' Joe shrugged. 'Maybe it was someone selling something.' Young, pretty girls never visited him.

'No,' Ellen said, sounding definite. 'She knew you because she asked for you. She said she'd call again. What was her name now?' She screwed up her face as she tried to remember. 'It was an unusual one.'

Joe waited, trying to appear polite but all the time scanning the sky for any little movement. He knew his birds should be in soon.

'It began with an M, that I'm sure of.'

'M?' Joe said, gulping.

'Mandy? No.' Mrs McGrath shook her head. 'Not Mandy.'

The last girl Joe had known whose name began with an M had screwed his life up. He didn't want to go there ever again.

'Maybe you'll remember it later,' he said, wishing she'd leave now. 'You go in and I'll give you a shout when the birds are in.'

'Mindy,' she pronounced triumphantly. 'That's what it was! A Mindy called for you yesterday.'

'I don't know a Mindy,' he said, feeling weirdly relieved. 'Maybe she was at the wrong house.'

33

'No, she knew your name.'

And then he saw it: a flash of white breast against the grey of the sky; a lone bird circling. His heart lifted as it always did to see one of his birds arrive home safely. He forgot about Ellen and instead whistled high and shrill. The bird stopped circling and arrowed down towards him. Joe laughed, but then the smile died on his face as Prince perched on the roof of the loft, his head cocked, observing him.

He whistled again. It was important to get him into the trap so he could remove the race ring from his leg and clock his time. Prince didn't budge.

Joe whistled once more and still the bird remained where he was.

'Eh, Ellen,' Joe said as politely as he could, 'would you please go inside? I think my bird is afraid of you. He won't come to me.'

He was losing precious seconds now. Other birds could be flying into their lofts and his bloody bird was hopping about terrified of this old woman with her washing basket.

'Please will you go in?' he asked again, trying not to sound confrontational.

'Oh, I don't know.' Ellen did not sound at all pleased to be ordered inside but, to his relief, Joe saw her moving towards her house. 'Being told to stay indoors because some birds are flying around? I don't know.'

'I'll let you know when they're all in,' he called after her, before whistling at Prince again. The bird obligingly hopped on to the trap and Joe, as gently as he could, removed the ring from Prince's leg and popped it into the clock. Ninety-four minutes, he reckoned. But it could have been faster if Mrs McGrath hadn't been around.

In the next ten minutes, more and more of his birds returned. He never tired of seeing them come home safely. Blurs in the sky that became more definite as they flew back to him. He loved watching them alight in the boxes or on perches and eat the special mix he always gave them after a race. It was what they flew home for. That and their mating partners.

34

After twenty minutes, all but one of his birds had arrived. Joe gave it another ten and then reluctantly concluded that it must have met with an accident on the way back. He hated losing birds but it was something that happened at nearly every race or every toss.

He shut up the loft and went to tell Mrs McGrath that she could now hang out her washing.

They arrived in Rossclare about an hour later. As Billy drove along the coast road, Lizzie rolled down her window a tiny bit. She loved the tangy smell of the sea that hit her whenever she came home. Once upon a time she'd have gone swimming, but nowadays she rarely ventured into the water.

'Close that window!' Aileen half shrieked. 'It's freezing.'

Lizzie did as she was told and stared out into the inky blackness as Billy drove up towards their parents' house. The gates were open and Billy pulled into the driveway. Immediately the front door was opened and their parents came out to meet them. They must have been sitting by the door waiting for them, Lizzie thought in amusement.

'Hello!' Polly Walsh half ran across to the car. 'Welcome!' She enfolded her son in a hug, which he returned. Then, turning to Aileen, she did the same.

'Hiya, Mam,' Lizzie said. 'I'm here, too.'

Her mother laughed. 'Yes, Lizzie, I wasn't forgetting about you.'

'And neither was I!' Her dad pulled gently on her hair. 'Come on in and have some dinner, yez must be starving. I believe the traffic is terrible.'

'Awful,' Billy said, joining the two of them. 'It took over three hours to get down.'

After dinner Aileen and Billy went to call on Johnny, an old mate of Billy's, and Lizzie was left to tell her parents all her news. She didn't mention about seeing Joe Jones – that'd put a right dampener on the weekend, she thought. Instead she sat back and answered their questions about Tom. They always asked about Tom. Lizzie reckoned they kept hoping she'd tell them it was over.

'And is he working at the moment?' her mother asked.

'He has a part in a play,' Lizzie said.

'Oh, really?' Her mother sounded impressed. Since Lizzie had started seeing Tom eight months ago, he'd been in two plays. 'Is it a good part?'

Lizzie swallowed. 'Eh, well, he says that being in this play is a big coup. The director is the business, you know.'

Her mother looked at her, a little impressed. 'And what does Tom do in the play?'

'And he has a few auditions lined up,' Lizzie said quickly. She was terrified that if she lied and said he had a great part, they'd want to come and see him. 'He's very hopeful.'

'Lizzie,' her father shook his head, 'that boy will never have any money. Would you not go and get someone who has prospects? I mean, did he even get you a Christmas present?'

'Of course he did.'

'What was it?'

'A CD and a kite.'

'Mmm, you always wanted a kite, did you?' Her parents exchanged meaningful looks.

'No. But flying a kite is good fun. Have you ever done it?'

'No.' Her mother was indignant. 'What on earth would I be doing flying a kite at my age?'

'Your mother's idea of fun is going out in the rain with a placard,' her dad said dryly.

'I don't do that for fun. That's called protecting the community. We're marching tomorrow actually, Lizzie.'

'Oh, Mam,' Lizzie winced, 'not another one.'

'Yes, another one. You can never have too many protests. And this is an important one, isn't it, Kevin?'

Her husband nodded, though Lizzie could detect a hint of resignation in his eyes.

So, obviously, could her mother.

'There's no need for that sort of a nod,' she snapped. 'It affects this area – you'd think you'd be more supportive.'

'I *have* been supportive,' Kevin said indignantly. 'I've made up your banners, haven't I? And I rang the local papers looking for publicity and asking people to turn up. Now what would you call that?'

Mrs Walsh harrumphed and folded her arms. Turning to Lizzie she explained, 'There is a plan in the offing to revamp the harbour – we don't think there'll be enough room for all the boats if it goes ahead. So we're protesting against it.'

Lizzie sighed. Nothing could happen in her mother's part of Wexford without Mrs Walsh expressing an opinion on it.

'Now, it starts at nine, Lizzie, so I'll expect you to be up.'

'Me?' Lizzie couldn't help looking devastated. 'But—but, it's the weekend now.'

'So put it to good use. It's a fine thing when you can sit and help perfect strangers on the phone all night but you won't help your own mother.'

Lizzie said nothing.

'Now, you'll be up the front with me, helping me carry the banner.'

'And what about Billy?'

'What about him?'

'Well, he's home, too.'

'He's down with Aileen. I can hardly expect him to leave her, can I? And she can't come; she couldn't walk half a mile in those high heels she wears.'

Lizzie made a mental note to invest in some stilettos.

'Now,' her mother continued, 'we're marching from the harbour into the planning offices and staging our speeches there.'

Lizzie stayed quiet and her mother, taking that in the affirmative, stood up and brushed some crumbs from her beige skirt. 'Now, I'm going up to print out some copies of the chant. I'll be down in a while.'

She bustled out of the room and Lizzie gave an exasperated sigh, looking over at her dad.

'She's happy once she's got a project to be concentrating on,' her father said mildly.

Lizzie nodded. She supposed it was better than the terrible grief that had engulfed them all that day fourteen years ago, when Megan had gone out the door and never come back.

'And d'you know what else?' her father said, as he poured himself a glass of wine and offered Lizzie the bottle to fill her own glass. 'She's begun clearing out Meg's old room.'

Lizzie froze with the bottle held in mid-air. 'Really?'

'Yeah, she thought that, I dunno, some grandchild or other might like to sleep there when he or she gets older.' He paused. 'Your mam's looking to the future, which is good.'

Lizzie gulped. It was good, but it was heartbreaking too. 'And what'll she do with Meg's stuff?'

'I don't know. Sort it out, I suppose. Give things away, keep things.' He paused. 'There are a lot of things in that room.' Then, smiling, he added, 'Your sister was a terrible hoarder.'

She was, too. Lizzie remembered how Megan had piles of clothes and would invite Lizzie into her room to do makeovers on her. There were masses of half empty perfume bottles standing sentry along the windowsill. And enough hair products scattered across the floor to rival any hair salon. Lizzie had viewed Megan's room much as Aladdin had his treasure trove. 'I wonder will she let me have a root around when she's got it cleared.'

'I'm sure she will.'

Lizzie sat back in the chair and sipped the wine. It was a nice wine, probably bought in honour of Billy and Aileen's visit. 'Well, I'm glad,' Lizzie said.

'Yes.' Her father nodded. 'So am I.'

There was no way she was going to mention Joe Jones now.

That night, as was usual after a race, the club was heaving. Most of the members were over sixty and had been in pigeon racing from their early boyhood. Joe was the youngest member and someone could always be depended upon to give him a slagging over his lack of girlfriends. Joe never minded, they didn't mean it anyway. Most of them agreed that it was easier to keep pigeons if you didn't have a wife.

He stood in line, waiting for the official to check his times on the clock. No one ever knew the results of a race until the times had been checked against the distances flown. He felt confident that Prince had flown well, though of course it was impossible to be sure. The was a great buzz of conversation going on all around him and, though Joe never really got involved with too many people, he savoured the friendliness of it, the banter without the malice or threats that had underlined so much of his time in recent years.

'Hiya, Joe.' Alan, the chairman of the club, greeted him as he reached the top of the queue. He held out his hand for the clock. Joe watched as he opened it to remove the rings. 'Feeling lucky?'

'I don't believe in luck.' Joe sank his hands into the pockets of his denim jeans and grinned. 'I just believe in good birds.'

'Hey, listen, we all believe in good birds,' Alan answered, laughing. 'But then you get married and you realise there ain't no such thing.'

'So cynical,' Cid, another ancient pigeon fancier, croaked from behind Joe. Looking up into Joe's face he asked, 'How did your birds do?' He rubbed his hands together gleefully. 'I fancy my chances big time tonight.'

'They did OK,' Joe said nonchalantly.

Cid was the kind of guy who always fancied his chances and it wasn't just with his pigeons. Tonight his lanky frame sported a cream linen suit and blue open-necked shirt. His thatch of hair was brushed sideways and lacked any sort of a style. 'You coming for a pint after?' he asked.

'Yep.'

'Joe, hiya!' It was Noel. He was the closest thing Joe had to a friend in the club. He'd been the one to introduce him to everyone and get him started off with his loft. A sort of father figure, he kept dispensing advice to him on caring for his pigeons – and on life in general. He was a great laugh for a sixty-five-year-old.

The three moved away to the back wall to make way for other

people who were just coming in. It was a big club and the race had been well attended.

'How'd your birds do?' Noel asked Joe.

'Aw—'

'Brilliant,' Cid interrupted. 'Aw, I think I'm in for a great season. I have one now that seems to have come into form at just the right time. You should see the eyes of her. Nice and bright.'

Joe exchanged a glance with Noel and both of them suppressed a grin.

'I had one that didn't come back,' Joe said then. 'It's a bit of a blow.'

'Good one?'

'Yeah. I was going to breed from him.'

Noel nodded sympathetically while Cid chortled. 'Can't say I'm sorry one of your better birds didn't make it,' he stated. And, at Noel's look of disbelief, he said defensively, 'Well, less competition for us, isn't it?'

'You are bleedin' unbelievable,' Noel said incredulously. Turning to Joe, he asked, 'Isn't he a right friend to have, saying stuff like that?'

Joe just laughed. Compared to the people he'd met, Cid was harmless. 'Aw, he can say what he wants; his crappy pigeons have never beaten mine yet.'

'There's always a first time.' Cid tapped his nose.

'Not for you there hasn't been,' Joe joked and dodged an elbow from him.

John limped over to join them. Apart from Joe, he was the youngest member. At forty-five, he'd taken to pigeon racing quite late, but he was highly competitive and a quick learner. Joe had gifted him a few pigeons when he was starting up and the two had remained good friends.

'OK, EVERYONE!'

Amid much shushing, the chairman of the club stood up. 'I've got the results here. I'm going to post them up but, as usual, I'll announce the top three. Right: in third place was John Daly's Lucy Lou.'

'Yes!' John's fist punched the air. It was his first top three result. 'Yes! Yes! Yes!' He grabbed Joe by the shoulders and said loudly, 'Third place – can you believe it?'

'Eh, no actually,' Cid said sourly, causing people to laugh.

'In second place was Jim Reilly's Autopilot.'

Jim's celebration was a bit more sedate. Ninety years of age and tottering along on a Zimmer frame didn't exactly allow for wild enthusiasm. He accepted the congratulations with a shaky nod of his head.

'And the winner of the first club race of the season is . . . Joe Jones' Prince!'

Joe grinned modestly as Cid gawked at him in disbelief. 'When are you ever gonna strangle that pigeon and give the rest of us a chance?' he said, causing more laughter, though Joe didn't think he'd meant to. 'I bloody mean it!' he shouted out above the noise.

'I'll strangle him when you realise that you haven't a clue about pigeon racing,' Joe answered back and people around the room clapped and jeered.

'Come on up here, Joe,' the chairman said.

Joe made his way to the front of the room, his head low. While he was delighted to win, being the centre of attention in a crowded room freaked him out. It took all his self control to stay calm as he accepted his prize. Then, as was the norm, he waved the cheque about and said, 'Right lads, the first round is on me.'

Lizzie lay staring at the familiar ceiling of her childhood. She'd turned in early and now couldn't sleep. She pulled the quilt her mother had thrown across the bed up to her chin. The quilt was an old one, depicting characters from a show she used to watch as a kid. She'd been thrilled when her mother had bought it for her, and Megan, six years her senior, had pretended to be jealous of her, begging her for it. And Lizzie, always wanting to impress Megan, had given it to her.

She'd adored her elder sister. She'd spent her early girlhood trying her best to imitate her: if Megan liked a band then Lizzie liked it too; if Megan said something was uncool than

41

Lizzie wouldn't have anything to do with it. But really, looking back, she and Billy were more alike than she and Megan could ever have been. Megs was a show stopper. Her dad had called her his princess. Megan would walk into a room and everyone would look at her. She had charm and glamour in spades. She also caused more trouble than anyone else in the house by being way too big for her boots in many ways. But it was impossible to be angry with Megan for long. For one thing—

Her phone suddenly started to ring, playing a loud dance tune Tom had sent to her. Lizzie hopped out of bed, knowing her mother would go spare. Calls late at night frightened her.

Tom had sent a text: *Nite nite. Sleep tite.*

Lizzie smiled and sent one back.

8

LIZZIE, YAWNING WIDELY, had been dragged from bed by her mother to join in the protest.

The start-off point was filled with about a hundred protesters. They were either fishermen or their wives. Some children also darted about, in and out between people's legs, totally hyper. Martha, her mother's best friend, was busy handing out placards and whistles. Lizzie's dad was distributing bundles of leaflets to a number of people who were, Lizzie supposed, meant to hand them to anyone who passed.

There were people on this protest who would turn up to complain about the colour of paint on a litter bin, Lizzie observed. Her mother was one of them and Martha Dowling was another. Her dad generally got involved, too, but it was only to please his wife. He knew his life wouldn't be worth living if he didn't support her. He was coming towards Lizzie now, a few stray leaflets in his hands. 'All set,' he winked.

'As set as a bowl of warm jelly.'

'Ha, ha.'

Lizzie knew she should just walk away. She was twenty-eight, she didn't have to do what her mother wanted any more. But in fairness, she conceded that this at least was a valid protest. It wasn't as if she was marching for the right of flowers to grow on grass verges or the retention of a horribly dangerous historic building. Though she had marched for that in the past. Nope, this was a bona fide protest.

'Elizabeth, here you are.' Her mother handed her a loudspeaker.

'Mam, I'd rather just use my ordinary voice.'

Her mother frowned. 'You could be more supportive, Lizzie,' she said crossly. 'I'll give this to Martha, she'll appreciate it.'

'Good idea,' Lizzie smiled, trying to charm her back to good form.

Her mother tsked a bit and went in search of her friend. She arrived back a couple of minutes later with Martha, who was looking delighted as she examined the loudspeaker.

'One, two, three, four!' Lizzie jumped as Martha's nasal tones were amplified all around the harbour.

'Who on earth do we deplore?' Lizzie's mother shouted out.

'Daniel O'Donnell!' some wise guy yelled.

Lizzie snorted back a laugh as her mother, putting the loud-speaker to her lips, said, 'If that man can't take it seriously, he can leave. Daniel O'Donnell is a fine singer!' The crowd cheered.

'Now, again!' her mother cried. 'Come on, everyone – who on earth do we deplore?' The crowd answered with the rest of the chant.

Despite her embarrassment at marching along, Lizzie had to admire her mother. Nothing put her off. She was a woman on a mission. She strode determinedly forward, loudspeaker planted firmly to her mouth, shouting at the top of her voice. It seemed she was oblivious to the slagging of some less well-informed members of the public.

'Hiya, granny,' someone said. 'I wouldn't mind docking my boat in you!'

Lizzie bristled. 'I reckon you've only got a dinghy,' she shouted back. The man laughed.

'Elizabeth.' Her mother was shocked. 'Have a bit of dignity. Don't give them the satisfaction.'

'Did you hear what he said?'

'No, I was too busy trying to get my point across. Now come on, lift the chin and lift the voice.' Loudspeaker back up, she shouted, 'One Two Three Four!'

'Isn't she marvellous?' someone said in admiration. 'If she doesn't get the council to refuse the planning permission, no one will.'

Lizzie wasn't quite sure that she'd use the word marvellous. Her mother was marvellous in the way a tank is marvellous at crushing cars beneath it.

The protest was growing louder as they turned on to the main street. The police were there to guide them along and they'd stopped the traffic to let them through. Motorists beeped their horns as they passed and that only made the protesters more determined. The chant grew in volume.

Lizzie snuck a glance at her watch.

'You go on off now,' her dad said, nudging her. 'We're nearly there. Your mother won't mind.'

'Sure?' She tried to sound as if she didn't mind.

'Don't try and sound as if you don't mind,' her father teased.

She didn't ask again.

9

LIZZIE, WITHOUT CONSCIOUSLY thinking about it, found herself at the gateway to Joe Jones' parents' house. Well, she supposed, she had to get to know about him if she was to – what? Her mind faltered slightly. If she was to know him, of course. If she was to . . . She paused. She'd cross that bridge when she got there. The fact that she felt compelled to find out about him at all scared her a little. It was an out of control thing, like the feeling she had for cigarettes. She knew it wasn't doing her any good, but she couldn't let it go.

Joe Jones had been an only child. His dad, Geoff, owned the newspaper in Rossclare where Megan had worked that last summer. Geoff also had his fingers in quite a lot of other pies and was by all accounts a hard man to please. Joe's mother had been a former model, always wearing the latest fashions, and she had regularly featured in the papers at social events. Since Joe had been imprisoned, they had withdrawn from life in Rossclare.

Joe had grown up, she recalled from the time of the trial, as a doted upon, slightly wild child. Lizzie's dad had known Joe, having let him work on his boat a few times. He was, by all accounts, an exceptional fisherman. Her dad used to say that Joe Jones could smell where the fish were.

The bus she'd caught after leaving the protest dropped her off just opposite the gates to Joe's parents' house. Her biggest fear was that Joe would be there, though if he hadn't noticed her at the Luas station, she felt confident that she wouldn't be recognised. It had been fourteen years, after all, and while his face at twenty was burned into her memory, he hadn't changed

– whereas she had. The only recognisable thing about her now were her eyes, which had been her only asset at fourteen. Now, while not exactly *Vogue* cover material, Lizzie reckoned that she was about a million times better looking than the gawky adolescent she'd once been. At sixteen, she had sprouted suddenly, growing almost overnight to her five-foot-eight. The sudden growth spurt had caused her to be as skinny as the rest of her family.

She stood for a second, observing the opened iron gates and the wide curved driveway beyond. At the top of it, somewhere, was the house. She'd seen pictures of it, a massive two-storey affair with a large garden front and back.

Joe Jones had grown up here, she thought, as she put a foot inside the gates. He'd walked this exact same path, played in that garden. He'd driven the cheap car she remembered up that tarmac driveway. Feck it, she thought suddenly, she was going to walk right up to the house. She'd come all this way and there wouldn't be another bus back for ages. She wondered what she'd do when she reached the front door. Maybe she could pretend she was looking for someone, that she had got lost or something. She just had to see, had to know what life was like for these people now. It shocked her to realise that she hoped they were miserable. The feeling crept over her like night-time and she flinched before shaking it from her head. She didn't hope they were *totally* miserable, just not happy in the way they'd once been.

'Just not happy like before,' she whispered, to push the really horrible thoughts away. Her steps fell into rhythm with the words and her heart beat along with it, too. For one weird moment, she saw herself as if from outside: a lanky figure in an over-large coat striding grimly towards a front door. How ridiculous was that? She paused. It *was* ridiculous. She was being mad. What on earth had she been thinking of? She swallowed hard and had just turned to go when she heard, 'Hello, can I help you?'

Lizzie jumped. A man, he had to be Joe's dad, had spotted her from one of the downstairs rooms and had opened the window to shout after her. 'Can I help you?' he repeated. He didn't sound too friendly.

'Eh, I'm not sure,' Lizzie stammered. She felt her face grow hot. 'Is this the – eh – Connor house?'

'No.' The man, very like Joe to look at, shook his head. 'No Connors here.' He paused. 'There is an O'Connor next door, though – would that be who you're looking for?'

Shit! Of all the names in all the world . . . Lizzie attempted to look blank and shrugged. 'I don't think so.'

'Well, you could try them. It's a bit of a walk, though, if you go back down the drive.' He paused and seemed to consider. 'I can let you across our back garden and into their front garden, if you like?' He didn't seem to think she was going to refuse as he said, 'Just a second, I'll meet you at the front door.'

Lizzie waited with a hammering heart for him to open the door. Thoughts of legging it as fast as she could raced through her mind, but it would only look more suspicious. Nope, she had to brazen it out.

'Now, you can come through.' Mr Jones, front door open, beckoned her inside. Lizzie fell into step behind him. Even though her heart was hammering so much she felt sick, she was strangely elated to be able to gawk at the house. And what a house it was. A light-filled, huge hallway dominated by a sweeping staircase and doors everywhere. She was about to comment on the beauty of the house when he asked, 'Are you a relation of the O'Connors?'

'Eh, no.' A light sweat broke out on her forehead. She hadn't bargained on being asked any questions. 'Just a friend. Though I don't think it's O'Connor I'm looking for.'

'Oh.' He gave a shrug. 'So do you want to try, just in case?'

'Who's that, Geoff?' A tall, slim woman appeared at a doorway straight in front of them.

Lizzie stared at her. This was obviously Joe's mother, Leah. Despite her expensive clothes, she didn't look as haughty as Lizzie remembered from her photos. Instead her face bore an inno-cent, almost childlike expression, which only emphasised her still beautiful features.

'Hello,' she said to Lizzie. 'We were expecting you?' She looked at her husband in mild confusion. 'Do we know this girl? She looks . . .' Leah frowned. 'Familiar.'

Lizzie felt her stomach heave.

'No,' Geoff's voice became suddenly softer and he crossed over to his wife. He smiled at her. 'This isn't a visitor for us. This girl is looking for a family called Connor. I thought it might be the O'Connors so I offered to let her out the back way.'

'Hi,' Lizzie said. Oh God, what was she *doing*? Her mother would have a fit. 'Sorry to barge in like this.'

'No trouble.' The woman smiled gently. 'It's a long walk back down the drive. But Geoff, I think the O'Connors are gone to Shirley's for the weekend.' She turned to Lizzie. 'That's their daughter.'

'Niece,' Geoff said, nudging her and grinning. 'Shirley is their niece, Leah.'

'Oh, yes, of course.' Leah tinkled out a laugh. 'Anyway, they've gone there until Monday night.'

'OK,' Lizzie said quickly, sensing an opportunity to escape. 'Well, the Connors I know don't have a daughter or a niece.'

Mr Jones grinned sheepishly. 'I suppose I should have asked you that.'

'He was never the brightest.' Mrs Jones smiled softly at him and he smiled back, looking oddly relieved.

'I'll, eh, go.' Lizzie indicated the front door and took a step backwards. 'Sorry to intrude like that.'

'How did you get here?' Mrs Jones asked.

'Bus,' Lizzie said. 'From, eh, New Ross.'

'Oh, but there won't be one for ages to take you back,' Mrs Jones said. 'And where do your friends live?'

Lizzie shrugged. 'I thought they lived here.' She managed a passable laugh. 'I'll have to ring them when I get back to my house. In, eh, New Ross.' Three lies in such short sentences, she thought. It's official, I'm going mad.

'You can use our phone?'

'I don't know their number offhand,' Lizzie gulped.

'Well, not to worry,' Geoff said, 'I'm going to New Ross in about twenty minutes. I'll drive you back.'

This was a nightmare. It served her right. 'I couldn't expect you to do that.' Her voice sounded like a terrified squeak. She swallowed hard and with effort brought it under control. 'You don't even know me.' Her jumper was sticking to her, she was sweating so much. And how on earth could she get home from New Ross?

'It's no trouble,' Mr Jones said. 'The buses that go by here are so few, you'd be lucky to get one within the hour.' They both looked expectantly at her.

'But you don't know me,' Lizzie spluttered out, unable to think of anything else to say.

'We're not exactly signing over our worldly goods to you,' Geoff Jones said in amusement, 'it's only a lift. And besides my wife is coming, too, if you feel unsafe.'

'Oh no, it's not that,' Lizzie stammered. God, they were nice enough people, though Mr Jones did have a terrible reputation. 'Right,' she continued, 'that's very nice of you, thanks.'

'I've just to make a few phone calls first,' Mr Jones explained, holding up his mobile. 'Back in a while.'

Lizzie squirmed. Jesus. Shit.

'Have a cuppa while you're waiting,' Mrs Jones said. 'Come on in.'

Now they were offering her tea. It served her right. She'd come full of anger and they were being very nice. She guessed it wasn't their fault they'd had a son like Joe.

'OK, thanks,' she said weakly, following the older woman into the most enormous kitchen she had ever seen.

'So, are you from New Ross?' Mrs Jones asked as she filled the kettle, indicating for Lizzie to sit down at a table that would hold about twenty people comfortably.

'New Ross. Yes.' She couldn't meet the woman's eye. She was too nice to lie to. So to avoid any more fibbing, she said hastily, 'You have a lovely house.'

That at least was true. Light poured into the kitchen, despite

50

the grey skies. It made the Italian marble floor tiles sparkle, throwing light up on to the expensive kitchen presses and gleaming stainless steel kitchen equipment. There was a huge utility room just off the kitchen; it looked at least as big as Billy's house.

'Thanks. It's a bit big for the both of us now, though.'

'Oh. Did you once have loads of children or something?' Lizzie was pleased at her casual tone.

'No.' Mrs Jones smiled, a little sadly, Lizzie thought. 'Just the one.'

'Boy or girl?'

'Boy.' Mrs Jones paused. 'All grown up now.'

'And is he still living around?'

Mrs Jones busied herself with the tea as she answered. 'No, no. He's left here. He's in Dublin. He works up there.' She placed a cup and some milk in front of Lizzie. 'There you are now. I'll get you some tea in a minute.'

'Thanks.' Lizzie poured some milk into her cup. 'Where does he work? I'm in Dublin, too, maybe I'd know him.'

Mrs Jones smiled. 'Big place, Dublin,' she said. Then went on, 'Oh, he works, you know, in lots of places.' She screwed up her eyes and looked up at the ceiling, as if trying to remember the name of where he worked. 'Lots of jobs,' she finished. 'Always busy.'

Lizzie shrugged. 'Oh, right.'

'And he races birds,' Mrs Jones went on. 'Stone mad about pigeons, he is.'

'Really?'

'Always was,' Mrs Jones went on. She began to pour the tea. 'Say when.'

'When,' Lizzie said as the tea reached the mid-way mark.

Mrs Jones poured herself a cup and sat opposite Lizzie at the table.

'And do you see him often?' Lizzie asked.

Leah shrugged. 'Oh, you know. Yes. Lots.' She flushed. 'Would you like sugar?'

She was lying. Lizzie decided not to ask any more. There was a silence then. Lizzie didn't quite know what else to say. She sipped her tea and tried to ignore the urge for a smoke.

'And are you originally from here?' Mrs Jones asked.

'Born and bred.'

'Oh. That's nice.'

'Yes. I love Wexford. Though I suppose Dublin is my home now.'

'Are you long up there?'

'A few years.' She talked then a little bit about the Life agency, though she got the impression that Leah Jones wasn't that interested. Well, who would be interested in a perfect stranger's life? she thought. But she kept talking away, just to fill in the silences.

Just before the clock hit the half hour Mr Jones arrived back, jangling his car keys, and asked her if she was ready to leave.

'You really are very good.' Lizzie stood up. 'But honestly, there is no need.' How the hell was she going to get home from New Ross? It was an hour from Rossclare at least.

'Not at all. I've to buy a few things there, so come on.' Then he looked at his wife. 'Come on, Leah, you too.'

'Me? I don't want to go out.'

'Well,' he smiled slightly and wrapped his arm about her shoulder, 'I want you to come out. I've a surprise for you.'

'Oh, well, in that case,' she laughed, as he helped her put on her coat.

'Come on, so,' Mrs Jones laughed to Lizzie. 'This man,' she indicated her husband, 'he hates to be kept waiting.'

They really were a nice couple, Lizzie thought. Not at all like she'd been expecting.

Mr Jones didn't talk much on the way to New Ross. He stared intently out the window, weaving in and out of traffic as rapidly as he could. The way he drove reminded Lizzie of the way Mark drove.

Leah sat in the front, saying very little, quite content to stare out the window and remark every so often on how cold everywhere looked. Geoff Jones answered her tenderly whenever she commented on anything and Lizzie was struck by how kind he seemed.

She wondered how they'd coped when Joe had gone to prison.

Just as the car reached the outskirts of New Ross, Lizzie said, 'You can let me off here, if you don't mind. This is great.'

Geoff indicated and pulled the car in off the road. 'Bye now,' he said.

'Yeah. Bye.' Lizzie climbed out and watched them drive away.

How the hell could she get home now?

She rang her dad on his mobile and, after expressing his surprise that she was in New Ross, he said he'd pick her up in an hour or so, after the protest had ended. Lizzie decided to wander into the town and see if she could find a good bookshop. She knew now what it was she had to do. Her plan was very simple.

It was all about finding the right bait.

10

Monday, 5th July

Well, Dad doesn't know it but he has done me a huge
favour with the job he got me. If he for one minute
suspected just how cool this job is, he'd have me out of
there double quick. Talk about perks!!!! Or pecs!!! Or
whatever you're having yourself . . .

Basically, I decided I might as well make the best of
this job so I dressed up for it. So glad I did now. I wore
my skirt that looks respectable until you cross your
legs. Massive split up the side. And I wore my high
shoes and my gorgeous white blouse that makes the
most of my cleavage. Our family are not blessed with
great busts but this blouse is great.

The first thing that happens is that I meet Geoff
Jones. Geoff owns the paper. He is like the richest man
in Wexford. Or the richest man in Ireland, I don't
know. Anyway, he looks rich. He was wearing a suit
and tie and his face was sort of cross and impatient.
He said hello and buzzed Joe (his son) to come and
collect me. Joe arrives up. Now, Joe is a handsome guy,
Tall, nice bod, cheeky chappie sort of grin. He's a bit
weird though. He likes hanging about with my dad for
starters and on top of that he's big into pigeons. But
as I studied him I thought to myself, yeah, I could
work with him. It must be like when you decide to get
married, you stare at your husband to be and think,

yeah, I could wake up to that face every morning. That's what I felt about Joe. He wasn't exactly horrible to look at.

But anyway, Joe brings me down to the office where me, him and another guy are to work and, without beating about the bush, Joe looked like a grey day on Rossclare Strand compared to the guy who was sitting in the office waiting for us. He was like a four star holiday to Ibiza. OH GOD! Beautiful wouldn't even describe him. Turns out his name is Dessie, he's twenty-three, so not too much older than me. He loves selling ads and he has white straight teeth, a gorgeous northern accent that sounds as if he swallowed a tub of cream, dark hair, fabulous dark eyes you could get totally lost in and smooth skin – though I haven't had the pleasure of running my hands over it. I have died and gone to heaven.

Alleluia!!!!

The job involves selling ad space in a newspaper. We ring up companies and try to get them to buy ads. The two lads could sell contraceptives to a priest. Me? I have sold nothing in three days. Joe said he'd give me some of his ads and I could pretend that I'd sold them. When I protested, he just said that his dad could hardly fire him for poor sales, could he?

I guess he had a point.

Then Dessie laughed and told me to take the ads, that there was no point in losing the best looking member of staff! I rang Aileen and told her this and she agreed that things were progressing nicely. I can't wait for her to meet Dessie when she comes down in August.

I really miss Aileen since her and her dad moved to Dublin on another wild goose chase for her mother (her dad is BONKERS!). Aileen told me she reckons that if her dad finds her mother that he will let her come back. AGAIN! Aileen's mother has left her and her dad twice now and her dad has let her come back both times. Aileen says her dad insists that this time will be her last chance but Aileen doesn't believe him. It's awful in her house, she says, as her dad is so upset. That's why Mam has invited her down for a month in the summer.

Anyway, my poor dad can't understand why I like my new job so much. Poor innocent man.

11

W HEN LIZZIE ARRIVED back from lunch on Monday afternoon she saw Tom lounging against the doorway of the
Life building. He glanced once or twice at his watch before
scanning the street.

Lizzie observed him for a second, wondering not for the first
time how it was that a man with none of the classically good-
looking features could be so damn attractive. Tom was tall, a bit
on the skinny side, his hair and eyes the darkest brown while his
face was vampire-pale. His nose was off centre as, according to
him, he'd fallen out of his pram when a baby and broken it. But
despite this, he had a presence about him that demanded attention; an energy he radiated which lit up those around him; an
intensity in his face and movements. The clothes he wore were
always a little quirky, too, and Lizzie loved that. People tended
to stare after Tom in the street for no obvious reason. They were
staring now as they passed. Staring at his faded brown cords and
purple and yellow trainers.

'Tom!' Lizzie called out eventually.

'Hey!' He strode towards her, grinning broadly. 'Well, so much
for surprising you.'

'What?'

'I turn up here at lunchtime all set to treat you to a five-euro
sambo and where are you?' He cocked an eyebrow. 'Gone.'

'Aw, sorry, I left early.' She gave him a gentle shove. 'You should
have rung.'

'Eh,' he joked, as if she was thick, 'then it wouldn't have been
a surprise, would it?'

Lizzie laughed. 'No, I guess not. So,' she asked, linking her hand in his, 'how'd your weekend go?'

'Good. Missed you.' He tweaked her cheek. 'Yours?'

'Same. And your line? Oops, sorry, play?'

'My line was fabulous, thanks for asking.' He paused and admitted almost shyly, 'I also got a second call back for the other play I went for. Main part.'

'No!'

'Uh-huh.'

'That is brill.' She hugged him and inhaled the gorgeous scent of his aftershave. 'Oh, I'm so proud of you.'

'Well, I have to get it first.' He took Lizzie's hands in his and looked at her, his eyes suddenly becoming serious. 'And I just want to say I'm sorry about last Thursday night. I totally overreacted.'

'It's OK. I was only—'

'Lizzie,' he interrupted, holding his hand up, 'just let me say this, OK?'

He sounded as if he meant business. 'OK,' she said cautiously.

Tom took a deep breath and said determinedly, 'I'm going out with you 'cause I like you. I mean . . .' He paused and, his voice faltering a little, said haltingly, 'I *really* like you.' He stressed the 'really'.

'I know. And I like you.'

'And I know that at the moment I can't bring you to fancy places, but one day I will, you'll see.'

'I don't care about that.' She was appalled that he would think it would matter to her. 'That doesn't matter.'

'It does to me.' He said it firmly, his black eyes holding her gaze and turning her on something rotten. 'You deserve much more than a sandwich in a greasy spoon, I know that, I'm not stupid. And I know that's why your folks hate me, but I swear, if acting doesn't work out, I'll give it up and get a real job.'

'You will not!' Lizzie said. 'I like greasy spoons, I like going to see you in plays. I like pointing you out to my mates and saying, that's my guy up there. I don't care what my parents think.'

'I do.'

His honesty floored her. She swallowed. 'Well, you shouldn't. If I'm happy, they're happy too.'

He tilted up her chin. 'One line is a start, Lizzie. Next time, I'll have more.'

God she loved it when he sounded all passionate and intense. 'I know. And you were great with one line.'

'Thanks.' He smiled bashfully at her. Touched his forehead off hers. 'Was I the best?'

It was a joke they had. It was her job to think up witty responses. 'Were you the best? Is there a massive big hole in the ozone that'll kill us all one day?'

He laughed. 'Eh, not one of your better ones, Liz.'

'Were you the best? Was Thin Lizzy the best band of all time?'

'So I wasn't the best?'

'Oh feck off, there's no pleasing some people.'

She punched him, he caught her hand and, pulling her to him, he kissed her.

'Well, it's a fine thing when I'm looking for my staff and they're out snogging their other halves in the middle of the street,' Mark joked as she walked by him to her desk.

'It's a fine thing when your boss is a peeping Tom,' Lizzie said back. 'I could report you, you know.'

'Yeah, right.' Mark rolled his eyes. 'So how is the famous actor?'

'Not famous enough, but he will be,' Lizzie said cheerily. Mark, like her parents, didn't treat her relationship with Tom as anything other than a fling.

'Yeah, but what will he be famous for?' Mark quirked his eyebrows. 'His ability to be an actor without actually getting any parts?'

'This is my boyfriend,' Lizzie said firmly. 'You are my boss.'

'I am.' Mark nodded contritely. 'Apologies. Sue me if it makes you feel better.'

'What do you want?' She wondered if any other bosses treated their staff the way Mark treated her. She guessed it was because they'd known one another a long time, since the beginning of

Life, so she supposed their exchanges were more frank than other people's working relationships. And while she liked Mark, he did his best to drive her mad sometimes. Still, she was well able for him. He joked that he employed her for her attitude. 'Well?' she demanded.

Mark regarded her for a second with amused eyes. 'OK, I'll stop teasing.' He stood up. 'I only wanted to see if there was any word from O'Brien's builders on the house?'

'I only sent out the email last week. I'll call them first thing next Monday. OK? Happy?'

'I'd be a lot happier if we had a house to buy,' Mark said. 'Still, it's early days I suppose.'

'Very early days.'

'I'd be happy with something concrete to go on,' he said.

'That's what your wife said when she flung you out the window, was it?' Lizzie giggled.

Mark snorted and said, 'My acrimonious relationship with my ex is not your business.'

'My relationship with my boyfriend is not yours,' Lizzie said sweetly back.

'Point taken,' he winked.

12

THE PHONE RANG. Lizzie took a deep breath and picked it up. 'Hello. This is Lizzie at Life. How can I help you?' She forced herself to sound alert, though it had been a very tiring night with non-stop calls since about seven.

Anna, whose phone had temporarily stopped ringing, was taking advantage of the lull to pull on her coat.

'Go,' Lizzie mouthed silently.

Anna made an 'are you sure?' gesture and Lizzie nodded.

'Hello?' she said again into the phone as the door closed gently behind her co-counsellor.

'Hi,' a shaky voice said back. 'I—I, well, I don't know who else to call.'

'That's fine,' Lizzie said gently. 'You take your time. How about just telling me your name for now.'

'My, my real name?' The woman at the other end sounded fearful.

'No, it doesn't have to be. But I'd like to call you something.'

'Sinéad,' the woman said. 'I always liked that name.'

'OK, Sinéad,' Lizzie said as softly as she could, hoping she sounded encouraging. 'Can you tell me what's wrong?'

The woman took a deep breath. 'Well, I don't know if anything is wrong, really,' she said hesitantly. 'I just rang you to find out.'

Lizzie remained silent. It was amazing how many people said that.

'I'm married two years, see,' the woman continued, 'and, well, things seem to have changed.' Her voice shook. 'At least I think they have. Or maybe they haven't. I don't know any more.'

'What kind of things?' Lizzie asked.

'All kinds of things.' Sinéad paused. 'Us. The way he is. Everything.'

The way he is. Lizzie bit her lip. 'Just take your time,' she advised. 'Explain it to me.' What the woman wouldn't realise is that she would be explaining it to herself, too.

'OK.' Another shaky intake of breath. 'Well, when we got married it seemed normal, you know.'

'Your marriage?'

'Yes. We were happy. He made me laugh. He bought me things.'

'Sounds good.'

'Oh, it was.' There was a long pause and Lizzie wondered if Sinéad had hung up but then she went on, sporadically halting after every couple of words as if she couldn't quite catch her breath: 'But now, well, I get on his nerves. I don't know how. I don't mean to. I never know any more what will annoy him. And I'd just like to know.'

'You'd like to know if it's normal to get on someone's nerves?' From experience, Lizzie knew where this was leading and she winced in anticipation at what she might hear.

'Yes.' The woman paused, then stammered out, 'No. I'd just like to know *how* I get on his nerves.'

'What kinds of things annoy him?' Lizzie asked.

'Oh . . .' Sinéad seemed to think. 'Well, yesterday I met a friend of mine, just for half an hour, and he got really upset about it. He said that this friend didn't like him and that I was betraying him by meeting her.'

'And were you?'

'No. Of course not.' Then, 'I mean, my friend doesn't like him but she never says it. We never talk about him. And anyway, I told him that his mother doesn't like me and it doesn't stop him from meeting her.'

Good for you, Lizzie wanted to say, but she couldn't. 'OK,' she said instead, 'and what was his reaction to that?'

'Well, that's why I decided to ring,' Sinéad sniffed. 'Just to see if it's normal.'

'See if what's normal?'

'Well . . .' Sinéad gulped audibly and Lizzie got the impression that she was just about holding it together.

'Take your time,' Lizzie said, 'I'm going nowhere.' Though if she didn't get out in ten minutes she was going to miss the Luas and probably Joe, too.

'He, eh, well, he hit me,' Sinéad blurted out. Then, 'Not hard or anything. Just as if he was sort of exasperated. Not a big hit.'

'He hit you,' Lizzie repeated, as if to emphasise the main words in the sentence. She tried to say it in a non-judgemental way, though she felt like killing the bastard. 'OK. So he hit you but it wasn't hard.'

'That's right.' Sinéad sounded hopeful. 'Not hard at all.'

'Do *you* think that's normal?'

'I don't know,' Sinéad said. 'That's why I rang.'

'Has he ever hit you before?'

Sinéad paused. 'No, and he swore he wouldn't ever again. I mean he begged me not to leave. He got down on his knees and apologised and even said I could meet my friend, even though it hurt him a lot. Like, he must be hurt a lot for him to hit me.'

'Do you hit him when he visits his mother?'

Sinéad laughed a little uneasily. 'Well, no.'

'Why?' Lizzie paused. 'I mean, if it's normal.'

'I just wouldn't.' She paused. Stopped. 'Oh.' Another pause. Then she said, half angrily, 'You think he's wrong, don't you?'

'I didn't say that.' Lizzie strove for a neutral tone. 'I'd just like you to think about why you don't—'

The line went dead.

Lizzie replaced the receiver. 'Damn.' Closing her eyes, she massaged them with the palms of her hands. Sinéad, like others before her, had rung hoping to be told it was normal. That's all she'd wanted. But Lizzie couldn't tell her that and Lizzie knew deep down Sinéad didn't really believe it either.

God, she hoped this woman would ring again. She hated to think of all those people out there who were in trouble.

'That bad, ey?' One of the night counsellors startled her as she came in.

Lizzie opened her eyes and smiled. 'It's been a busy night, all right.' She indicated the book. 'I've a call to write up, but I'll do it tomorrow. I'll just scribble Sinéad in to remind myself.'

Five minutes later she was out on the street, her eyes searching for Joe in the straggly crowd. As before he passed her out, his head bent against the chill April air. He strode along as if he hadn't a care in the world. Well, Lizzie thought, soon he'd have a lot of worries – an awful lot. She would make sure of that.

She shivered slightly and couldn't decide if it was in antici-pation or fear of what she was going to do. Was it fair? some part of her wondered. After all he'd served his time, but what was a couple of years in jail compared to being dead? She grit her teeth and remembered how he'd admitted that, yes, he had been the last one to see Megan alive. But instead of saying that he'd been responsible for her death, he had made up some stupid theory that had fallen apart in court. Lizzie remembered his face when things had started to go wrong for him and it was that which had kept her sane until now. Maybe it wouldn't have hurt so acutely if he'd admitted what he'd done, but he hadn't. If he'd apologised or said sorry, but he hadn't. Lizzie blinked back angry tears and put all her concentration into gripping her bag firmly in her hand and walking after him as fast as she dared. If he didn't hurry, they'd both miss the Luas. She thought how funny it was that no one on the street knew that the guy passing them out was a convicted criminal. She wondered what they would do if they knew. Would his neighbours try to get him out of his house? Would that sweet, nosy neighbour still believe that he was a 'good lad'? Would she ignore him? Would she care? Lizzie wondered what secrets the people walking towards her were carrying and if she would care.

The late-night Luas was just pulling up as they arrived. Joe hopped into a half empty carriage and Lizzie hopped in after him, her heart beginning to pound.

* * *

Joe thought it odd that the girl with the oversized bag chose to sit beside him. After all there were a lot of free seats on the tram, but she had plonked herself right beside him, hitting off him in fact and causing him to bang his head against the window.

'Oh, sorry,' the girl said, not sounding that sorry in Joe's opinion, 'I do apologise.'

Something about the tilt of her head made him catch his breath. A tug of something at the edge of his brain, which dissolved as she bestowed on him another apologetic grin. She was cute in a dishevelled sort of way. He liked the way her hair was lots of different colours. It looked cool and sort of funky.

'No worries.' He rubbed his temple. 'I'll send on the medical bill.'

She gave a light laugh, showing him a glimpse of her even white teeth. He smiled back and turned away again. Women as pretty as this one made him uncomfortable.

'I hate the window seat,' she went on in a breathless sort of voice, 'I get sick.'

'Right.' He nodded without looking.

The tram began to move slowly out of the station and the girl beside him started to fidget, her elbow banging off his body in quite an annoying way. Joe attempted to move away but, as he was crammed up against the window, there was nowhere to go. He glanced sideways to see what she was up to. She seemed to be wrestling a rather large book out of a bag. The book looked way too big for the bag and she was pulling at it as if she were trying to wrestle a fish caught in a net. In the end, with a massive wrench, the book came free and fell with a bang on to the floor. People jumped.

The girl looked mortified. 'Sorry,' she called out to the carriage in general.

Joe watched in semi-amusement as she pulled the book on to her lap. To his surprise, it was a pigeon book. A completely crap one, but a book about birds all the same.

'It's probably too heavy a book to be bringing about with me,' she said conversationally to him, for some reason, 'but it just looked so interesting, I had to have it.' She flicked a hand through her mad-coloured hair.

'It's actually not a great book, if you don't mind me saying.' Joe surprised himself by replying but he couldn't help it. It was a combination of the attractive girl and the subject matter. 'It's . . . you know.' He waved his hand about and felt a blush creep over his face as he said shyly, 'Too technical, really. You want to know about birds, you have to work with them.'

'Oh.' She looked surprised. 'Right.' A pause. 'Do you keep pigeons?'

He considered being evasive. The last thing he wanted to talk about was himself, but she looked so interested. And what would be the harm? If it was another guy, he'd have no problem talking. 'Yeah,' he nodded. Then, sensing that more was expected of him he added, 'I started off years ago, my granddad used to keep them, but I've only got back into it in the last few years. I've about eighty birds now.'

'Wow. Cool.'

He smiled shyly, 'You?'

The girl shook her head. 'No. I'd love to but I'm living with my brother and he'd hate it.'

'Why?'

'He's just not into birds. He thinks they're dirty and smelly.'

'Rubbish.'

'Yeah, that's what I say, but it's his place.' The girl paused. 'I'd love to be involved someway without having to keep them myself.' She sighed and passed her palm over the open page of the book. 'This is the nearest I can get.'

Joe felt sorry for her. He knew what it was like not to be able to pursue the hobby. 'You could join a club,' he suggested.

'A club?'

'Yeah.' Joe nodded, warming to the topic. 'That way you could maybe help someone out with their birds or help out on race nights. Every club always needs a hand.'

'Really?'

'For sure.'

The girl paused. 'Are you in a club then?'

'Ranelagh racing club.'

'Would they be interested in me joining, just to help?'

Joe half grinned as he thought of all the members and not a woman among them. He thought of this striking girl walking in on top of them on a Friday night. 'Absolutely,' he nodded. 'Though you could change your mind.'

'No, I wouldn't. I'd do anything just to be near the whole scene.'

'Would Ranelagh be near you?'

'I live in Dundrum, so I could catch the Luas.' The girl paused. 'Would you give me directions?'

'Sure.'

Lizzie watched as Joe drew a map on the cover of her book, his shaved head bent in concentration. She felt sick being so close to him and yet sort of elated, too. Her plan had gone so much better than she'd anticipated, but obviously asking about his birds was the way to this guy's heart. From his closed up demeanour when she'd sat beside him to the animated look on his face now, she knew that if she played her cards right she'd be home and dry. He hadn't changed much since she'd last seen him, she thought. His hair was shaved and his face was more mature, more chiselled. But she'd spent so much of her thirteenth and fourteenth years hoping to catch a glimpse of him with her dad that she'd know him anywhere.

'We meet again tomorrow,' he said, disturbing her thoughts as he handed her back her pen. 'Seven o'clock. I'll introduce you, if you like.'

She widened her eyes in appreciation. 'Would you? Oh, thanks.' Biting her lip, she added, 'You have no idea how much this means to me.'

To her surprise, his eyes darkened a little as he said solemnly, 'Yeah, I do. I was like you once.'

He'd never been like her. Never, Lizzie thought. 'It was such a weird coincidence sitting beside you tonight,' she said as brightly as she could.

'Aw, fate is a weird thing,' Joe said, smiling broadly. Then the smile faltered a little as he stood up abruptly. 'Sorry, my stop. See you tomorrow if you decide to come.'

'Oh,' Lizzie waved her pen about, 'I'll be there.'

'By the way,' he held out his hand, 'I'm Joe.'

Her skin crawled as she took his hand in hers. His grip was firm, his hand warm. 'Lizzie,' she stammered.

'Bye, Lizzie,' he smiled again. 'See you tomorrow.'

That night Lizzie dreamed that someone was coming after her. She knew they had a coat or bag or something to cover her with. Once they covered her, they were going to take her away.

She woke up at five and couldn't go back to sleep.

13

T OM'S PHONE WENT straight to voicemail. She had deliberately rung him when she knew he'd be at the theatre.

'Hi Tom, it's Lizzie. I might be late meeting you after the play
tonight. Don't wait for me, I might be held up. If so talk tomorrow
morning. Break a leg. Lots of hugs.' She blew a big smoochy kiss
down the receiver, feeling a tiny bit guilty to be standing him up,
but she'd make it up to him next time.

Flicking her phone off, she tucked it into her bag and left to
catch the Luas to Ranelagh.

'Hi, pigeon girl.' A horn blared beside her. Lizzie looked up from
Joe's map, which she had been following, to see Joe in a battered
red car, leaning out the window. His good-looking face grinned
broadly at her. 'Want a lift the rest of the way?'

'Eh, yeah, thanks.' Lizzie tried to conceal the quiver in her voice.
This was it. This was her big chance and she couldn't blow it.
Joe leaned over and unlocked the passenger door for her. 'Just
give it a huge pull and it should loosen up,' he advised.

Lizzie yanked the door hard and it came away from the frame
with a squealing of metal.

'Hasn't been used in a while,' Joe said, looking suddenly shy
as she sat in beside him, her long legs almost folded under her
in the confined space.

The back seat was down and a number of covered wicker
baskets, containing what she assumed must be pigeons, were
aligned behind her. 'Are they your birds?' she asked, suddenly
interested to see them despite herself.

'Uh-huh.' Joe was concentrating on getting the car back into the flow of traffic. 'They'll be racing tomorrow from Wexford. I bring them down on a Friday to be entered for the race.'

'OK.'

'Eh, look under your seat there,' Joe said. 'If you can bend down.'

Lizzie swallowed hard. Was she completely mad, getting into a car with a convicted murderer? 'Why?' She winced at the fright in her voice.

Joe shot her a quick glance. 'I, eh, well, I found an old book of mine, thought you might like it. It's under the seat.'

'Oh, right.' Lizzie bent down and retrieved an old battered book, a picture of a pigeon on the front. *Pigeon Racing*, it was called. 'Oh,' she gulped, 'thanks.' She didn't know what else to say. If it were anyone other than Joe, she would have been incredibly touched at the thoughtfulness, but all she wanted to do was wallop him with it. 'That's so good of you.'

He flushed. 'Yeah, well, that book you had yesterday, it's not great. It's all technical, there's nothing about, you know, giving the birds affection and stuff. That book,' he nodded in its direction, 'has it all. It was one of my first books.'

Lizzie feigned interest and flicked through some pages. There were pictures of breeders, all old and wrinkled and wearing really odd clothes.

'It's a really old book – the photos are dated, but the stuff in it is sound.'

'Are you sure you trust me with this?' Lizzie asked.

'It's only a book,' Joe said, grinning. 'And anyway, if I don't get it back I'll hunt you down on the Luas.'

'You'll get it back, I promise.' Lizzie tucked it away in her bag. 'God, I can't wait to read it.'

'There's a very good chapter on training the birds,' Joe said, sounding animated. 'You'll love it.'

'I bet I will.'

A silence fell between them.

'Do you work in town?' Lizzie asked eventually, hoping the

70

question would sound natural after what they'd just been talking about. 'Are you on the Luas every night?'

'Just on my late nights,' Joe answered. 'I'm assistant manager at Fortunes Gym on D'Olier Street. I'm also a swim instructor there. You?'

'I'm in charge of fundraising at Life. I also counsel.'

'Life?'

'You haven't heard of Life?'

'I heard it's something you have to survive,' Joe joked.

Lizzie flinched. Not everyone survives, she felt like snapping at him. 'It's like the Samaritans,' she said, making a huge effort to sound pleasant. 'We help people, or at least we hope we do.'

He looked impressed. Lizzie wondered if she should push the 'I am a good person' angle. 'It's great – but sad at times, too.'

'I'll bet it is,' he nodded. A pause. 'I'd never be able to do it, that's for sure.'

'It's not for everyone.'

'Yeah,' he said, 'I suppose not. Fair play to you. It's a good thing to do.'

In the ensuing silence, Lizzie studied him out of the corner of her eye. Here was a man who looked so perfectly relaxed, so perfectly at home behind the wheel of his battered car. He drove along, his weird greeny hazel eyes scanning the road ahead, the tiniest of smiles on his lips. He smelled of soap and air and fresh clothes. She wanted to banish that complacent look from his handsome face, so she asked casually, 'You're not from Dublin, are you? You sound like a Wexford man.'

It worked. His grin died and he winced. 'Wow,' he said, sounding taken aback but trying not to, 'good guess.'

'That's because I'm from there, too – you still have the twang.' Lizzie smiled disarmingly. Time to cheer him up. 'So, what part?'

'Rossclare,' he said, and she caught the wariness in his voice. 'You?'

She was tempted to say Rossclare, too, and get him worried

71

in case she might know who he was, but instead she lied: 'New Ross. Do you miss it?'

'Nope.' His answer was final. He gazed with a fierce concentration out the windscreen. It was obvious he wasn't used to talking about his home place.

'Me neither,' she said. 'Dublin is great, isn't it? Do you go out much?'

'Naw.' He shook his head. The smile crept back on to his face. 'The pigeons need a lot of looking after. I have a neighbour, a lovely woman, but for some reason my birds keep shitting all over her clothes.'

It was his bewildered tone that made her laugh, despite herself.

'No shit,' Joe said, then grinned even more. 'Or like maybe lots of shit.'

She laughed again, not able to help it. But perhaps that was a good thing.

He indicated and pulled into a small car park, which was already filling up. Men with baskets identical to Joe's were carrying them carefully into a small red-bricked building. 'So, here we are. You tag along with me if you want and I'll introduce you to everyone.'

'OK. Thanks.' She smiled at him.

'And you can keep that book until you're finished with it. Any questions, just ask.'

'Yeah, great.'

'Come on, so.' He climbed out of his car and slammed the door. Going around, he popped open the boot and pulled the baskets from it. 'You can carry one, if you like.'

'Can I?' She tried to make it sound as if she thought it was a big deal.

'It's not a big deal,' Joe said, sounding amused. 'It's only a basket.'

'Sure, of course.' Lizzie pulled the basket from the back and followed Joe into the building, where they joined a queue.

Lizzie was a bit taken aback to see that the age profile of the members of Ranelagh pigeon club was triple her own. They were old, like her parents. And everyone seemed to be sneaking glances at her. And it was all men. Everywhere. Not a woman in sight. Her unmarried Aunty Betty would love it here.

'Are there no women here?' she asked Joe.

'Nope.' He turned to her and smiled a little. 'And they're all dying to ask who you are only they haven't the nerve.' He winked. 'I'm just waiting to see how long it takes.'

Jesus, Lizzie winced. This was worse than she could have imagined.

'See that skinny guy there with the suit?' Joe said under his breath. 'That's Cid. He'll be the first to crack.'

Lizzie said nothing. Cid looked a little creepy. A weird little grasshopper of a man. The queue shuffled along. At the top a man seemed to be calling out 'Red hen' or 'Blue cock' or words like that. The interest in Lizzie seemed to intensify but Joe didn't introduce her, instead he kept looking forward and ignoring the stares. He was enjoying this, Lizzie realised.

'Hey, Joe.' The skinny little man called Cid scurried over to them, just as Joe had predicted. He was wearing a bright suit that only emphasised his wasted frame. 'Are you going to introduce us to the lady or not?' His eyes roved up and down Lizzie in appreciation.

'Oh, yeah,' Joe said as if it had just occurred to him. 'This is Lizzie, everyone. She'd like to join the club.'

A murmur of approval seemed to sweep through the room.

'No!' Cid gawked at her in surprise. 'Wow!' He nodded to the basket she was holding. 'Are they your birds?'

'No, his,' Lizzie said, indicating Joe.

'Don't you have pigeons?'

'Not yet, but someday I will. I haven't the space at the moment. I'm hoping to learn too.'

'Is he going to show you his loft?' He looked at Joe.

'I dunno,' Lizzie answered as she saw Joe flush.

'You going to show her your set-up, Joe?' Cid asked.

'I dunno,' Joe shrugged and shifted his basket from one hand to the other. 'If she wants. Or she could go somewhere else. It's up to her.'

'Well, if he won't,' Cid said as he stuck out his hand, 'I certainly will. My lofts are the best you'll get. I'm Cid with a C and I'm pleased to meet you.'

'Likewise,' Lizzie smiled.

'Are you going out with Joe?' someone shouted from the back of the queue.

'No, she is not,' Joe said, rolling his eyes. 'I met her on the Luas and we got talking.'

'He has no girlfriend, you know,' the same guy said. 'And you'd be ideal. We're all looking for a woman who doesn't mind her husband loving other birds.'

'Aw lads, will yez feck off,' Joe muttered to a splutter of laughter. 'They're juvenile,' he said to Lizzie. 'Don't mind them.'

'So what is it you want to do, Miss?' An old man on a walking frame was peering at her now. He had bright blue eyes in a faded face. 'Help out, is it?'

Lizzie gulped. She hadn't really decided, preferring a wait and see approach.

'Anything,' she said. 'I'd just like to be involved in some way or other.'

'Well, you leave Joe with his birds and go up to the chairman and ask him what you can do.'

'I was going to introduce her,' Joe said. 'Will yez gimme a chance?'

The old man shook his head. 'You boys have no idea about manners these days,' he said in slight exasperation. 'Letting the girl stand there feeling awkward. Come with me.' He gallantly offered his arm. 'I'll do the honours.'

His offer was met with good-natured cheers and whistles and Lizzie smiled. 'I'd be delighted for you to do that,' she said.

'You'd want to watch him,' Cid said. 'There's a lot more to that walking frame than meets the eye.'

'Have you no respect?' the old man said back sternly. 'Come on, Miss.'

Lizzie took his arm and, feeling as if she were trapped in a bizarre world, allowed him to lead her to the top of the queue.

Ten minutes later she was ensconced behind a desk, writing down details of all the birds entered for the race. Her hand was aching but she found to her surprise that, despite the boring work, the lads were great fun. In fact, she was having so much craic with them that she failed to notice Joe had left.

'Shit,' she muttered at the end of the night. She should have known that he'd go once his pigeons had registered. Now she was stuck writing reams of numbers while the purpose of her visit had vanished.

'Now,' Alan, the chairman, said to her as the last fancier left, 'thanks a lot, Lizzie.' He started to fold the pages of entries away. 'I hope we'll be seeing you in future.'

'Oh, you will for sure,' Lizzie nodded. 'When do you meet next?'

'Tomorrow night for the results.'

Lizzie's heart sank. Tomorrow was out.

'But every Friday and Saturday usually. It's been great to meet you Lizzie and, eh, just a word.' He paused and Lizzie looked at him. 'If you are going to learn from any one, let it be Joe.' He tapped his nose. 'They're all great here, they'll all help out, but Joe is the real deal. Stick with him and you won't go wrong.'

'I'll try,' Lizzie smiled.

'Now, he's a quiet lad but he's helpful. You stick with him.'

'OK.' Lizzie smiled her thanks, her heart pinging. She'd be doing that all right. 'Thanks. See you next week.'

'Bye now.' Alan smiled at her.

Later, in her room, she pulled Joe's book from her bag. Opening it she saw an inscription, written in gorgeous flowing handwriting, the kind they didn't teach any more: *To Joe, my best little grandson. All my love, Granddad Jones.* Beside it, in a big childish scrawl was: *Property of Joe Jones. Aged 10. Wexford. Ireland. Europe. The World.*

Lizzie stared at the writing, a lump in her throat. One so proud, the other so innocent. It wasn't too late to stop, she thought suddenly. She could just vanish from Joe's life as suddenly as he had appeared in hers.

But, then again, he wasn't ten any more. His granddad was long gone. Life had changed them all. Her family had been ruined and all because of him. No, Joe was right. Fate. That's what it was. As she remembered his laughing face from earlier, she grit her teeth and clenched her hand around a page of the book, almost ripping it. How could he laugh when he'd ruined so many lives? How could he move on and grow old while Megan would remain forever young? How could he eat and sleep and love and live while it would never happen again for Megs? How could he laugh?

Well, Lizzie thought, glaring at the book, her eyes filling with tears, he wouldn't be laughing for much longer.

14

Monday, 12th July

I sold my first big ad today. I can't believe it. I rang up a company from the phone book. Jefferson's, they were called. When the girl answered, I asked to speak to their marketing person. (I'm getting better at sounding confident.) Anyway, the upshot of it was that they are to take out a full-page ad in the paper for six weeks – that's six full-page ads!!! They asked for a reduced rate in return for supplying us with a free gift for every edition of the newspaper.

A FREE GIFT!!

Dessie was really impressed. Him and Joe even gave me a clap. I felt as proud as if I'd just performed open heart surgery.

Thursday, 15th July

The free gift is four thousand packs of tampons.

They arrived today and I swear I nearly got sick. Dessie and Joe nearly got sick laughing. The boxes are everywhere. In the office, in the hallway, in the toilets. Imagine sitting in a small cramped space with two blokes and about four hundred tampons. It's just not funny.

'I somehow don't think we'll be needing a free gift,' Dessie laughed to Joe. I said nothing, just tried to ignore them.

Then Geoff arrives down to the office. 'This paper,' he says, 'does not give out free samples of—' and he couldn't say the word.

'Of what, Dad?' Joe asked innocently and Dessie snorted with laughter.

I tried to hide behind my computer screen.

'Ladies' things,' he spluttered.

Then he says, 'There better be a good explanation.' And he glares at the lads.

They started to laugh again. It was OK for them.

I was about to open my mouth to explain when Joe says, 'Sorry, Dad, my fault. I thought they sold, eh, tam . . . bourines,' he finished weakly.

'Feck off.' Dessie was coiled up laughing.

'Tambourines,' his dad said. 'Are you kidding me?'

I couldn't let Joe take the blame, even though it made sense. His dad couldn't get rid of him. 'It wasn't his fault,' I said. 'It was my fault. I did it. Joe had nothing to do with it.' And then I started to cry. I don't know what was more embarrassing, crying or seeing all those tampons scattered about the place.

'Oh for Jaysus' sake,' Geoff said then. 'Will you stop it?'

Dessie handed me a tissue from a box on his desk.

'I never asked what the free gift was,' I hiccupped.

'Anyone could have made that mistake,' Joe offered feebly. Dessie agreed.

Geoff looked disbelievingly at them. 'Anyone could have ordered thousands of free gifts like that?' he scoffed. 'Really?'

'I'm sorry,' I sniffed. 'I suppose I'm fired.'

'You should be,' Geoff said, 'but you're honest at least.' Then he shot a look at Joe. 'And you,' he said, 'don't take the blame like that again. I need to know how good my workforce is. One more chance,' he said to me. 'But you ring up Jefferson's and you tell them to

78

take their gifts back and you tell them we'll run the ads for free.' With that he turned on his heel and stalked out of the office.

I had just lost the company over eight grand.

15

THE DOORBELL RANG. Lizzie took the stairs two at a time, hopping lightly from one step to the next.

'I'll get it, it's for me!' She opened the door and Tom stood, dripping wet in the porch, holding what was once an impressive bunch of flowers. Lizzie took a look at him and started to laugh.

'Eh – hello?' he grimaced. 'Getting wet here?'

'Oops, sorry.' She cocked her head to the side. 'It's just being wet suits your personality.'

'Bitch!' Tom strode into the hall and hit her playfully with the flowers. Petals flew everywhere. 'They were meant to be for you,' he said as he studied them. 'They cost me a fortune.'

'Prices in the garage gone up then, have they?' Lizzie grinned as she took them off him.

'I got them in a shop, actually.'

'Aw, they're lovely.' She smiled at him. And they would have been, too, if they hadn't been heavily rained on before being decapitated. 'What's the occasion?'

'You.' He pointed at her. 'And me.'

'Aww.' She thumbed to the kitchen and lowered her voice. 'I can't even put them in water just yet. Aileen is giving Billy a big romantic surprise dinner in there.'

'I'll be able to do that soon.' Tom shoved his hands into the pockets of his jeans and grinned. 'Who only went and got cast in the hottest new play to hit the Dublin scene in years?'

'*No.*'

'Uh-huh.' He nodded self-deprecatingly.

'Brilliant!' Lizzie attempted to hug him with the flowers in her hand but it wasn't entirely successful, more blossoms detaching themselves and falling to the floor.

They both laughed a little. 'You want to put them somewhere where they won't die,' Tom advised. He followed her into the TV room, adding, 'The director of this play is massive. If I impress him he'll cast me again, you know what I mean.'

'So you have the main part?' Lizzie found a vase at the back of a press and pulled it out. She began arranging the flowers as Tom sat watching her.

'Not the main part,' Tom shrugged, 'it's another part. About a hundred lines this time.' He smiled at her. 'So you'll even be able to blink and not miss me.'

'So I could fall asleep and maybe still catch you?'

'Technically, yeah.' He hunkered down behind her and wrapped his arms about her waist before dropping a kiss on the top of her head. Sighing contentedly, he added, 'This could be it, Lizzie, my big break. I could actually start making a few bob now.'

'Fantastic. So, what do we do to celebrate?'

Tom grinned. 'What we always do. Have a pint.'

They ended up in the local pub. Both of them were soaked through.

'I'm wrecked,' Tom said, splayed across the seat. He pulled a ragged twenty from his jeans and handed it to her. 'Go and get me a pint, would you?'

'Not able for all that rain,' Lizzie teased him.

He laughed. 'My mammy would kill me,' he nodded. 'No hood. No coat.' Tom's mother doted on him, as Lizzie had found out when she had met her briefly.

Lizzie took his money and ordered two pints. Carrying them back to the table, she noted he did actually look very tired.

'Are you OK?' she asked as she put his drink in front of him. 'You're not about to have a heart attack on me or anything?'

He opened an eye. 'Would it bother you if I did?'

'Eh, yeah,' she said as if he were stupid, 'your pint would go to waste.'

81

'Ha, ha.' He took a deep swallow of it and sighed. 'I'm grand. It's just going straight from one play into another, it's never happened to me before. I think I'm in shock.'

Lizzie grinned. 'Take more than that to shock you.'

'I wouldn't bet on it.'

'What's the biggest shock you've ever had?'

'Oh, I dunno,' Tom said airily, looking upwards. 'A girl in a pub trying to knock my drink out of my hands 'cause I skipped her imaginary queue.'

She laughed and thumped him affectionately. 'Seriously?'

He didn't answer.

'Can't think of anything?'

'I'm trying to choose,' he said back. 'It was either my first bungee jump or my first parachute jump.'

'A bungee jump?' Lizzie gaped at him. 'You did a bungee jump?'

'Yep. Me and Domo did it.' Domo was his best friend. 'It's a real head rush. I've done a few of them now. But the first one is the scariest.'

'Wow.' Lizzie was impressed. 'I don't think I'd ever do that.'

Tom gawked at her. 'You are organising a parachute jump. That's just as scary, I reckon.'

'Eh, note the use of the word "organising",' Lizzie grinned. 'No way am I doing it myself.'

'You don't know what you're missing. Seeing the ground rushing towards you, it's a blast.'

'I'd have my eyes closed.'

'What would be the point? You're jumping anyway, might as well enjoy the view.'

'I like the view right now,' Lizzie grinned cheekily as Tom's eyes twinkled back at her.

'Am I the nicest view you've ever had?' he asked.

'Is chocolate ice cream with nuts and whipped cream the nicest dessert ever?'

'Is it the chocolate ice cream they serve in Rocco's?' That was their favourite restaurant.

'Yep.'

'Ta.' He kissed the tip of her nose and pulled her tighter towards him.

Lizzie snuggled in beside him, her clothes beginning to steam in the heat. 'You are perfectly mad, d'you know that?'

'Yeah, mad about you,' he said back, his dark eyes appraising her.

'Aww. Cheesy.'

Tom absently began to play with a strand of her hair. Finally he smoothed it down and said, 'I'll be rehearsing a lot for this play and then we'll be performing and touring, so I won't get to see too much of you, d'you mind?'

'Nope,' she grinned. 'I'll come and see you every night.'

'That'd be expensive.'

'Well, I don't intend on paying. Naturally you'll get me complimentary tickets.'

'Cheapskate.'

'Absolutely.'

They smiled at each other and it suddenly dawned on Lizzie how happy she felt. Completely content. Just sitting here, sipping a pint with this guy she'd known for the last eight months, was as good as she reckoned it could get. She didn't feel the need to impress him or entertain him or anything. Maybe it was because he didn't try to impress her either. He had very little cash, a crappy bedsit and no car. He also had a weird way of looking at the world, which charmed her. It was so easy being with him.

'I'm gonna miss you,' he said after a bit. 'But I'll ring you when I can and we'll go out as much as I'm free, will that be OK?'

'Yep.' Lizzie drank some more. 'So, when do rehearsals start?'

'Next week. You'll have to come to the flat and help me learn my lines.'

'Will do.'

There was a slight pause before Tom said, with an attempt at sounding casual, 'You can stay over if you like.'

Lizzie's heart pinged. Tom had never asked her to stay over

and she hadn't pushed it, fearing the rejection. 'Why now?' She tried not to grin too much.

''Cause I know I'm going to make it now,' he said seriously. 'Before this, I wasn't sure and I didn't want you not having stuff from me that maybe some other guy could give you. So I thought I'd play it casual, to let you escape if you wanted.' He laughed, a little embarrassed.

'That is the nicest thing anyone has ever said to me.' Lizzie snuggled into him.

'You sad person.' Tom shook his head.

'So when would you like me to call over?' Lizzie asked.

'Oh, now, I'd better play it hard-to-get.' Tom screwed up his face. 'How about, I dunno, tonight?'

'What are we sitting here for?' Lizzie pulled him to his feet and, laughing, they left the pub.

The rain had stopped. They walked back to Billy's, arms about each other, so that she could pick up some clean clothes for work.

'Hi,' Lizzie called as she pushed open the front door. 'It's only me and Tom. We're heading back out again.'

'In here,' Billy called back.

Lizzie raced upstairs, grabbed her clothes and toothbrush and ran back down. Poking her head into the kitchen she was about to call out a cheery 'goodbye,' but something about the way Billy was sitting alone at the kitchen table, a cold cup of coffee in front of him, stopped her.

'Hey,' she said softly, going in to him. 'Are you OK?'

'Aileen is eight weeks pregnant, Lizzie,' he said flatly.

'Pregnant? No way!' Lizzie shrieked delightedly, making Billy jump. 'Wow! When did you find this out?'

'About two hours ago. She told me over dessert.'

'And where is she now?'

'Gone to tell her dad the great news.'

There was something about the way he said 'great' that made Lizzie flinch. She cast a glance at Tom, who was standing in the hallway. Billy followed her gaze and suddenly noticed her packed bag.

'Hey, hi, Tom,' he said, attempting to sit straighter. 'How's things?'

'Congratulations,' Tom said.

'Huh?' Billy looked at him then nodded. 'Oh yeah, right, yeah, thanks.' He turned to Lizzie. 'Right, well, you'd better be off, so.'

Lizzie shot a look at Tom. 'Eh, see you, Tom,' she said weakly.

Tom cracked a grin. 'Right. Talk again. OK?'

Lizzie's heart sank as Tom turned to go, but there was no way she could leave Billy alone like this. Something must have happened to make him look . . . the only word she could think of was devastated. She ran out after Tom and kissed him briefly. 'Sorry about this,' she whispered.

'No worries. You look after him, ey?'

'Will do.'

She watched glumly as Tom strode up the driveway and round the corner. God, even the set of his shoulders and the length of his stride was a turn on. Still, there'd be more nights, her first priority was Billy.

'So,' she said as she went back in to him, 'spill.'

'I thought you were heading out,' he said.

'Naw. Much prefer to be with my weirdo brother who's going to be a daddy.' She punched his arm playfully. Then, when his only response was a glum shrug of the shoulders, she asked uncertainly, 'It is great news, isn't it?'

Billy said nothing.

'Is it not yours?' she asked then.

Billy laughed unexpectedly. 'Jesus, Lizzie!' he spluttered incredulously. 'Of course it's mine!' He rolled his eyes. 'Thanks.'

'No, I meant—' She pulled back and studied him. 'Well, you don't sound happy about it, that's all.'

Billy's grin died and he sank his head in his hands. 'Oh God, I dunno,' he sighed, before admitting dejectedly, 'I don't know how I'm meant to feel. For one thing, we really can't afford it, Lizzie. We're only scraping by as it is.' He bit his lip. 'Jesus, what a mess.'

'Billy,' Lizzie said firmly, not able to believe he'd just said that, 'Aileen is pregnant with your child and you're acting like this.' She tried to read his face but his eyes were downcast. 'I hope you didn't say that to her.'

He met her gaze. 'I'm not stupid. No, I pretended to be delighted, didn't I?'

Lizzie heaved a sigh of relief. 'Good.'

'She was afraid to tell me, you know.'

'Because of the money issue?'

'Suppose,' he shrugged.

'She would have had to tell you eventually.'

'Yeah.' He didn't sound convinced. 'Still, it explains why she's tired all the time. I was beginning to worry about her.'

'Did you give her a hug and say you were thrilled when she told you?' Lizzie asked.

'Yes!' He sounded defensive. A pause before he added, 'I don't know how convincing I was. I was sort of in shock.'

Lizzie glared at him. 'You don't know how convincing you were?' she snapped. 'Convincing? You're having a little baby, for God's sake! Why would you have to be convincing?'

'Because . . . Because . . .' He shook his head. 'Jesus!' Then, 'It'll be expensive. Everyone says babies are expensive.'

'You will afford it.' Lizzie touched his arm. 'People just do, Bill,' she went on gently. 'For one thing you won't have to pay a babysitter. I'll be here.'

He smiled briefly. 'Thanks.'

'I mean it,' she said. She gave his arm a squeeze. 'You worry too much, that's your problem.' He said nothing. 'Have you told Mam and Dad yet?'

'No.' He shook his head. 'Apparently the first twelve weeks are the risky ones, anything can happen so . . .'

Lizzie barely let him finish. 'But Aileen's telling her dad. Come on, Bill.' Lizzie dashed into the hall.

Billy followed, smiling a little at her excitement. He was glad she was so thrilled, it would boost Aileen up no end. Maybe he should just do as Lizzie advised and wait and see how things panned out, though he really didn't know how to be happy about it. 'OK, you dial then.'

'Me?' Lizzie grinned. 'Really?'

'Really.'

Billy watched his sister dial, her slim finger jabbing buttons with a feverish excitement. He watched her face light up as the phone was answered at the other end. 'Dad, hi? How's things? Is Mammy there?' Lizzie's face dropped. '*What?*'

'What?' Billy asked, his heart turning over in fright.

Lizzie put her hand over the receiver. 'Mam is on an overnight protest.'

'What?'

'What is she doing, Dad? Is she out in that rain?' Lizzie listened then relayed the news to Billy: 'Her and Martha and a few other hard liners are staging an all-night vigil for the harbour. The cops are going to be there, too. Dad says he has to go off now to bring them soup.'

Billy laughed loudly as Lizzie glared at him. 'It's not funny, Bill.' She turned back to the phone. 'No, Dad,' she placated, 'it's not funny . . . you're joking? Wow.' Back to Billy. 'Apparently she's staging it every night from now on. And in a while they're going to chain themselves to the walls permanently.' Lizzie listened patiently as her father continued on with his story and, finally, she said, 'Well, if you need anything, ring here, OK?' He said he'd need a new heart with all the stress, before grumpily asking her why she was ringing.

'Well,' Lizzie tried and failed to keep the delight from her voice, 'we've a bit of news ourselves, Dad. I'll let Bill tell you.'

To her amusement, Billy blushed as he took the phone. 'Hiya, Dad. Yeah, that's mad about Mam . . . No, I'm sure she'll be fine, I'm sure it's not a breakdown. You know Mam.' His face broke into a grin and in a voice that struggled to keep laughter at bay he said, 'No, Dad, I can't see anyone attacking her, she'll be fine. Hasn't she Martha to protect her, ey? And aren't you going down with soup, too?' He paused and shoved his fist into his mouth to stop laughing. 'Eh, my news?' he went on, the smile sliding from his face. 'Well, I suppose it's mine and Aileen's news. She's, eh, well, she's going to have a . . . a baby.' It was hard to say it. Saying it made it real. Pause. 'Well, thanks, Dad. And yes, we're fine for money, we'll manage, I'm sure . . . November, apparently, but she's to get a scan done to make sure . . . Yes, we have enough money. Honestly.' Billy rolled his eyes.

Lizzie half smiled. Her dad was worse than Billy when it came to worrying about money.

'No, Aileen isn't here . . . Yes, Dad,' Billy went on patiently, 'she is happy, she's only gone out to tell her own dad . . . Why didn't I go with her? I dunno, I just didn't think . . . Yes, Dad, I suppose I am happy about it. Can you tell Mam? . . . OK. Good. I'm sure tomato soup is grand . . . Well, just shove it in the saucepan and heat it up and bung it into a flask. I dunno how long for, it'll say on the packet.'

Lizzie started to giggle.

Billy flapped his hand at her to go away in case he'd laugh. 'Bye, Dad. Yeah. Bye.' He clicked down the receiver and turned to Lizzie.

'Poor Dad having to make soup,' Lizzie said, trying to sound sympathetic.

'Poor Mam having to drink it,' Billy chortled. 'He'll probably single-handedly kill off the whole protest himself.'

It was good to see him laughing, Lizzie thought, as it dawned on her that Billy hadn't laughed in months.

16

IT WAS TEN when the phone rang. Joe had just finished checking on his pigeons and bedding them down for the night. Wondering who could be ringing him at that hour he bounded into the kitchen, thinking that it might be one of the lads from the club.

Ellen's number was flashing and Joe hesitated. The last thing he needed was to be shelling out more money for that woman's clothes. Half of the time, he reckoned, he didn't even owe it to her, but he tried to avoid rows with the neighbours if at all possible. Damn it anyhow, he figured as he picked up the receiver, there was no way he was paying her anything this time.

'Hello.' He hoped his voice sounded suitably cold.

'Joe,' Ellen whispered, 'is that you?'

'Eh, yeah.' He paused. 'Is something wrong?'

'I think there's someone downstairs,' she whispered. 'I'm in bed and I can hear something in the kitchen.'

'D'you want me to check for you?' Joe asked.

'Yes, please.' The woman took a shaky breath. 'I didn't call the police because they'd take ages to come so I'll ring them now.'

'Yeah, do that. And don't worry.'

'I'll try not to.'

Joe barely let her finish her sentence. He raced out the door and into his back yard. Taking the dividing wall at a leap, he found himself in Ellen's beautifully manicured garden. It was so long since he'd actually seen a patch of ground so lovingly tended that it stopped him in his tracks. His mother had always been into flowers and plants. Joe swallowed hard, before remembering why he was there.

He crept slowly towards the kitchen window, keeping to the shadows. The kitchen was in darkness. He wasn't quite sure what he should do. Should he hammer on the door and frighten whoever was in there, and hope they made a dash out the front way? But what if they ran upstairs? Would it be better to be quiet and surprise whoever it was?

And then he heard it. The unmistakable sound of someone opening a drawer. And what was worse, they were making no attempt to be discreet. Joe decided that the only thing he could do was to make a run at the back door and break his way in.

Creeping as silently as he could towards it, he saw the door was slightly ajar. A pane of glass, carefully removed, lay against the back step. Joe, not really having a clue what he was at, crept silently into the kitchen. A figure, back to him, was rifling through a kitchen drawer. Joe, careful not to make a sound, leaned toward the countertop and picked up a place mat. Taking a deep breath, he flung it through the kitchen door, where it clattered on to the wooden floor of the hallway. The burglar looked up in a panic and turned to flee out the back. In a flash Joe was on him. He landed a punch to the boy's face and blood spurted out his nose and down his chin.

'Ow!' the lad said, clutching his nose. 'I'll have you for assault!'

'In your dreams,' Joe said. He grabbed the boy's free arm and twisted it up behind his back. 'What the hell do you think you're doing, ey?'

'Nothing.'

'Nothing? You broke in here, you took glass out of the back door, you made a mess of the kitchen. And you're doing nothing?'

'You can't prove it was me.' The boy, who was small and thin with a starved-looking freckly face glared at him. 'I can say it was you.'

'No, you won't,' Ellen, wrapped in a big towelling dressing gown, said from the door. 'You won't say it was Joe. I'll confirm that it was you.'

At those words the boy's face fell. 'I was only looking for money,' he grouched. 'It's not a big deal.'

Joe, without even being aware of it, twisted his arm harder.

'Ow,' the lad winced, 'lemme go! You're hurting me arm and you've broke me nose.'

'Aw, sorry about that,' Joe said in mock concern. 'Have you called the police, Ellen?'

'They're on their way.' Ellen walked slowly to the seat furthest away from the boy. She was pale and had started to shiver.

'Put on the heat, Ellen,' Joe advised gently. 'You've had a shock. This guy is going nowhere.'

Ellen stood up and made her way to the heating box on the wall. She flicked the switch and had to support herself against the counter with both hands before she shuffled her way back to the chair. Joe gave the lad an extra shake in frustration. Ellen needed a cuppa and a rug or something and he couldn't get it without letting go of the boy.

'Take deep breaths,' he said.

The boy inhaled deeply.

'Not you,' Joe said crossly. 'You, Ellen.'

'Me ma is going to kill me,' the boy spoke up. His voice had lowered a notch on the toughness scale. 'She'll murder me, so she will.'

'No, she won't,' Joe said.

The boy looked at him.

''Cause I'm gonna do that for her'

He was rewarded with a small smile from Ellen before the boy began to struggle again.

Very faintly, just then, there was the sound of a police siren. Despite the fact that he was in the clear, Joe's heart skipped a beat and he unexpectedly felt like vomiting.

After the police had gone, Ellen insisted on making Joe a cuppa. He agreed because he reckoned it was more for herself than him. She was still pale and still shaking. He watched her in concern as she padded about the kitchen in her big pink fluffy slippers. They were the kind of slippers a teenager might have liked.

'Ellen, are you OK?' he asked. 'Maybe I should make the tea.'

'No.' She held up her hand. 'It's the least I can do after what you did.'

'I did nothing,' Joe said firmly. 'He was just a kid. He hadn't a clue. He'd have run if you'd even tackled him.'

She allowed herself a smile. 'I don't think so,' she murmured.

'Well, *I'm* scared of you.' Joe spread his palms wide. 'Every time my phone rings I think I owe you more money.'

Ellen laughed. 'Oh, you!'

Joe grinned and watched in amusement as she placed biscuits on a plate and cups on saucers. It was all very formal. She poured the milk into a jug and gave him a place mat. Finally she carried a massive pot of tea over to the table.

'Anyone else joining us?' Joe joked.

'Oh, I always make a big pot,' Ellen said. 'My late husband and I used to spend our days drinking tea and I just got used to making it like this.' She carefully poured him a cup, her hand shaking with the weight of the pot. 'Now, there.' She turned to her own cup and poured and, lastly, set the pot on the table between them. 'Sláinte,' she said.

'Yeah,' Joe lifted his cup. 'You, too.'

They sipped in silence, Joe not really knowing what to say to the woman. Their discussions normally cantered around his pigeons and he didn't really want to go there.

'I'll be telling everyone down at my club what you did for me tonight,' Ellen said.

'Club?'

'The old folks,' Ellen went on. 'It's great. I'm one of the youngest there. I'll be telling them all about you. You're a credit to your parents, so you are.'

Joe choked on the hot liquid. Tea spluttered out all over the table. Ellen, after making sure he was OK, went to get a dishcloth to wipe up.

'Sorry about that,' Joe said. Jesus.

'I never had children,' Ellen went on as she wiped up the tea, 'but if I had, I'd have been proud to have a boy like you. Wait until I tell all my friends what you've done.'

Joe squirmed. It was so long since anyone had said anything positive to him that he felt weirdly emotional.

'Yeah,' he murmured instead as he stared hard at his tea, 'thanks for that, Ellen. But really, it was nothing. He was only about fifteen. Hardly a hardened criminal.'

'But he could have been,' Ellen said, and unexpectedly she shivered. She lay back in the chair and closed her eyes. 'Oh, sorry, oh,' she waved her hand about, 'I feel a little faint all of a sudden.'

And she collapsed, hitting her head off the kitchen floor.

17

Friday, 23rd July

Joe asked me out for a drink tonight after work. I was knackered. I'd sold one ad, which is a bit pathetic since I'd made about a million phone calls. I don't have the ability to bullshit the way the lads do. Joe jokes that Dessie bullshits so much that he's carved out his own hole in the ozone layer. Well I think it's a joke, I don't really get it.

Anyway, Joe asked me if I wanted to go for a drink and I said that as long as the drink came with free uppers, I'd be OK. He laughed and was about to say something else when Dessie came back. Dessie looked from one to the other of us and said, 'How 'bout ye?'

I love the way he says it with his cute accent and his lovely glittery brown eyes and his quirky smile.

'Joe and I are going for a drink,' I said. 'D'you want to come?'

Dessie rolled his eyes and, sneaking a peek at Joe, said, 'I don't think this fella wants me around.'

'Of course he does,' I said. 'Don't you, Joe?'

'Well, I didn't ask you 'cause I know that you normally head off at the weekends to see Denise,' Joe answered. And the way he said it was kind of pointed.

Who is Denise? I wondered, as my heart sank quicker than a cork in water.

'Well not this weekend,' Dessie said as he grabbed his jacket from the chair and checked his pockets for money. 'She's coming down tonight so I might as well join ye in the meantime.'

And so the three of us went for a drink. I think Joe was a bit pissed off about something.

When he was up at the bar ordering, Dessie asked me what I thought of him. Of Joe. I said that I thought he was OK. Dessie grinned and said airily, 'Well, I reckon that Joe thinks you're more than OK.'

How awful was that? 'I don't fancy Joe,' I blurted out. I stressed the 'Joe' to show that I fancied someone, though.

Dessie quirked an eyebrow and said nothing.

Joe came back with the drinks and I'm sure he was wondering why I barely said a word to him. I just couldn't think of anything to say. I didn't want him to get the wrong impression and have to fend him off. As it happened, he left after one drink. He said he had to look after his granddad's pigeons as his granddad wasn't too well at the moment.

'Joe,' Dessie said with a grin, 'how many times do I have to tell you, you won't get a girl talking about other birds in front of them.'

I giggled, but Joe just seemed to glower at him as he pulled his jacket from the chair and left.

'So,' Dessie said, when Joe had gone, 'have you any plans for the weekend?'

'No.' Then I realised that probably sounded a bit pathetic. Who would be interested in a girl whose life is a social vacuum? 'Not yet,' I added.

Dessie looked at his watch. 'I have to go now and meet Denise from the bus or she'll give Salome a run for her money.'

'Salome?'

'Yeah. And I'll be John the Baptist.' Dessie laughed a little.

I laughed too, but I hadn't a clue what he was on about. Maybe it's a northern thing.

18

A NNA, AS USUAL, was in before her and had put the kettle on for tea. Kneeling on the floor beside Anna's chair, a small girl was bent over an array of half-naked dolls. She looked up as Lizzie came in.

Anna indicated her little girl, 'Lizzie, meet Chloe, my daughter.' Then, apologetically, she added, 'My babysitter is sick. I had to bring her with me.'

'No probs.' Lizzie crouched down beside the small, dark-haired little girl. 'Hi, Chloe, I'm Lizzie. It's nice to meet you at last, your mammy talks about you all the time.'

The child looked solemnly back at her out of large brown eyes.

'Are they Bratz?' Lizzie asked, indicating the dolls.

A nod.

'They're cool.'

'This is Cloe,' Chloe volunteered shyly, holding up a blonde-haired doll. 'Only she spells her name different to me. She's my favourite.'

'Mine too,' Lizzie agreed. 'I'm going to be an aunty soon. My brother is going to have a tiny new baby. It'll be about,' Lizzie put her palms a foot or so apart, 'that size. D'you think it'd like those dollies?'

'A baby would be too small,' Chloe said, looking to Anna for reassurance. 'Maybe if it's a girl and when she's bigger.'

'Oh right, OK,' Lizzie nodded. 'Thanks for that.'

Chloe nodded, smiling slightly.

'She'll probably fall asleep in a bit,' Anna said softly. 'I'll get a taxi to bring us home.'

'No worries,' Lizzie said. 'Is your babysitter really sick or what?'

Anna made a face. 'Yeah, a stomach bug, I think. I've had to cancel a night out tomorrow just in case she's not better.'

'I'll babysit for you if you're stuck,' Lizzie said.

'Oh no, I couldn't . . . I wasn't dropping hints or anything . . .'

'Where and when?' Lizzie asked. At Anna's doubtful look she continued, 'I want to get some practice in for when my own little niece or nephew comes, so you're doing me a favour.'

'I somehow doubt that.' Anna grinned a little.

'The offer is there,' Lizzie said. 'It'd be no bother. I'm not going anywhere, I haven't seen Tom since last weekend, he's so busy.' Tom had called her and apologised. When he wasn't rehearsing, he was working in a pub. Lizzie wondered if they'd ever get it together.

Anna winced. 'You sure?'

'Positive.'

'Well, OK.' Anna grinned delightedly. 'Thanks.'

'No bother.' Lizzie gave a cheeky grin. 'So you won't mind answering the phones tonight while I bond with your daughter over a few Bratz?'

'Aw yeah, I knew there had to be a catch . . .'

'Lizzie, for you.' Anna handed Lizzie the phone.

'Hello?'

'Hello, is that Lizzie?'

'Yes,' Lizzie confirmed. 'Who's this?'

'I'm, eh . . .' There was a slight hesitation. 'Eh, Sinéad, I think I said. I rang you a few weeks ago.'

As Lizzie remembered their conversation, she felt a mixture of relief and apprehension. Relief that the woman had rung back and apprehension as to the reason why. 'Of course, Sinéad,' she said. 'You were a bit concerned about your husband's behaviour, weren't you?'

'Well, I don't know if concerned—' Sinéad stopped and said instead, 'I just wanted some advice.'

'OK.' Lizzie picked up a pen. 'And would you like to talk again?'

'Of course I would,' the woman sounded a little annoyed, 'that's why I rang.'

Lizzie ignored her tone. As if she were treading across a minefield she said carefully, 'Great. That's good, Sinéad. I'm glad you rang again. What can I do?'

The question seemed to throw Sinéad. 'Eh, well . . .'

Lizzie waited.

'I just . . . I don't know. I just . . .' Sinéad's voice trailed off.

'Just talk if you want to,' Lizzie said softly. 'I'm not going to tell anyone. You can just say what you like and not worry, OK?'

'Oh,' Sinéad said, just as softly, 'you've no idea how . . . how good that sounds to me. No idea.'

'If it sounds good,' Lizzie said, 'then go for it.'

Sinéad sniffed and seemed to be wiping her nose hard. 'I'm, well, I'm confused,' she said haltingly. 'I just don't know any more.'

'What don't you know?'

'He says I'm being silly, that I'm too emotional.'

'Silly about what?'

'About everything.' A pause. 'For instance, just as an example, I want to do up one of our rooms and no matter what I pick out he says it's horrible. He says I shouldn't be allowed to decorate a doghouse, never mind his home.'

'Well, people do disagree on stuff like that,' Lizzie answered, trying to be fair.

'But—, but, I'm an interior designer by trade,' Sinéad said shakily. 'People pay me a lot of money to do up their houses. I did up ours when we first moved in.'

'And did you tell him this?'

'He says people in general are stupid.'

'He sounds like he doesn't like many people,' Lizzie offered.

'Oh no. He's very popular.' A note of anger crept into Sinéad's voice, which made Lizzie feel better. 'He's Mr Residents' Committee, Mr Tidy Towns, Mr Important In Work. He can charm everyone.' She paused. 'Well, everyone except my friends.'

'So he's different at home to when he's out?'

'Yes, I suppose.' Then, as if afraid she'd revealed too much, Sinéad said hastily, 'But he hasn't slapped me since that one time. He's just, well, it always seems that he's picking on me.'

'Is this a sudden change?' Lizzie probed. 'He wouldn't just be having problems in work, would he?'

'No, he's very successful in work,' Sinéad said almost bitterly. 'And after I talked to you last, well, I began to think and, well, I realised that, in fact, I've changed a lot since I've been with him.'

'In what way?'

'I used to be so confident.' The anger drained out of Sinéad's voice and instead it started to shake, as if she were trying very hard not to cry. 'So sure of myself. So decisive.'

'And you're not any more?'

'Last week I stood in the shopping centre,' Sinéad sniffed, 'and I couldn't even decide what washing powder to buy. I looked at them all and read all the packages, and I was afraid to pick the wrong one so I bought them all.'

Lizzie said nothing.

'All of them. And when he came home I put a wash on and he asked what powder I was using because that was a silk shirt of his I was washing and I opened the press and I took out the powder for silks and he told me I was stupid and that I should have got it dry cleaned.' She took a deep, shaky breath. 'No matter what I do, it turns out wrong.'

He was a bully, that's what he was, Lizzie wanted to tell her. But of course she couldn't. She hated that about her job. She'd have loved to wade in and tell Sinéad to dump him. Instead she asked, 'Do you feel you're being undermined?'

'I don't know what I feel,' Sinéad said, her voice lower but under control again. 'Maybe it's normal after four years of marriage. Maybe he's just bored with me.'

'So why won't he just say that?' Lizzie suggested gently, trying to get the woman to think. 'Surely it's less hurtful than what he's doing now?'

'Maybe he doesn't think so.'

'Maybe you should ask him.'

Sinéad considered this. 'Maybe I will,' she responded. 'Maybe that would be a good idea.'

'Let me know how you get on.'

'OK.' Sinéad paused. 'And thanks. Sorry for snapping at you.'

'Snap away,' Lizzie responded cheerfully, 'it's what I'm here for.'

'No,' Sinéad said with a firmness that surprised Lizzie. 'No one should ever be there for that.' Then she hung up.

Lizzie waited at the corner of the lane until she saw Joe coming along the street, then, as if she had just emerged from the Life office, she breezed out into his path, pretending not to see him.

'Hey,' he said with slight uncertainty, 'Lizzie?'

She turned and he jogged up beside her. 'Thought it was you.' He pointed up the lane. 'Is that where you work, yeah?'

'Yep. A small office, right at the top of the building.'

He fell into step beside her. Then hesitated. 'You don't mind?'

'No, why should I?' she asked archly, trying out a slightly flirty tone. 'You can be my security walking up this street.'

He grinned, 'Sure, yeah. D'you get nervous walking on your own at night in the city?'

'Naw, not really.' Lizzie studied him. Despite the initial hesitation at walking with her he was now quite relaxed, his hands swinging loosely beside him as his stride matched hers effortlessly. 'But it's nice to have company.' She pulled out her cigarettes, she needed one badly.

'Yeah, I guess it is.' He eyed her. 'Especially when that company has a packet of fags in her hand and the other person is gasping for one.'

Lizzie managed a laugh and flicked open the box. 'Want one?'

'Yeah, thanks. I ran out and hadn't time to buy a packet.' He put it to his mouth. Lizzie fished a lighter from her pocket and flicked it on. It spluttered out. She tried again.

'Hey, your hands are shaking,' Joe exclaimed. 'Are you OK?'

'Just cold,' Lizzie lied. Terrified would be more like it. This whole scenario was progressing almost too well. She attempted to flick the lighter again but, instead, Joe gently took it from her and lit his own cigarette, before lighting hers.

'Thanks,' she nodded. Then, 'I'm surprised you smoke, with you running a health centre.'

He grinned. 'Yeah I know, but I can't seem to give them up.'

'Me neither.'

Joe grinned at her and Lizzie was suddenly aware of how attractive he must have seemed to Megan. He was handsome, but it wasn't just that – there was an easy charm about him, his casual way of dressing, his soft way of talking, his semi-bewildered way of asking questions. It was a potent combination. And yet, as far as she was aware, he wasn't seeing anyone.

That was a bit odd, she thought.

They arrived at the Luas and both of them finished their cigarettes almost at the same time. 'Filthy habit,' Joe smirked as he ground his fag out before picking it up and dumping it into the bin.

'Disgusting,' Lizzie agreed lightly. 'One is no good, better off smoking two at a time.'

Joe laughed.

The Luas pulled up and, without discussion, he sat in beside her. Lizzie dragged her bag on to her lap and slid out his book. 'Thanks for this.' She attempted to hand it to him. 'I learned a lot.'

'You can hang on to it if you like,' Joe said, waving her away. 'You might need it when you start up.'

'Oh, thanks very much. I will, so.' She tucked it back into her bag.

'That's some bag,' Joe remarked, eyeing it in amusement. 'I reckon you could fit a pigeon loft in there.'

Lizzie smiled. 'Probably,' she agreed. Then, 'You weren't down at the club last week. I was hoping to ask you something.'

'Naw, I couldn't make it,' Joe said, suddenly looking uncomfortable.

'Oh.'

There was a pause.

'My next door neighbour, she's an old woman, had a bit of a turn. I was doing good Samaritan.'

Lizzie flinched. Good Samaritan, was he joking? She wondered if his neighbour knew what he was really like.

'She was in hospital for a couple of nights and she's out now. She's a little better, but I'm still checking up on her. But I hope to be down tomorrow night with the birds.'

'Well, I'm out tomorrow,' Lizzie said. 'But if you need a hand any other time, I can help.' Then she added, 'With the birds, not your neighbour.'

Joe shrugged. 'Aw—'

'Alan told me to learn from you,' Lizzie gabbled before he turned her down. 'He said you were the best.' Oh God, she couldn't let this pass her by. He had to let her help. It was the only way she could think of to get into his life and earn his trust. At Joe's obvious embarrassment, she touched him lightly on the arm. 'Please?'

He flinched and Lizzie pulled her hand away. Maybe she'd pushed too hard.

'Do you know much?' he asked.

'I'm a quick learner and I really am interested,' she lied. She was surprised at herself. When she was with this guy she could just switch off any conscience she had. But it was the memory of him in court, the lies he told, that made her able to do it. It was like fuel to an engine starved of oil.

He studied her, his head cocked to one side. Eventually a small grin curved the corners of his mouth. 'OK,' he nodded, 'you're on. But I dunno if I'm the best.'

Lizzie's heart hammered suddenly, making her feel sick. This was it. The beginning of the end for Joe. 'Well, Alan said you were,' she said firmly. 'So, when would you like me to start?'

Joe shrugged. 'Next Friday, if you like? You free from around six?'

'Yeah.' Lizzie tried to look thrilled. 'Oh thanks, Joe. You're a life saver.'

'Hardly.' He tipped her a grinning mock salute. With an effort of will she smiled back.

Some fisherman he was, she thought scornfully. She'd fed him the bait and was now reeling him in the way her dad had taught her long ago, very gently, with no sudden jerks.

She hoped her dad would be proud of her.

19

CHLOE WAS ASLEEP at last. She had been great fun but an awful kid to get to bed. Lizzie had played with every single one of her toys and now they all lay scattered about the floor, making the previously immaculate room an untidy mess. As best she could Lizzie tidied up, she didn't want Anna arriving back to this chaos. Each time she'd dragged out something new, Chloe had said innocently, 'It's OK, my mammy doesn't mind. She lets me do anything.' Somehow Lizzie doubted that.

Anna's house was small but brilliantly compact. There was a tiny hall with a small but functional kitchen, a small playroom and a television room. It was the TV room she was in now. Pictures of Chloe adorned the walls. Chloe as a baby, Chloe in her first school uniform. There was also a photograph of Anna with a very striking-looking man. The picture looked as if it had been taken on holiday somewhere, possibly Spain. Both of them wore T-shirts and shorts. Anna looked so much younger, her hair shorter, defining her pixie-like features. The man was stunning, that was the only way Lizzie could describe him. Tall and wearing a white T-shirt that showed off his muscular, tanned arms. His hair was coal-black, as were his eyes. He was smiling but something about the way he smiled struck Lizzie as odd. Whereas Anna looked radiant, the man looked merely tolerant. His arm was wrapped about Anna's shoulder protectively and she was gazing up into his face. There was no doubt in Lizzie's mind that this man was Chloe's dad – the little girl was the image of him. Lizzie wondered what had happened. Anna still wore her wedding ring but it was obvious there was no man in this house.

Lizzie went into the kitchen and flicked on the kettle. Anna had left biscuits out and it touched Lizzie to see that they were her favourite: Ginger Nut. She opened the packet, took four, and, carrying them plus a large mug of coffee, she sat down to watch the late-night Saturday movie.

Anna had offered to let her stay over if she wanted and Lizzie had jumped at it. It would be nice to give Billy and Aileen time to themselves, and Aileen's happiness at finally declaring herself a mother-to-be was a bit wearing. She'd purchased baby books and had enlisted Lizzie in drawing up lists of possible names. Lizzie had discovered that Aileen's taste in baby names was horrendous. One possibility was Linford, seeing as it was a cross between Dublin and Wexford. Rufus and Clementine were two other options, as they were so 'unusual'. Billy had told Lizzie to let her at it and that, when the time came, he'd talk her into calling the child a name that it might actually want to have. Lizzie didn't envy him the task. Aileen had also bought another book chronicling the day-by-day development of the foetus in the womb. Every morning Billy was treated to just how much his child should have grown in the night and whether his new offspring had any teeth or fingernails yet. Billy's attitude reminded Lizzie of the guy in Anna's photo – he was tolerating it. Lizzie wanted to shake him, to tell him to get a grip, but Billy had always found change difficult, so maybe he just had to get his head around it in his own time.

Lizzie had just drained her mug and decided to go upstairs to bed when the front door opened. It was Anna. Lizzie went into the hall to greet her. 'Hi, good night?'

Anna nodded and came quietly towards her, following her back into the sitting room. 'Not bad.' She sank into the sofa. 'It was just dinner with a couple of friends, nothing too major. How was Chloe?'

'Active.'

Anna gave a splutter of laughter. 'She was dying for you to come,' she said. 'The novelty of someone new.'

'How is your babysitter now? Is she better?'

Anna paused and flushed. 'To be honest, Lizzie, she was never sick,' she said, sounding mortified. She shifted uncomfortably on the sofa. 'I, eh, had a row with her.'

'What?' The thought of Anna having a row with anyone was weird.

'Yep,' Anna nodded glumly. 'I'm sorry I lied. It was just easier than explaining everything.'

'You don't have to explain, so long as you don't row with me.'

Anna smiled a little. 'No fear of that.'

'Well then,' Lizzie nodded, 'forget it.'

'It was my mother,' Anna blurted out. 'She is great, taking Chloe from school and everything, but last Wednesday I had to call a halt to it.'

'Oh, well, we all row with our mothers,' Lizzie said, thinking of her own parents.

'Not like this.' Anna sighed.

'D'you want a coffee?' Lizzie asked, unsure if Anna wanted to continue along this subject and deciding to give her the opportunity to change it.

Anna waved her away. 'No thanks, I drank enough coffee tonight to refloat the Titanic.'

There was silence.

'Can I tell you something, Lizzie?' Anna asked, breaking the silence. 'I'd really like your opinion, you're a good counsellor.'

'Not as good as you.'

Anna rolled her eyes. 'I think the beauty of being a counsellor is that you feel good helping others because you're completely unable to help yourself.'

Lizzie giggled. 'Ouch!'

'Seriously, though,' Anna cocked her head to one side, 'I'll bet you decided to do what you do because you wanted to help people.'

'Yep.'

'So something must have happened to make you feel that way.'

Her perception floored Lizzie. She gulped and shrugged and muttered an, 'I suppose'.

107

'Have I upset you?' Anna was suddenly contrite. 'Oh, sorry. I didn't mean to.'

Lizzie waved her concern away. 'No, it's just, you're so right.' She licked her lips. 'My, well . . .'

'You don't have to tell me,' Anna said softly. 'It's just something that happens. I went into it because my husband killed himself.'

Lizzie's head shot up. 'What?'

Anna nodded. There was no trace of self pity in her eyes or face. Just an acceptance. 'Yep.' She crossed to the fireplace and took down the photo that Lizzie had noticed earlier. 'That was him. Mick.'

Lizzie took the photo. 'He's gorgeous.'

'I know he was,' Anna said. 'I was mad about him. I reckon if we'd lived to be a hundred together, I'd still be mad about him. He was great fun, he could make everyone laugh, he was the clown at every party and yet, look at him there, that's who he really was, I think. The camera caught him just before he painted his grin on.' She replaced the picture. 'That's why I keep that photo up, not the others.'

Lizzie said nothing.

'Christmas Eve, I walked into our old house, I was seven months pregnant with Chloe and I found him hanging from the attic. No note, nothing. And everyone saying that they'd never have guessed.'

'Oh God, Anna . . .' Lizzie voice trailed off.

'It was terrible,' Anna said matter-of-factly. 'And I was grieving and I was so bloody angry too, Lizzie. I hated him for what he'd done. It's weird, you hate yourself for being angry but you can't help it and you've no one to direct it at. My mother was great at that time. She was there when the baby was born, helping out, doing all sorts of stuff for me and I truly appreciated it. Then, about four years ago, I decided that enough was enough and I was going to get some good out of it. Squeeze out the good, you know?'

Lizzie knew.

'So I got counselling, and after I decided to become a counsellor myself.'

'Good for you.'

'And I've moved on, but my mother can't. She won't tolerate me mentioning him. The last straw came this week when Chloe asked her why she didn't like her daddy. I never even knew Chloe noticed. Well, my mother's answer was that Daddy had done a very bad thing and that he wasn't a good daddy at all. I went ballistic. I mean, I flipped. I told my mother she was poisoning the image of him that I'd tried to build up for Chloe.' Anna paused and took a breath. 'I've told Chloe the truth, that her daddy wasn't well, that his mind was so sore that he had to stop it from working. And she accepted that but now she's on about her daddy being bad. Do you think I'm being unreasonable, Lizzie?'

Lizzie bit her lip.

'Sorry, sorry, sorry.' Anna gave an embarrassed laugh. 'I'm putting you on the spot. Sorry. It's just so hard to judge yourself, you know?'

'I don't think you're being unreasonable in trying to explain to Chloe,' Lizzie said carefully, 'but I suppose your mother had to pick you up off the floor when it happened and she hates him for what he did to you. She's still angry.'

Anna blew air out through her lips and nodded. 'I know you're right. But I can't have it affect Chloe, you have to see that.'

'I do.'

'I've told her that unless she starts to talk about him in a nice way, I can't let Chloe visit.'

'Sounds OK, but maybe *you* should still visit.'

'Peacemaker Lizzie,' Anna teased.

'Hardly,' Lizzie said back.

There was a small pause before Anna said, 'I could do with that coffee now, what about you?'

'If you could go back and find out what was on his mind the day he did it, would you?' Lizzie suddenly found herself asking. 'Like, if you had a chance to solve that mystery, would you do it?'

'Nothing I would have said could have prevented him doing it if he'd wanted to,' Anna mused.

'But if you had the chance . . .'

'Then, yeah, like a shot.'

Lizzie nodded, satisfied. Anna wouldn't ever get the chance, but she just might, she thought.

'Why?' Anna asked.

Lizzie shrugged. 'I just wondered when the desire fades, the wanting to know, you know?'

'It never does.' Anna gulped hard and left the room for the kitchen.

And that was what was so hard to live with, Lizzie thought. You could accept death eventually, but you could never accept the not knowing.

20

J OE SAT IN his car in the Luas station car park. He'd agreed
to meet Lizzie there as he reckoned it would be hard for
her to find her way to his house; there were a lot of twists
and turns on the way. It was spitting rain and the night was a
dingy one. She'd have been freezing by the time she found his
place.

He wondered a little at the wisdom of letting the girl help him
out – after all, he didn't really know what she was able to do. But
she appeared so enthusiastic, just like he used to be. Just like he
still was, he supposed. He decided to give her a break. And besides,
he needed the help: he could hardly abandon Ellen, could he?
He guessed he could have asked Noel or John for a hand, but
Joe didn't really like asking for help, so Lizzie's offer had come
at just the right time.

He spotted her suddenly, dressed in a bright red coat, standing
in the car park looking around. He gave a *bip* of the horn and
she ran lightly towards the car.

'Hi.' She climbed in beside him and he got a whiff of straw-
berries. 'Were you waiting long?'

She was so bright and fresh and clean-looking that Joe had to
turn away suddenly. He fired the engine and shook his head.
'Naw.'

'The Luas was delayed,' Lizzie went on, 'some problem with
the line. But still, here I am.'

'Yep.' With an effort he turned to face her and smiled. She
was dressed in a pair of denims and a tight blue top with a
big daisy on the front. 'Do you have a change of clothes?' he

asked. 'You look, eh, a bit dressed up for cleaning out the pigeons.'

Cleaning out the pigeons? Lizzie tried not to shudder. She hoped it didn't mean what she thought it meant. 'These are my old things,' she lied.

They didn't look old, Joe thought.

'It's really great of you,' Lizzie went on, settling her enormous bag at her feet. 'But you'll have to tell me everything and explain it all to me, won't you?'

Joe grinned. A girl after his own heart.

Lizzie's phone rang just as Joe pulled up outside his house. He climbed out of the car as Lizzie fished the mobile from her bag. It was Tom.

'D'you mind?' Lizzie asked.

'Naw, fire ahead, follow me in.'

'Tom, hi,' she said into the phone.

'D'you remember me?' he laughed. 'The guy who is failing miserably to get you into bed?'

Lizzie grinned. 'What's the story?'

'I'm free later tonight, if you are? Sorry about the short notice but I rang the pub and told them I was sick. I've a rehearsal for about two hours and I can meet you after, if you like?'

Well that was bloody typical. 'Eh, I might be able. I'll ring you later – OK?'

In the background, there was a ring on Tom's intercom. 'Yep. OK. Talk then. Love you.'

She turned the phone off.

'Anyone important?' Joe asked as she stepped out to join him.

Did she want Joe to know she had a boyfriend? No, she decided. The less he knew about her the better. 'Nah.'

'Right.' Joe indicated the house. 'Well, here we are.' He pulled his keys from his pocket and strode up the overgrown driveway, a crooked gate squeaking violently as he pushed it open. His driveway was more a narrow little path bordered on each side by some grass. 'Home.'

'You own this place?' Lizzie asked, following him. 'Like, you have a house?' For some reason she'd been convinced he'd been renting it, or at least sharing it with others.

'Yep. All mine,' Joe nodded.

It'd be rude to ask how on earth he could afford to own a house, wouldn't it? Instead she went for a fake, 'I'm impressed.'

Joe shrugged. 'Yeah, well, I was lucky. My grandfather left me his pigeon loft when he died and I sold it. With the money I made, I bought this.'

'You sold your grandfather's pigeon loft?' Pigeons could buy you a house – she hadn't known that.

Joe squirmed. 'Yeah, pretty crappy thing to do, but I had no choice.'

'Did you not?' Lizzie reckoned she'd have sold it, too, if it was worth that much.

Joe turned abruptly from her and inserted the key into the lock. 'I wasn't in a position to keep it then,' he said over his shoulder.

'It must have been some loft.'

'The best.' His tone held a note of pride. 'Just like mine will be one day.'

In your dreams, Lizzie thought, and suddenly shivered. But it was typical. There he was, a bloody convict and he had his own house, and poor Billy and Aileen, who had done nothing to anyone, were struggling like mad to pay off their massive mortgage.

She followed Joe into a bare hallway, devoid of any personal effects, and into an equally bland kitchen. The walls were a sunny yellow, but that was about as cheerful as it got. The floor was covered in horrendous brown tiles and the worktops were cheap Formica.

'I haven't exactly got the hang of the whole interior design thing yet,' Joe explained wryly. 'I much prefer getting the latest gadgets for the loft.'

He unlocked the back door and waited as she followed him into the garden. 'You'll love the whole set up,' he promised. His face had changed, Lizzie thought in surprise. He seemed suddenly animated, not at all the careful, cautious guy he'd displayed so far. His step was light and she followed him across the grass.

The lofts dominated the small garden. They were like mini sheds, from inside which came soft cooing noises and the sound of flapping wings.

Joe unlocked the loft and beckoned Lizzie to follow him.

Lizzie took a deep breath before entering. Birds were not her favourite creatures, especially not pigeons. If it had been a loft full of robins or sparrows perhaps it might have been better. She took a hesitant step inside and the scent of pigeon assailed her nostrils. She did her best to keep her face from betraying anything. Oh Jesus, she thought.

Joe seemed oblivious to it. She was aware that he was waiting for her reaction, so she uttered a 'Wow' and hoped it sounded sincere. Her eyes fell on a long, low feeder on the ground. A pigeon fluttered by her towards it and Lizzie flinched.

'That's the hopper,' Joe explained. 'I let them feed themselves from that all day, every day.'

'What's in it?' Lizzie couldn't identify the dry, brown-looking stuff.

'Barley malt,' Joe explained. 'I get it from a brewery. It's great stuff, the birds love it. It has to be watched, though, in case it gets wet or goes off. It causes fungal spores to develop.' He pointed upwards and started on about the ceilings and the wood and paint and stuff. He talked about feeding the birds and what he gave them. Lizzie couldn't make head nor tail of it but she nodded along anyway.

'The important thing to remember when racing birds,' she heard Joe say when she tuned back in, 'is to give them a reason to want to come home. With the cocks, most fanciers will work the widowhood system. Basically they fly home to their mates, whom they haven't seen all week.'

'Oh, that's cruel.' Bit like her and Tom, she thought wryly.

Joe grinned. 'Not really. Cid down the club reckons he'd be quite happy to only see his wife once a week.'

'Ha, ha.'

'Another thing they fly home for is food.' Joe shook the little dish. 'I give them corn and seeds when they come back.'

'So they need a reason to come back.'

'Yeah.' Joe reached in and took out a bird. 'No point in coming home if there's nothing good at the end of it, ey?' His comment had a desolate ring, even though he directed it at the pigeon he was holding. He held the bird tenderly in the palm of his hand, its head against his stomach. His finger ran down the length of the pigeon's body. 'And, of course, you need to love them enough so that they want to fly back to you.'

The words hit Lizzie with such force that she gasped.

Joe looked at her sharply. 'You OK?'

'Fine, yeah.' She swallowed. It was weird to hear him talk that way. Really unsettling.

'Here.' Joe smiled and held out the bird towards her. 'See what you think of him.'

Lizzie gently took the pigeon from his hands. Oh God, this was harder than she'd thought. What if it took a dump all over her brand new T-shirt? She hadn't really thought out the whole 'helping him with his pigeons' issue at all.

'Eh, great,' she tried to say with enthusiasm. She was convinced her finger was sticking up its backside, which was disgusting.

Joe grinned, all white-toothed admiration. For the bird. 'See how well balanced he is.'

'Well balanced?'

'Yeah.' Joe, much to her horror and revulsion, gently took her hands in his and helped her lift the bird up. Lizzie tried not to shiver. 'See how his body follows a line. He's balanced. And look at his wings.' He pulled a wing for her to examine. 'Nice coverage, see?'

'Oh, yeah.' Lizzie hoped she sounded as if she knew what she was talking about.

'Very good coverage. I see that now. That helps him fly well, doesn't it?'

Joe shrugged. 'I think so,' he nodded. 'Other people have different ways of telling. Some use eye-sign. They basically look into the bird's eyes and swear they can tell if it'll be any good.

Some like a low-lying tongue in the mouth. But I reckon you can tell just by holding a bird. See how he just sits so nicely in your hand.'

The bird wasn't sitting too nicely in Lizzie's hand. He was getting a little edgy and his head was moving a little too much for her to feel happy about it. And her finger was definitely in the wrong position. Which might explain why the bird was uneasy, too . . .

'Can I let him go now?' she asked, trying not to sound as if she actually wanted to.

'Yeah.'

They both watched as the bird flew and eventually came to rest in a box.

'His name is Prince,' Joe said. 'My best racer. I'll probably breed off him next year, but for now I just love seeing him take to the skies and fly back home.'

'And he stays in that box all the time?' Lizzie asked.

'Yep, that's his home. See the ring he has on his legs? That tells who he is. Every pigeon has to have one of those.'

'So that's how you know he's Prince?'

'Well, no. I just know it's him from the way he looks.'

Lizzie doubted that. As far as she could see, every bird in the place looked exactly the same.

'And the way he moves,' Joe added.

'I see.' But she didn't.

'So,' Joe looked expectantly at her, 'we'll basket them first.'

'OK,' Lizzie nodded. 'And, eh, how do you do that?'

'I usher them into the corridor and they have no option but to go into the basket. Watch.' He gently went about encouraging the birds to leave their perches and, one by one, they waddled across the loft and into the narrow passageway.

'Now,' Joe said, 'I'll go out and place a basket at that ledge and you get the lads to move towards it. We should get it done in the next few minutes, OK?'

'Sure.' Lizzie didn't feel that confident. She watched Joe leave and, when he was outside, he called to her to usher the pigeons towards the basket.

116

'Hup,' Lizzie called feebly, feeling stupid. 'Hup.'

The birds continued to peck the ground and wander around.

'Hup,' Lizzie called in a crosser voice. 'Come on!'

Joe was grinning from the other side. 'You're way too polite,' he laughed.

'HUP!' Lizzie shouted and immediately there was a frantic fluttering of wings as birds took off in every direction.

Lizzie screamed as they whirled around her head and Joe raced in, half laughing, half concerned.

'You'll give my birds a heart attack before the race.'

'Sorry,' Lizzie said meekly, kicking herself for screaming. He'd probably feck her out now. 'I guess I need more help than I thought.'

'I guess you do,' Joe agreed, an amused smile dancing on his lips. He tapped the skin next to his eye. 'Watch.' With a clap of his hands and a whistle, the birds stopped their frantic flapping and, like obedient children, started to walk towards the ledge. Lizzie, despite herself, was amazed at the way they obeyed him.

'Respect and trust,' Joe said. 'That's what you have to give them and they give it right back.'

He went outside. Lizzie followed and saw him latching up the basket and setting it on to the ground.

'Now, do you feel like trying again?'

'Do you feel like letting me?'

'Sure.' He observed her. 'You're learning, right? No point in giving up now, ey?'

'Yeah, no point in giving up at all,' Lizzie replied, and the way she said it came out sounding really strange, threatening even. Joe shot her a glance but she managed to disarm him with a smile, turning away quickly in case he saw that she wasn't really smiling. She squared her shoulders and turned towards the loft. 'Now, for the second time.'

'Be firm without being cross,' he advised.

'OK.' God, why couldn't he have a more likeable hobby? she wondered. Like stamp collecting or football? Something she could support without getting her hands dirty or making a fool of herself.

She walked as enthusiastically as she could back into the smelly loft and confronted the pigeons.

'Ready when you are!' Joe called.

Lizzie clapped her hands and there was a small commotion. The birds eyed her warily.

'Come on now,' Lizzie said in her best school teacher's voice, 'come on.'

A couple of birds alighted on the perch.

'In you go.' Lizzie whooshed them with her hands and, to her amazement, they obeyed.

'Yeah!' Joe gave a little cheer and Lizzie smiled, slightly stunned.

The other birds, sensing what was wanted, copied the first two and, to her delight, they were soon all basketed.

'You have the knack,' Joe said as he clipped the other basket shut.

Lizzie couldn't figure out if he was joking or serious.

Joe put the second basket beside the first. 'Now,' he said, 'I'm just going to go next door to see how Ellen, my neighbour, is. D'you want to clean out the boxes?' He made it sound like an honour.

Clean out the boxes? Lizzie looked questioningly at him. 'Clean out the boxes?'

'Yeah, scrape out all the droppings. I'll be back in a bit to help you.'

'Scrape out the droppings?'

'Yeah,' Joe nodded. 'Don't worry, it's easy.'

She wasn't worried. Just horrified.

'I normally do them on a Friday,' Joe went on, 'when the birds are in the baskets. This is what you do, see?' He took a bag from his pocket, pulled out a wooden tray that was resting under a pigeon box and, with a palette knife, scraped the droppings into the bag. 'See. It's easy.'

'Sure is,' Lizzie said as brightly as she could. She wondered if he had gloves anywhere.

'You can use these.' Joe, as if reading her mind, pulled some thick gloves out of his pocket. 'When you finish, you can wash your hands in the kitchen. There's disinfectant under the sink.'

'OK, cool.'

'Brilliant.'

She watched Joe go back into the house, wash his own hands and grab a bag of groceries. He came back out and hopped over the back wall. Lizzie ducked inside the loft in case she was spotted by the old woman who lived next door. She stared around at the empty loft, all its boxes now empty. And it was up to her to clean it. Well, there was no better way to earn trust and respect than doing what she was told. By the time she was finished, she'd have taught Joe a lot about trust and respect.

'Hi, Ellen, how's things today?' Joe called out as he set the bag containing some milk and bread on the kitchen floor. He poked his head into the dining room, where Ellen lay on an old, faded sofa. 'Will I make you a cuppa?'

Ellen nodded. 'Thanks, pet. How much do I owe you for the groceries?'

'Aw, nothing. It's only bread and milk.'

'You didn't get it free, though, did you?' she asked sharply as Joe turned to go and put on the kettle.

'No, but it was only a couple of quid.'

'My purse is over there.' Ellen pointed to her black bag. 'Take the money out of that before you leave, Joe. I mean it.'

Joe said nothing. Instead he boiled the kettle, made Ellen a sandwich and brought it all in to her on a tray. Setting it beside her, he sat in a chair opposite. She still looked a bit shaken, even though it had happened a couple of weeks ago. He supposed that when you got old it became harder to get over something like a burglary and collapsing on to the hard tiles of your kitchen floor – she had given her head a right wallop. It was difficult, though, juggling the pigeons, his job and Ellen. The neighbours on the other side were pretty good, too, at helping out, so between them they were muddling along.

'How you feeling?' he asked her.

'Oh, much better.' Ellen took a bite out of her sandwich and chewed slowly. 'You really don't have to be so attentive, Joe. You've got your own life.'

'Yeah,' he nodded, 'and in my life I've agreed to keep an eye on you, so button it.'

She smiled a little. 'My Sam would have liked you,' she said approvingly. 'In fact, he was a lot like you even to look at.'

Joe knew she thought that already. There were pictures of Ellen's Sam all over this room. They beamed down at him from the mantelpiece and from the walls. A big old photograph of the couple was framed and sat underneath the television. He didn't think he looked too much like Sam, but he never bothered contradicting Ellen.

'He died when he was about your age,' Ellen remarked then. She lifted the mug to her lips with a shaky hand. 'What age would you be, about thirty?'

'Yep.'

'I don't know,' Ellen smiled a little. 'No one gets married any more. Sam and I were married eight years when he died. It was a terrible shock.'

'Yeah, it was pretty young to go all right,' Joe nodded. He wished Ellen would open a window, the air was stifling. 'Will I open a window?'

'No,' she waved him away, 'I like to keep them closed.' A pause. 'He was crossing a road and a man knocked him down. Right in front of me.'

Joe made sympathetic noises. It was awful to see something like that, he was sure, but he prayed like hell that she wouldn't start crying. How would he cope with that?

But Ellen had obviously done her crying a long time ago. 'It took me ages to get over it. I wasn't right for a long time.'

Joe said nothing. He didn't think he was expected to. Ellen seemed to have decided to reveal little bits of her life to him. He supposed they didn't have much in common so it was the easiest thing to talk about. He'd heard about her two dead sisters, her dead parents, a friend who had gone to America and who she'd never heard from again, and the boyfriends.

'They put the man who knocked him down in jail,' Ellen said then, and Joe flinched.

120

'Did they?' he managed to say, his throat dry, hoping that Ellen wouldn't see the sudden way his own hands had started to tremble ever so slightly.

'Yes. But you know, Joe, I never blamed him. It was a dark night and we were on the road at a corner. It was just bad luck.'

He stared at her.

'So I went to see him and told him that. It was about a year later and the man cried and cried and said he didn't care how long more he was to spend in jail – that hearing those words was his freedom.' She took another sip of tea. 'It's the thing I feel I really did right in my life, you know? Sam would have approved.'

'Eh, yeah.' Joe stood up suddenly, not wanting to hear any more. 'I better go Ellen, I've someone helping me with the birds and—'

'They want me to meet the boy who tried to rob me,' she said then.

'What?' Joe looked at her incredulously.

'It's some kind of thing they do. You can meet with the people who do these things and talk to them and explain how it affected you. They think it does some good.'

'Do they?' Joe rolled his eyes and jammed his hands into his pockets. 'I hope you told them to get lost.'

'No. I said I'd like to meet him. He's only thirteen.' She regarded Joe over the rim of her cup. 'But I'll only feel up to it if you come along. Will you come along?'

Joe bit his lip and didn't quite know how to answer.

What felt like an eternity later, amid much gagging, Lizzie eventually had the boxes cleaned out. It was hard to believe that such small creatures could create so much shit, she thought, as with a final scrape the last of it fell into the bag. Tying a knot in the top, Lizzie dumped the bag outside the loft door and, holding her hands as far away from her body as she could, she marched into the kitchen.

She pulled the gloves gingerly from her hands and plunged her palms under the warm water. The plumbing in the house was almost as bad as at Royal Lawns. The water gurgled alarmingly as it splashed into the sink. Lizzie pulled open the press underneath and found the disinfectant. As she took it out her eye fell on another bottle, tucked into the left-hand corner. Lizzie reached in and cautiously took it out. It was a large bottle, and the label on the side announced that if a few drops of this were regularly added to the pigeons' water supply, it would ward off some disease or other. Lizzie couldn't even begin to pronounce the disease. Her heart skipped a beat. She glanced quickly out the window and, without giving herself time to think it over, twisted the cap on the bottle and shook a few drops into her hand. The liquid inside was the colour of water.

Should she?

She stood for a second with the opened bottle in her hand, the dilapidated clock on the wall tick-ticking the time away. Looking back later that night, it seemed to Lizzie that in this moment she was poised on a cliff edge. If she did nothing and put the bottle back in the press, she'd take a step back from the precipice. But instead she did what she knew she was always going to do and flung herself over the edge, hoping to God that when she eventually landed it would be soft. She turned the bottle upside-down and watched as the liquid flowed out. Oh God, it was slightly darker than water, she noticed then. And it smelled.

Hastily Lizzie turned on the tap to let the stench swirl on down the sink. And, leaving about a quarter of the liquid in the bottle, she put it under the tap and refilled it with water.

Now see how healthy his pigeons stay, she thought, as she gave the top a final vicious screw on.

Joe was preoccupied when he arrived back. He complimented Lizzie on a job well done and said nothing when she told him that she couldn't make it to the club that night as she had other plans.

'Yeah, OK, thanks for your help. If you like you can come over tomorrow and watch the birds come in from the race,' Joe offered, but without his earlier enthusiasm.

'Sure. Maybe.'

Lizzie refused his offer of a lift and insisted that she could walk back to the Luas. It was funny, but the reality of what she'd done had made her feel a little sick and she just had to get away.

21

Tom's flat or 'apartment', as he mockingly called it, was in the city centre. It wasn't exactly situated in the most sought-after area of the city either, Lizzie thought as she neared it. It had the run-down look of Royal Lawns without any potential for charm.

She hadn't known she was on her way here when she'd jumped on the Luas after leaving Joe's. It had been a blur, dumping the stuff down the sink, leaving his house, her thoughts whirling about like mad. Feeling euphoria, feeling guilty, feeling good, feeling like she was the worst person on earth. She hadn't bargained on the guilt at all. She certainly hadn't felt guilty up until now, but then again, she hadn't actually done any harm up until now.

Lizzie stood for a bit, just up the road from Tom's place, looking at his window on the second floor and seeing the dim light through the thin, tatty curtains. She thought she saw Tom move about. She even fancied he looked out and saw her, but it was probably only her imagination. She needed his company tonight, she thought to herself. Tom was calm and reasonable and the norms of society never seemed to bother him. Sure, hadn't she met him after he'd tried to skip the queue in a bar? He wouldn't think anything of what she'd done. Or would he? She didn't know. But, she thought, she'd probably do it again, and the knowledge made her feel worse about herself. After all the pigeons hadn't done anything to her personally. But then again, Megan had done nothing to Joe and look what had happened to her. Once she thought of Megan, her heart squeezed slightly. Hardened. And she found that by focusing on her sister, the pigeons suddenly ceased to matter.

Still, she just needed to see Tom right now. She had planned on going home from Joe's and asking Billy and Aileen all about their baby scan, which had happened earlier today, but she just couldn't talk babies when she'd done what she'd done. No, she had to see Tom. He'd make her feel good again.

She hadn't rung him to say she was on her way. Maybe she should have, but he'd rung her earlier so she knew he was free. She hoped his rehearsal was finished; she didn't want to stand around outside his flat, waiting for him. She just needed him to . . . Lizzie wasn't sure what she needed from him. His easy company, she guessed. Just to be able to sit beside him and feel special. Tom always made her feel like that.

Lizzie started to walk across the large green towards his place, ignoring the stares of the teenagers who had congregated in a large group over at a run-down swing. They watched her from behind a broken-down fence as she passed. She had just got to the door of the apartment block and was about to buzz up when she saw Tom jogging down the stairs.

'Hey,' his grin was crooked, delighted, showing his uneven front teeth, 'I thought it was you. What are you doing here?'

'Just thought I'd surprise you.' She tried to match his grin. 'Surprise!' she sang.

Tom's grin widened. 'I didn't expect you so early, thought you had things to do.' He jammed his hands into his pockets and rocked back on his heels, his over-long hair, just the right side of mussed, falling over an eye so brown it was almost black.

'Yeah, but I'm finished now.'

'Brill.' He winked and ushered her in front of him as they climbed the stairs to his second-floor flat. 'Come on up, I have some beers in the fridge.' He paused. 'Or do you want to head out?'

Lizzie knew he hadn't much spare cash and that he wouldn't like her paying. 'Nope. Here is fine.'

He looked relieved. 'OK.' He pushed open his front door and strode ahead of Lizzie into the apartment.

'You should really lock your door,' she chided gently.

'Yeah?' Tom spread his arms wide, 'And, eh, what exactly would a potential thief actually steal?'

He had a point. His place reflected its owner: broke but optimistic. It was bright; a bit too bright – Lizzie would never have considered yellow and red on opposite walls. He had themed the walls with a green and purple mat that the previous occupant had left behind and had also painted his kitchen presses a purple, to match the mat and to hide the filth of the wood. The whole effect was enough to induce a migraine, but Lizzie was used to it.

The sound of a toilet flushing startled her. 'Have you company?' she asked.

'Just Imogen from the play,' Tom said. 'I told you I had a rehearsal, remember?'

'Here?'

'Uh-huh. We need to work a lot together. So we just met to talk about it.'

Tom turned back to rummage in the fridge and eventually located two cans behind some mouldy cheese. He handed Lizzie one and, taking it from him, she sat down on his sofa, feeling it immediately sink underneath her.

'Hey, Imogen, do you want a can?' Tom called as a very pretty blonde girl emerged from the bathroom. She had blonde bouncy curls and a clichéd good-looking face: peaches and cream skin, rosebud-red lips and long lashes fringing eyes of navy blue.

'No, thanks.' Her gaze fell on Lizzie and she smiled, the dimples on her cheeks adding to the irritating wholesomeness of her. 'Hello,' she said. 'I'm Imogen, the love of your boyfriend's life.'

'In the play,' Tom laughed.

'Hi,' Lizzie said. She couldn't imagine Imogen trying to poison pigeons. The girl looked as if she should be the angel on a Christmas card.

'We're having a laugh, aren't we, Tommy?'

'Yep.' Tom sank on to the sofa beside Lizzie. 'Can we finish up now though? I wasn't expecting Lizzie so early.'

126

'Sure.' Imogen picked up a colourful coat from the table. 'Nice to meet you, Lizzie.'

'Bye,' Lizzie nodded and watched the girl move her shapely bum out the door.

'Lovely girl,' Tom remarked as he took a slug of beer.

'Is she, *Tommy*?' Lizzie teased, poking him in the chest. She rolled her eyes. 'Tommy, how are ya!' she scoffed.

He grinned. 'I just thought Tommy Lynch sounded a better name than Tom Lynch.'

'Once it's you it sounds good to me.'

Tom laughed and wrapped a companionable arm about her shoulders. 'Cheers.'

'Yeah cheers, you poseur!' They clinked cans and were silent for a bit.

'So, how come you're here early?' Tom asked.

'Are you complaining?'

'Nope.' He leaned in and kissed the tip of her nose.

Lizzie felt tears in her eyes. She didn't deserve that. Right at that moment, she felt like the most horrible person on earth.

'Hey.' Tom, noticing, lowered his gaze to meet hers. 'What's the matter? Have I done something? Are you OK?'

'Yeah.' Lizzie blinked rapidly and put her can down on the floor. 'I'm fine.' She cupped his face in her hands. He was the sexiest guy. He oozed it without even knowing it. The way he walked, his voice, the slow, easy grin. He could make her forget what she'd done. Maybe even make her regret what she'd done. 'Kiss me,' she muttered. 'I mean, *really* kiss me.'

Tom grinned. Gently he covered her two hands with his own and brought his lips to meet hers. Their foreheads touched and he squeezed her hands, letting his lips gently press on hers. Lizzie, he was convinced, was the love of his life. He adored her no nonsense, no bullshit manner. He liked the way she dressed and the way she looked and the way she made him feel. He liked that she needed space and didn't crowd him the way other girls might have done, and he prayed every night that she wouldn't suddenly go off him because he had feck all to give her.

'That's not a real kiss,' Lizzie murmured, grinning.

He regarded her with his chocolate-coloured eyes. He landed another soft kiss on her lips. She smelled a little funny, he thought. A sharp smell. But she tasted lovely.

'Yeah,' Lizzie said, 'like that, only longer.'

'OK.' He nodded, untangling his fingers from hers. With one hand in her spiky hair and the other at the back of her head, he kissed her as he'd wanted to for so long. He felt the length of her body as she pressed herself to him. She had her hands up his T-shirt now and was pushing herself so hard against him. There was something desperate in it, though. It wasn't like Lizzie. She normally teased him by pulling away from him and driving him mad until he had no choice but to grab her. Tonight she wasn't doing that. He pulled away.

'Lizzie,' he asked, his breath ragged, 'are you OK?'

'Yeah. What's the matter?'

'Nothing.' He frowned slightly, his body telling him one thing but his mind telling him something else. 'Are you planning on staying?' he asked.

'Are you planning on letting me?' She didn't wait for an answer and leaned back into him. He couldn't help it. He ran his hands over her face, over her body, his face pressed to hers, his mouth not able to get enough of her. 'Oh God,' he groaned.

'Let's keep going and see what happens,' she whispered.

'You know what will happen,' he said back, trying to stop the shake in his voice.

'Good,' was all she said.

She smiled at him impishly and there was no turning back.

Lizzie awoke to the jingle-jangle of her phone. Tom groaned but remained sleeping. Lizzie sat up and immediately the sound of the phone stopped. She glanced across at Tom's alarm clock and saw that it was three in the morning. Jesus, who the hell would be ringing her at that hour? She lay back down and the phone started to ring again.

It was the loudest ring tone ever. It was the loudest phone ever.

She decided that she'd better turn it off and crept out of bed, padding barefoot and semi-naked towards the bedroom door.

'Oh, let me guess,' Tom's sleepy voice arrested her, 'this is the part where you sneak off and leave me a thank you note.'

'No,' Lizzie turned to him, 'this is the part where I switch off my mobile phone and try to get back to sleep.'

'So you're coming back?' Tom said as he chewed his lower lip and regarded her. 'Good. I like the sound of that.'

Lizzie blew him a kiss. She left the bedroom and fished her mobile out of the bag. *You have one missed call: Billy.* Jesus, what the hell was he doing ringing her at three in the morning? Then it dawned on her, maybe it was something to do with the baby. All sorts of horrible scenarios ran through her head, so she hastily dialled him back.

'Lizzie!' Billy's voice shot down the phoneline at her. 'Where are you? What happened to you?'

'Nothing. I'm at Tom's.'

'You never said you were meeting him.'

She laughed slightly. 'Who are you, my secretary?'

'No, I'm your brother and I was worried about you.'

'Jesus, Billy, I'm twenty-eight, give me a break.'

'Are you planning on staying there?'

'I am planning right now on hanging up. You gave me a fright ringing at this time in the morning.'

'You gave me a fright, too, not coming home.'

'I thought something was wrong with the baby,' Lizzie went on, ignoring him.

'Babies,' Billy said.

'And I thought—' Lizzie stopped. 'What did you say?'

'Aileen is expecting twins.' His voice was flat.

'Twins?'

'Yep.'

Lizzie wasn't sure what to say. He hadn't been that enamoured with one baby. 'And how is Aileen? How does she feel?' she asked instead.

'I dunno. She's left me.'

129

'WHAT?'

From the bedroom she could hear Tom jump up. He appeared at the door and looked questioningly at her. Lizzie waved him away but, yawning, he filled up the kettle and plugged it in.

'She said,' Billy took a deep breath, 'well, she said she saw my face when the nurse announced it. So she left.'

'You mean she left the hospital?' It was too early in the morning to take all this in, Lizzie thought. It must be some sort of a weird dream.

'Yeah,' Billy confirmed, his voice shaking a little. 'She left the hospital and came home and packed a few things and moved over to her dad's.'

'What the hell did you look like?' Lizzie barked crossly. 'For God's sake—'

'I don't know what I looked like,' Billy barked back. 'I was just shocked, you know? Two babies.'

'OK,' Lizzie sighed deeply. 'Let's get this straight—'

'I am not one of your counselling projects,' Billy said curtly. 'I only rang to see if you were safe. You are. So I'll go.' He hung up.

Lizzie stared at the phone. 'The nerve,' she fumed. She dialled his number again but he didn't answer.

'What's up?' A cup of tea appeared over her shoulder.

'Sorry for waking you.' Lizzie, suddenly shy, pulled her T-shirt down as far as it would go. She took the tea from him and her T-shirt moved up again. Tom came round and sat in beside her, a mug of tea in his own hand. 'Aileen has left Billy, apparently.'

'No way!'

'Yes way.'

As she told Tom the story, she found it hard to meet his eyes. Yes, last night had been bloody great, but now, with Tom looking at her as if he truly loved her, she felt . . . she didn't know. Weird would describe it best. Yesterday she could have accepted it. Today she knew that she wasn't as great as he thought she was. What she had done to Joe's birds was horrible. The love in Tom's eyes for her was a lie. She couldn't live like that, but she couldn't let

Tom go either. And she couldn't not find out the truth from Joe or punish him for what he'd done.

'Do you want me to bring you home?' Tom asked, interrupting her thoughts.

Lizzie hugged the mug between her hands and for the first time met his concerned gaze. 'I just want you to hold me,' she said. 'Don't look at me, just hold me.'

Tom didn't ask why, he just got the big duvet and put it around them both and they sat, his arm about her shoulder, watching the sun steal through the window.

22

MARK HAD INSISTED on coming along to Lizzie's meeting with Jim, the builder. Lizzie hoped that Jim would sell a house to Life at cost price. Jim did not get on with Mark.

'He specifically requested that you not be there,' Lizzie eventually admitted. 'You annoy him, Mark.'

'Yeah,' Mark nodded. 'Success annoys people like Jim O'Brien. But I am the director of Life, I know more about it than you, Lizzie, and if he asks detailed questions, what will you say?'

'I'll tell him, as I always do, that I'll find out the information and get back to him,' Lizzie said through gritted teeth, knowing that the battle was lost. If Mark wanted to come, then Mark would come. She supposed it was the reason he had got Life up and running. He didn't listen to reason so, while he annoyed people, he also at times managed the impossible.

'Mark,' she had one more go, 'a house is a big ask. If Jim can give us a house, I think we have to respect his wishes.'

'Rubbish.' Mark made a dismissive gesture with his hand. 'He has houses coming out of his ears. No, he'll be impressed that I took the time out to come.'

'He won't!'

'Calm down,' Mark shook his head. 'Don't go all hormonal on me. Honestly, you haven't been yourself at all these past few days.'

'Don't you dare say I'm hormonal.' Lizzie removed her coat from the hook at the door and pulled it on. 'Well, seeing as you're determined to come and jeopardise our chances of getting this house, you might as well give me a lift in your fancy car.'

'Will do,' Mark nodded imperiously, holding the door open for her as she marched out of the office.

Lizzie didn't say much to him on the way. It was true what he'd said, she wasn't herself. Part of it was stress: Billy was going mental as Aileen wouldn't talk to him and had refused all his calls – she was being a bit over the top, Lizzie had to admit; plus her mother was going mad in Wexford between worrying about Billy and fighting with the local police force. And on top of that, she had Tom totally under her spell and, while she loved him, she felt as if she were deceiving him. But worst of all was that she just didn't think she had the stomach to see Joe any more. Oh, she wanted to. She wanted to make him pay so badly it hurt, but after she'd poured the bird medication down the sink she also realised that living with a revenge agenda was quite difficult, too.

Could she stop seeing him?

She wasn't sure, and the more she thought about it the more confused she became. But maybe, if she stopped seeing Joe, she could get on with her life with Tom.

Or could she?

Could she ever go back to the woman she was before she'd seen Joe? She'd already taken one step away from that person and it wasn't something she could reverse. Did she want to keep going?

'Bloody wanker!' Mark startled her by blasting his horn at a driver in front who had the audacity to indicate and pull into the line of traffic. His horn blasting was followed by a finger gesture which the other motorist replicated enthusiastically.

'Jesus, Mark, will you calm down? We need to be able to concentrate when we get there. Now,' she tried to focus herself, as she really couldn't afford to blow this or they'd be left high and dry, 'let me do the talking and the schmoozing. You sit and listen and don't speak unless you're spoken to, all right?'

He shrugged a little.

'All right?' Lizzie asked a little more sharply.

'Yeah.' He sounded like a sulky adolescent. Then, 'I don't know what your problem is.'

Lizzie ignored that. Instead she asked, 'How's Stella?'

Stella was Mark's girlfriend. His first since his wife had left him five years ago. Instantly his face changed. 'Aww,' he said, 'she's fantastic. She's some woman. Brilliant.'

'She must be,' Lizzie joked, 'putting up with you.'

'Cheeky,' Mark pretended to swat her. 'I'll have you know, I could charm the birds outta the trees once upon a time. My wife, before she ended up hating my guts, chased me. She was a very forceful woman.'

'Imagine.' Lizzie rolled her eyes. Mark was oblivious to how forceful he could be.

'You don't want to imagine that!' Mark snorted. 'Still, she got her comeuppance. Ran off with the guy we bought our car off and then he ran off on her. Gave her a nervous breakdown, so it did.'

'Oh, that's terrible.' He'd never told her that bit before.

'What goes around comes around,' Mark said cheerfully. 'I had one when she left, so it was only right that she should have one, too.'

'I see your compassionate side is still missing in action,' Lizzie remarked drily.

'You can only have compassion when someone is at least a bit sorry,' Mark huffed. 'Was my wife sorry that she ran off with our car salesman? Did she say sorry for taking all our money out of the bank before she left? Did she admit she'd been conned? Eh-eh,' he made a sound like a buzzer and continued in a faux American accent, 'I don't think so.'

And with those words, he answered Lizzie's dilemma about Joe.

23

Saturday, 31st July

Joe had a party tonight on his dad's new boat. He invited me and told me to bring anyone I liked. I just brought Billy as I wasn't sure how many people I'd be allowed to bring and anyway, Mammy told me that if Billy didn't go then I couldn't. Not that I minded. Billy is great at mixing, just like me.

We went in Billy's new car. Well, it's new to him. In reality, it's a couple of years old and he imported it from England. It's black and has sort of flames painted along the sides and two big exhausts poking out the back and when it goes it ROARS. All his friends are dead impressed by it. I don't know what kind of a car it is but when Mammy saw it, she nearly collapsed. He got a major lecture on speeding and on all the people who have died on Wexford roads and Billy being Billy pretended to take her seriously before asking me and Dad and Lizzie if we wanted to sit in it.

Dad and I sat in the back because Lizzie is as mad as Billy and she insisted on sitting in the front. Well, with Mammy watching anxiously from the driveway, Billy drove nice and easy away but once we were on the open road, he put his foot down and I'm not joking when I say we went from ten to a hundred miles an hour in about five seconds. Billy had the radio on and the windows open and Lizzie was whooping from the front seat. I swear that girl would do anything. Dad was shouting for him to slow down and Billy was pretending that he couldn't hear, what with all the noise from the radio. I just pretended to laugh but it was terrifying – like those video games where all you can see is the road whipping by. Billy's car is so low to the ground that it was all I could see from the back seat. Billy and Lizzie are totally fearless – it's like they think they're invincible. Of course, when Billy did eventually slow down, Dad went ballistic and threatened to take the car off him. Billy just laughed and Lizzie turned round and said in this big bored patronising voice, 'Dad, he's got his own job and his own money and you really can't tell him what to do any more.'

'Sad but true, Dad,' Billy chortled.

'Well,' Dad said back, 'if you go and break your mother's heart by dying on the roads or by killing someone else, I'll never forgive you.'

'He won't.' Lizzie is a great one for sticking up for us. Because she's the youngest she gets away with murder. It's handy sometimes. Lizzie has charm. She has Dad wrapped around her finger. She has all men wrapped around her finger. I have the looks, I don't mind admitting, but Lizzie has the wit. Fellas actually try to impress her. Despite me having the better figure and a nicer face they don't hardly look at me. Aileen says that maybe guys feel as if I'm out of their league and that's why they don't approach me and while I'd like to believe this, I don't think it's true. I always find myself being not quite who I am with lads, trying to be funny or trying to be smart (which is a big mistake for me to do, believe me). Lizzie, with her roundy figure and cheeky grin, is just herself and it works. I never had a boyfriend at her age and it wasn't from lack of trying. Lizzie has guys queuing up to go out with her.

Anyway, I'm going off the point. But it's nice to write things sometimes. Just your thoughts, not what exactly happened, because sometimes they can be two very different things, right? But anyway, suffice to say we left a sulky Lizzie behind when we went to the boat party. (I think she has the hots for Joe because she keeps asking me about him in work. He's miles too old for her. Mam would go mad!) Billy drove, accompanied by about a million instructions from Mammy about not drinking and driving. I reckon that he drove so fast we got to the party five minutes before we actually left!

The place was heaving. And everyone was so dressed up. All I had on was a red summer dress, very short, and a pair of high red sandals. I broke out in a bit of a sweat when I saw how everyone else was so glammed up. Billy didn't seem to notice that he was the only one in jeans and a T-shirt and because Billy didn't care, I suddenly didn't either. If it was OK for Bill, it was OK for me.

It's a gorgeous boat, and I hate boats. It was so new it was still a shining white, its name 'Rossclare Rossi' painted in swirling script all along her hull. And it has a kitchen and toilet and everything. There was music playing and a bar all set up. Lights had been strung all across the deck. Joe was somewhere in the middle of a bunch of people. I know because I could hear him laugh.

Billy and I made our way to the bar and Billy got a water while I had a vodka. And then I saw Dessie. And he saw me and he raised his arm and waved. So I took a massive gulp of the vodka.

'Hi.' Dessie, in a brilliant blue T-shirt and a pair of white cotton trousers came over. God, he looked so dazzling, as if he'd been washed in Daz.

'Hi, Dessie,' I said and I knew I sounded breathless as

if I was about to have an asthma attack or something. 'This is my brother.'

'Billy.' Billy stuck out his hand. 'I've heard all about you from Megs.'

I wanted to kick him.

Then Billy said in a really untactful way, 'I'll leave you to talk to Dessie then, will I, Meg?'

I shrugged. What are you meant to say to a thing like that? He winked at me then mooched off, and was soon chatting up this blonde model-type girl who was way out of his league.

Dessie smiled at me and I smiled back and took another gulp of vodka.

Next minute, up Joe comes. He was manky drunk. I've never seen Joe drunk and this probably sounds terrible, but it suited him. He was smiling, showing off his lovely white teeth. Normally Joe is really quiet, not in a shy way, just in a sort of self-contained way that makes you think he doesn't need people.

'Hey,' he came between Dessie and me and slung his arms about our shoulders, 'how's my two work buddies?'

'You're drunk,' Dessie laughed. 'Jesus, will you stop breathing in my face?'

'Sorry.' Joe straightened himself up, still keeping his arm around me. 'Great crowd, isn't it?'

'Yep,' Dessie said, scanning the deck. 'Not bad.'

'So,' Joe said into my face and boy, did he reek of beer, 'you got here.'

'Naw, I'm just an apparition,' I said. I'm witty when I don't fancy someone, which is unfortunate 'cause I think guys like funny girls, which is why all the guys I don't fancy fancy me.

'And what an apparition,' Joe said, shaking his head. 'Gorgeous.' Then he asked, 'So where is the real Megan?'

'At a real party,' I said back.

And they laughed. I was actually quite proud of that comment.

'Where's Denise tonight?' Joe asked Dessie. 'I thought you were bringing her.'

Dessie rolled his eyes. 'Massive row,' he confirmed. 'Again. In fact, I think it's definitely over.' He didn't sound that upset over it.

'Yeah, sure!' Joe laughed, unconcerned.

'I was meant to go up to visit her this weekend.' Dessie locked eyes with me. 'So when I asked her down she refused to come, and I said that I wasn't going up as Joe needed me at his party to give it a bit of street cred.'

'Wanker,' Joe said easily, a big lazy grin on his face. 'You'd really want to treat her a bit better, Dessie.'

'Like you would?'

I think there was what would be called a tense silence? Then a very drunk girl wearing what looked like half a dress slithered up to Joe and wrapped an arm in his. She reminded me of a snake shedding its skin.

'Joey, will you show me where I can find the crisps?' She batted her eyes at him.

'Show her there, Dessie,' Joe said, ignoring the girl and keeping his arm around me.

'She asked you,' Dessie said.

They locked eyes.

'Please, Joey?' The girl had her hand on Joe's arm and was running a taloned finger up and down. 'I want you to.' She slipped an arm about him. 'Please.'

Joe sighed. 'Come on, so.' He left us, the girl clinging on to him and barely managing to stagger in her high heels.

'She's mad about him,' Dessie snorted. 'Every time we go out, she throws herself at him. Of course Joe is too honourable to lead her on, but I keep telling him that's what the girl wants.'

'Who is she?' The girl had wrapped her arms about his neck and was attempting to slow dance with him.

'Jessica is her name. She's been after him for years. Joe has quite a fan club, you know. Jessica is at the helm.'

Both of us started to laugh as Joe, reaching behind the bar, managed to grab a six-pack of crisps and thrust it at her, before making his escape.

'A fan club?' I have to say I was surprised. He didn't strike me as the kind of guy girls would go for.

'Oh yeah.' Dessie screwed up his face. 'Even Denise had a thing for him when we met her first.'

How could someone, given the choice, fancy Joe over Dessie? I wondered.

'She said it was because he didn't try to impress her.'

I rolled my eyes. 'What girl wants a guy who doesn't try to impress? If I had a boyfriend he'd have to be impressing me all the time.'

Dessie looked at me in amusement. 'Yeah?'

'Oh yes.' I knocked back the rest of my vodka. 'Or at least he'd have to try.'

'How would he try?' Dessie was regarding me curiously now. 'What impresses a great-looking girl like you?'

'Compliments like that for a start,' I said.

Dessie bit his lower lip and grinned. 'So, compliments. Stuff like being told that you have the sexiest pair of legs on this boat?'

'Uh-huh.' My head was beginning to spin, I don't know if it was Dessie or the vodka, but whatever it was it was cool.

'And that red is your colour and your eyes are gorgeous and that your mouth looks as if it was made to be kissed and . . .'

He went on like this, throwing out compliments as if they were sweets for me to eat. And I thought with each compliment he was moving closer to me. Or maybe it was me moving closer to him, I don't know. If we'd got any closer, I'd probably have had a heart attack. In fact, I'm convinced that Dessie was about to plant a kiss on my lips when the engine of the boat suddenly roared to life, jerking me forward into Dessie's arms. People cheered.

'And off we go!' Joe yelled above the cheering.

'Oh, I am sorry,' I lied as I tried to untangle myself.

'I'm not.' Dessie took his hands from my arms and looked in amusement at me. 'That was quite nice.'

'You have a girlfriend,' I blabbered out. I wanted to appear moral, even if I didn't feel it.

'I do.' Dessie assumed a glum sort of look. Then added, 'For now.'

What did that mean? I wondered. It sounded good though.

The boat sped up and a girl beside us yelped.

'Isn't Joe a bit drunk to be driving this boat?' the girl asked us. I could have killed her for interrupting what was a good line of conversation.

Next thing there was the sound of a speed boat, which actually turned out to be the coastguards. Someone must have rung and reported Joe for taking the boat out whilst drinking. A man with a loudspeaker ordered Joe to bring the boat in.

'Oh-oh,' Dessie sounded slightly amused, 'someone's in trouble.'

The long and the short of it was that the party ended pretty abruptly – Joe was hauled off by the police and Dessie and a couple of others went with him.

Just as Dessie left he turned to me. 'Thanks for keeping me company tonight,' he said. Then he ran to catch up with Joe, who was being treated rather roughly by the coastguards.

I can't wait to see him Monday.

And Billy assures me that Dessie looks as if he's really into me! Though I couldn't say the same about the blonde he'd been chatting up.

24

JOE WAS ALMOST sick as he accompanied Ellen into the police station. For the last five years, since his release, he'd avoided even going past police buildings and now, here he was, in one again. It was still the same as he remembered. The desk, the forms, the noise and bustle. At least this time, though, he was there as a law-abiding citizen. But it still didn't stop him from thinking that he'd be arrested on some misdemeanour he didn't even know he'd committed.

'Hello,' Ellen, full of purpose, marched up to the desk, 'I'm Ellen McGrath and this is my neighbour, Joseph. We're here to meet with,' she unfolded a piece of official-looking headed paper and read out, 'Anthony Carter.'

'Aw, Anthony Carter,' the policeman repeated, in a not-too-promising sort of voice. 'Yes, he's in here. Come on.'

Joe followed Ellen as she went after the policeman. He had to take deep breaths as he was shown to a small interrogation room. Walls bland and white. Bland brown desk. Bland brown chairs. Anthony was sitting in one of the chairs, twisting his stick-thin fingers one about the other. He glanced up nervously as they came in. Then, as he saw Joe, he said loudly, 'That's the fella that broke me nose, Ma.'

Anthony's mother, thinner than her son, was sitting beside him and a woman guard was on his other side.

'Shut up, Anto,' his mother hissed nervously.

'Ellen and Joe,' the guard said, 'welcome.'

Ellen was right, Joe noticed – Anthony was younger than he'd thought the night of the break-in. Sitting here now with his mam, he looked no older than his thirteen years.

Ellen slid into a seat opposite the boy whilst Joe remained standing. He couldn't help it. Much as he wanted to sit down, he was afraid that if he did, he'd never be let out of the room. Stupid, he knew.

'Would you like to sit down, Joseph?' the guard asked.

Joe shook his head and gulped audibly. 'No, ta.'

'It helps if we all sit,' the woman said in a slightly firmer voice.

Joe winced, and then nodded. He pulled out a chair and sat, a little away from the table, rubbing his hands nervously up and down his jeans.

'OK,' the guard said. 'Now, I'd like to introduce you both to Anthony's mother, Ann.'

'Hello,' Ann said. Then, in a rush, 'Thank you both for agreeing to this. I know it couldn't have been easy.' Her eyes met Ellen's. 'Especially for you.'

Ellen managed a smile. 'Well, if Joseph hadn't agreed, I'd never have come.'

Anthony's mother swallowed hard. 'OK. Right. Well, thank you, Joseph,' she said. Her voice wobbled.

'It's Joe,' Joe said, without quite knowing why. He guessed he felt sorry for her. A little, anyway.

'Joe,' she repeated.

'Now,' the guard went on, 'Anthony has thought a lot about what he has done, haven't you, Anthony?'

'Uh-huh,' Anthony said. He was staring at his hands.

'What does "uh-huh" mean?' the guard asked.

'It means "yes",' Anthony said defensively. 'Everyone knows that.'

'It would help if you'd say "yes" or "no"' the guard said.

'You answer properly now, Anto,' his mother ordered, poking him in his arm.

'Sorry,' Anthony muttered. Then, lifting his head slightly from the desk, he said, 'I'm sorry for what I done.'

There was a silence.

'Would you like to say anything, Ellen?' the guard asked.

Ellen swallowed and opened her mouth but nothing came out.

'Ellen?' the guard pressed gently.

'She collapsed,' Joe said suddenly, startling everyone. 'She collapsed after you were taken away, Anthony, d'you know that?'

Anthony was like a rabbit caught in headlights.

'Joe—' Ellen began, but Joe held up his hand to silence her.

'No, Ellen, let me tell him. She collapsed, Anthony, and she had to be brought to hospital. If I hadn't been there, she could have died, d'you know that?'

Anthony shook his head.

'Yeah,' Joe nodded as he moved nearer to the table. 'Would you like a death on your conscience, Anthony? Would you?'

Anthony shook his head.

'Is that a "no"?' the policewoman asked.

'Because I'm telling ya, Anthony, living with a death on your conscience is no joke. Even if you hadn't meant it to happen, it's no bloody joke. Even if you didn't even know it happened and you found out, it's no joke. So think hard before you decide to rob anyone the next time, ey?'

There was a silence. Joe scanned the room. Ellen was staring at him, looking almost as shocked as Anthony and his mother. The guard was trying to smile to normalise the situation – this outburst was not part of the rehabilitation plan.

Joe stood up and made his way to the door.

'I'm going out to get some air,' he said as he pushed the door open. 'You carry on.'

Lizzie had asked Billy if she could borrow his car to go into town.

Billy, who was still shell-shocked by Aileen leaving him, had barely registered the request, so Lizzie had taken advantage of that before he could change his mind. She grabbed the keys and, hopping in, fired the ignition. The car chugged a little before finally getting going.

Billy's car was a wreck, she thought as she pulled out into traffic. A one-litre ten-year-old shuddering piece of metal. Still, it did manage, after a fashion, to get from A to B. Driving it was an experience, as everyone on the road seemed to want to pass

145

it out. If the car was a person it would be the class nerd, shaking and shivering in a corner as it watched all its super buddies glide along through life.

Lizzie hoped she knew where she was going. She'd consulted the internet for directions and found a Dublin street map online. She was looking for Duke's Road in Dun Laoghaire. She knew roughly how to get to Dun Laoghaire but, beyond that, she was lost.

Twenty minutes later she pulled up by the side of the road to ask someone.

'Oh yes,' the man said, grinning, and, sounding almost delighted, announced, 'it's *miles* away.'

Lizzie's heart sank.

'You're way out of your way,' he went on. Then, pointing, he said, 'Now, go down to the crossroads down here, then turn left. Right? Then take a right and another left. Right? Then after that you'll come to a roundabout, don't take the first right, take the second one and you'll be on the right road. It's straight on from there. You can't go wrong.'

But she did. Lizzie cursed in frustration. Jesus, she should have asked Tom to go with her, he could have read the map. But Tom was very busy at the moment, so she hadn't really been able to meet up with him. They'd gone for a drink once or twice, but Lizzie had feigned tiredness and come home early. She knew he was wondering what was up and why they hadn't spent the night together since, and she knew she'd have to confront it sooner or later. Make a decision. But for now, all she wanted was for Tom to still be in her life, to be her normality, even if it was on the fringes. The thought of losing him hurt her, but so had the thought of not knowing what had happened to Meg.

And then she saw it, like a little miracle: Duke's Road, printed on a signpost at the beginning of a lovely leafy avenue. Wow, Lizzie thought as she drove up Aileen's dad's street, she had no idea that Aileen came from such a fancy area. Big detached houses with large front gardens. Nice.

She pulled up outside number 13 and saw that there was a

146

car in the driveway, so someone must be home. Taking a deep breath, she hopped out of Billy's car.

'What just happened in there?' Ellen startled Joe as she came up behind him. He was having a smoke outside the door of the police station.

'Nothing.' He blew the smoke out in a long, thin stream and watched it being carried away on the calm air. 'Just, I dunno, lost it for a second, that's all.'

'Really,' Ellen said, not sounding as if she believed him. 'OK. Are you ready to come back in?'

Joe met her gaze. 'Can you carry on without me? I'll wait here for you and bring you home, but that bloody place,' he indicated the station behind him, 'gives me the creeps.'

Ellen stood beside him and touched him gently on the arm. 'I'm just going to say this once, Joseph,' she said calmly. 'You helped me, and if you ever want me to return the favour, I will.' A squeeze. 'OK?' Then she turned on her heel and left him staring after her. It wasn't until he turned to take another drag of his fag that he realised he had a huge lump in his throat.

Aileen's dad was the biggest man Lizzie had ever seen. In fact he was even bigger than the last time she had seen him. His huge shoulders seemed to fill up the whole door frame. A giant fist was curled about the front door, holding it open.

'Lizzie,' he said, his eyes widening. 'Nice to see you.'

Well, at least he wasn't going to give her an ear-bashing about her brother, Lizzie thought in relief.

'Thanks, eh . . .' She tried to think of his name and couldn't.

'Abe,' he supplied with a small smile. Then, indicating the hallway behind him, he lowered his voice and said, 'Have you come to talk some sense into herself?'

'Well,' Lizzie shrugged, 'I don't know if sense is the word, but I know Billy misses her and is trying to ring her.'

Abe nodded. 'She won't talk to him. I keep trying to make her, but she won't.'

That didn't seem too promising. 'Can I see her?' Lizzie asked.

'Oh, be my guest.' Abe stood out of the way to let her by. 'She's still in bed, though. She spends her time in bed when she's not at work. When I try to talk to her, all I get is hysterics.' He winced. 'There are some things fathers just aren't good at.'

'There are some things none of us are good at,' Lizzie joked feebly.

'Well, when you've finished, you're welcome to join me for a cuppa,' Abe said. 'I could do with someone to talk to who's not going to blame men for all the wrongs in the world.'

Oh God, it sounded as if Aileen was really furious, Lizzie thought. She gave Abe a weak smile and slowly ascended the stairs.

The landing was wide, with doors leading off it in all directions. Luckily there were signs saying Bathroom, Dad's Room, Spare Room, and then one that said Aileen's Room. It had a picture of ballet shoes on it and a teddy. It had obviously hung there for years and years as it was faded and dusty.

Lizzie knocked gently on the door.

'Go away, Dad, I already told you I feel sick.'

'It's, eh, me, Aileen,' Lizzie said timidly. 'Lizzie.'

'And what do you want?' The sound of pounding footsteps followed by an opening wrench of the bedroom door. 'Huh,' Aileen turned on her heel and flounced back towards the bed, 'have you come to plead for him?'

'He doesn't even know I'm here.' Lizzie took a hesitant step inside.

'Yeah. Sure.' Aileen had her face buried in the pillow again. 'Well, you can tell him from me that he's wasting his time calling me. I am never going back to a man who does not want his own children.'

'Aileen,' Lizzie tried to keep her voice nice and calm, 'of course he wants his own children. And he wants you.'

Aileen's body stiffened. Then relaxed. Then she turned over on the bed and slowly sat up. 'You didn't see his face, Lizzie. You weren't there.' Her voice sounded teary. 'Oh God, it was so humiliating.'

A big tear trickled down her cheek and she furiously scrubbed it away. 'I don't even know why I'm crying,' she said half savagely. 'I hate him. I hate him.'

She sounded as if she did too, Lizzie thought despairingly. 'What did he look like?' she asked instead.

'Has he not told you what happened?' Aileen asked.

'Nope.' Lizzie took the chance of moving in beside her on the bed. 'You know Billy, he doesn't talk about stuff like that.'

'Oh, I know him all right,' Aileen's tone was bitter, 'and I wish I didn't.' Her hand touched her tummy briefly. 'My poor little babies.'

Lizzie waited, saying nothing.

Eventually Aileen spoke again. 'We were getting a scan done,' she said. 'The first one. And you know how excited I was, Lizzie. I just couldn't wait to see our little baby on the monitor. Billy said he couldn't wait either. And in we went and the nurse rubbed the gel on my stomach and got the little roundy thing so that she could see the baby and next thing, she turns to us and says, "Oh my God, there are two little ones in here." And I laughed and turned to Billy and, oh, Lizzie, you should have seen him.' She sniffed and shook her head. 'The nurse didn't know where to look. He was like a statue and his mouth was wide open and his face was white and he says, "Two" as if he'd never heard the bloody number before and the nurse nods, that's right, she says, two. Twins. You're having twins, congratulations. And he tried to smile but he couldn't, Lizzie. He physically couldn't. I saw it, Lizzie. And so did the nurse. And when I walked out of there I told him I was leaving. And he asked why and I just said, because I saw the way you looked. And he didn't say anything because he knew what I meant. He knew.' More tears.

Lizzie patted her on the back in a lame gesture of support. 'He's awful sorry, Aileen,' she said softly. 'I suppose at the time he couldn't help it. It was a shock to him. But he's sorry now.'

'It's too late to be sorry,' Aileen said in a vicious sort of a whisper. 'The damage is done. Some things you just can't take back.'

Lizzie's hand froze mid-pat. Naw, she thought, she couldn't mean it. Aileen and Billy were like her Mecca of relationships. They were mad about each other. Weren't they?

'I know he's your brother and everything,' Aileen said, 'but he's not the Billy I used to know.' She looked at Lizzie. 'D'you remember the way he used to be, Lizzie?'

Lizzie shrugged. Of course she remembered.

'He used to be mad,' Aileen said softly. 'Totally mad. Sometimes a little too reckless maybe, but Jesus, Lizzie, he lived. He was fun. He drank, he made me laugh.' A pause. 'Now he only makes me miserable.'

'He just worries.' Lizzie tried to stick up for Billy. He'd be heartbroken if he could hear Aileen, she was sure of it. 'You've got the house and a mortgage and he worries.'

'He never used to.'

'No,' Lizzie said softly, 'I know that. But ever since Megan—' She didn't finish.

'Ever since Megan,' Aileen repeated, then shook her head. 'Well, Lizzie, Megan was my friend too and I miss her and I loved her, but you have to keep going.'

Lizzie said nothing.

'You loved her too,' Aileen said, 'and you've kept going.'

Lizzie gulped. Megan's death had changed everything. The way things like that do, she supposed. She had moved on, but she'd changed, just like Billy had.

'Billy has moved on too,' she said eventually.

Aileen said nothing.

'He loves you, Aileen, he's so miserable and so sorry and you won't even talk to him.'

'He humiliated me. He humiliated his own children.'

'He never meant to.'

'And how would you know? He never even told you what happened.'

'Because I know my own brother.' Lizzie's voice rose despite herself. 'I know Billy.'

'Yeah, well,' Aileen shook her head, 'I just need to be away

150

from him now because I feel like I could kill him.' She sniffed and turned back to her pillow. Lizzie sat like a spare not knowing what to do.

'You can go now,' Aileen said. A pause. 'Thanks for coming over.'

'It was his first robbery,' Ellen filled Joe in on the way home. 'He's only thirteen, the poor pet.'

'The poor pet?' Joe almost laughed.

'Oh, don't take that tone,' Ellen said, a little annoyed. 'You didn't stay to hear why he'd done it.'

'Ellen, he broke into your house, he tried to take your money. You collapsed. And he's the victim?' Joe looked at her in disbelief.

'Keep your eyes on the road,' Ellen said primly as she fluffed up her hair and adjusted her skirt. 'His father died, if you must know. There is no income going into that house and the poor child needed money for next year's school books and his mother didn't have it.'

'Are there not grants for that sort of thing?'

'What little boy is going to know about grants?' Ellen looked at him in surprise. 'Honestly, Joseph, I'd never have had you down for a cynic. I'd have thought you'd have compassion.'

'I have compassion for you,' Joe said patiently.

'Well, I have compassion for Anthony,' Ellen replied. 'And I have asked him to help me with little jobs after school to earn some money for his books.'

'You *what?*' Joe almost crashed into the car in front of him, he was so shocked.

'Yes, I did. And his mother said he was a great lad really and the lady guard who was there, the, whatever you call her – facilitator – thought it was tremendous.'

'Tremendously stupid,' Joe replied. 'I mean, how do they know it was his first robbery? He took the glass out of your door pretty good. I'd say he was a pro.'

'Are you trying to frighten me?' Ellen turned from him. 'Because I won't be put off, Joseph. There are some things that you just

151

feel are right to do. That's all there is to it. And anyway, everyone deserves a second chance.'

Joe said nothing. Maybe she was right, who knew. She was obviously feeling a lot better anyway, now that she was back to arguing with him.

'What are you smiling at?' she asked archly.

'You. You're back to yourself again, having a go at me.'

Ellen laughed. 'Joseph, if I was fifty years younger, I'd have a go at you.'

'Christ!' Joe spluttered. 'You dirty old woman!'

25

LIZZIE HADN'T COME on a Saturday night to the pigeon club before and the place was buzzing. Who would have thought that a few birds flying about the place could cause such excitement? She stood for a second in the door, unsure of what she should do, when, to her relief, Cid called across to her. 'Oy! Gorgeous! Over here.'

A few lads laughed. Lizzie wasn't sure if it was at the 'gorgeous' reference. That would be a bit insulting.

'You watch that lecher,' some guy laughed as she passed him.

'Watch him?' Lizzie raised her eyebrows. 'I can hardly bear to look at him.'

There were whoops and cheers at that and even Cid smirked.

Joe was standing beside Cid and two other men. He grinned at her as she approached.

'Hey, how's it going?' he asked. He indicated the two men she hadn't met before. 'This is Noel and this is John.'

'Hi.' Lizzie shook their hands. Noel was around sixty-five, with a big smiley face, whilst John was younger, maybe in his forties. He seemed to have a bad hip or leg as his body was slightly lopsided.

'Haven't seen you in a few weeks,' Joe remarked. 'I thought I'd frightened you off.'

'Nope,' she made herself grin back, 'just really busy these last couple of weeks, that's all.'

'Yeah. I never even spotted you on the Luas or anything.'

She'd been leaving later to avoid bumping into him, but now that her mind was finally made up, she wasn't going to shy away any more. Step two of her plan was riskier, but focusing on Megan dispensed with any qualms of conscience she'd experienced. And her conscience was like a bold child, rearing up when she least expected it. Thinking of Megan was how she'd learned to tame it.

'So how're the birds?' she asked.

Before Joe could answer, Alan held up his hands for hush.

'Right everyone, we've the results here.'

Immediately people began sussing each other.

When there was relative silence, Alan said, 'I'll read out the top three, as usual, and post the rest on the board. OK, it was a close call today. The times are all within seconds of each other. Here we go. In third place was Jim's Autopilot.'

'Again?' Cid bit his lip in frustration as Jim smiled amicably around.

'In second was Peter Doyle's Judas.'

'No way!' That was Peter. He'd never been placed before. 'Brilliant!'

'And first place . . .' Alan rolled his eyes and joked, 'This is getting boring now, it's Joe's bloody Prince. Yet again.'

There was laughter and congratulations. Lizzie expected Joe to be jumping around the place but he just smiled in a half embarrassed way as he went up to accept the cheque.

'It's getting boring for me, too,' he said to the room at large, 'having to finance the drinks every week.'

Someone clapped.

'That bloody bird can't be normal,' Cid grumbled. 'Jaysus, it won almost everything last year and now it's at it again.'

'Be happy for your friend,' Noel said back, patronisingly. 'You know, smile a little.'

Joe arrived back. 'You coming to the pub with us?' he asked Lizzie. 'I'll get you a drink. My way of saying thanks for cleaning out the birds the other week.' He turned to the others. 'I swear, the boxes were never as clean as when she did them.'

'You can do my box if you like,' Cid scoffed, poking her.

'I can give you a box if you like,' Lizzie said back, causing the lads to laugh.

'You've a very sharp tongue on you for such a pretty girl,' Cid muttered.

'You'll never know anything about her tongue,' Noel spluttered. 'You dirty auld fella!'

'Awful,' Joe rolled his eyes as he held the door open for Lizzie. 'You can't bring them anywhere.'

The pub wasn't too crowded and the five of them found seats around a small table. Joe handed the barman his cheque and asked to have the change out of it once he'd ordered for everyone.

'You won again?' the barman asked in amusement.

'Yep.'

'OK. No worries. Now what's everyone having?'

Joe carried five drinks down to the table. He was glad Lizzie had come back, he was afraid he'd put her off or scared her away or something. That would have been a shame as all he'd wanted to do was show her how wonderful the birds were. She was chatting easily to John and he marvelled at her ability to fit in. It had taken him weeks to build up the courage to even assume that he could sit with a particular group at a table, but, he guessed, he hadn't always been like that.

'Now,' he said, putting down the drinks. Everyone helped themselves.

'To Prince,' John said, stealing a sly glance in Cid's direction. 'A prince among birds.'

'Yeah,' Cid raised his own glass, 'let's hope he gets some disease and dies.'

Lizzie flinched as the others threw beer mats at him and told him to shut up.

'You OK?' Joe asked in an undertone. 'Don't mind Cid, no one takes him seriously. He's not a bad guy half the time.'

'Telling you what,' John said as he put his pint down, 'it'd be the worst thing to happen though, wouldn't it? It happened to a friend of mine. All the pigeons died on him and he had to knock the lofts down and rebuild.'

'It would have been the best thing for my marriage, though,'

155

John said dryly as they all laughed. He turned to Lizzie. 'My wife hated the pigeons. She kept saying I loved them more than her.'

'She was right, though, wasn't she?' Noel smirked.

'Yeah well, birds don't nag, do they? They don't tell you to put the top back on the toothpaste or to put the lid down on the jax. Nope, me and my birds, a match made in heaven.'

'Yeah, you've so much in common,' Cid nodded, 'all yez do is eat, shit and drink.'

'Exactly.'

'If my birds died, I might as well be dead,' Noel went on. 'I'm years building up that loft.' He looked at Lizzie, 'D'you think we're all mad?'

'No,' she said. 'I'd feel the same, I suppose.'

'Joe,' Cid said seriously, 'you make that girl fall in love with you.' He turned to Lizzie, 'Jesus, where were you when I was looking for love all those years ago? I had to settle for the wife, I couldn't find a decent woman to put up with me at all.'

'Eh, newsflash,' Noel said. 'Not entirely your pigeons' fault, I wouldn't say.'

Cid stood up abruptly and glared at Noel. 'I dunno why I always sit with yez,' he snapped. 'All I get is insults. I'm going over to another table.'

'You sit with us because,' John began to sing: 'We are the winners. You are the losers.'

'May your pigeons turn around and cripple your other bloody leg,' Cid said crossly as he pushed his way out, his pint held aloft.

'Ouch!' John said mildly, rubbing his bad leg. 'That hurts, Cid.'

'Aw, fuck off!'

Noel looked at his watch. 'Twenty minutes tonight,' he chortled. Then, at Lizzie's questioning look, he said, 'The time it takes for Cid to get insulted and leave.'

She grinned. 'That's not nice.'

'Neither is he,' John said.

Lizzie didn't know whether to agree or not.

* * *

The night ended around twelve-fifteen. Lizzie had no idea that she'd spent that long in the pub. She'd meant to leave in time to catch a Luas home but there was no hope of that now. Despite herself, she'd found the lads very entertaining. And Joe continued to surprise her. He was far quieter than she'd anticipated. He never got involved in the arguments or slagged anyone too harshly. He laughed a lot, though, and it transformed him. It gave him the look of someone who could be great craic. If she hadn't known better, she'd have assumed that he was really quite gentle. But people who were gentle didn't hit women, did they?

'How are you getting home?' Joe asked as he saw her preparing to leave. He glanced at his watch. 'The Luas has stopped, hasn't it?'

'I'll walk,' Lizzie said more cheerily than she felt. It was about three miles in the dark. She supposed she could ask Billy to pick her up but he was so bloody moody at the moment, she didn't want to risk it. Plus he was drinking a lot more since Aileen left, and she didn't want him arrested for drunk driving.

'You will not,' the three men said together, looking appalled.

'Where do you live?' Noel was putting on his coat.

'Dundrum.'

'Aw, that's only about five minutes from my place. I'll drive you.' He jangled his keys. 'I've only had one pint, promise.'

'You sure it's not a problem?'

'Yep.'

'OK. Thanks.' They really were a nice, if odd, bunch of men, Lizzie thought as she made to follow Noel.

'Oh,' Joe called after her as he jumped up from his seat. To her surprise he looked a little awkward. 'I'm, eh, going on a training toss early Tuesday morning if you like.'

No matter how early it was, she'd be there. 'How early?'

'Well, probably six o'clock. I'm driving about thirty miles out of the city, letting them go, and then driving to work. Should make it into the city for nine. Does that suit you?'

'Yeah. I'll be at your place for six.'

'Naw, I'll pick you up from yours,' Joe said. 'Sure, you'd never make it over to me. What's the address?'

So she told him to meet her on the main road – there was no way she could risk Billy seeing him.

'OK, see you then.'

'Hey Joe!' Cid yelled loudly from a nearby table. 'You play your cards right with that young wan and you might be able to poker!'

Lizzie laughed as Joe flushed. 'I apologise for that,' he said, rolling his eyes.

'No worries. See you Tuesday.' She ran to catch up with Noel.

'Joe must like you,' Noel remarked as they emerged into the dark night. He pressed his keys and immediately the lights flashed on his car. A big sturdy Volkswagen.

Lizzie said nothing, just sat into the passenger seat.

'He doesn't normally bother with new members.' Noel started the car and pulled out of the car park on to the road. 'If you want your own loft, you're in with the right guy there.'

'That's what Alan said.'

Noel smiled. 'That's what anyone will tell you. Listen and learn, Lizzie.'

'How is he so good, d'you reckon?' Lizzie asked, wondering what story Joe had spun for the club.

Noel shrugged. 'Some people just are,' he nodded. 'Joe says he learned a lot from his granddad, though I can't say I ever heard of the man. Joe just has that something. You don't see it often but, when you do, you recognise it. Staf Van Reet has it. You ever heard of Staf Van Reet?'

Lizzie shook her head.

'You've never heard of Staf Van Reet?' Noel looked at her in amazement. 'Van Reet?' he repeated.

Lizzie flushed. 'Eh, oh yeah,' she gulped. 'Van Reet. Sorry, I thought you said Venret.'

Noel smiled. 'Jesus, I got a shock there. Van Reet pigeons are only world famous. I met Staf once,' he said then. 'Bought an egg from him. One of the best pigeons I ever had.' He then went into a very boring monologue about the Van Reet line of birds, and how exactly his bird was related to some big fancy pigeon.

It was going to be a long drive home, Lizzie reckoned. And then, very uncharitably for her, she thought: no wonder hardly any of these men had wives who stuck around. Before feeling ashamed of herself.

Noel dropped her off at a house that wasn't hers and, bipping his horn, he drove off. Lizzie, making sure he was out of sight, immediately ran down towards Billy's place. Even though the night had been stressful, she'd learned one thing – Joe was definitely the golden boy of the club. So that was something else she'd have to change.

26

TUESDAY MORNING SHE was standing at a bus stop, waiting for Joe to show up. It was early and the sun was peeping above the houses opposite. Lizzie yawned. She hadn't been sleeping too well. Despite her resolve of the other night, she had been tempted, yet again, to walk away from today, to walk away from Joe.

Her determination seemed to crumble whenever she was with Tom. It was as if she had to learn to function on two levels. The girl she was when she was with Tom was the real Lizzie: funny, affectionate and happier than she'd been in a long time. Being in his company eased the conflict in her head, his love was like heat on ice, making the hardness inside her dissolve and grow warm again. Then, when she was apart from him, her thoughts inevitably turned to the next meeting with Joe and her overpowering desire to build up a trust with him, only to abuse it as brutally as she could. These thoughts hardened her resolve once again. She felt as if she was see-sawing between two mind sets, trying hard to keep her balance. On Sunday night, as Tom had kissed her, she wondered if he would still love her as much if he found out what a vindictive person she could be. As his lips teased hers, as his black eyes burned into hers, she'd seen her vendetta as something crazy – but then she was steadied by the sudden thought of Joe's pigeons flying disastrously in their next race because they hadn't been getting their medication. Then, as Tom murmured in her ear how much he loved her, she thought about how great she'd feel if she could just wipe that bewildered grin from Joe's face; as Tom ran his thumb down her jawbone and caressed her chin, she wondered how Joe would cope if she played a few mind games on him. So this morning she had got up and dressed and headed out of the house to meet Joe, almost as if she was being pulled along by some sort of magnetic force.

A *bip* and she turned to see Joe waving at her from the front seat of his car. He looked incredibly awake, bright-eyed and sunny, so much so that she felt a stab of pure malice.

'Hey,' he greeted her as she sat in beside him, 'you look tired.'

'Yeah, I am.' She found it hard to look at him.

Joe pulled out into traffic. 'I love the early mornings,' he said, and there was a smile in his voice. 'No one around to hassle you, not much traffic, it's cool.'

'So where do you take the pigeons?'

'Well, I take John's and Noel's birds, too. We do it every third week for each other. I generally drive to Kildare and let them go. There's a field that I pull into, the guy who owns it doesn't mind. It's flippin' magical when you see them take to the air. You'll see.'

Lizzie didn't bother to reply. God, why did he enjoy life so much? She wished so hard for him to be miserable. To calm herself she concentrated on looking out the window, as the city gave way to the open fields of the countryside.

'You're very quiet,' Joe remarked after a bit. He sounded a little uneasy.

'I'm just tired,' she said. Then, on impulse, she decided to tell him about Billy. She knew from experience that sometimes if you shared information with people they were more open to sharing with you. And who knew what she might find out then? So, despite her misgivings, she blurted out, 'I'm worried about my brother. He's split up with his girlfriend. And she won't talk to him at all.'

It was the wrong thing to say. Joe seemed to tense up and his hands gripped the steering wheel tighter.

'Sorry,' Lizzie managed a small laugh, 'you don't need to hear that. Sorry.'

With what seemed to her a huge effort of will, Joe's face relaxed into a smile. 'Naw, it's terrible to break up with someone.

161

I have to say, I wouldn't be the best relationship counsellor in the world.'

'No? Why?'

He shrugged. 'Well, relationships aren't exactly top of my agenda at the moment. It's kinda hard to meet women when you've your head stuck in the sky looking at pigeons.'

Lizzie laughed. 'Yeah, I guess so. Have you no girlfriend, then?'

'Nope.' He didn't sound as if he wanted one either.

There was silence then. It began to spit rain and Joe turned on the wipers. The steady swish of them lulled her and she felt her eyes closing, before realising where she was and jerking awake.

Joe laughed. 'You can sleep if you like.'

'And miss the pigeons? No chance.'

He seemed to like that answer because his grin broadened.

They arrived at the field and Joe jumped out and pulled open the gate. Driving his car through, he stopped just at the entrance. 'OK, Lizzie, hop out and pull out the baskets for me, will you?'

Lizzie did as she was told, taking a basket in each hand and handing them to Joe. He carried them into the centre of the field and Lizzie followed up with two more.

'Now, you ready?' His eyes were gleaming. 'This is just like the coolest part. Lift open the baskets and just let them out.'

Lizzie copied what he did and watched as the birds hopped out on to the baskets, looking around before taking to the air, where they circled before heading for home.

'See the way they circle,' Joe said, pointing. 'That's so they can get their bearings. See that guy?' He pointed to a white pigeon that was still going around and around, 'He's going to get lost if he doesn't move soon.'

They watched the bird for a bit, until finally he seemed to make up his mind and head back in the direction they had come.

Lizzie studied Joe as he watched the last bird fly out of sight. 'It's brilliant, isn't it?' he said, finally taking his eyes from the sky. 'If I were to drive home now, some of those birds would be back before me. It's amazing.'

'Yeah, isn't it?' She supposed it was, not that she'd ever thought about it.

'Come round to my place next Saturday, if you like, and you can wait with me.'

'I might be going home next week,' she said. 'I haven't been home in ages so I'll let you know.'

'No worries, sure there are lots of other Saturdays.'

'Do you not go home at the weekends at all?' Lizzie kept her voice deliberately casual as they walked back with the empty baskets to the car.

'Nope.' His answer was abrupt as he placed his baskets in the boot and took hers from her.

'D'you go home during the week then?' She relished his discomfort.

'Nope.' He walked round the side of the car and hopped in.

Lizzie joined him. 'Oh.' She watched him start up the car, his face flushed, his hand trembling slightly as he inserted the key into the ignition. Then she said, 'Sorry if I said something I shouldn't.'

It worked. He turned to face her, the car juddering slightly. 'No, you didn't say anything you shouldn't. I just don't visit my parents, that's all.'

'Oh.' Pause. 'Right, well, moving swiftly on . . .'

Joe smiled a little. God, he was so predictable. 'They don't like me, I don't like them.'

'Oh.'

'Yeah.' He shrugged a little. 'Oh.'

He said nothing more as he got the car out of the field and on to the main road. Instead he flicked on the radio and began tapping his fingers to the beat of the music.

He bought her breakfast in a small cafe on O'Connell Street. He had the full fry-up while she settled for a cup of coffee. She wanted nothing from him, not his coffee nor anything else. She watched him as he ate his food with relish, putting tomato sauce on his sausages.

163

'That is disgusting,' she teased. 'You really are the worst person to be working in a health centre.'

He laughed loudly and nodded. 'I know. I'm such a hypocrite.'

He got that much right at least.

'How come swimming?' she asked then. 'Are you really good at it?' God, it was great, she knew just how to make him uncomfortable. Everyone in Wexford knew that Joe was a class swimmer. He could have saved Meg but instead he had chosen not to . . .

Joe swallowed a mouthful of sausage and shrugged. 'I'm OK,' he said modestly. 'I teach it because it's important for everyone to learn.' He looked down at his half empty plate and shoved it away from him. 'Right, are we ready to go?'

'But you haven't finished.'

'Yeah, I have.'

There was a message to ring Jim O'Brien when she got into work. Lizzie's heart lurched as she saw his name on the pad along with his mobile number. Without taking time to shrug off her coat, she picked up the receiver and dialled him. Oh God, she prayed, please let him donate the house. Please. Please. Please.

The phone started to ring at the other end and Lizzie held her breath.

'Hello?'

'Jim, it's Lizzie.'

'Hi, Lizzie, just give me a second to go somewhere quieter.' She was cut off into the limbo land of on-hold before Jim's voice came back to her a few seconds later. 'Hello, darling!'

'Jim, hi yourself.' He'd called her 'darling', that couldn't be too bad.

'I'm calling you about the house, Lizzie.'

'Yeah, sorry I wasn't here. I'm a bit late in this morning. I was out with a friend early. I—' She was babbling. She sounded nervous. She stopped. 'Anyway,' she breathed.

'Anyway,' Jim said back. Another pause. 'I was thinking about your proposal, Lizzie, and, well, I'm afraid—'

'Oh, Jim.'

164

'I know, darling. But things are tight here. You've no idea. I've had to let lads go all over the place as the houses aren't selling. I am sorry that you're going to have to take one off my hands.'

'I almost had—' She paused. 'Sorry, what did you say?'

'A five-bed, middle of Kildare. It's two hundred thousand cost.'

'You beauty!' she yelled. 'Jim O'Brien, I love you!'

'Yeah I know, but I'm married.'

'Mark will be thrilled!'

'Don't make me feel bad about this, Lizzie, for Christ's sake.' She laughed out loud.

Now all she needed was to raise the cash. Four hundred people had to parachute jump. Lizzie began to make some phone calls.

She gave herself the rest of the day off to celebrate. Mark wouldn't dare to give out to her. She had lined up a prime slot on the Declan Darcy radio show to promote the jump, but unfortunately the researchers wanted Mark to speak as he was the founder. Lizzie had a feeling that the interest in the jump would be minimal once Mark started to rant on about people not caring about each other. She'd have to brief him on what to say.

She was busily working out in her mind the most tactful way of doing that when she passed a pet shop. There were pigeon baskets displayed in the window and Lizzie, sensing the ideal opportunity to smuggle one home while Billy was out at work, went in and bought one. Ten minutes later, she was on the Luas on her way home to store the basket in Billy's garden shed. She also had a handy supply of unsalted peanuts and corn, which the pet shop owner assured her every pigeon would love. She knew what she was going to spend the rest of her day doing now. And little did Joe know just how helpful his book was.

She spread the peanuts and corn on the tiny little bird table out in Billy's back garden. Then she sat in the kitchen and waited.

165

Finally, after fifty minutes or so, the pigeons landed. Three of them.

Lizzie grinned.

Life was only going to get better.

27

THERE WAS A clattering noise coming from Ellen's back garden. Joe, sitting out in the weak sunshine waiting for his birds to return from the race, heard it. It sounded like metal on metal. A bird distracted him as it flew overhead, but it wasn't a pigeon.

Joe groaned. Where were they? Noel had rung over an hour ago to say that the birds had been released, and Joe was expecting to see his first bird any time now. He hoped Lizzie would make it; she had agreed to come over, telling him that her plans to visit home were on hold as her brother didn't want to go home now. She'd been a bit evasive and he'd been glad. He didn't know what he'd do if she told him any personal stuff, he'd been a long time out of that loop. And yet . . . it'd be . . . he tried to think . . . normal. And healthy. Joe sighed. Lizzie was great company, she made him smile and if he were a regular bloke he would like that, but the fact of it was that he wasn't totally normal and getting friendly with a girl would mean telling her all sorts of stuff and he didn't think he was ready for that. Still, he thought wistfully, it must be nice for her, able to go home when she felt like it. His birds had been released from Wexford this morning and it gave him a weird feeling inside.

His thoughts returned to the noise in Ellen's garden. He decided to risk looking over the wall. It was Anthony. The boy was inexpertly digging a flowerbed. His shovel had just struck a rock or something and he was cursing under his breath.

'Anthony,' Joe said loudly, and tried not to grin as the lad jumped.

Anthony's eyes narrowed. His face assumed a sulky teenage look that Joe remembered from his own childhood.

'It's Anto,' he barked out, leaning on the spade and glowering.

'Digging the garden, ey?'

'No,' Anto snapped, 'I'm having it off with me girlfriend.'

Joe laughed loudly and Anto gave a reluctant half smile.

'I asked for that,' Joe said.

Anto said nothing.

'You do a good job for Ellen, do you hear?' Joe assumed a stern voice. 'She's not in the best of health and I'm telling you don't give her any trouble.'

Anto glowered some more and started to dig again.

Joe, satisfied that he'd said his piece, turned his gaze back to the sky.

Lizzie pulled up in the back lane a few doors down from Joe's house. The basket, containing some pigeons, lay at her feet. They were stupid birds really, she thought. She'd baited them with good food all week and crept closer to them each time until they weren't too bothered by her presence. Then yesterday, before Billy had come back from work, she'd walked up behind them and thrown a towel over their heads, just like Joe's book had advised. It had been a bit messy trying to lift them up and put them into the basket and she was afraid she might hurt them, but she hadn't. The birds didn't seem too distressed either, she thought – they were cooing away to each other and no fights had broken out.

And now, stage two of her master plan: she didn't know if it would work, it was all a bit of hit and miss but it would definitely have some sort of an effect. And if it didn't, she'd just have to try something else. She left the car engine running because if it did work, she reckoned she'd have to make a quick getaway.

Joe had told her that the first birds should arrive in about an hour. So here she was, watching and waiting.

*　　*　　*

Joe looked at his watch. Lizzie was late. She'd sent him a text to say she was on her way and hoping that she wouldn't miss the action. He'd sent her one back to say that she'd want to hurry.

He prowled around his garden, unable to relax, when suddenly he saw a flash of grey against the sky. He knew instinctively that it was one of his. He knew by the way it flew, perfectly balanced, beautiful to look at, by the way it hovered and by the way it started to dive. It was coming in. It was coming in.

And then suddenly, from nowhere, three birds took to the sky. Three birds right in the path of his bloody pigeon. Joe groaned. Who the fuck was releasing pigeons now? Jesus. He watched in despair as his bird mingled with the others, circled with the others. Precious seconds ticked off his time. Joe whistled frantically. His pigeon heard but was caught up in the circle of flight with the others. More seconds lost. Jesus Christ! He whistled again and, to his relief, his bird dived. Joe's heart dived with it.

Damn it anyway!

Lizzie parked her car and made her way along the street to Joe's house. She had to be careful not to grin too much. It had been great! Her three birds were now just grey blurs in the distance. She hoped they knew where they were going. She hoped they'd make their way back to Billy's back garden, where there was a huge supply of peanuts waiting for them. She hoped like mad that the lone pigeon she'd seen had been Joe's. She reckoned it was as it had been making straight for the house when she'd done what she'd done. And nope, she didn't feel guilty at all, which was a relief. Well, there was nothing to really feel guilty for, was there? No one had been hurt. Nothing had suffered, except, hope-fully, Joe's race results.

She walked up to Joe's and noticed that the back gate was open.

'Hiya,' she said as she pushed it inwards.

There was no answer.

She walked further into the garden and was there just in time to see Joe shoving the pigeon's race ring into the clock.

'Aw, don't tell me I missed it,' she said, creasing her brow up in disappointment.

'You did.' He was grumpy.

'Oh, sorry about that.'

'No,' he waved his hand, 'I'm not mad at you. I'm mad at whatever idiot released some birds just as my fella was coming home.'

'What?'

'Yeah,' he half laughed in disbelief, 'Prince came in and three bloody birds from I dunno where just launched themselves at him. They flew off that way.' He indicated the south. 'I swear to God, if I find out who it was I'll kill them.'

Lizzie flinched. Her stomach lurched suddenly as the realisation crashed in that she was playing a very dangerous game here.

'Hey, are you OK?' Joe looked at her in concern. 'You've gone very pale. D'you want a drink or something?'

'No, I'm—'

'Hey!' She was immediately forgotten about as he spotted another bird. 'Look, up there, d'you see it?'

Lizzie glanced up and, sure enough, there was another grey spot against the brilliant blue of the sky, closely followed by two more.

'Get ready,' Joe grinned widely at her, his disappointment forgotten, 'it's going to be mad now.'

And, despite herself, as bird upon bird came into the loft, responding to Joe's whistle, Lizzie was weirdly moved. Just to see them all returning home safely after their journey across the country was miraculous. Joe was kept busy taking the tags from their legs. As Lizzie watched, she became aware of a thin, hungry-looking lad peering over the wall. The boy was cautious at first, before abandoning all semblance of shyness and sitting up on the wall, gaping in wonder as birds flew around and alighted on perches.

'Wow!' he said.

Joe glanced up at him but said nothing, so Lizzie didn't either. After about twenty minutes Joe reckoned that all the birds were in, and he turned to Lizzie and smiled.

170

'Well?' he asked. 'What did you think of that?'

'Savage,' the young lad answered. 'It was brilliant. Do you own all them?'

Joe paused and studied Anto. 'Yep. Why? Do you like birds?'

Anto reddened and shrugged. He jumped back down off the wall and disappeared.

'Was that a "yes"?' Lizzie laughed.

Joe laughed, too, and asked her if she wanted a cuppa.

Later that night Lizzie called round to Anna, who had invited her over for a drink and a sleepover. Feeling like a kid going to a slumber party, Lizzie had packed her overnight bag.

She felt better leaving Billy on his own now. Whilst he still continued to call Aileen on a daily basis in the hope she'd crack, his drinking had eased off after she'd told him she was worried about him. But he was still miserable. She wished Aileen would just give him a chance. She was being very harsh, Lizzie thought, and Aileen wasn't normally like that.

'Hiya.' Anna met Lizzie at the front door, her fingers on her lips. 'Shush, I've just got her to bed.'

'At nine-thirty on a Saturday? A seven-year-old?' Lizzie feigned mock horror. 'She should have been in bed hours ago.'

'I like her company,' Anna confessed. 'It's lonely here at the weekends.'

Of course it must be, Lizzie thought suddenly. How awful to sit night after night on your own, looking at pictures of what was and what might have been. She touched Anna briefly on the arm and dumped her overnight case on the floor.

'You're in Chloe's room,' Anna continued to whisper as she led Lizzie into the television room. 'She's in with me tonight. She's so excited.'

Lizzie laughed.

'Now,' Anna held up two bottles of wine as Lizzie sat on the sofa, 'red or white?'

'Red.'

Anna uncorked the bottle and poured them both a generous

glass. Then she produced a big bag of sour cream crisps and some dips.

'Yum,' Lizzie pulled a handful of crisps from the bag. 'Do you know, this is the most sophisticated thing I've done in weeks. I never realised before how Aileen ran the house. Dinner and tea and all sorts of food. Now there's only some mouldy cheese and a rotten tomato in the fridge.'

Anna laughed. 'Well maybe, sweet thing, you should invest in some grub.'

'I know, but I've had a lot on.'

Anna cocked her head to one side and smiled, 'Tom wearing you out, is he?'

'I wish. I haven't seen him, to be honest. Nope, I'm busy soft soaping Mark for his radio interview next week.'

'Soft soaping Mark?' Anna grinned. 'You'd normally eat him for breakfast.'

'Well, I'm not in the humour for breakfast.' Lizzie said back. 'Oh Anna, if he goes on air and alienates half of Ireland, I'll never forgive him.'

'He won't. He's changed a bit since he's been seeing Stella. He'll be grand and anyway, if he does, it's not your fault.'

'Suppose.' She heaved a sigh and looked at Anna. 'So, how about you? Any news?'

Anna crunched on a couple of crisps and regarded Lizzie. 'Well, not much really. A Sinéad rang the helpline when I was filling in on Friday, looking for you. She refused to talk to me.'

Lizzie frowned. 'Sinéad?'

'I looked her up on the database. Husband seems to be a bit of a bully.'

'Oh yes,' Lizzie nodded, remembering. Sinéad hadn't rung in a while. 'And how did she sound?'

Anna shrugged. 'She wasn't on long enough for me to gauge that but, at a guess, I'd say a little upset.'

Lizzie sipped her wine. God, it was gorgeous. She wondered idly how it was that when she chose wine, it never tasted as nice. She could spend up to twenty quid on a bottle and it was still awful.

'I hope she rings back,' she said.

'She will, I think,' Anna nodded.

'Mammy?' A cute face with a head of curls peered round the door. 'Mammy, I can't sleep.' Chloe, however, was looking directly at Lizzie. 'Hi,' she said with a beaming smile. 'I met you before.'

'You did, that's right.'

'Chloe, I think it's bed time,' Anna said gently.

'But I can't sleep.' Chloe was still gawking at Lizzie. 'Is your brother's baby born yet?'

'No,' Lizzie felt a pang as she answered. 'And you know one thing? It's two babies now.'

'Two? No way? How?'

'Like twins.'

'Two ladies are having babies.'

'No. One lady is having two babies.'

'Two babies in her tummy?' Chloe was wide-eyed.

'Yes.'

'How did two babies get in there?'

'Eh . . .' Lizzie looked desperately at Anna. 'Well, eh—'

'Yes, Lizzie, how *did* two babies get in there?' Anna grinned.

'So, Chloe,' Lizzie said, 'how have you been? I hear you're making your first holy communion this year.'

Anna chortled, but it worked. Chloe nodded vigorously. 'Yes, and I went to my first confession.'

'Yeah?' Lizzie grinned. 'And what would a little girl like you have to tell? You don't have any sins, I bet.'

'I do. I did something Mammy told me not to. And I told a lie.'

'Did you?' Anna grinned. 'Well, there's a surprise.'

'And the priest said it was OK, that it wasn't really a sin and that if I wanted to tell you, I should.'

'Good for him.' Anna leaned against the table and looked fondly at her daughter. 'So are you going to tell me?'

Chloe looked from one to the other of them.

'OK,' she said, sounding quite excited. 'Well, it was that Nana rang the other day and I told her I would try and get you to call her. But it was lie because I know you're angry at her.'

173

'Oops,' Lizzie made a face, 'maybe I shouldn't have heard that.'

'Nana rang the other day?' Anna said, her voice slightly cross. 'The sneaky thing, trying to get you to do her dirty work.'

Chloe frowned. 'No, it wasn't dirty. She just said—'

'You don't talk to her again, do you hear?' Anna said.

Chloe gulped hard and Lizzie thought she was about to cry. 'But I like my nana. She's nice.'

'I know you do,' Anna glanced at Lizzie ruefully, 'but it's me she should talk to, not you. So tell her that next time, OK?'

'You said I can't talk to her.'

'Well, you can. Only not about me. Tell her to ring me if she wants to talk, OK?'

Chloe nodded.

Anna tousled her daughter's long dark hair. 'Sorry for getting cross. You were good to tell me.'

'That's what the priest said: it's good to tell your mother things.'

'Does he want a job working the phones at Life?' Lizzie giggled.

Prince had clocked fourth. Joe grinned and clapped as the winner waved his cheque in the air and said that the drinks were on him.

'Hey, what happened to Prince today?' Cid asked, barely able to conceal his delight.

Joe shrugged. He was tempted to tell the others about the three pigeons being released just as Prince came in, but it just sounded like an excuse. He didn't want them to think he was a bad loser. He knew the truth and that's what mattered. He grinned to himself. Sometimes that wasn't what mattered at all, actually. It was what people believed that counted. Still, he'd gone beyond caring what people believed.

'Just an off day,' he murmured as he made his way up to the list that Alan had pinned on to the wall. Glancing down it, he almost groaned in frustration. The top three were within a second of each other. Prince was two seconds behind them. He'd lost at least thirty seconds with what had happened. Maybe more. Prince had won that race, of that Joe was certain.

'An off day, would you listen to him?' Cid scoffed. 'Face it, Joe, Prince is worn out. He's suffering burn out.'

'He was only two seconds behind the winner, Cid. Where were your lads?'

'Good point,' Noel said. Then, feigning surprise, he jabbed the list of times. 'Oh look! Your first is three minutes behind. But they're not suffering burn out though, are they?'

'Nope,' Cid said defiantly.

'Incineration, I'd call it,' Noel went on.

As Joe, John and Noel started to laugh, Cid announced that he wouldn't sit with them that night.

'Ten seconds,' Noel grinned as he glanced at his watch, 'now that's a record.'

Anna was talking about her husband. She'd got on to the subject when Lizzie asked her if she ever stopped thinking about what could have been.

'You never quite stop,' she said. 'In the beginning it was harder, though, especially when Chloe started to do all the cute baby stuff. I just felt so angry that he was missing out.'

'I feel like that about my sister,' Lizzie said. 'Angry that she's missing out.' She paused as Anna looked at her with interest. Lizzie never talked about Megan. Well, not to anyone besides her family and Tom. And the fact that she'd told Tom made her know he was special.

'My sister was, you know, killed.' She took a breath. 'Murdered,' she clarified.

'Oh, Lizzie.'

'Yeah, and I can't stop thinking about her. Like not all the time any more, but in flashes. When I moved to Dublin I thought, oh wow, she'd love this, and every time I go out, it's like she's with me. I reckon she would have lived in the pubs.' Lizzie smiled a little. 'She hated school and Mammy used to worry so much about her but Dad always used to say that with her looks she'd marry "a really rich fella who'd keep her in the style to which she was unaccustomed".'

Anna smiled. 'What age was she?'

'Nineteen,' Lizzie said softly. It seemed so young now, looking back.

Anna shook her head.

'You should have seen her, Anna,' Lizzie said wistfully. 'She dressed like she belonged in Hollywood. Well, I always thought so. I was fourteen and a big frump; she was like this rainbow in the house. Mammy used to always say her skirts were too short and her make-up was too thick. And she'd say back it wasn't her make-up that was thick, it was Mammy.'

Anna laughed and Lizzie did, too.

'Her and Mammy were always fighting. But when she . . . she died, the house was just way too quiet. I couldn't wait to leave.'

'Did they get someone for it?'

'Yeah. A neighbour. My dad was very fond of him, it broke his heart. The town was divided though, some said he was guilty and others said no way. He was, though. He told lie after lie on the stand and got caught out on them all. He said she'd been drunk for a start, and yet there was no alcohol found in her system. Big bloody liar, trying to make out she'd been drinking. And he also said she was meant to meet another guy that night, but the other fella denied texting her and no text was ever traced from him. Such a liar.'

Anna said nothing.

'Every time I think of him, I just,' Lizzie paused and unclenched her fists, 'well, I hate him, Anna.'

'I'll bet you do.'

'He was freed after only twelve years. Twelve years. I don't know why.' Lizzie took another gulp of wine. It was partly to calm her and partly to stop the huge rage inside her breaking out. 'He killed my sister and he's free to walk about now. My mother was devastated all over again.' She paused. 'I saw him,' she bit her lip and went on, 'a few weeks ago.'

'Oh, God. Did he see you?'

Lizzie shook her head. She'd probably said too much. It was the wine. She put down her glass and decided not to drink any more. 'I just saw him and wanted to kill him, Anna. It's like he's brought it all back.'

Anna opened her mouth to say something but stopped.

'What?' Lizzie asked.

'You have to let it go,' Anna said quietly. 'You know that, don't you?'

Of course she knew that. But she also knew that she couldn't. Maybe when she'd destroyed him she might just manage to do it. 'It's hard. I mean, I really hate him,' she said again.

'I hated Mick too, at times, for a different reason obviously, but I hated him for what he'd done to us,' Anna nodded as Lizzie looked at her. 'He'd devastated our world just as that man devastated yours. But, in the end, it was a choice I had to make. I had to get on with my life. I decided that I wanted a good life for me and Chloe. And do you know what I realized, Lizzie?'

'What?'

'I realised that love and hate aren't the opposites of each other at all.'

'Are they not?' Her feelings for Joe and Tom were certainly polar opposites.

'No, they're not,' Anna said. 'Hate is much more powerful than love. It eats into your soul far more than love. I hated Mick with more intensity than I'd ever loved him. Isn't that scary?'

Lizzie nodded. She knew Anna was right. She spent way more time thinking about Joe than Tom these days.

And it *was* scary, but she couldn't help it.

28

Fab!!!

Fab!!!

Fab!!!

Wonderful news. Dessie kissed me. And not just in my steamy imagination. It started like this . . .

We had the office to ourselves all week because Joe is out apparently being fined and cautioned and in shit with his dad. It was awful actually because Joe's dad, in the interests of public information, had to run a piece in the paper on Joe driving the boat whilst being drunk. It was only a column on page four, which wasn't too bad because Dessie said any other paper would have run it at least on page two if not front page.

I took full advantage of the week alone with Dessie and wore my shortest skirts and tightest tops into work. Mam, of course, had to get her dig in and asked me if I was selling myself as well as the ads. So I told her that I would if the price was right, which made her go mad. Anyway, Dessie complimented me every single day on what I wore.

Then on Friday I wore a glittery skirt, just over my knee, a little glittery top and a white fake-fur jacket. I also put on my highest heels, which I can barely walk in. And anyway, I tripped over the phone cord which runs along the floor and crunch, I was right over on my ankle. That cord is a total danger. Oh, the pain. Dessie jumped up. I think he was in the middle of a big sell, but he abandoned it and rushed over to me and lifted me up and I clung on to him and I have to say, he wears this delicious aftershave. He carried me to the chair and took off my shoe. My toes looked all cute as I'd painted them in gold. He put his hands around my ankle and the pain was awful but, to be honest, he could have broken it and I wouldn't have told him to stop. Then he asked me if I could walk and I said yes, if he supported me, so he lifted me up and we stood there, body to body and I didn't move for a second and neither did he. His eyes looked into mine and then there was this sort of swelling romantic music but it was only my mobile phone, which we both ignored.

'You OK?' he asked and his voice was all husky.

'I am now,' I said and I smiled at him.

'Me too,' he said and he cocked his gorgeous head to one side and asked if I was trying to lead him astray, what with me pressing myself into him and that.

'I have hurt my ankle,' I played it really cool, 'it's you taking advantage of me.'

'You are gorgeous,' he said.

'I try my best,' I said back and he laughed.

Then he said, 'Joe is mad about you, you know.'

'And you?' I asked. (My mother would have freaked.)

'I just lust after you,' he grinned.

It wasn't exactly a great answer but, to be fair, I think he was joking. 'Lust away,' I said back.

Then he kissed me, but it was very brief because my ankle was really sore so he had to stop.

I haven't heard from him all weekend but anyway, I can't go out because my ankle is all strapped up.

179

Monday, 9th August

Dad drove me into work as I couldn't get the bus – my ankle is still strapped up. Mammy was all self-righteous and only just stopped short of saying I told you so.

Anyway, I actually got in early and when I walked into the office, there was Joe, already at his desk. He gave me a really embarrassed grin as I stood in the doorway with no idea what to say to him.

'Welcome back, sailor boy,' I stammered out eventually.

He sort of laughed and shrugged and said that he felt about as welcome as an STD, which made me laugh. His dad is really coming down heavy on him, he said then. He told me that no matter how much he apologises his dad keeps going on about it, so he's moved in with his granddad. He says he would have moved in anyway as his granddad isn't well and his mother asked him to keep an eye on him. So he figures in the short term, until his dad calms down, that it's the best place to be. Then he asked me what happened to my ankle and I told him, leaving out the part where Dessie kissed me. I only told Aileen that. And she says she can't wait to see the two lads when she comes down. Anyway, then Dessie arrived in and started singing a song about a drunken sailor and Joe laughed and threw a pen at him which unfortunately hit his dad, who had just come in.

'Sorry,' Joe said. But he was trying not to laugh.

'Get to work!' Geoff flung a list of names on Dessie's desk and told him to ring them all by the end of the day. 'I'm not paying you to mess,' he shouted.

Then he turned on me. 'What are you looking at?' Stupidly, I could feel tears forming in my eyes so I looked down at the desk. It's not that I was scared, it was just his shouting was so unexpected.

'Hey,' Joe said, standing up. For the first time I noticed how scruffy he looked. Obviously no one was doing his washing for him. His T-shirt was an old one – I know this because it said 'The Eight Legged Groove Machine' on it in black writing. His jeans were creased and looked as if he'd slept in them. 'Don't take it out on her. It's my fault. Shout at me.'

Geoff strode over to Joe, who, to give him credit, didn't flinch. He poked him hard in the chest. 'Oh, don't worry,' he said in a really menacing voice, 'I'll be shouting a lot at you. You look a disgrace. Be cleaner tomorrow.'

Then he marched out, slamming the door after him.

Joe heaved a sigh and sat back down, without looking at either of us. He flicked on his computer and stared hard at the screen. Dessie and I didn't know what to say and none of us could look at each other.

'Bastard,' Joe muttered after a bit.

There was an awkward silence until Dessie said casually, 'How much would you bet on your dad spontaneously combusting before the day is done?'

We laughed.

'If I thought he would I'd help him along,' Joe answered, grinning. He pointed at Dessie's sheet of numbers, 'Anyway, give us some of your numbers, Dessie, and we'll make a start on ringing these people.'

We all took some numbers and began to work.

And then, about an hour later, just as I was actually making some progress and selling some space to a toilet paper company that had recently moved premises, the door was flung open. The handle of the door smashed itself off the opposite wall and we jumped.

'You piece of shit!'

'Pardon?' the person at the other end of my line said.

'Sorry, it's just—'

'Slimy little toerag.'

'Can I ring you back?' I asked and then, without waiting for an answer, hung up.

The girl in the doorway, there was no doubt about it, was Dessie's northern girlfriend. Or ex-girlfriend. At least, I hoped she was his ex. I knew it was her though, because despite the fact that she was dressed like some throwback to the eighties, she was gorgeous. And totally furious. She was wearing skin-tight black jeans and biker boots. This was teamed with a shocking pink string vest top over a black long-sleeved T-shirt. Her spiky hair complemented her spiky attitude.

'You snake in the grass!' she said, still not moving but pinning a very guilty-looking Dessie with her enormous hazel eyes. In fact her eyes looked like they didn't belong with the rest of her.

I shot a glance at Joe, who was watching the unfolding drama with interest.

'Hi, Denise,' he said.

That threw Denise a little. 'Hi,' she said, before turning back to Dessie. 'Snake in the grass,' she repeated slowly, glaring at him.

'And, eh,' Dessie attempted a bit of a grin, 'what sort of a snake would that be then, Dee?'

Joe spluttered on a laugh, then tried to make it sound like a cough.

'What sort of a snake?' Denise swaggered into the room. 'Why, the sort that strangles its victims, that sort! The sort that slithers around and sneaks up on its prey and looks and acts ugly. That sort.'

'Are you insulting my good looks?'

I laughed then and she whirled on me. 'What are you laughing at?' She looked me up and down. 'I suppose he's chasing you now, is he?'

I went bright red.

'Dessie,' Denise shook her head, 'what is it you see in her?' She swaggered towards me. 'I suppose it's the lack of an outfit, the display of white flesh, the big red guilty-looking face.'

'Hang on a second,' I said, not wanting to be outdone, 'you can't talk to me—'

'Denise, can we take it outside?' Dessie said.

'Would you like to go out with a guy who tells you he's coming to visit and then doesn't turn up? Two weekends on the trot?' She was still focused on me. 'Is this the reason, Dessie?'

Well, I thought, he hadn't been with me this weekend just gone.

'You could have come to the party. It was a great one.' Dessie ignored the question. 'Joe even got arrested.'

'Thanks, Des,' Joe nodded, 'glad you enjoyed that part of it.'

'If I had my way, I'd have you arrested,' Denise spat at Dessie as she swaggered across the room, her head jutting out like a rooster on the attack. 'You asshole. You think you're so smart, don't you?'

How could he go out with such a person? I could hear my mother now going, 'Where is her dignity?' and she'd have a point.

'Have you come all the way down here just to shout at me?' Dessie asked calmly.

'Yes.'

Joe made motions for us to leave. He stood up from his chair and beckoned to me. I didn't want to go, but it was none of my business and that girl was scary.

'Megan and I will go on an early lunch, so,' Joe said, attempting to keep his tone light. 'One hour, Dessie.'

I pulled my jacket from the back of my chair and followed Joe from the room.

'Is that the, eh, girlfriend?' I asked Joe when we were sitting down in the pub with some coffee in front of us. I hated calling her Dessie's girlfriend. It gave me a chill. And made me feel like a heel for kissing him. I mean, I

183

wasn't so desperate that I had to become a boyfriend stealer.

'Uh-huh,' Joe nodded, then took a gulp of coffee and began to splutter. 'God, that's hot!'

I half laughed. What had he expected? 'That's coffee for you.'

'Smart arse,' he grinned.

'She seems,' I tried to be tactful, 'kinda bossy.'

'Nah, Denise is sound,' Joe nodded. 'She wouldn't be as bad if Dessie treated her right.' He paused and regarded me with speculative eyes. 'Dessie likes to mess her around. He likes to show her who's boss. So then she messes him around. It's the way they work.'

'Has he broken up with her?'

'Oh yeah,' Joe laughed, 'loads of times.'

That wasn't what I meant. I wanted to know if it was all off NOW. Only I couldn't ask because Joe was giving me a strange look, up and down as if he was considering what to say next. 'Whenever Dessie has other fish to fry,' he said, 'Denise gets the boot. He calls it being honest with her.'

'Dessie goes on fishing trips?' That was news to me. All I bloody needed was another fisherman in my life.

Joe spluttered out some more coffee. I think he was laughing before he suddenly went all serious again. He said quietly, almost as if he didn't want to, 'I think he's after you now.'

'Me?' I gave a huge smile that, I hoped, conveyed surprise. 'Me? Why?'

Joe didn't smile back. He didn't even sound as if he particularly wanted to tell me this.

'Why?' he repeated, looking intently at me. 'Because he can.'

I opened my mouth to say something but nothing came out. That was a bit insulting.

'Sorry,' he winced, 'that sounded awful.' He put his

coffee on the table and leaned in towards me. His eyes are a bit weird, I noticed then: one is hazel; one is a deeper shade, nearer brown. He shifted about on the seat, 'Look Megan, I'll be honest with you, OK?'

I wasn't sure I wanted to hear this.

'I liked you a lot. I got you the job in the newspaper by lying to my dad and telling him you could sell wool to sheep farmers. I wanted to get to know you. Like when I go fishing with Kev (that's my dad and it was weird to hear him say Kev), I don't only go because I like your dad, you know. I used to keep hoping I'd see you.'

I gawked at him.

'I take it that's a look of horror,' he joked half-heartedly. Without waiting for me to reply, he went on, 'Anyway, once Dessie saw I fancied you, he started going after you, too.'

This was mad. 'Why would he do that?'

'To hurt me. To hurt Denise.'

Joe was mad. Paranoid. 'You've lost me,' I said.

'About a year ago, Dessie and I had a falling out over Denise. She fancied me, he fancied her. He accused me of trying to move in on her, which was crap, but anyway, he eventually got Denise and she's mad about him, but I dunno, he doesn't quite trust it. So he treats her like shit to pretend to her that he isn't as mad about her as he is. Right now he's trying to piss her off by chasing you, and into the bargain piss me off too.' He paused, then asked, 'You like him, don't you?'

I didn't answer. Instead I said, 'I thought you two were mates.'

'It's just the way Dessie is,' Joe explained. 'He hates that she fancied me first. He hates when I sell more ads than him. He hates when I get more bonuses than him. Everything is competition. You just happen to be the prize this time.'

185

I was speechless. The prize?

'Now, I'm pretty sure I haven't a hope in hell with you.' Joe gave this rueful grin. I think that's the right word. 'But trust me, leave Dessie well alone. Dessie is out for Dessie.'

I have to say he sounded sincere.

'I'm just letting you know, Megan,' Joe said after a bit. 'I know you like him but he'll use you.'

'Well, eh, thanks for that, Joe,' I said. 'And I do like you, you know – just not—'

He waved me away. 'Don't even finish that sentence,' he half grinned. 'I'll live with the disappointment. I was playing out of my league anyway.'

Why do men always talk about sport? I decided not to mention the kiss with Dessie. I would tell Dessie not to mention it either. I was not going to be used, that was for sure.

'Dessie is a good mate,' Joe went on then, as if he was sorry to have said anything bad. 'I just don't want to see you get hurt, Megan, that's all.' To my surprise, he blushed, as if saying something so personal was embarrassing for him.

So I told him that I appreciated his thoughtfulness and that I would definitely think about what he'd said. Then I gave him a quick peck on the cheek.

Then, 'What is this?' from Geoff Jones, who had just walked into the pub. He was fuming. 'Didn't I tell you to stay in work?' He glared pointedly at Joe. 'I go into the office and Dessie is there having a slanging match with some girl who doesn't even work in the place and the two of you are—' He narrowed his eyes. 'Are what?' He glared at me.

'Having a discussion,' Joe answered for me, standing up and pulling on his jacket. 'We're going back now, Dad.'

'Well your office discussions must be interesting affairs,' Geoff growled.

Dessie was busy making calls when we got back as if nothing had happened.

'So?' Joe asked him. 'What's the story?'

The story was that Denise had gone, but not before having dumped a cup of coffee all over him. And then Dessie says, 'So we can take up where we left off on Friday, Megan, ey?' And he winked at me.

And yes, I felt bad for Joe, who I hadn't been honest with. He tossed me a hurt look before leaving work early, but the minute he was gone Dessie certainly did take up with enthusiasm where we'd finished. And Joe is wrong and Cher is right: it's in his kiss. Dessie likes me.

29

LIZZIE STEPPED INTO Joe's kitchen. It looked different. Cleaner. Or something.

'Did you do something to this place?' she asked, looking around.

Joe grinned sheepishly. 'Eh, just washed the floor. Wiped down the counters. The place was in a bit of a state.'

'Good job.'

Joe watched as she glanced around the room, glad suddenly that he had made an effort. He didn't want her to think he lived like a pig, though apparently pigs were very clean. Lizzie looked good, he thought. Cute. The more he was with her, the more he liked her. It scared him a bit. She chatted about home a lot, which in the beginning had made him uncomfortable, but now he liked to hear her talk on.

'So, d'you want a cuppa before we start?'

'Sure, great.'

Lizzie carefully laid her paper down on the table where he could see it. Just before she'd come, she'd managed to pop into a shop and buy the *Rossclare Read*. She was sure it would give him a jolt. She watched as Joe flicked on the kettle and took some milk from the fridge. He really had made an effort, she thought. Even his fridge looked cleaner than the last time.

'So how have my favourite birds been?' she asked.

He turned around and his grin was so sunny that she had to catch her breath. 'Good, though I didn't enter them in any races this weekend. They all seem a little tired or something. I can't quite put my finger on it. Hopefully, it's just a little bit of burn out.'

'Oh.' She quashed her momentary guilt. 'That's weird.'

He shrugged, not appearing too concerned. 'I've checked them for funguses and stuff, so they're clean. I don't think it's much to worry about. He carried her cup to the table and put it down. And then, just as she'd hoped, his eye caught the paper. His cup jerked a little, slopping coffee over the sides.

'That your paper?' he asked, sounding as if he was trying to be cool about it.

'Yeah. I just got it when I saw that piece about the harbour in Rossclare. D'you want to read it?'

'Eh, no, no, it's cool.' His hands trembled slightly as he laid his cup down. Well, Lizzie fancied that they trembled. If she hadn't known who he was maybe she wouldn't have noticed.

'Do you know anything about the harbour?' Lizzie asked innocently. 'Aren't you from Rossclare?'

'I'm out of the place too long now.' Joe didn't look at her. He carefully poured milk into his tea. 'I dunno what's happening down there at all. I—' he stopped. Drank some tea.

'You what?' Lizzie asked.

His eyes met hers. 'I used to fish out of there. Before,' he indicated the room, 'well, before I came to Dublin.'

'You were a fisherman?'

'Uh-huh.' He nodded. 'Loved it. Would have stayed but came up here instead.'

'Why?' Lizzie could barely contain her excitement. Maybe he'd confess. Maybe he'd tell her everything. Maybe then she could—

'Just did.' He stood up, his back to her. 'Now, I definitely have some biscuits. Hang on until I find them.'

'But if you loved fishing . . . ?'

He ignored that. Instead he pulled a packet of Ginger Nut from the press and tore open the wrapper. 'Hope you like these. They're my favourite.'

They were Lizzie's favourite until right at that moment, when she found she couldn't eat a single one.

*   *   *

189

Twenty minutes later, after not getting any more information from him, Lizzie stood in Joe's back garden, prepared to clean out the boxes. She hated this job. It was smelly and dirty and she really wasn't in the humour for doing it. But for her next plan to work she needed to get access to his coup. She watched with hungry eyes as he unlocked the loft and left the keys dangling from it. Before she had a chance to take them, he had handed her a bucket and palette knife. Soon she was scraping away, trying not to look too revolted.

Joe was humming tunelessly, relishing the whole experience. All she needed was for him to leave her alone for a few moments, that was all. But he didn't. He seemed determined to stay as if to make up for the first time when he'd left her on her own. Oh, how she wished she'd had the foresight to take action then, but she'd been teetering on the brink a few weeks ago – now, she was finding it easier to slip into her role as interested pigeon-girl. The more she played her part, the more she believed in it. She knew she had to find out what happened that night just to have some peace. Either that or ruin his pathetic life . . .

Finally they'd finished cleaning and Joe began clearing up, taking her bucket from her and mooching about as he washed it out. Lizzie watched him and when she was sure he wasn't looking, she gently reached over and removed the bunch of keys from the lock. Now all she had to do was to get out as quickly as she could before he noticed that they were gone. With a bit of luck, she could drop them in his garden later on and he'd think they had fallen from his pocket. She excused herself and went inside to wash her hands. As she reached for the disinfectant, she noticed that the bottle she'd filled with water was now mostly empty. Those pigeons were not getting their medication and she grinned.

'Hey, Lizzie!'

She jumped as Joe came in behind her.

He took a step back, looking as startled as she felt. 'Sorry, I didn't mean to frighten you like that.'

'No, it's fine.' Had he sneaked up behind Megan before he killed her? she wondered, as a sudden wave of nausea hit her.

190

'Hey, are you OK?' Joe scanned her face. She had gone very pale. 'D'you want to sit down?'

This was her chance to leave. 'No, no, I think I'll go home. I don't feel well at all.' And she didn't.

'Do you want me to drive you?'

'No! No, it's fine.' Lizzie shakily made her way to the door.

'Right, if you're sure.' Joe accompanied her into the hall and held the door open for her.

'Thanks.'

'Oh, just before you go, you haven't seen my keys, have you? I can't think where I put them.'

'No,' Lizzie shook her head. 'I remember you leaving them down all right.'

'Leaving them down? Are you sure? I thought I left them in the lock.'

'Naw, I'm sure you opened the lock and took them out.' Lizzie felt her stomach heave a little more with the lie and she knew that she had to get away. 'Listen, I better go and get back home. Talk to you during the week, OK?'

And then she came face to face with the old woman who lived next door to Joe, who was just coming up the steps with a young lad in tow. Lizzie tried to avoid looking at her but the old woman was sharper than she appeared.

'Mindy,' she said. 'Hello.'

Joe let out a splutter of a laugh. 'That's Lizzie, Ellen. Her name isn't Mindy.'

Ellen frowned. 'No, I met her a few weeks ago and she told me her name was Mindy. Isn't that right, love?'

'Sorry, excuse me,' Lizzie pushed past her and ran down the garden path, not knowing what else she could do.

'She's not well,' she heard Joe say to the woman.

Joe stared at Ellen, who was staring after Lizzie.

'She definitely said her name was Mindy,' Ellen said. Then added, 'And she said she wasn't interested in your birds.'

'Yes, well, Lizzie *is* interested in the birds,' Joe replied, wondering if Ellen was going a bit funny and mixing people up. 'So it couldn't be her.'

Ellen didn't seem convinced but instead of pursuing it, she pulled Anto towards her. 'Well,' she said as she shoved him forwards, 'here's another person who is interested in your pigeons.'

Joe looked blankly at her. Then looked at Anto. 'So?'

'See?' Anto glowered at Ellen. 'I told you he wouldn't let me near them.'

'You want me to let you near my pigeons?' Joe looked at him. 'You bloody well tried to rob a house and you want me to let *you* near my birds?'

'No. No, I don't. You and your birds can rot for all I care.' Anto shoved his hands into his pockets and, pushing past Ellen, he stomped off.

'Oh, Anto, come back, come back!' Ellen called after him. She whirled on Joe. 'It took him all his courage to come here today,' she snapped, 'and now look, you've ruined it!'

'I've ruined nothing,' Joe said, stunned. 'For God's sake—'

'He loves birds. His dad used to keep them before he died. Anto helped him out.' Ellen raised her eyes to heaven. 'He is a child, Joe. You are an adult. You should give him a chance.' Then she, too, stomped off.

Joe looked after the two of them in amazement. The whole scene had been totally unexpected. Maybe if he'd been prepared for it, it might have made a difference. He might have had time to think about it, but Jesus, to let a wild kid like that near the most precious things he had? That would be stupid.

Wouldn't it?

Four o'clock. Two hours since the light had gone off in Joe's bedroom window. Lizzie, too nervous and keyed up to feel tired, walked up the road towards his house, looking very carefully to her left and right. All was still, there was no one around, no one looking out on the street. Very carefully, keeping to the deepest shadows, Lizzie slunk into Joe's front garden and was soon engulfed by the gloom to the side of his house. She gently unlatched the side gate and let herself into his back garden.

Silence.

Carefully she unlocked the door to the racing loft. The birds wouldn't react until first light. Lizzie crept into the loft and, taking a tiny bottle of water from her pocket, she poured it on to the malt in the hopper.

She felt detached suddenly. An onlooker. She was fully aware of what she was doing but there was no emotion behind it: no elation, no guilt. There was just the instinct to strike out. She wondered, still in a detached way, when it would hit her. Or was she beyond feeling bad for what she was doing? 'I am making his birds sick,' she told herself. Nothing. It was a relief but it was a little scary, too. Revenge, she thought, must be a little like taking exercise. The more you did, the more you were capable of doing and the less it hurt. Finally, she thought, she was wrestling control back from the man who had ruined her past.

She left the loft door unlocked and then dropped Joe's keys on to the grass. And tucked her new spares into her pocket.

Joe found his keys in the grass in his garden the next morning. He couldn't understand why they were over next to his side gate. He didn't remember being near it – all he'd done was go between the loft and the kitchen. And what was even weirder was that one of his lofts was unlocked. Not open, which was good or all the birds would have flown.

Still, Joe vowed, he'd just have to be more careful next time.

The guilt hit her the next day as she showered. She wasn't thinking about anything when the reality of what she had done leapt out. She had stolen into a garden in the early hours of the morning and . . . Lizzie pushed it out of her head, not wanting to confront it, afraid that if she did she might lose her nerve. She squirrelled the guilt away in a small corner of her mind and squashed it down.

30

'WHAT IS THE situation with you and Aileen?' was the first thing Mrs Walsh demanded of Billy when he and Lizzie arrived home to visit at the weekend. They hadn't been down in a while, and Polly Walsh had rung wondering idly if her children were abandoning her.

Billy glared at his mother. 'I am sorting it out.'

'Oh, are you indeed,' Mrs Walsh ignored Lizzie as she struggled to pull all the bags out of the car, preferring instead to follow behind her son as he stomped into the house, 'and how are you doing that exactly?'

'Mammy, it really isn't your business,' Billy said in exasperation as he strode into the kitchen and flicked on the kettle. 'It's my life.' He nodded at his dad, who was at the table reading the paper.

'When a woman is carrying two,' Mrs Walsh took a deep breath and said again, in a louder voice, '*two* of my grandchildren, I think it is my business if my son is not with her.'

'She is not with me,' Billy corrected.

Lizzie sat at the table alongside her father. He glanced at her over the pages of his paper and she shrugged.

'Well, you get her back.' Mrs Walsh began banging cups as she took them from the press. 'You tell her you want her back. I will not lose my grandchildren!'

'I'm only in the door, will you leave it?!'

'It's bad enough setting up house with a girl you didn't marry, but when you get her pregnant and then decide you want to opt out of fatherhood, that beats all.'

'I didn't decide to opt out!' Billy's voice rose in exasperation. 'Mam, I am thirty-four, I don't need this shit from you!' He stormed on by her and out of the kitchen door, slamming it hard.

'Charming!' she shouted after him.

There was a silence.

'I told you to wait until after dinner before mentioning it,' Mr Walsh said calmly. 'What did you hope to achieve by having a go at the chap the minute he walks in the door?'

'I hoped to bang some sense into that stubborn head of his, that's what I hoped,' Mrs Walsh snapped.

'He has tried to talk to Aileen,' Lizzie offered meekly, 'but she won't listen to him.'

'Oh, that's it, stick up for your brother, go on. That's all you ever did.' Mrs Walsh laid both her hands on the table. 'Well, I'm telling you both,' her voice trembled a little, 'I lost a daughter once and I will not lose my grandchildren.'

'Oh, Polly,' Mr Walsh put his paper down and stood up. 'It's not going to be like that. Come on.' He held his arms out to his wife. 'Come here, come on.'

Lizzie left the two of them and went in search of Billy.

He was round the back, his hands sunk into his pockets.

'Hiya,' she said.

He didn't answer.

She pulled a packet of cigarettes from her pocket and offered him one. He shook his head. 'Naw, ta.'

She put one between her lips and struck a match.

'If Mam sees you smoking she'll kill you.' Billy managed a small grin.

'She won't care. She's only interested in you at the moment.' Lizzie took a long drag and blew out smoke circles as Billy watched.

'You've always been a really cool-looking smoker,' he said, half admiringly. 'It suits you.'

She grinned. 'Tom hates me doing it.'

'Tom loves everything you do,' Billy scoffed.

'Just like you did with Aileen.'

He shrugged. 'Aw, I dunno.'

'You did.'

There was a small silence before he said quietly, 'Lately I'm thinking that we only got together because Megan died. We both needed comfort. And then it was too hard to break free, you know.'

Lizzie gawked at him, shocked. 'You don't mean that!'

He shook his head despairingly. 'I don't know what I mean. I just wish she'd talk to me.' He looked at her. 'I can't go on like this, Lizzie, being ignored.'

'You have to convince her that you want the whole of family life, that's what you have to do,' Lizzie said as she took another drag of her fag. 'You just have to keep at it.' Then, because he seemed in a relatively mild mood, she added, 'And you have to get your life back on track, Billy, and start buying food for the house and looking after yourself again. I mean, look at that shirt, it's manky.'

Billy plonked down on the grass and said nothing for a bit. Lizzie sat down beside him, knowing he'd talk eventually. This was the first real conversation they'd had since Aileen had left, mainly because, unless drunk, Billy never talked about things that upset him and tended to leave the room every time difficult stuff got broached.

'I just can't care about stuff like that,' Billy admitted quietly as he looked down at his shirt. 'Like, if Aileen hadn't left, I'd never have thought the stuff I'm thinking now. And the stuff I'm thinking about now just, I dunno, paralyses me.'

'What stuff?'

'Me being a father,' Billy murmured. 'It's not something I wanted, Lizzie. I mean, Aileen is right, I didn't exactly cheer when I was told there were twins on the way.'

'And now?' A feeling of dread was spreading through Lizzie. She hadn't expected Billy to be like this.

'I don't know.' He gave her an anguished look. 'I can't sort my head out, Lizzie. I mean, I was happy in our flat with Aileen, but oh no, she wanted a house we could barely afford and I went along with it. Then, just as I was getting used to having all our money swallowed up by a mortgage, she's pregnant. I feel like she's hijacked my life. She's trying to make me into something I never wanted to be.' He pulled up a fistful of grass and observed it as it blew off on the breeze. 'It's not something I'm sure I *can* be.'

'It's something you are now, though,' Lizzie said quietly, 'whether you want it or not.'

His answer was to get up and leave.

Just like always.

Later that evening Martha called in. Billy had gone to bed early after refusing to talk to anyone about Aileen, and Lizzie and her parents were watching the Lottery show on the TV. Someone had just won a car and Mrs Walsh was remarking on how awful the woman looked: 'If I was going on television, I'd definitely dress up a little bit more. I mean, where did that woman get her shoes from?'

'Hello? Hello? Anyone home?' Martha had let herself in the back door. 'Polly? I've got the banners and handcuffs for the march tomorrow.'

A march? Tomorrow? Lizzie's heart sank.

'Oh, good,' Mrs Walsh called. 'Come in here, Martha. Let's have a look.'

Martha appeared round the door with two enormous signs and four pairs of silver handcuffs.

'We're chaining ourselves to the harbour railings,' her mother announced proudly. 'They'll have to forcibly remove us. They've ignored our night-time protest so it's time for tougher measures.' She turned to her friend, 'Now, Martha, put that stuff down and have a coffee.'

'Oh, lovely.' Martha put her placard on the floor and rested her handcuffs on top. As she received a cup, she said, 'Oh, I've another bit of news for you.'

'Yes?'

Lizzie could tell that her mother didn't really want to hear Martha's bit of news. Her eyes had swivelled back to the screen where the contestants for the following week's show were being drawn out.

Martha sensed this too and said dramatically, 'Leah Jones has Alzheimer's disease.' Then, once she'd got their attention, added, 'Apparently.'

Her mother and father were all ears now.

Martha nodded, delighted that her titbit had got such a reaction. 'Yes. I heard that she got lost yesterday in town and didn't know who she was or anything. Geoff had to collect her from Dunnes stores and he told a girl there that she was having tests for it. But I mean, you don't go getting lost if there's nothing wrong with you, do you?'

'Oh, poor woman,' Polly Walsh said.

'Yes, and she isn't even that old,' Martha nodded vigorously. 'And,' she went on, lowering her voice for maximum impact, '*apparently*, now I heard this from Julia who's a good friend of Angela who knows the wife of a friend of Geoff's, and she said that Joe Jones will not even come down to see his poor mother before she forgets him altogether.'

'No!' the two of them gasped.

'Now.' Martha looked around, then sat back in the chair. 'Isn't. That. Awful?'

'Yes,' Mrs Walsh said. Then added, 'But I'm not surprised. Any fella that can—' Her voice faltered and she bit her lip and stopped.

'Exactly,' Martha agreed. 'Exactly.'

'Poor Leah, though,' Mrs Walsh said then. 'She's had it tough and now that.'

'Huh, I don't think that's tough,' Lizzie surprised herself and the others by saying. 'Makes it easier for her to forget what her horrible son did, doesn't it? Wouldn't you like to be able to forget, Mammy? Wouldn't you?'

'Oh, now, Lizzie,' her father said softly, 'there's no use being like that. Only makes you hard.'

'Being hard is OK,' she said. 'Means you don't get hurt.'

'Means you don't feel,' her dad said. 'There is a difference.'

'Not from where I'm standing.' The bitterness in her voice surprised her. 'I feel all right. I feel glad, so I do. Serves them right. They have their son. We don't have Megan. That woman can forget, we can't. Where's the justice in that?'

There was a silence.

'Come on,' Mrs Walsh said gently, 'don't go upsetting yourself, Lizzie. I know I wouldn't ever want to forget little Megan.'

'Trouble and all as she was,' Mr Walsh smiled.

That made them chuckle.

31

LIZZIE DIDN'T THINK she would ever forget the sight of her mother being hauled off in the back of a police van. She stood with Billy on the fringes of the protest, holding a placard which read NEW HARBOUR PLANS HARBOUR DISASTER, as she watched her mother screaming at the crowd not to give in. Not to give way. Everything she said was met by cheers and whoops.

A youngish looking policeman was laboriously cutting through the handcuffs that bound her to the harbour wall. Each time she moved he winced, afraid that he'd cut her. Finally he dispensed with the saw, pulled apart the broken cuffs and hauled Polly Walsh to her feet. Some guy up front was busy snapping pictures.

'Where is my husband?' Polly demanded, scanning the crowd.

Mr Walsh sheepishly put up his hand. He had, under pressure, extricated himself from his own set of handcuffs and so had Dolly. Martha however, like her mother, had remained staunch until the end.

'You're supposed to be in chains!' Polly yelled at him.

'Someone has to feed the chickens,' Mr Walsh said. 'I'll follow behind, love. OK?'

'I wouldn't like to be in Dad's shoes when Mam gets hold of him,' Billy said wryly.

Lizzie laughed slightly but stopped as she saw her mother being manhandled into the back of a van along with Martha. Her dad suddenly looked concerned.

'Do you want me to come with you to the police station, Dad?' Lizzie asked, worried at his troubled expression.

He waved her away. 'No, no, the two of you go back. I don't

know how long this will all take.' He shook his head. 'I just hope she knows what she's doing.' Handing his placard to Dolly, he began to walk towards his car, Billy and Lizzie following.

'Now,' he said when he reached it, 'feed the hens and lock up the coup. I'll be back as soon as I can.'

They watched as he drove away, then they, too, drove towards home.

Later that night, when their dad still hadn't returned, Lizzie went to pack in preparation for leaving the next day. As she climbed the stairs she saw that the door to Megan's old room was ajar. Since Megan had gone, Lizzie hadn't wanted to venture past the threshold of the room, finding all Megan's old stuff hard to look at without getting upset. It was as if time stopped in that room the day Megan had died. All her old bottles and perfumes and clothes waiting for their owner to come back. Like a dog that refuses to accept its master is dead.

She tentatively approached the door to close it when she noticed a figure sitting on Meg's old bed.

'Bill?'

He looked up and Lizzie wasn't sure if he'd been crying or not. 'You OK?'

He nodded, swallowing hard. 'I just came in to talk to her,' he said.

'Did you?' Lizzie pushed open the door a little and ventured in herself. The room was much barer than it ever had been. Her mother had been busy, stripping all the posters from the walls and taking the bed linen off the bed. Bits and pieces of Megan's make-up and hair products were all tidied away in a box. Her fireplace had been cleaned and the brass sparkled. The floor-boards had been varnished.

'It's not like her room any more,' Billy said as Lizzie sat in beside him.

'No, Mam is clearing it out. Or at least she was.'

'It's good, I suppose, that she can do that.'

'Yeah,' Lizzie nodded. 'She's trying to move on, I guess.'

Though, even as she said the words, Lizzie wasn't sure if they were true.

'I miss her, Lizzie,' Billy said. 'I thought it would get easier but sometimes it just hits me.'

Lizzie rubbed his arm and blinked hard. She knew what he meant.

'She was the noise in the house, wasn't she? It all went when she went. Mam used to say that Megan was like a cat, always landing on her feet. She never worried about her, did she?'

Lizzie shook her head. 'She only worried about her catching cold in the short skirts she used to wear. D'you remember Mam told her the breeze going up her legs would give her kidney disease?'

Billy snorted back a laugh. 'And she told Mam that was impossible as your kidneys are in your chest.'

'She meant lungs.'

'She was awful thick, wasn't she?'

They laughed quietly.

'I miss her, you know.'

'Yeah.'

The curtains had been washed, too. There was no sense of Megan in the room now. Whatever smell of her that had been there had disappeared.

'Since she died, I just think my life has gone all wrong.' Billy's voice broke slightly.

'Aw, Billy,' Lizzie pulled her brother into a hug. He clung to her, not crying but holding her as if he were drowning. 'It's just this stuff with Aileen, it'll work out, you'll see.'

He said nothing, just let her hold him, which was scarier than any words would have been.

32

'NOW REMEMBER, MARK, it's important not to preach.'

Lizzie yawned. All her late nights were catching up on her, but it was worth it. Each time she saw Joe, he looked, she fancied, slightly more bewildered than the last. Finding his lofts open most mornings would do that to a fella, she reckoned. Now it was time to really start putting the heat on, but for right now, her priority was to tutor Mark before they went on air.

Mark looked at her in exasperation. 'Who are you? My PR woman?'

'You could do with one.'

He ignored that. 'Look, the radio station asked for me. They didn't ask for you and they didn't ask for me to parrot your words on air. They asked for me and me is who I will give them.'

'If I asked for an alligator to come into my radio studio, do you think it'd be reasonable to expect it to be in a cage so it couldn't bite me?' Lizzie asked.

Mark frowned. 'I'm not sure where this is going,' he said. 'Are you saying I'm an alligator?'

'Yep.'

He rolled his eyes and smirked. 'Stella calls me a tiger. Her big, furry tiger.'

'Please,' Lizzie said, revolted.

'Ah, jealous, are you?' Mark nudged her. 'Is your poncy actor boyfriend not being all he should?'

'*Tom*,' Lizzie stressed the name, 'is very busy doing his play. He rehearses during the day and he works in a bar at night. He is not poncy, the same way your girlfriend is not sane. Now can we get back to the task at hand? You are going to give an overview of—'

'Oops.' Mark looked at his watch. 'Time to go. And try not to be jealous that Declan Darcy doesn't want to talk to you, it's OK. You'll get over it.' He patted her patronisingly on the shoulder as she came around the car to join him.

'Mark, take this in the spirit that it's meant: go fuck yourself.'

'Nope, I've got Stella, remember?' He winked at her and Lizzie had to smile, though inwardly she was praying hard for the man not to make a national joke of himself.

They were ushered into the studio and given headphones to put on. Declan nodded a greeting and explained that he would talk to them after his newspaper spiel at the beginning.

'We just take a quick gander through the papers and I make a few witty comments and the like,' he said.

Mark nodded confidently. 'No problem, Declan,' he replied, sounding really official. 'We've all the time in the world.'

What a lick-arse, Lizzie wanted to hiss, though she probably would have said the same herself.

The countdown to the programme began. The music banged out a fanfare and suddenly Declan was transformed from a weird-looking middle-aged schoolboy to super smooth DJ.

'Hi, folks,' he began in his Dublin accent, 'welcome to the best radio show in the land: mine. Declan Darcy. Now, let's have a look at the papers today.' He picked up the bundle from his desk and immediately snorted with laughter. 'Well, folks, no matter what paper you pick up this morning, variations of this photo will feature in them all. I'm looking at the *Indo* – and what a picture! What an amazing sight! Godzilla is only in the ha'penny place compared to these two ladies. Martha Dowling and Polly Walsh were arrested in Rossclare after they tied themselves to the harbour wall and refused to move. They're protesting against the development of Rossclare harbour. Well, I have to say, Polly, you've a face to ground a thousand ships.'

He gave a cackle of laughter as Lizzie sat frozen in her seat.

She took a quick glance as Declan casually threw the paper across his desk. Oh God, her mother looked pure evil. She wouldn't be pleased with that photo. Her hair was sticking up in all directions and her teeth were bared in a grimace. Lines criss-crossed her face, making it look like some bizarre road map.

'That's one scary-looking bird,' Mark whispered.

Lizzie ignored him. She barely heard the rest of Declan's opening speech. It had been a terrible weekend. Her mother and Martha had remained in custody and were due up in court in the next few days. It was all very stressful, especially on her dad, whom her mother was refusing to speak to since he'd unchained himself from the railings.

'An' now,' Declan said with a flourish, his hoarse voice crashing through Lizzie's mournful recollections, 'I've a special guest in the studio today, accompanied by his secretary.'

Under the table Mark kicked her and Lizzie made a face at him.

'This man is probably a stranger to most of you but by the end of our slot, let's hope you'll all know him a bit better. He's the founder of the Life counselling service. Mark Delaney, welcome to the studio.'

'Thanks, Declan, and can I just say that the woman beside me is not my secretary, she's actually the fundraiser for the charity. I know she looks like a secretary, but she's not.'

Declan gave a huge guffaw of a laugh and Mark smiled politely, unaware he'd just insulted every secretary in the land.

'So now, Mark, first tell us a bit about Life.'

She'd tutored him on this one, Lizzie thought in satisfaction.

'Basically Life is an over-the-phone counselling service. Every call only costs ten cents, no matter how long the duration. We counsel on everything from bereavement to relationship break-up. I've a team of volunteers who work twenty-four seven to bring this service to the public. Some of them are professionals who want to give something back and others, like Lizzie here, are amateurs. Well, that's the wrong word, she's had training but she doesn't do it for a living.'

205

Lizzie squirmed. Oh God.

'Who trained you, Lizzie?' Declan asked, pouncing on her.

'A professional is employed to train each new batch of coun-sellors,' Lizzie said, making her voice sound as efficient as possible. 'Then each new person is monitored for a few months and their performance is assessed. We have a very high stan-dard of care.'

'Nice one,' Declan said before turning, to Lizzie's dismay, back to Mark. 'And what made you set it up, Mark? You were,' he rummaged about in his pile of papers, 'the owner of a stationery company, were you not?'

'Stationary being right,' Mark scoffed, 'in that the company wasn't going anywhere.'

Declan laughed, as did his researchers behind the screen.

All he had to do was follow what Lizzie had told him, but oh no, he was determined to go his own way. Lizzie sat back, folded her arms and waited for him to blow it, like he'd blown so many meetings before.

'Yeah,' Mark said when the laughter stopped, 'I owned the company with my wife, we set it up together. Then of course she decided that she was going to wreck our marriage by having an affair and we had to divide up everything, including the company. Well, I don't mind telling you, Declan, it was a hard time. I had a fistful of cash and nothing to spend it on and I had to look at my wife all shacked up with her new man.'

'Terrible.'

Lizzie winced. She hoped Mark wasn't going to tell of the time—

'And I knew I reached a low when I started ringing all the weird chatlines. I mean, those women have great voices but . . . *ugh*.' Mark shuddered. So did Lizzie, for a different reason.

'I just wanted to feel connected to someone, you see,' Mark went on. 'Anyone would have done me, even that woman at the front of today's paper.' More laughter. Lizzie bristled. 'But the end came when I tried to talk back to these women, to tell them how I was feeling, and they hung up on me. One of them even called me weirdo. *Me?*' Mark's voice rose in indignation. 'There she was, a bloody granny in a house in Russia or somewhere, doing all her heavy breathing while she was, I dunno, minding her grandchildren or something, and she tells *me* that *I'm* weird.'

'Mad,' Declan said. 'So you decided to set up your own helpline?'

'Yep. After having the biggest breakdown of my life. You might not think it, Declan, looking at me. I mean I seem so together, but in those days I was really fraying around the edges, d'you get me? After it happened, I decided to set up a helpline for breakups and then it just evolved. People ring us for everything now. Even if they just feel lonely, like I did.' He paused. 'Loneliness is the root of a lot of our problems, you know. Even my horrible wife was lonely, I understand that now.'

There was a pause when he'd finished and, to Lizzie's surprise, someone in the studio started to clap.

Declan beamed. 'Great story, Mark. Well told. So tell us, why are you here now? What is Life's next project?'

'Oh,' Mark said magnanimously, 'I'll let Lizzie explain that. She's the brains behind the fundraising.'

Lizzie jumped. Shit! He hadn't told her was going to let her speak. She looked at him and he smiled cockily at her.

She gave him a grin back.

His loft was open again. That was three times this week. Joe took his keys from his pocket and inserted the key into the lock.

Click.

It was working perfectly. It didn't make sense. He had definitely locked up last night, he had even written a note when he had done it and stickered it on the wall inside the loft. He opened the loft again, stepped inside and nothing . . . the note was gone. Had he even done it in the first place?

His head swam and he had to sit down. And it was then he noticed the malt.

It was wet.

How on earth . . . ?

He looked wildly around for a leak, for a reason for the dampness.

None.

He'd have to ring in sick. He needed to check his birds for spores.

His boss would go mental.

The show ended, and Declan wished them all the best, before saying, 'And Mark, we've had an amazing response to you from our female audience.'

'Yeah?'

'It seems a lot of women out there want to know if you're available.'

To Lizzie's amusement Mark blushed. 'I'm not, as it happens, but if they'd like to meet me they can sign up for the parachute jump.'

Wow, that was slick, Lizzie thought, pleased.

'There now, girls, you heard it here. CKY Radio and Declan Darcy.'

As Declan played 'Parachute' by Something Happens, Mark turned to Lizzie. 'There now, see, I wasn't so bad, was I?'

'No, actually,' Lizzie nodded, 'you were pretty great.' There would be no stopping him now, she thought, half amused – he'd be unbearable.

Later that night, to distract himself from the fact that he seemed to be losing his mind, Joe attempted to do a bit more on the clean-up of his house – it really was a state. He hadn't much noticed before Lizzie arrived on the scene, as no one ever visited him at home, but when she'd stepped into his kitchen he'd suddenly seen it through her eyes.

He was now tackling the dining-room floor. He couldn't actually remember ever cleaning it. The pigeons lived in a tidier environment than he did. To his relief he hadn't found any traces of spores among them, but he'd have to keep a check on it. And they really didn't seem as active as they had been. Maybe the older ones were just a little tired from all the racing.

He had just managed to spray some disinfectant on to the floor when his phone rang. Wiping his hands along his old jeans, he went into the hall and, without looking at the caller ID, he picked it up.

'Hello?'

'Joseph, it's Dad.'

Joe froze, his hand seemed to be stuck to the receiver.

'Joe?' his dad said again. 'Are you there? I need to talk to you.'

'I've nothing to say to you, Dad. I'm out of your life now. Don't ring me again.'

He vaguely heard his dad shouting out something to him as he replaced the phone on the hook. He stood for a second looking at the phone before it began to ring again. Joe walked away from it. He just couldn't go back, not after all that had happened. Not after what his dad had done to him. He had a new life now – OK, it was a little lonely and not the sort of life he'd ever wanted, but it was working out all right. He was happier than he'd ever thought he could be. He had no desire to see his parents ever again.

The phone continued to ring for the next hour, but he ignored it.

Her mobile phone rang at nine that night. Picking it up, she was surprised to see Aileen's number displayed. With fumbling fingers she pressed the accept button. 'Hello, Aileen?' This was a surprise.

'Oh, so you're still talking to me then?' Aileen said shyly.

'Of course I am,' Lizzie said warmly. 'How's things?'

'Not too bad,' Aileen answered. 'I'm not as sick as I was in the beginning.'

'Great. Good.'

There was an awkward pause.

'Anyway—'

'Can I—'

'You first,' Lizzie said.

'I was just going say that, well, I saw your mother on the front of the newspaper today.'

'You and about a million other people,' Lizzie answered glumly.

Aileen gave a weak laugh. 'Well, I just rang to say I hope she's OK and that you're OK and . . .' Her voice trailed off a little. 'And that . . . that Billy's OK with it.' She had difficulty saying his name.

'I can put you on to Billy,' Lizzie suggested gently. 'He'd be glad to hear from you. You're the only one he ever talks to about stuff anyway.'

'Oh no, no, I don't think so.' Aileen sounded suddenly scared. 'No, I just thought, you know . . .'

There was a silence.

'I don't want to be sweet-talked into going back,' Aileen admitted after a bit. 'I can't be like my dad, Lizzie.'

'Your dad?'

'Yeah. He . . .' Aileen swallowed. 'You know, kept taking my mother back. And she kept leaving him. I can't be like that.'

'Oh, Aileen,' Lizzie felt a rush of sympathy for her, 'Billy wouldn't leave you. He loves you, he's just—' She paused. After what Billy had said at the weekend, she didn't know any more. She would have bet her life on him loving Aileen, but now . . . She gulped. 'Anyway,' she said, 'it's great to hear from you.'

'Yeah, and I rang also to apologise for the way I behaved the day you called by. I was horrible.'

'You were, but you were upset.'

'I was.'

Her voice dipped. 'My dad is driving me mad.' She sounded like Aileen all of a sudden, girly and giggly. 'I'm going to have to look for somewhere to live. He keeps reminding me of how hard it is to be a single parent.'

'You won't be a single parent,' Lizzie said, 'Billy will be there. He's not running off.'

There was a pause.

'And I'm going to be here all the way,' Lizzie offered. 'Like being an aunty is a responsible job, too.'

210

'Would you like to come in for the scan?' Aileen said suddenly. 'I'm going on Thursday and my dad can't come, so will you go instead?'

She'd take Thursday afternoon off. 'I would totally love to,' she declared.

33

AILEEN WAS WAITING for her at the entrance to the maternity hospital. She smiled uneasily as Lizzie walked up toward her. Lizzie beamed back.

'Come here!' Lizzie enfolded her in a hug before holding her at arms' length and scrutinising her. 'You look fab,' she announced emphatically. 'Being pregnant suits you.'

Aileen laughed a little. 'I'm getting so fat, I can't fit into anything any more.'

'You're not fat!' Lizzie waved her away. 'And your skin looks so great.'

'Thanks.' Aileen nudged her. 'I'm glad you're here. My dad would never think of saying anything like that.'

Lizzie grinned and linked her arm. 'Come on, Mammy, let's get you inside.'

They walked down the corridors, following signs for the antenatal clinic. There was a large queue of pregnant women in front of them. Some women had partners with them, while others were on their own. Aileen and Lizzie sat down and waited. A few people looked curiously at them. Lizzie's phone started to ring. She smiled apologetically and flicked it open.

'Hello?'

'Hey, gorgeous!'

'Hi, Tom.'

'You free Saturday? I've got the night off.'

Lizzie winced. Of all the nights – there was no way. It had been too carefully planned. 'Eh, I'm going out with Billy, Tom.'

'Can't you cancel? I've got a surprise for you.'

'No way. Sorry.' She felt awful lying to him. Since she'd started her campaign, as she called it, the guilt she was experiencing wasn't so much at what she was doing to Joe, but rather at the way she was deceiving Tom. He loved someone who was beginning to disappear. Each time she'd stolen into Joe's back garden at four in the morning, part of the girl she'd been and who he loved seemed to steal away, too. She knew she didn't deserve him or, worse, that he certainly didn't deserve her. It was becoming an effort to pretend that she was the same as she used to be.

'OK,' he sounded disappointed, 'you're coming to see the play next week though, ey?'

'I wouldn't miss it for the world.'

'Well, I'll catch you after, so.'

'Yeah.'

She hung up and found Aileen staring at her with her mouth open. 'You're cancelling Tom in favour of Billy?'

Lizzie shrugged. 'He's a bit down.'

Aileen flushed and the two sat in silence until a nurse called: 'Adrienne Lowry?'

A very pregnant woman stood up and waddled towards the doctor's office. The queue moved up a seat.

Eventually, after about an hour, Aileen was called in. Lizzie watched in fascination as Aileen's stomach was spread with gel and a scanning device was pressed to her belly. Immediately the *whoosh whoosh* of the heartbeats sounded.

'Oh my God!' Lizzie put her hands to her mouth as sudden tears sprang to her eyes. 'Is that their little hearts?'

The doctor smiled. 'Yes. And see here: there they are on the monitor.'

Lizzie gawked at the monitor, where she made out some kind of moving blurs. They didn't look much like anything.

'Hello, babies,' she waved. 'Hello.'

Aileen laughed and the doctor smiled, then she began clicking buttons on a computer and taking measurements. Lizzie turned to Aileen. 'This is brilliant, thanks for inviting me. Isn't it amazing?'

'Yeah,' Aileen nodded. 'That's what I think, too.'

Lizzie was about to say that Billy would love it, when she stopped herself. There was no point in getting involved. She just had to take what she was given and be grateful for it. It was up to Billy and Aileen to sort themselves out.

'Would you like a print-out?' the doctor asked.

'Oh yes, please,' Lizzie said.

'I meant for Mum?' the doctor said, amused.

Aileen laughed. 'That'd be lovely.'

'Can you do two?' Lizzie said impulsively as Aileen shot her a dark look. 'I'll pay for it if I have to.'

The doctor smiled slightly. 'Well, don't tell anyone else, will you?'

'Cross my heart.'

'Why did you ask for another scan picture?' Aileen said as they sat over two cups of coffee.

'To show Billy.' Lizzie stirred some milk into her cup. 'He'd like a picture, I'd say.' She knew Aileen was annoyed but was trying to ignore it.

'I was wondering when Billy would be mentioned,' Aileen said crossly. 'I was wondering when you'd sneak him in.'

'I wasn't trying to sneak him in,' Lizzie said honestly. 'He's already involved and no matter what you think, Aileen, he is their daddy.'

Aileen ran her finger around the rim of her cup. 'We need to sort out what to do with the house.'

'What?' Lizzie felt sick. That sounded so bloody final. So awful. Watching Billy and Aileen split up was like watching her own parents do it, she thought. They were her family when she was in Dublin.

'Aileen, don't be hasty,' she said. 'Please think about it. You're throwing something great away – for what? For a look that was a spur of the moment thing? It's, it's . . .' she sought for the right words, 'ridiculous.'

Aileen glared at her before gathering up her belongings and standing up. 'I'm going now. Tell Billy that my dad will be in contact to sort the house out.'

214

'Tell him yourself,' Lizzie fired back.

Aileen nodded, as if it was all she expected from her, and said, 'I'll make my own way home.'

'Aw, Aileen—' Lizzie pleaded after her. Aileen flapped her away.

Even a smoke wouldn't be any use now, Lizzie thought glumly, as she faced down the stares of the other customers.

Another night off work. His boss was not going to be pleased, but John and Noel had both said they were available to come over that evening and Joe needed their opinion. It was the first time, aside from when he'd started up, that he'd asked for help.

'Thanks for coming tonight, guys,' he said as he let the two men into his house.

Noel whistled softly as he looked around. 'Oh, someone has discovered the duster!' He grinned slyly. 'I wonder why.' He marched ahead of Joe into the kitchen and laughed loudly as he remarked, 'Wow, much nicer than when we were here last.'

'That was ages ago,' Joe flushed.

Noel ignored him. 'The floor all cleaned up and everything. It wouldn't have anything to do with a pretty young wan who's just joined the club, would it?'

'Feck off,' Joe answered without looking at him. 'I just never had time to clean up before.'

'Course you didn't,' John joked. 'And it was driving you mad, wasn't it?'

'Like I said, feck off,' Joe answered pleasantly as he pushed open the back door to let the lads into the garden. His pigeons were up, flying around. As he crossed to the loft a number of them came swooping down, landing on his shoulders and head. Joe affectionately flapped them off.

'I can't quite put my finger on it,' he explained. 'They're in good form, just not as good as before.'

John scanned the birds. 'They look good to me,' he remarked.

'They're lethargic,' Joe said. 'It's not something anyone else might notice.'

'You giving them their antibiotics?' Noel asked.

215

'Yep.'

'What sort?'

'The bottle is in the kitchen.'

Noel turned and followed Joe back into the house. Joe took the bottle from his press and shook it. 'Not much left.'

Noel examined the bottle before unscrewing it. He swirled it about, then sniffed. 'Not much of a smell from the stuff,' he remarked.

'It's nearly gone,' Joe said.

'No, come here. Smell.' Noel thrust the bottle under Joe's nose and Joe sniffed. Then sniffed again. Then he tipped the bottle towards his lips and tasted a liquid drop.

'Jesus,' he winced, 'it's water. Or as good as. Taste, Noel.'

Noel took a sample taste. 'There's your problem, Joe. The stuff is too weak.'

'Yeah, but how?' Joe sniffed again.

Noel shrugged. 'Happened to me once. Well, not that exactly, but I had to go away for work one time and the wife told me she would give them their treatments and she didn't. The birds were in bits when I got back.'

Joe barely heard him. His mind was reeling. How could that have happened?

'Stuff must be faulty,' Noel said, taking it from him and dumping it down the sink. 'Surprised you didn't notice. You think you'd notice that it didn't smell.'

'Yeah well, I normally don't go shoving my nose into it.' He watched as Noel rinsed out the bottle. 'You got any more?' Noel asked.

'Yeah. Yeah I have. I'll do it now.' From the back of the press he pulled another bottle, opened it, and assured himself that it was all right before diluting it for the birds.

'Who's the kid?' Noel pointed at a skinny boy perched on the wall, who seemed to be having an animated discussion with John.

Joe glanced up. 'He's a lad who works for Ellen, my neighbour. He does odd jobs for her. Hey, what the hell is John doing?'

John had handed Anto one of Joe's pigeons to hold.

Joe was about to race into the garden when he noted the reverent way Anto took the bird and held it close to his chest. He watched as Anto ran his index finger along the length of the bird's body with a gentleness that belied the rough look on his face. John was nodding and encouraging him.

'Boy knows how to hold a bird,' Noel said admiringly.

'Yeah,' Joe answered, not at all sure what to do. He had to go outside, though – that was Prince Anto was holding. As he stepped into the garden, Anto flinched and hastily handed the bird back to John. John was left startled as Anto hopped down from the wall and ran off.

'Nice kid,' he remarked. 'Loves the pigeons.'

Joe didn't answer. Instead he held up the medicine. 'We found the culprit. Or at least we think we did.'

'No way!' John let Prince go and whistled softly. 'Gone off, was it?'

'I guess,' Joe nodded. He started to dole out the fresh anti-biotics. 'We'll find out Saturday week when I fly them again.'

'Cid will hate that. He came third last week.'

'No!' Joe grinned. 'I wish I'd been there.'

'No, you don't.' John shook his head. 'He was unbearable. I left early.'

The other two laughed before starting to look for the source of Joe's damp.

'Hello, is that Lizzie?'

She recognised the caller's voice. 'Sinéad.'

'Yes, that's right.' Sinéad sounded relieved.

'I haven't heard from you in a while, how have things been?'

'Not good,' Sinéad answered bluntly. 'I tried to ring you before but you weren't there and then things calmed down again and now, well, he hit me. Again. Last week.'

Lizzie remained silent.

'And I ended up with a bruise the size of a fist on my face and I couldn't go outside the door for days.' Now the woman's voice wobbled.

'And what happened?' Lizzie asked gently.

'I told him that he couldn't do that,' Sinéad said, sniffing. 'I told him that I was not going to let him hit me. Like since I talked to you, I was thinking back. And I've changed so much. I used to have loads of friends. I used to see my family. Now there just seems to be the two of us. And I'm nervy all the time. All the time.'

'What did he say when you stood up to him?'

'He said sorry,' Sinéad said. 'And, well, he sounded as if he meant it. So I said it was fine so long as he didn't do it again. And he said that I just made him so angry and I said I'd try not to make him angry and then tonight, well, I let a cup drop because he raised his voice and then he made me clean it up and then he told me he could see a piece under the chair and would I get to it and so I did, and then I'm under the chair thinking, why am I doing this? Why doesn't he do it if he saw it? And I pick up the cup and he says I better buy a replacement one and I said that they were willow pattern and couldn't be replaced so he took them all out of the press and smashed them up one by one. Just picked them up and smashed them. One by one. And I jumped each time he did it, I couldn't help myself. Then he told me to clean them all up.'

Lizzie gritted her teeth. It took all her will power to keep quiet. 'Did you clean them up?'

'No,' Sinéad said. 'They're still there and he's gone out and said he hopes it'll be clean when he gets back and I just want to run away.'

'You want to run away,' Lizzie deliberately raised her voice in the hope of catching Anna's attention.

Anna glanced up and Lizzie beckoned her over.

'Yes, I'm so scared but I'm not cleaning up, I'm not.'

'Well then, get out right now and tomorrow go and see if you can get a barring order against him. It'll stop him coming near you.'

'Just leave now? Where will I go?'

Lizzie gave her the address of a women's refuge and told her she would ring in advance to say Sinéad was on her way.

'It's Lori,' Sinéad said tearfully. 'That's my real name.'

'Well, Lori, you'll be safe. I promise.'

'Will you come and see me?' Lori asked.

'Come and see you?'

Anna shook her head.

'Eh, Lori, I can't. I'm not allowed.' Lizzie hated having to say that to her. 'But there is a lovely woman in the shelter who'll take care of you. Her name is Julie, all right?'

'Oh.' Lori sounded devastated. 'Right, thanks.'

The phone went dead.

Lizzie heaved a sigh and flopped back on her chair.

'Well done.' Anna gave her a brief hug. 'Good girl.'

Lizzie didn't feel as if she'd done any good at all. 'I wish I could just go and meet her,' she said.

'Yeah, and the next time someone calls you'll want to meet her. You know you can't, Lizzie.'

She didn't answer.

Despite the fact that they didn't find any source of damp, it was a good night. It had been so long since he'd had people over for a chat and a few cans that he'd forgotten how much fun it could be. They talked all night about birds and races and form.

It was Joe's kind of night.

34

'HE'S WELCOME TO help me with the birds if he likes,' Joe said to Ellen as he took a chair in her fussy sitting room. From the look of the place it didn't seem as if Anto was doing much cleaning at all. Dust lay on everything.

Ellen smiled and her face suddenly appeared younger. 'Oh, I knew you'd come around.' She stood up and pinched Joe on the cheek. 'You're a good boy really, aren't you?'

'I'm stupid is what I am,' Joe said, half in jest. He shrugged a little. 'He seems to know how to handle a bird and that's good enough for me for the moment.'

'So now you'll have two helpers: that pretty Mindy and a very happy Anto. Aren't you Mr Popular all of a sudden?'

'Lizzie, Ellen, her name is Lizzie.'

'Does she have a sister?'

Joe shrugged. It occurred to him suddenly that he knew nothing much about Lizzie. Maybe he should ask her. Girls liked when you showed an interest in them. And despite not wanting to get involved with anyone, Joe suddenly realised how involved with people he was becoming. Ellen, Noel, John and now Anto. He wasn't too sure if he liked it. Though he knew that he liked Lizzie – there was something about her. He wouldn't mind being involved with her. He shifted about uncomfortably on the seat.

'Anyway, I'll be getting back. You can let Anto know that the next time he's here, if he does a good job cleaning out this room, he can have half an hour with the birds.'

'This room is fine.' Ellen sounded indignant. She looked about. 'I don't let him in here. These are my important things that only I touch.'

'Oh, right,' Joe shrugged. 'Well, get him to do something for you and I'll inspect it.'

'You are so self-righteous,' Ellen said crossly. 'He does his best. He's only a small boy. He can't clean really well. He doesn't need to be judged, just accepted.'

'You'd better look out or you'll collapse,' Joe said, amused at her cross voice.

'Collapse?'

'Due to your bleeding heart.'

'Get out,' she pushed him towards the door, 'you dreadful man. Get out.'

Joe laughed. It occurred to him that he was laughing a lot more than he used to.

Two in the morning. Lizzie was psyching herself to get out of the car when her phone bleeped. *Can we meet 2morrow? Tom.*

She winced. She'd planned on calling to Joe tomorrow. So she texted back: *Morning only.*

OK. R u having a good night with Bill?

Yep. Great. C U tomorrow.

She wondered what he wanted, but it would be good to see him all the same.

Putting her phone in the glove compartment, she stepped out of her car. Then, opening the boot, she pulled her pigeon basket from it. Carrying the basket, she pulled her black jacket around her and, making sure she wasn't being observed, slipped quietly up Joe's driveway and into his side entrance. She slowly pushed open the gate. It squeaked a little and she winced. A little oil the next time.

Closing it after her, she crept across the silent garden. She knew where it all was now and she hurried as quietly as she could across the grass. Then, very gently, she inserted the key and pulled open the door.

Nothing stirred.

Slowly, with that sense of detachment growing stronger each time she came here, Lizzie opened the lid of the basket.

35

L IZZIE AWOKE TO the sound of the phone the next morning.
Groggily, she glanced at her watch. Her head felt muzzy, as
if her mind was caught in a thick fog. Eight-thirty. Who would
ring on a Sunday at eight-thirty? Oh God. Her stomach heaved
as she remembered what she had done the night before. Maybe
it was the police. Or Joe. She felt suddenly sick.

She wouldn't answer it. She lay in bed, the duvet pulled up to
her chin, and let the phone ring out. It was a relief when the
noise stopped, but it started again a minute later. Joe hadn't got
her home number, she remembered, so it couldn't be him. She
felt sick again with relief.

A sudden vision of the panic she would feel if she were caught
out unnerved her. But she wasn't going to be caught. There was
no way. Joe was becoming friendlier as time went on. Why, one
day last week, after she'd yet again cleaned out his pigeon coup,
he'd told her about his day at work in a sort of halting way, which,
under other circumstances, would have been charming.

Downstairs the phone continued to ring.

Lizzie listened for a second wondering if Billy was going to
get it, but when she heard nothing from his room, she stumbled
from her own bed. She'd barely slept the night before, high on
adrenalin.

'Hello?' she said sleepily, hoping to convey to the caller that
early on a Sunday was not a time to ring anyone. She yawned
widely.

'It's me.'

'Dad, hey.' He sounded cross or worried, she couldn't decide.

'I'm worried, Lizzie.'

'Why?'

'It's your mother. She's refusing to apologise for what she's done. She was up in court Friday.'

Her mind had to play catch-up. She yawned again. 'Court?'

'Yes, I didn't want to worry you or Billy. It was on the news last night. Did you see the news last night?'

'No.'

'Well, I thought she'd apologise, see, but she didn't. Told them she'd fight all the way.'

'Did she?' Well, that was no surprise.

'So the judge asked her how she'd like to fight from behind bars and, Lizzie,' he sighed, 'she's in a cell here awaiting a trip to Mountjoy.'

That woke her up. 'You are joking!'

'Six months until she apologises.'

'Oh my God.'

Her dad said nothing.

'But—but, sure she's not a danger to anyone.'

'No. Only herself. It's like she's on self-destruct. I have been up all night worrying about her. I can't sleep, I can't eat. Oh, this has been coming a long time.'

'Are you OK?' Lizzie asked.

'No, I'm not. Haven't you been listening? I can't sleep, I can't—'

'OK, calm down. Look at this rationally. I—'

'You're my daughter, Lizzie, not my counsellor. There is no rational explanation for your mother's behaviour. Even Martha says it.'

'Martha apologised?'

'She did. On Friday, and she thought your mother would too, but oh no, that'd be way too normal for your mother.'

Lizzie didn't know what to say. Her dad sounded very agitated and it wasn't good for him to be like that.

'Anyway,' he went on, 'I need to visit her when she's up there, so I'm going to have to come and stay. Will Billy be OK with that?'

'Of course he will. Look, Dad, we'll all go and visit her.'

'She's going to be in today's papers,' he said glumly. 'Front page again. And the funny thing was she used to have no interest in the harbour.'

'Dad, get some sleep, and eat something, for God's sake. We'll sort it out.'

'If you saw the way she was carrying on, you wouldn't be able to sleep either.' He muttered a 'goodbye' and hung up. Lizzie vowed to ring Martha to get her to keep an eye on him.

Joe sauntered to the shops at the end of his road to get the Sunday papers. He loved Sundays: drinking coffee in the local coffee shop, having a read of the newspapers and then going back to his lofts and setting up the bird baths.

The woman behind the counter had his order ready before he'd asked for it. A large black coffee and a fry-up.

'For someone who eats that every week, you're still the best looking thing in the place,' she chortled as she handed his breakfast over to him.

She said that every week, too.

'For someone who makes such great food, I'm surprised you're still single,' Joe said back.

'I'm waiting on a proposal from the right man, so get your skates on, young fella.'

'I'm not great on skates,' he shrugged, grinning.

'Good, you can fall down. I can fall on top. We can see what happens.'

Joe laughed and carried his breakfast to the table. Sitting down, he wondered a little glumly why it was that all the women over fifty liked to flirt with him. Did he look so safe and boring that all he could manage were a few suggestive comments from older women? Aw well, he thought as he cut into a massive sausage, he had to take what he could get.

He opened up the paper and, with a clatter, dropped his knife on to the floor, making the people at the table beside him jump. There she was again: Mrs Polly Walsh. This time she had her head held high and the headline was NO BACKING DOWN. Joe stared and stared at her. He'd spent so long trying to forget this woman who had stared empty-eyed at him all through his trial that now, seeing her again, it made his head reel. Truth was, prison had been a cakewalk compared to the trial. All those people he'd been friendly with staring at him with horror. And he hadn't deserved it – that was the worst thing. At least he didn't think he deserved it. Not fully. Only no one understood that.

Joe shoved the paper away from him and stared for a second at his breakfast, before standing up and walking out.

'Lizzie,' Billy called, knocking on her door.

Lizzie groaned and rolled over. She hadn't been able to go back to sleep after the bombshell news about her mother. She was wrecked.

'I'm awake,' she yelled back.

Billy came in looking worried, about to say something, before he suddenly froze. Too late Lizzie realised what he had spotted on the floor beside her bed.

'Is that,' he sounded hoarse, 'is that . . . where did you get that?'

Lizzie said nothing as he bent down and picked up the scan of the babies. After visiting Joe's last night she'd suddenly wanted to look at something that made her feel good, she hadn't felt much of anything in such a while now, so she'd taken the scan out and studied the two innocent little shapes curled up around one another. Two pure little lives about to begin. She'd fallen asleep with it in her hand. She watched as Billy stared at the flimsy piece of film paper. If Aileen could see his expression now, she'd never have walked out, Lizzie thought. Billy brought his eyes to meet hers.

'Are they my babies?' he said eventually.

Lizzie nodded.

'How?' His forehead crinkled up. 'How did you—'

'Aileen invited me to go for a scan with her.'

She watched as Billy took that in. His expression flinched in momentary hurt.

'You never said,' he muttered.

'I thought I should go, see how she was and then tell you.'

'Then why didn't you?' There was no mistaking the hurt in his voice now.

'Because,' Lizzie took a deep breath, 'we had a bit of a row.' She tried to think of a way to airbrush it. 'I, eh, told her she was being unreasonable and she stormed out. I was afraid to let you know.'

Billy didn't seem to care. Instead he continued to study the picture, before running his finger over it.

'Did you see them move?' he asked quietly.

'Yeah.' Lizzie climbed out of bed and came to stand beside him. She, too, looked at the picture. 'They're just perfect, aren't they?'

He nodded. 'Can I keep it?'

'I got it for you.'

'Thanks.' He looked at it again before suddenly remembering what he'd come in for. 'Tom rang looking for you last night. He seemed under the impression you and I were going out together, so I told him you'd just left to go to his place.'

Oh shit.

When Joe got back, Anto was in the back garden, peering into the racing loft.

'Oy!' he shouted out at him. 'What are you doing here?'

Anto jumped and turned to face him. 'Ellen said that you said that I could help,' he shouted back, a little belligerently.

'Yeah. I didn't say you could creep into my garden and spy on my birds.' Even as he said it Joe knew he sounded childish. It was the shock of seeing Megan's mother in the paper. And his edginess about the lofts being mysteriously open now and again.

'I'm not spying on your birds,' Anto spat back. Then, 'But you're a bit stupid all the same.'

Joe gawped at him. 'Pardon?'

'Feral pigeon in your loft. How did you let her in?'

227

'There isn't a feral pigeon in my loft!' Joe sputtered at the boy's cheek. 'I'd know a wild pigeon if I saw one.'

Anto said nothing, just pointed smugly at a grey, tatty-looking bird that was pecking away at the food in the hopper. Joe did a double take. A wild bird? In his loft? How the hell . . . ?

'Jesus.' He scrabbled in his jacket pocket for his keys. Hastily he unlocked the loft and, with Anto's help, shooed the pigeon out. These wild ones were riddled with disease. Joe felt a little sick. If his birds had caught anything . . . Grudgingly he turned to Anto. 'Thanks.'

Anto shrugged cockily. 'You should be more careful.'

'I am careful,' Joe said through gritted teeth. 'I don't know how it got in there.'

He took the hopper from the floor and, with Anto following, he rinsed it out, dried it and put more food into it for the birds.

'I definitely didn't see it last night,' he said, half to himself, as he deposited the hopper back on the loft floor.

'Maybe it got in through a trap or something,' Anto suggested.

Joe barely heard him. His heart suddenly skipped a beat as his eyes scanned the loft. Oh shit. Oh no. But he couldn't have.

'It could have squeezed through that trap there,' Anto inserted his hand into the trap and frowned, 'but nah, no bird would—'

'Prince is gone,' Joe said, staring wildly about. 'He's gone.'

'Is that the bird I held the other day?' Anto asked. 'The really good-looking one with the tiny dent in his wing?'

Joe nodded. He was pacing wildly now, picking up birds and discarding them, alarming some who hopped hastily out of his way.

'Oh God!' He felt sick. 'He's gone.'

'Did he come in yesterday?' Anto asked.

Joe nodded. He was sure he had. Definitely he had. Or had he? Maybe he was thinking of the day before. But if Prince hadn't come back, he'd have noticed last night. His best bird. Of course he'd have noticed. But then again, sometimes important things went by your notice. Like Megan that time. Or the way he kept forgetting to lock up. He shook his head. There had to be a mistake. He was upset because of the paper. He took deep breaths. Prince *couldn't* be gone. He turned to Anto, who was starting at him in apprehension.

'We are going to go through every bird here,' he said, suddenly firm. 'We'll pick them up, look at the ring and put them in a basket. Prince is bound to be hiding somewhere.'

An hour later, having double-checked, Joe was forced to admit that Prince was nowhere. He whistled and Prince didn't come. He held up food and Prince didn't come. In the end, he let Anto bathe the birds and he went inside and tried his best not to vomit.

Tom looked wrecked, as if he hadn't slept. He came into the house, hands buried deep in the pockets of his pin-stripe suit jacket, which he wore with a bright red shirt and a loosened skinny black tie. His jeans had holes in the knees and a pair of bright red trainers completed his unconventional look. He looked effortlessly cool, Lizzie thought with a pang.

'Hey.' She attempted a grin.

He shifted from foot to foot. 'You didn't go out with Bill last night then, ey?' was all he said.

'No.' Lizzie flushed.

'And you didn't go out with me.'

'No.'

'So,' Tom was deliberately casual, 'where did you go, ey? And why did you tell me that you were going out with Billy?'

Lizzie walked into the kitchen and he followed. She'd thought in vain all morning, trying to come up with a plausible excuse. But she knew she couldn't lie to his face. She couldn't tell the truth either. For one thing he'd despise her for what she'd already done, and for another, he'd try and talk her out of it and there was no way she was going to stop. Not now. And then he might tell Billy and all hell would break loose.

'Well?' Tom asked again.

'I just had somewhere else to go,' she tried to say with confidence. 'Nobody's business but mine.'

'Fair enough,' Tom said, nodding. An edge of steel crept into his voice as he asked, 'So why lie to me? And why pretend that you were out with Billy when I texted you at two o'clock?'

'Were you trying to set me up?' She felt a flash of anger. 'Trying to make me incriminate myself?'

'I was trying to see what the hell was going on.' His voice rose. With an effort of will he lowered it. 'So, what *is* going on? Are you going to tell me?'

'One little white lie,' Lizzie said. 'For God's sake.'

'And if it had been me telling you that one little white lie?'

She flushed. 'What exactly do you want me to do, Tom? I'm not going to tell you where I was. I can't tell you where I was, where I might be again if you ring. I'm sorry, but I can't.'

He looked stunned. 'So where does that leave us?' he asked, dazed.

'You have to trust me.' She knew she was clutching at straws.

'You lied to me, Lizzie.'

'I said I'm sorry!'

'You didn't, actually.' Then slowly he muttered, 'Have you met someone else?'

Not in the way you mean, she wanted to say.

'No. Are you saying you don't trust me?'

There was a silence. 'I love you, Lizzie. I don't want to lose you.'

'Then let me go out with who I want, when I want.' Even as she said it she knew it was unfair.

'I do. You never normally lie about it. How would you feel if I did that?'

She glared at him. 'I wouldn't send you texts hoping to catch you out.'

'That is not the issue here,' he snapped, asserting himself suddenly, 'and you know it. You lied, Lizzie, and yeah, it is kinda hard to trust someone who tells you lies. How many other times have you done it, ey?'

'Everyone lies!' she shouted at him. 'Are you so brilliant you never told a lie in your life? For God's sake!'

There was a pause. 'I never told a lie to you,' he said simply.

It brought her up short. She swallowed hard. 'I'm sorry.'

'So?' He looked hopefully at her.

'I can't tell you, though.' She winced as his face fell. 'You . . . you, well, you don't want to know.'

His shoulders slumped and he stared down at the foot of one red trainer. 'D'you remember when we met first and I had to work nights and you'd come and sit at the bar keeping me company as I served the customers?' At her nod he said quietly, 'Well, you don't do that any more.'

'I didn't know you missed me that much.'

'Yeah, well, I do.' His eyes met hers. 'You're lying to me and I can't go out with someone who does that, Lizzie. I just can't.'

What was he saying? 'What do you mean?' she whispered, dreading his answer.

'You know what I mean.'

The words seemed to drop into the ocean of silence that followed, sending out ripples. Lizzie shook her head.

'Don't, Tom. Don't say that.' Her voice broke a little.

'What else *can* I say?' He looked hopelessly at her. 'You won't tell me where you've been. I will accept anything, Lizzie. Anything. If you're seeing someone else and regret it, maybe we can work it out. Just tell me.'

It was those words that made her realise Tom was way too good for her. He didn't deserve a manipulating woman like her, a woman who kidnapped prize birds and was cruel to animals. Even if he did understand, which he wouldn't as he'd never do what she was doing, she couldn't let him believe she was something she wasn't. The time had come to choose, she realised. Tom or Joe. She couldn't live with both now. And it would be better for everyone if she chose Joe. Holding on to Tom would suffocate them both. Her with guilt and regret for allowing Joe to escape, and Tom with despair at her unhappiness.

'I can't tell you,' she said, trying to keep her voice level. 'I just can't. You deserve better than me, Tom. You're right.'

He blinked. One. Twice. 'Is it drugs or something?'

'No.'

'Just tell me.'

For a second she was so tempted. For a split second, as she took in his brown eyes and the cute little scar just above his lip. For one second she wanted to blurt it all out, to cry in his arms for as long as it took to feel clean again, to have him hold her and tell her that she wasn't going mad, that it was OK to hate so much that you shook in the morning and felt your heart grow smaller with every passing thought of revenge. That it was OK to do bizarre acts and feel nothing. Maybe she could live with just letting it go. The thought glimmered for a second, shining like a beacon.

Just for a second, though, and then the feeling passed and she was swamped once again with steely resolve. She wanted to go mad if it meant wiping that grin from Joe Jones' face. If she could drive Joe mad, her own sanity would be worth it.

'Just go, Tom, will you?'

He stood for a second or two, then gulped out, 'You really want this?'

Of course she didn't, he was the most precious person in her life. But it would be for the best. She wasn't sure she even had enough space in her to love him any more. 'Yes. I think so.'

'Fine. Fine, so.' He sounded hurt and pissed off in equal measure. 'See you, so.'

'Bye.' She didn't look at him as he left.

She waited until the front door slammed before bursting into tears.

And she didn't think she was just crying for Tom.

She cried for about twenty minutes. Then, as she wiped her eyes with some kitchen paper, she consoled herself with the thought that everything would be easier now. She wouldn't have to lie to Tom and she could pursue Joe with a clear conscience. And yet she felt sick, like someone who had won the lotto but lost the ticket.

But then she remembered Prince sitting in his basket in the garden shed, waiting to be released, and thought of Joe, who surely must be searching frantically for him by now, and the sick feeling hardened into something more concrete, something she could use. Doing what she was doing would ease the pain of losing Tom and hopefully banish the pain of losing Megan.

She had made her choice and now she'd have to get on with it.

From under her bed she retrieved the new heavy-duty secateurs she'd purchased at the local hardware shop and went down to the shed in the back garden. She had to be quick, Billy had told her he'd be back in an hour – he'd left to give her time to talk to Tom.

The cat from the house next door was busy pacing up and down outside the shed and Lizzie hastily shooed it away. A big black tom, it was lethal where birds were concerned. Lizzie closed the door of the shed behind her and took a second to get used to the gloom. Very gently, she took the basket from behind some old sheets where she had hidden it. Thank God Aileen was gone, as she'd never have got away with it otherwise. Billy never came in here now and, as a result, the garden was as wild as the rest of the greens on the estate. Inside the basket, the bird cooed expectantly.

God, she'd love to see Joe's face this morning with his wonderful bird gone AWOL. She was going to ring him later and she knew exactly what to say, too.

Joe had rung the club to get them to put out the word that his bird was missing, just in case Prince showed up in someone else's loft, which, if he had, meant that he wasn't really fit for racing any more. He found it hard to believe that Prince would do that, though. He was such a good bird. Lizzie had rung, offering to come over and help with the birds, and had been shocked when she heard that Prince had disappeared. She was sitting here now in his kitchen, her hair braided in two quirky tiny plaits, having made him a cup of tea and brought along a packet of Ginger Nut, which was very thoughtful of her. She looked a little rough, though.

'Are you OK?' he asked Lizzie hesitantly. 'You're very quiet.'

Lizzie flinched. 'Fine,' she said.

Joe recoiled. Maybe he'd overstepped the mark. He wasn't good with this stuff, having spent all of his twenties in jail.

'It's just, you know, your eyes look all swollen and sort of red and—' He shuddered to a stop. 'I'll shut up now.' He managed a small grin.

Lizzie shrugged. She knew she looked awful, that's what happened when you cried. She'd wondered how long it would take for Joe to ask, though. For a while she'd been afraid he'd ignore her huge swollen eyes and blotchy complexion.

'It's all over with my boyfriend.' Her voice wobbled and she sniffed. A tear plopped into her coffee. She wasn't acting in front of him, for a change.

Joe winced. 'Oh, right.'

'Bet you wish you hadn't asked,' Lizzie said wryly. 'The last thing you need right now is an upset female in your kitchen.'

'You in my kitchen I can handle.' He smiled a little awkwardly. 'Your boyfriend must be mad.'

'Thanks,' she said softly.

'No worries.'

She smiled back but her eyes filled up again. Hurriedly she blinked the tears away, but not before Joe noticed and turned away too, staring out the window, his eyes automatically drifting skywards.

Lizzie observed him, her tears vanishing as she took in his devastated profile. This was better than she'd hoped. He was devastated. Of course he could never be as devastated as she had been fourteen years ago, but still, there was more to come. A lot more.

He turned back to her and gave a half-hearted grin.

'Thanks for coming,' he said, crossing over and touching one of her braids. It took every ounce of her will power not to shudder. And he didn't let it go. Instead he was staring into her face with a weird sort of look.

'Stops me thinking.' She said it as breezily as she could.

'Yeah.' Joe pulled away abruptly, looking confused. 'Thanks again,' he said, 'and sorry about you losing your boyfriend.'

'Sorry about you losing your pigeon.'

They sort of smiled at each other, before he turned back to the window.

36

Billy left for work the next day at seven. For once Lizzie was awake. Not that she'd been able to sleep. Her mind seemed to be constantly buzzing. When she heard Billy's car leave, she ran downstairs and out into the back garden. The neighbour's cat was pacing up and down outside the shed again and Lizzie had to shoo it off.

She took the pigeon basket out and opened it. Prince blinked in the light and hopped up to the rim of the basket. Lizzie had to admit that he really was a beautiful bird.

She looked at the cut on the bird's leg and winced – she hadn't meant for that to happen. She'd tried to treat the bleeding yesterday and it did look better today.

'Sorry,' she whispered.

Then she wondered why she felt sorry. She had stolen this bird's medication, watered its food and now all of a sudden she was feeling guilty? She rubbed her face with her hands. Most days it was easy and she could switch off, but actually seeing the damage on Prince's leg and knowing that she had directly caused it was a reminder of what she was at. A brutal reminder that she didn't want to face. She had never hurt anything before. Ever. She cried when her dad's chickens died, for God's sake, and now she had cut this bird's leg. Still, it should heal – she'd read that birds, especially pigeons, healed quickly.

'Off you go,' she said gently and Prince took flight in one fluid movement. He circled above the garden awhile before getting his bearings, then, like an arrow, zoomed back towards his loft.

* * *

Joe was pulling on his jacket when he noticed the bird outside, perched on top of the racing loft. He glanced out the window and did a double take.

He was back!

Wherever he'd been, he was back!

Joe wrenched open the back door and whistled. Prince immediately flew to him and it was then that Joe noticed the cut on his leg. And with horror he noticed that someone had removed the bird's ID tag.

It took a second for it to register as his mind tumbled with every possible scenario. Prince could never race again. His ID was gone. He'd never race again. He was only good for breeding now. Jesus. And on top of that, someone had deliberately removed the tag. Someone had taken Prince, somehow, and removed his ID. Who the hell would do that?

His relief at Prince coming back was suddenly tempered with anger.

There was only one person he could think of.

'So how did the meeting go?' Mark demanded as Lizzie hurried in to work, two hours late.

Lizzie flushed. She didn't like lying to Mark. She'd never lied to him before.

'Not too good,' she said. 'Not even a donation.'

'So why did he want to meet you?'

Lizzie forced herself to look at her boss. 'I have no idea.'

'Who was it?' Mark laid his hands flat on her desk and poked his head in towards her. 'I'll ring them up, give them a piece of my mind. I'll tell them not to waste my valued employee's time.'

'Eh, no,' Lizzie shook her head, her back turned, 'not a good idea. Who knows, maybe in the future . . . ?' She let her voice trail off. 'Now, I've a few things to do, so if you wouldn't mind.'

'Well, I suppose you're still talking to me so I should be grateful for that,' Mark said jovially.

'Sorry?'

'Well, dating an acting superstar has probably gone to your head.'

'What?' Was the man finally cracking?

'You. Dating a superstar.' He spoke as if she were stupid. He looked at her encouragingly. 'Has he not called you?'

'Who?'

'Your fella, the hotshot actor.'

Lizzie swallowed hard. She didn't want to have to tell Mark, but—

'He's in the paper today with some blondy wan hanging off him. Is he in a play or something?'

'Yeah, it's opening tonight.' Of course, she couldn't go to that now.

'Hang on there now, I'll just get the paper.'

'No, don't, it's—'

But he was gone. She could hear him rummaging about in his office, throwing files and pens everywhere as he searched for that morning's paper.

'Here we go.' He sauntered into the room. 'Now, what do you think of that?'

She thought Tom looked bloody gorgeous, that's what she thought. He was staring out of the page with a wistful, lost look in his eyes and Imogen, all blonde bouncy curls, was staring up at him with such a look of devotion that it made Lizzie catch her breath. If she wasn't careful, Imogen would nab him. Then she realised that it didn't matter. He wasn't hers any more. The real-isation was a physical pain in her chest.

'I'd watch that girl.' Mark jabbed the page. 'Still, your fella doesn't look too interested. But then again, blonde is what most fellas go for, except for me of course. Now, I'm more a—'

'He's not my boyfriend any more,' Lizzie said, surprised at how calm she sounded. 'It doesn't matter.'

'Not your boyfriend?' Mark gawked at her. 'Did he break up with you because he got famous? Were you not glamorous enough for him? Jesus, if that's the case I'd punch him for you, Lizzie.'

'There's no need. It was a mutual thing.'

'Mutual, my arse. You certainly don't look like it was mutual. You look horrendous. You have for ages now.'

'Thanks.' She handed him back his paper. 'Now can this vision of horrendousness get back to work?'

'Just say the word.' Mark tapped his nose. 'He wouldn't know what hit him.'

'Yes, well the debate is currently on as to what exactly you are,' Lizzie quipped with a small grin.

Mark grinned back. 'You need any time off you just tell me, OK?'

'Ta.'

'No worries.' He patted her on the shoulder and left.

Eight o'clock. There was a sharp rapping on his front door. Joe yawned widely and stretched. He hadn't slept that well the night before, worrying about Prince and where he could be. The knocking came again. Furious hammering. Through the glass, he thought he made out Ellen's silhouette, though why she should seem angry at him he couldn't fathom.

He opened the door and grinned, 'Yes?'

'Joseph, you did it again, didn't you?'

'Sorry, I'm not with you.'

'You let your birds out in the morning. Here.' A blouse, covered in bird droppings was thrust in front of him. 'Look at what they did.'

She was back to herself anyway, he thought in amusement.

'Ellen, I don't let the birds out early on your washing days, you know that. It wasn't me.'

'Oh.' She looked at him in abject disappointment. 'I never had you figured for a liar, Joseph. Never.'

'I'm not lying.' He attempted to smile at her but she wasn't having it.

'Anto had to whistle your birds in,' she said, as if talking to a very slow child. 'They were out all day, flying about, in and out of the loft. Anto said it was very bad management, if you don't mind me saying so.'

'Naw, I never—' Joe shook his head. 'The loft was locked.'

'Are you calling *me* a liar now?' Ellen tut-tutted. 'Joe, I'm very fond of you, even if you are a little odd. But your birds were out. Anto said it looked like you forgot to lock the loft or something.'

He *had* locked the loft. He always locked the loft. But then again, he'd forgotten a couple of nights these past few months, too. 'Anto called them in?'

'Yes. He's a very nice boy, despite everything. It took him a while, though – he tried to mimic your whistle or something. He had to lock your loft up with some string. You should check it. He also said to tell you that he thinks your stray bird has come back, but that she's got nothing on her leg.'

'His leg,' Joe corrected automatically. He swallowed hard. 'Ellen, sorry if they were out. I'll double check the loft next time.' He glanced at her blouse. 'How much—'

'Oh, nothing,' she flapped him away, 'I wouldn't expect you to pay, it was a mistake. But those birds scare me, Joe. Just try and keep them in next time.'

'Yeah. Right.' He *had* bloody locked it. He had.

'Anto wants to know if he can help tomorrow.'

'Sure.'

'Thanks.' Ellen reached out and unexpectedly caught his arm. 'Anto is happy being with the birds, his mother told me so.'

Joe nodded. He had to get away. He needed to think.

'Why do you think I offered him the job?' Ellen smiled slyly.

He should have known, Joe thought as he managed a smile back.

Though Lizzie knew she wasn't going to go to Tom's opening night, she rang up the theatre to get tickets for the play during its run. She'd get a seat right at the back, so Tom wouldn't see her but at least she could sit and look at him. She could stare at his face and listen to his voice, see him walk and smile and pretend that he was hers again.

Just for one night.

*　　*　　*

240

Joe didn't get much time to think because, ten minutes later, another person hammered on his door. What now? he wondered irritably. He was still trying to figure out how the birds had got out. The lock seemed secure, so it looked as if—

As Joe approached the front door, he froze. It wasn't Ellen this time. Or his neighbour from the other side. The silhouette in the frosted window was a tall person, a man. Grey coat. Grey hair. It couldn't be. Joe swallowed hard and wondered if he should pretend to be out. But his car was in the drive, an upstairs window was open.

Maybe he just wouldn't answer.

The doorbell rang. Once. Twice. Three times. And then, to his dismay, his dad's voice yelled, 'I know you're in there. Open up or I'll say what I have to right here in the street.'

Joe wrenched the door open and stood in front of the man he hadn't seen in fourteen years. His breath caught in his throat as he took in the fact that his dad had aged. The face was lined, the back no longer as erect. The clothes not as slick as they used to be.

Geoff's hand dropped limply from the bell as he, too, looked at the son he hadn't seen.

'Well?' Joe said, trying to keep his voice steady, trying not to betray the weird emotions flooding through him. His hand held the door frame, barring the way in.

His dad coughed. 'Can I come in?'

'No.'

Geoff flinched, pursed his lips and sighed a little. 'OK. Fine. I didn't want to have to tell you like this, but if that's the way you want it—'

'What do you want me to do?' Joe asked, bewildered. 'You let me down. You were prepared to believe that I—that I—' He couldn't say it. The words stuck in his throat.

'I wasn't prepared to believe anything,' his dad said. 'But I had to say what I'd seen.'

'It wasn't what it looked like.' Joe raised his eyes upwards to stop the stupid tears that had sprung into them unexpectedly.

241

'Anyway,' he swallowed hard, 'I'm sure you haven't come to talk about that again, have you?'

Geoff shook his head. Then asked, 'Please can I come in?'

His dad in his house? 'No.'

His father bowed his head, his shoulders slumped. 'OK,' he nodded, 'fair enough. I, eh, just came to let you know . . .' He gulped. 'Well, I just came to tell you that your mother, well, she isn't too well.'

'What?'

'She—' His dad wiped a hand over his face. 'She's got early onset Alzheimer's. She's forgetting things. I thought you might like to see her before . . .' His voice faltered. 'Well, before she forgets you, Joe.'

Joe's hand dropped from the door. His mind whirled. His mother? She'd written to him every week when he was inside and he hadn't replied. Short letters. Funny letters. Sad letters. He'd read them all but he'd never written back. Not once. But she'd remembered him. Every single week.

After a pause, he said dully, 'Maybe better for her if she does forget me. Why would she want to remember, ey?'

His dad met his eyes. 'She loves you, Joe. We never believed you did anything, never. And her, most of all.'

Well, that was crap for a start. His father had twisted all the nice stuff he'd done into evidence against him.

'Please think about it,' Geoff said. 'You might regret it one day.'

'I can add it to the pile, so,' Joe made his voice hard. He nodded to his dad. 'See you.'

He closed the door on him, watching as his father turned and slowly made his way down the drive.

Joe stayed standing in the hall for twenty minutes before realising that tears were dripping off the end of his chin.

37

Thursday, 12th August

Aileen arrived two days ago. She's staying for a
month. Unfortunately I have to work for the next
week, but then I have holidays. Billy and Lizzie have
promised to look after her in the meantime. Billy
especially seems to be taken with her in a massive
way – I have never seen Billy offer to let any girl
drive his car, but when Aileen said she'd love to drive
it, Billy said OK. Lizzie and I gaped at each other,
then Lizzie said that Billy must have found it
tough.

'Found what tough?' Billy asked.

'Your personality transplant.'

We all cracked up and Billy went bright red –
another first. Then Aileen patted him on the head and
told him he was great and he said, 'See, see? Someone
appreciates me.' Then, to my horror, Dad offered to
bring her out on the boat and before I could warn her
she'd agreed to it. That made Dad think she was
great, too. Aileen is great, she sort of fits in with
everything in our house, just blends in as if she's
always been there. She says I'm so lucky to have
such a nice family and I suppose I am – though they
can be right pains sometimes.

Friday, 13th August

At the moment in work it's just me and Dessie, as Joe's granddad is sick and Joe is minding him and looking after his birds, too. I think he's deliberately not coming in to avoid being with me and Dessie. There's nothing to avoid really. Nothing has happened in work since, though Dessie did say he'd meet me in Dancesplash tomorrow night. I told him I'd text him when I got there if he gave me his mobile number and he said he'd give it to me but he forgot. He has mine, though. I gave it to him but he hasn't texted me yet.

Joe came to dinner in our house tonight. Even though he's not at work, he still managed to go fishing with my dad. And Dad invited him in for tea and in he came and, right through the meal, he totally ignored me. It was a bit hurtful so I told him I was sorry if I hurt his feelings but he didn't have to ignore me.

And he says, 'I'm not ignoring you. I just have nothing to say to you.'

I said, 'You ARE ignoring me.'

He said, 'Get over yourself, will you?'

And I said, and this was a good one, 'Well, there's no fear of me getting over you.'

So he upped and left and, of course, I had to try and explain why to Mammy and Dad. I said some rubbish about him being worried about his granddad and they muttered about how kind he was. But I told Aileen and Billy the real story. Aileen said he must be more hurt than he was letting on and Billy said that I was a bitch to say what I did. I feel a bit mean now.

Sunday, 15th August

Last night was great. Talk about dreams coming true.

We all went out clubbing. Aileen sat in the front seat

of Billy's car and shrieked obligingly as he drove like mad. It actually looks more dangerous than it is – Billy knows the roads we travelled so well. He knows when they widen so there really is no possibility of crashing. Lizzie, me and Billy's mate Johnny sat in the back and laughed at Aileen. She kept turning round and telling us to shut up. We arrived at the club and tumbled out of the car. Aileen told Billy that her legs were shaking so much she could barely walk. Billy gallantly offered to support her and she obligingly hung off him, all high heels and short skirt. Then she turned round and gave me a great big wink. I think she's quite into him, too.

Johnny looked a little glum. 'You're taken,' he said to me. 'Your friend seems to be taken. Who is left?' He glanced at Lizzie.

'I will call you,' Lizzie said, 'when I've exhausted all my other options.'

'Oh, I'd say you'd exhaust your other options all right,' Johnny chortled.

Lizzie belted him with her, quite frankly, horrendous red handbag.

The club we go to is over-eighteens and Mammy lets Lizzie go with us on condition that she won't drink. But of course Lizzie does. She can lush them back and it doesn't seem to take an effect on her. I think she shows off just to be in with Billy and me. I sometimes worry about her but Billy laughs and says there's no point, it's her parents' fault if she's out drinking at fourteen years of age. Anyway, loads of her friends get in too and she normally spends her night yabbering away to them and shrieking with laughter over silly things. I don't know how they're even let in, they don't even look eighteen.

Inside the place was heaving, but we grabbed a few seats in a little quiet corner that no one else wanted to sit in. And then I saw Dessie and I was so relieved as I hadn't heard from him since Friday and I had no way of contacting him. He waved and I walked over to talk to him, Billy whistling after me like the headcase he is.

'So, how you been since I last saw you at work?' Dessie asked. He was lounging against the wall and his eyes were all sparkly and his teeth all white and my heart flip-flopped like a pancake being tossed in the air.

'I've been good.' My voice shook a little. I was mad for him to touch me.

'I've been terrible.' He made an anguished face.

'Yeah. How?'

'Missed you.'

'That's the cheesiest line ever.'

'Aw,' he said, as the tip of his finger brushed the tip of my nose, 'but did your mother never tell you that cheese is good for you?' His brown eyes held mine like a hypnotist's. He moved in closer. His hand briefly touched mine.

I grinned. 'She did tell me that but I find cheese disgusting.'

'What do you like, then?' His voice was smooth as that shiny material that's impossible to sew.

'You,' I said. My mother would have had a fit. According to her, you should never tell a fella you like him. Well, I said, are men mind-readers? Are they psychic? She said, 'Well, I never told your father that I liked him. Men like a challenge.' I said back that Dad certainly found her a challenge and she had freaked. As usual.

'You like me?' Dessie feigned surprise.

'I certainly do.'

'How much?'

So I snogged the face off him.

Then we went outside to his car. Suffice to say that it wasn't just for driving.

Mam would have double freaked!

Monday, 16th August

Today in work was a bit mad. Seeing him respectably dressed. All nice and neat. I grinned at him as I came in and he grinned back.

'Thanks for Saturday,' he said.

'Thank you,' I said back. 'You've got a nice car.'

He laughed at that.

And that was it. That was all he said about it. I thought we'd be sneaking little kisses and little touches, but nothing. Instead, he indicated his desk. 'Got piles of work to do.'

My heart sank quicker than my sponge cakes had in home ec.

Then he said, 'Joe's granddad died Saturday night, did you hear?'

'No. Poor Joe.'

'Yeah, he found his granddad dead in an armchair when he got in from feeding his birds.'

'Oh God.'

'So he won't be in for ages now. You and me will have to sell a lot of ads to make up for him. Plus the funeral is tomorrow so I have to go.'

'I'll go, too.'

He didn't offer me a lift. I thought he would.

As it turned out Mammy, Dad, Lizzie, Billy and Aileen went to the funeral as well. The whole crowd from the paper were there and some of them had blagged lifts from Dessie, so maybe he couldn't have offered me a lift anyway.

Joe was up the front looking totally gutted, as were

his parents. His mother is a beautiful woman. Joe kind of looks like her. He's got her blonde brown hair and nice skin. I sat with my family and apologised to Aileen for bringing her to a funeral.

'Oh, it's cool. Billy has taken a half-day from work, so he's bringing me on a drive. We're getting lunch out. Your mother says she might come too but Billy hopes she won't as he'll have to drive really slowly to stop her nagging.'

I laughed.

My mother grimaced and pointed up the church at the coffin.

Friday, 20th August

I called over to Joe today. In his granddad's house. I felt I had to as I'm on holidays now. And by the time I get back to work the funeral will have been forgotten about and I might never get the chance to say sorry to him. And I don't want to be fighting with him now that he's so upset over his granddad.

It was a very weird experience. Joe is weird. Weirder than I thought.

He was out the back, sitting on his own on a kitchen chair, a can of lager beside him. He was looking at the birds. There seemed to be birds everywhere, some flying about, others locked up in these little sheds and making cooing noises. The grass was all squelchy and my heels sunk right into it. A bird shat on my shoulder.

'Shit!' I said, startling Joe.

'Literally,' he said wryly and we both kind of smiled at each other.

'Here, let me get a cloth.' He went into the house and I followed him. He located a smelly cloth under the sink and handed it to me. He watched as I wiped the stuff off my shoulder. It was disgusting.

'So,' he said, 'what brings you here?'

I put the cloth down, my hand STUNK! God, the hygiene in this house was not hygienic, to say the least.

'An apology to you,' I said, 'plus I want to say that I'm sorry about your granddad.'

He smiled, sort of wearily. Or warily – anyway, as if he wasn't quite trusting me.

'Well, apology accepted. Life's too short and all that, ey?'

'Yep.'

There was a pause then.

'D'you want a cuppa?' Without waiting for an answer, he shoved on the kettle. Out of the blue, he said, 'It was sudden in the end. Better for him. Better for me.'

'You must have got a shock.' I assumed it was the right thing to say. I've never had a friend who had someone who died on them before.

'Uh-huh. But he looked happy. Peaceful even.'

'God, he couldn't have been that happy.'

Joe laughed and shook his head and told me I was great.

'And how are you?' I asked then. He looked pretty rotten to me.

There was a slight hesitation before he admitted, without looking at me, 'Crap. But I just have to get on with it.' He passed me a cuppa and asked, 'How you getting on with Dessie?'

The subject change wrong-footed me. I didn't want anyone to ask that. Billy, Lizzie and Aileen kept teasing me and I had to pretend that we were having great fun in work. I embroidered the small positive things and tried to believe them myself. But work was just work. More work than before, in fact.

'Well?' Joe asked.

'Well, we're working loads. Dessie takes his work seriously as you know—'

'He's gone all cold on you, hasn't he?' Joe said. I don't think he was being mean.

'No!' I laughed a little and waved my hand in the air and hit it off the table which hurt like hell.

'That looked sore,' Joe remarked.

'It's fine. We're fine. Work is great.'

He said nothing to this.

'Anyway,' I went on, making things worse for myself now that I think about it. 'Dessie and I have a working relationship when we, eh, work and anyway, what we have is like nothing to do with you. So butt out.'

'I said nothing,' Joe answered. I think he was a little bewildered.

'And,' I said, 'if you for one moment think he used me – well, you're wrong.'

'I never said that either,' he said.

'Oh shut up!' I said. I actually think I shouted it.

'Hey, Meg—' Joe grabbed my arm, which was not a good idea.

'Let me go!' I shouted. 'You pontificating know-it-all!'

He actually laughed which made me furious and I slapped him.

And in walked his dad.

To my absolute shame, I burst into tears and ran out.

I don't know what happened after that.

38

A NTO WAS ENTHUSIASTIC, that was for sure, Joe thought. Even though the boy didn't talk much, his eagerness was evident in the way he did whatever was asked of him. Joe laughed to himself at how Anto talked to the birds as he deposited them in their basket. He knew all their names and could mimic Joe's whistle so that the birds flew to him sometimes.

'That's great,' Joe said as he closed the lid of the basket on the final pigeon.

'Can I come with you tonight to register them?' Anto asked, following him to the shed. 'I used to go with me da all the time.'

Joe said nothing, reluctant to commit himself. He might end up having to bring the kid all the time then.

Anto turned away. 'Forget it.'

'I didn't say no,' Joe muttered.

'You didn't say yes.'

'You're a cheeky little brat, aren't you?'

'Feck off.'

Joe laughed and Anto turned and glared at him.

'OK,' Joe relented, feeling sorry for him, 'you can come if your mother says it's OK. But you better behave.'

Anto didn't smile. 'Are you only messing with me?'

'Nope.'

'Right. Thanks.' He didn't say it in a delighted way. Joe admired that. It was like a, 'Hey, don't put yourself out, I don't care'.

'So,' Joe attempted some ordinary conversation, 'how many pigeons did your dad have?'

Anto shrugged. 'Not as many as you. And none as good-looking as Prince. But one of his birds came second in a race once.'

'Yeah?'

'He won money and we went to the pub and he bought drinks for everyone and Mam went mad and Dad said,' Anto assumed what Joe supposed was his dad's stance, '"That's the way it's done".'

'It sure is.' Joe put the basket of birds on the ground. 'You have to share your winnings. Bet you miss him, huh?'

Anto nodded. 'We had to sell his birds. I was really angry about it.'

Joe remembered selling off his granddad's birds. It had been horrible, too. 'I bet you were,' he nodded.

'You would have liked my da,' Anto said, following behind Joe like an over-eager puppy. 'And he might have liked you. A little bit anyway.'

'Gee, thanks,' Joe deadpanned.

Anto sniggered.

Getting in to see their mother was like getting into Fort Knox. They had to produce their visitors' passes, they had to flash ID and finally they were led into the visiting room with the strict instruction that it was non-smoking.

'This just gets better and better,' Lizzie grumbled.

'I thought you'd be glad there was no smoking,' her father said.

Lizzie sighed. 'This might be a good time to tell you, actually—' she began.

'Here's Mam,' Billy announced loudly, poking Lizzie in the ribs.

She didn't know what had come over her. Trying to upset her father by admitting she smoked, just as his prisoner wife was being escorted in to see him? But surely her smoking would be the least of his problems now. And besides, she was twenty-eight and entitled to ruin her health if she wanted. Not that she did, but she liked a smoke.

'—you?'

252

Lizzie suddenly realised that her dad, Billy and her mother were all looking at her.

'Sorry? What?'

'She hasn't been herself since you went to prison,' her father said reprovingly to his wife.

'Oh, don't blame me because she's got thin,' her mother snapped back. 'I was asking how you were, Lizzie.'

'Fine,' Lizzie said.

'Well, you don't look fine.' Her mother looked her up and down. 'Big black circles under your eyes, white face. Are you working too hard?'

'It's off with Tom,' Billy said for her. 'She's been a bit upset.'

Even the mention of his name made Lizzie weepy.

'And him about to make it big!' Her mother threw her eyes skyward. 'I saw him in the paper. What happened?'

'Just broke up,' Lizzie said. 'It doesn't really matter.'

'*He* doesn't really matter.' Mrs Walsh patted her daughter's hand. 'You don't pine after him, now. I always said there's something wrong with a man who pretends to be somebody else for a living just to be clapped by a bunch of strangers in a silly room with curtains.'

Lizzie smiled. 'Nice to see you haven't lost your practical side in here, Mam.'

'Not at all. Here isn't so bad.'

Billy was looking around. His eyes came to rest on a small, slim, blonde girl across the way. 'Is she a prisoner, too?' he asked.

'Yes. She's in because . . . Oh now, what did she tell me?' Mrs Walsh screwed up her eyes. 'Oh yes, she's a teacher and she had an affair with a sixteen-year-old boy. It was in the papers, apparently.'

'Lucky boy,' Billy grinned as his mother slapped his arm.

'Disgusting, it is,' she snapped. 'But I must say, she's a very nice girl. She's helping some of the others to read in here. And the boy she slept with comes to visit her, which is nice I suppose. No hard feelings.'

'No, it's not his feelings that'd be hard,' Billy snorted.

Lizzie giggled too.

'It's no wonder Aileen left with that sort of filth for a brain. Have you heard from —'

'So, when are you going to apologise?' Kevin Walsh demanded, cutting short the exchange. 'Or am I going to have to get used to living on my own for the foreseeable future?'

Polly Walsh looked aghast. 'Apologise? Me? I'm not going to apologise. They'll have to let me out sooner or later. They can't keep me in here with all these people who've broken the law.'

'*You've* broken the law,' her husband said.

'I have not!' His wife glared at him and some people visiting the blonde woman glanced across, before quickly averting their eyes. 'I have only stood up for my rights as a free Irish citizen.'

'By breaking the law.'

'Well, I won't be apologising,' Mrs Walsh folded her arms.

'Wonderful.'

A silence descended on the four of them.

'They've all sorts of weirdos in here,' Polly Walsh said after a bit, when she realised her husband was no longer going to talk. 'The woman in the cell with me, she's in because she burned her ex-boyfriend's house down.'

'Christ!' Billy exclaimed.

'She said he had it coming. He was having this big affair with a work colleague and he kept telling her he was on business trips and stuff and then she found out.'

'How?' Lizzie asked. Her mother had a great way of telling a story. Normally by embroidering the details, though Lizzie had a feeling that the stories behind the people here wouldn't need improving.

Mrs Walsh lowered her voice. 'Well, she decided to go away for a weekend with a few friends and then had a huge row with one of them and decided to come home. And what does she find?'

'What?' Billy and Lizzie asked together.

Their dad had crossed his arms and was feigning disinterest.

'Her boyfriend in bed *with another man*. He was gay on top of

254

it all! He said he was just experimenting. She said, "Experiment with this", and she lit his curtains on fire and the place went up like a house of straw. Apparently.'

'God.'

'Yes. She's sorry about it now, of course. And her ex-boyfriend has forgiven her, as well he might, but she's in for another few months. I told her that she should have just got on with her life and not let her ex ruin it for her. She said that's what she's going to do.'

'And what did she tell you?' Mr Walsh asked in a very superior tone of voice.

'Nothing. I'm right and that's it. I'm not for turning.'

'So you're saying that we'll have to trudge up here week after week to see you?'

'No. Only if you want to.'

Mr Walsh sighed.

'Of course we want to,' Lizzie intervened, 'but it's just we'd like to see you out, Mammy.'

'I'd like to be out,' Mrs Walsh said. 'You've no idea of the awful people in this place. But at the same time I can't give up on my principles. We are what we do, you know.'

Lizzie winced.

'Oh, well that's it then, isn't it?' Mr Walsh rose to his feet. 'You're obviously a woman who puts a harbour plan before the good of her family.'

'Before *your* good, you mean,' his wife scoffed. 'Just because you have to make your own dinner now and clean up after it, that's all you're worried about.'

'Don't be ridiculous.' Mr Walsh leaned his hands on the table and glared at his wife. 'I'm well capable of cooking a meal. I just don't like you being in this place, that's all.'

'I don't like being here either, but I will stay as long as I have to.'

'A simple sorry and you can continue with the protest. Martha is organising something for this weekend.'

'Well she might,' Mrs Walsh sniffed. 'She abandoned ship pretty quickly.'

255

'Look, Polly—'

'No, I'm not discussing it. I'd rather talk about how you all are. Billy, I believe, before your father interrupted—' she shot her husband a withering look, 'that we were discussing Aileen. How is she?'

Billy flinched. He hated talking about Aileen just as much as Lizzie hated talking about Tom.

'She refuses to take my calls,' Billy said, 'so I don't know how she is.'

'Wonderful!'

'Yes, well maybe if you weren't behind bars you'd have a better chance of sorting your kids out,' Mr Walsh said with a hint of triumph.

'You're their father, you sort it out.'

'Eh, newsflash,' Billy said, 'I can sort myself out, thanks.'

'And how are you managing the mortgage?' Mrs Walsh asked.

'Aileen's still paying her share,' Billy said. 'She has to if she wants to keep it going.'

'Well, aren't we a wonderful bunch?' Mr Walsh said wearily. 'Mother in jail, son separated from his pregnant girlfriend, daughter split from boyfriend and father at home trying to stay sane.'

'Oh, don't be so negative.' Mrs Walsh dismissed him with a wave of her hand. 'We're going to have two grandchildren; Lizzie has split from a man who bought her a kite; and you have a wife who sticks to her principles. You always were one for looking on the gloomy side, Kevin.'

'No, I've always been a realist,' Mr Walsh said. 'You, on the other hand, have lived all your life with your head stuck firmly in the sand.'

'Here.' Billy, to stop the argument in its tracks, shoved forward the picture of the baby scan. 'It's the twins.'

They watched as Polly slowly reached out and picked up the scan. She brought her face close to it as she wasn't wearing her glasses. Her features softened and her mouth opened in an expression of wonder. Her eyes caught Billy's.

'Beautiful,' she whispered. 'I can actually see the two of them.'

'Yeah.'

'Oh, Billy, you have to get that girl back. She was good for you.'

Billy winced once more but didn't deny it.

'I think this one is the image of you,' his mother said then, pointing at the baby on the left. 'He has your nose.'

'That's his foot, Mammy. You're holding it upside-down.'

It made them laugh.

It was no use – he had to talk to someone. After Anto left he tried to distract himself by doing all sorts of stupid things. Making his bed. Cleaning the windows of the house. He even swept the kitchen floor. But all the time thoughts of his mother kept flitting in and out of his head. She was ill. She'd forget him. Maybe it was for the best. How could it be for the best?

There was only one person he felt he could ask, but he wasn't sure how he could explain it right. He didn't want Ellen to judge him. But she'd forgiven the man who had killed her husband and was presently trying to rehabilitate the boy who'd broken into her house, so surely she could listen to him.

He made it to her front door and had his hand up to press the doorbell, when he suddenly felt violently ill. There was no way . . .

'Joseph?' Ellen had obviously seen him. She had the door open and was peering at him in surprise. 'What do you want?'

He stood like a thick, with his mouth open and his hand half in the air. 'Aw, nothing. It's fine.'

'Are you OK? You've gone a little pale. How's Anto? Is this about Anto? His mother says he's like new since you've let him help you. I must say it's a very good thing you're doing Joseph and I—'

'It isn't about Anto.'

'Oh.'

'Can I come in?'

Without saying anything she stood aside and let him into her hall.

257

'Would you like a cup of tea?'

He needed more than a cup of tea but he nodded anyway. In silence he followed Ellen into her kitchen and sat at her table as she bustled about getting biscuits and milk and putting them in front of him. Finally she handed him a huge mug of tea and sat opposite him as he poured some milk into it.

'What's the matter?' Her voice was suddenly gentle. 'You look upset.'

This could be the last time he might ever sit at this table, Joe thought in a detached way. He'd come to like Ellen and her spiky ways. Even though she was old, he liked her company.

'My dad called to see me the other night,' he said haltingly.

Ellen's mouth dropped open. 'I thought you had no parents,' she said.

Joe shrugged and looked into his cup. The tea was still and he could almost see the reflection of his face.

'I haven't talked to them in a long time,' he muttered. 'They let me down.'

'Oh.'

He wrapped his hands about the mug. 'Anyway, my dad, he told me that my mother is ill. Alzheimer's. He wants me to visit her before she forgets.'

Ellen said nothing.

Joe brought his eyes to meet hers. 'I don't know what to do.'

There was the longest pause. Ellen seemed to be thinking.

'You do,' she said simply.

'No, I don't.'

'Can you forgive them for how they let you down?'

'He says he didn't mean to. That he had to.'

She said nothing.

'I think it's crap.'

'Joe, do you want to tell me the whole story?'

He shook his head.

'Look,' Ellen said, 'I can't tell you what to do. You have to decide. I can't even advise you because I don't know what they did to you. If they hit you or abused you, then I wouldn't worry

258

about going to see them. But sometimes . . .' She paused. 'Sometimes we think people have let us down and they haven't.'

'They let me down.'

'Anto was angry at his dad for a long time because he died. That's the way kids think, you know?'

'I wasn't a kid.'

'Oh.'

'I was twenty.'

'I see.'

Only she didn't. She couldn't possibly see. This wasn't at all what he'd hoped for. He needed someone to tell him what he should do. He couldn't decide. He hated what they'd done, but he loved them too.

'My dad,' he began, swallowing hard, wondering how he could explain without shocking her. 'Well, I was up in court a few years ago. My dad testified against me.'

'Should he have?'

'I didn't do it, if that's what you mean.'

'Do what, Joe?' Ellen's voice had gone quiet. She touched his arm. 'What did you not do?'

He flinched. No one had touched him in so long. Not in a caring way, anyway. He swallowed hard and closed his eyes.

'They—they accused me of . . .' He couldn't say it, he could never say it.

'Go on.'

'A girl was found on the beach, washed up and the last person she'd been with was me. On my dad's boat.' He met Ellen's eyes. 'She was dead. Apparently someone had hit her across the head. It wasn't me, Ellen. I swear.' He dashed his hand across his face. He hadn't talked about this in years. He'd never talked about it, actually.

Ellen looked shocked, he'd known she would.

'My dad testified that I'd had a row with the girl a few days previously. He testified that I liked her and that I'd been a little aggressive towards her during the row. I'd only grabbed her arm, Ellen.'

259

There. It was out.

'Joe,' Ellen said softly. 'Anyone who knows you knows you'd never do that.'

'The jury didn't. I got life.'

'Oh, you poor lad.'

'I didn't do it, Ellen. I don't know how she ended up on that beach. I kept thinking I was in a nightmare and I'd wake up, only it got worse. My dad put the nail in my coffin.'

'What could he do, Joe? If he lied, I'd imagine it would be because he didn't believe you. He probably thought he had no choice. He probably thought telling the truth was the best thing.'

Joe said nothing. He hadn't looked at it like that. If his dad had lied, maybe that would have been because he believed the evidence damning. Instead, he'd told the truth and been devastated when Joe was convicted. He'd written but Joe had ignored his letters, refusing to have any visitors.

'You sometimes have to look at things from a different angle,' Ellen said, 'in order to fully understand.'

'Thanks for believing me,' Joe said quietly.

'Of course I believe you!' Ellen looked at him as if he were bonkers. Then added, 'Can I give you some advice?'

He shrugged.

'I often wondered why you never went out. Why you never had a girlfriend. Why all the people who call to your house are older then you. Now I know.'

'Yeah, I'm a complete saddo.' He said it with a small grin.

'No,' Ellen shook her head. 'You're still living as if you're in prison. You have to get back out there, Joe. Start to live again.'

He supposed she was right. But it was harder than anyone knew to step back out into the world again. Even getting a job was a huge task. His parole officer had arranged it for him. Another person who'd thought he was innocent. Walls, though, became safe after a bit.

'Do you think I should go home?' He asked the question he'd come to ask.

'Joe, you are obsessed with birds that fly home to you. You

spend your Saturdays looking into the sky to see them arrive.
Why is that?'

He swallowed. This woman knew more about him than he
knew himself.

'It's just brilliant to see.'

'Yes,' she said.

He knew that was the end of the conversation.

39

'L IZZIE, IT'S LORI.'
    'Oh, hi,' Lizzie grinned, delighted the woman had rung.
She had been dying to find out what had happened her. 'You
sound happy.'

'I am,' Lori said. 'Thanks to you.'

'Oh now, you did it yourself. I just listened.'

It was so good to have a happy ending, Lizzie thought. Things
like this rarely happened. Callers, once they had their lives sorted
out, forgot about ringing again, which Lizzie supposed was a
success of sorts. But it was good to know. To be told. To have a
definite end to a problem.

'And so did Larry. That's my husband. He is so apologetic, you
wouldn't believe.'

'Pardon?' Her heart gave a quick flip over. 'Your husband?'

'Yes. He came over last week and begged, I mean *begged* me
to lift the barring order and I said "no way".'

'Good for you.' Her heart slowed down a bit.

'And yesterday he came again, with flowers and tickets to
Barcelona. I've always wanted to go there and he remembered
that. And he said he would do anything, *anything* to see us back
together again.' She paused before adding, 'He can't live
without me.'

'And you said?' Lizzie desperately hoped her instinct was wrong.

'I said . . . well, I sort of made him sweat, like I had a right to
do, but in the end, we got back together.'

'Why?' Lizzie's voice came out sounding quite sharp. Across
the office, Anna glanced at her. 'Why did you do that? Are you

262

so cheap you can be bought off with a tacky bunch of flowers and some tickets?'

'They were not tacky flowers!'

'This man bullied you. Is he going for anger management?'

'Well,' Lori swallowed, 'well, yes. If you think he should.'

'Lori, what do *you* think? For God's sake—'

Anna firmly disconnected the call.

'What did you do that for?' Lizzie whirled on her. 'The woman is insane. Do you know what she did? She—'

'Lizzie, you are there to listen. From what I heard, this woman just wanted you to do that. You can't go abusing people.'

'Yes I can, especially when some woman is about to make a huge mistake.'

'No, you can't.' Anna gently shook her head. 'You know you can't.' She paused, and then asked, 'What is wrong with you, huh?'

'What is wrong with you, more like?'

Anna said nothing.

'Sorry,' Lizzie mumbled, bowing her head. 'I'm sorry. I know I shouldn't have done that, but when someone is doing something stupid, and you can't warn them, what can you do?'

'In my experience, Lizzie,' Anna said, 'people will always pretty much do what they want to do. You can talk to them all you want but in the end they'll do what suits.'

'I don't believe that.'

'I begged my husband not to take his life.'

Lizzie swallowed hard.

'I knew he was depressed, I knew he wanted to die and I begged him, Lizzie.' Anna sat on the desk. 'I pointed out all the good things to him, but it made no difference. He wanted . . .' She paused. 'No, I think he felt he needed to die.'

'He wasn't well.'

'Neither is Lori. She's in love. It's another type of insanity. Only she can get rid of that man and you have helped her do it once. She'll ring again. You'll see.' Anna looked at her sympathetically. 'Come on, Lizzie, cheer up.'

Lizzie swallowed hard. Anna was right, she knew that. 'I'm sorry. I'm a bit all over the place recently.'

'I noticed. Is it Tom?'

'Partly.'

Anna squeezed her arm. 'Want a coffee?'

'Yep.'

'Sit tight.'

They smiled at each other.

Graham, the owner of the health centre, called him in just as he had pulled on his parka jacket. A few of the women from his late class called out a 'goodbye' to him as they left and Joe waved.

Since the chat with Ellen, he'd made more of an attempt to try to connect with people, to be the way he was before. But he knew, of course, that that would never happen. But then again, no one was ever the same as they were when they were younger. And, if he were honest, he preferred some aspects of himself now. He had always been quiet, and now he accepted he was quiet instead of having to fight against it by drinking too much and doing stupid things. He accepted the fact that he didn't have a magnetic personality like Dessie and that was OK, too. He realised he had finally accepted himself. And he was kind of proud that he had survived twelve years in prison.

'Joe,' Graham beckoned him into his office, 'come here a second, would you?'

'Yeah?' Joe stood just inside the door, his hands sunk deep into his jacket pockets, trying to give the impression that he really would like to go home.

'It's just a warning to you not to ring in sick at short notice again, OK?'

'Yeah,' Joe dipped his head, 'sorry about that. I couldn't help it.'

'Joe, I know you've been in prison,' Graham went on. 'I know what for. You told me at your interview. You also told me you were innocent and you also told me you would work hard. I wasn't sure whether to believe you but my brother, the do-gooder in the family,' he raised his eyes and Joe tried not to grin, 'told me to give you a chance. He said I wouldn't regret it. Now so far I haven't regretted it. Don't make me. OK?'

Joe swallowed hard and nodded. He loved this job. He couldn't lose it. It was important to him to teach people how to swim. So that they wouldn't drown and be washed up on a beach somewhere.

'Go on, then.' Graham paused. 'You're the best teacher here, Joe. Just so you know.'

'Ta.'

'And the best assistant manager we've had.'

'Good.'

'Hop it, right.'

He met Lizzie at the Luas stop. She seemed to be in glum form.

'What's up?' he asked.

'Nothing.' She wouldn't look at him. Then she asked, 'How did your birds do on Saturday? Sorry I couldn't be there.'

'I had a second and a fifth.'

'Second?' She seemed surprised. 'I thought Prince was out of action.'

'He is, but Hero came good for me. And if he hadn't spent so much time hopping around the place when he got back, I might have got a first.'

'Great.' She knew she didn't even sound convincing. But honestly, what was she to do now? Kidnap Hero? She was running out of options. No matter what she did, Joe just seemed to bounce back. Tougher measures were called for.

'You're in a bad mood,' Joe remarked, sounding amused, as the Luas came to a stop. 'Bad day?'

'You could say that.' She wished he'd get lost. It was all his fault she felt so lousy. Joe followed her on to the train and sat in beside her. To her annoyance, he actually seemed happy.

'You must have had a good day,' she said.

He shrugged. 'No, I didn't. My boss gave me an earful just before I left.'

'Oh.'

265

'Listen, Lizzie, are you up for doing me a favour?' He nudged her with his elbow and smiled at her.

Unbearably upbeat. Lizzie wanted to slap the handsomeness from his face. She wanted to tear his eyes out. She wanted to cry. But she couldn't.

'A favour?' she asked.

'Yeah. It's a bit of a biggie. I just thought you might like to do it. If not, I'll ask one of the lads in the club.'

'What is it?'

'I'm heading away for a night next week. Would you feed the birds for me? Anto will probably be around, too, so you'll have help. I can leave you instructions and stuff.'

Lizzie nodded. 'Sure. No worries.' She attempted a smile. 'Thanks for thinking of me.'

'Thanks.' Another grin. 'Glad that cheered you up.'

Oh, she thought, it certainly had.

40

The foyer of the theatre was crowded, which was a relief. At least, thought Lizzie, I can blend. She unwound her bright orange scarf from her neck in an effort to do just that. Pushing her way through the throng, she ordered a glass of wine at the bar before finding a corner in which to drink it.

The place was buzzing, which was good sign. Tom had told her once that when a theatre foyer buzzed, it signalled that the play was a success. Lizzie hoped it was true. Up on the walls there were pictures of the production. Small groups of people were gathered around some of them, chatting and making remarks about the actors. A black-and-white of Imogen and Tom locked in an embrace caught her eye and she told herself firmly that it was only acting.

'Hey.'

Lizzie's wine slopped out of her glass. She hadn't noticed Domo, Tom's best friend, at all.

'Hi,' she said faintly.

'How's things?'

'OK.' Lizzie wondered if she should she ask about Tom. About the play.

The silence dragged a little until Domo broke it by muttering, 'Good to see you, you know.'

Lizzie lifted her gaze from the contents of her wine glass and smiled. 'Good to see you, too.'

'I suppose I shouldn't say this,' Domo said awkwardly, 'but he misses you like hell. Like he doesn't say it, but we all know because he's back to the way he was before.'

'Before?'

'Yeah, before you came along. Jesus, he could be a miserable bastard.'

Lizzie couldn't imagine Tom being grumpy – well, not unless he got teased about having one line in a play. The memory was bittersweet.

'He's probably just stressed,' she offered.

'Oh, he's stressed all right.' Domo rolled his eyes as he finished his drink. Placing the empty glass on the sill behind he said, 'Anyway, he'll be glad you came, I'd say.'

'Have to support him, see what all the fuss is about.'

Domo grinned. 'It's a good play, I saw it the opening night. Are you going to come for a drink afterwards?'

'No, no, I don't think so.' She smiled. 'I don't think Tom would appreciate it.'

'I think he would.'

Lizzie shook her head and was saved from answering by the announcement that the play was about to start.

Domo bent over and kissed her cheek and asked her to think about it.

She said she would, but knew she wouldn't.

In the pub things were a bit strained. Try as he might, Joe could not shake the feeling that Cid had something to do with Prince's tag being removed. Of course he couldn't just blurt it out or say anything, Cid would have him up for slander or something. But the guy was doing his head in. Ever since it had happened, Cid had been making jokey comments about Prince retiring early from competitive sport.

'I've heard of women retiring from their career to start families, but this is ridiculous,' he chortled.

'Shut up,' Joe said quietly.

'Aw, will you relax, I'm only having a laugh,' Cid said.

'My bird is out of action because *someone*,' Joe stressed the 'someone', 'took his tag off and in the process hurt his leg. I don't think that's particularly funny. Do you, John?'

John held up his hands. 'Look, maybe we'll change the subject.'

'I'm only having a laugh. Can you not take a joke, Joe?'

'I've taken a lot of shit from you,' Joe said firmly, 'but I'm not taking any more.'

'Shit from me?' Cid looked genuinely bewildered. 'What shit have you taken from me? I helped you build your lofts. I gave up my Saturday once to help you build them.'

'Yeah, once I wasn't winning you'd do anything to help, ey? I wonder now if you have a spare key to my loft, seeing as you fit the locks.'

'Aw, Joe,' Noel made placating motions with his hands, 'you can't—'

'And what is that supposed to mean?' Cid pushed back his chair and, standing up, poked Joe hard in the arm. 'Go on, what are you saying?'

'He's saying nothing, sure you're not, Joe?' Noel glared at him.

'I'm just saying,' Joe stood up, too, 'that it's very funny that now I'm winning, my bird suddenly goes missing. That you somehow think it's a laugh.'

Cid's eyes narrowed. 'Come again?'

'You heard me.' Joe gave him a shove. 'And you know what else? The only other time you got placed was when my birds didn't race. And another time Prince didn't win, it was because someone let a fecking load of pigeons up when he was flying in.'

'Joe!' Noel stood now. 'Will you stop!'

'Now that,' Cid rolled his eyes and appealed to the table, 'is mental. You're some liar, d'you know that?'

Liar. If there was one thing he hated being called it was a liar. He lunged out and caught Cid by the scruff of his jumper.

'Don't you ever call me a liar, you little toerag!' He shoved Cid from him and Cid was about to lunge towards him when he was caught by Noel and held back.

'Let me at him. How dare he! That is – is – slander, so it is!'

John put a restraining hand on Joe's arm. The barman came hurrying over.

'That is enough,' Noel said firmly to Joc. He turned to Cid, 'And you, you stop annoying him, right?'

'I'll sue you!' Cid shouted, his face red and furious.

'Yeah, right!' Joe shouted back.

'Out!' The barman said. 'NOW!'

Lizzie didn't want the lights to go on at the end of the play. She had sat in the dark, watching, her heart sore as Tom wowed the audience. His beautiful resonant voice was clear as sunlight in a blue sky as it flowed out over the auditorium. It was like listening to a brilliant musician as he played his instrument. And he domin-ated every scene: Tom was the actor everyone looked at, even when he wasn't doing anything. Imogen, who played the love of his life, was not so brilliant, Lizzie thought with something approaching delight. And no way was she being bitchy. The people sitting beside her, right at the back, thought so, too. She over-heard them wondering how Imogen had got cast.

'Probably sleeping with the director,' the man scoffed. 'Oh no,' the girl with him said, 'I read in some column or other that she's dating Tommy Lynch.'

Lizzie flinched. But Domo would have told her if Tom was seeing someone. Or would he? Well, he certainly wouldn't have asked her for a drink afterwards if that were the case.

As the second half got under way, she tried to imagine how she would feel if she was still seeing Tom. How proud and happy she'd be watching him. She'd probably go most nights and, by the end of the run, she'd know all his lines by heart. She'd defin-itely have dragged her parents along and he'd have impressed them big time.

But it was stupid speculating like that, she chided herself mid-way through the second half. Watching Tom perform was akin to looking at a train she'd narrowly missed. Waving from the plat-form as the life she could have had trundled on by. She wasn't with Tom any more – she was just a member of the audience. She didn't realise that tears were trickling down her face until just before the end.

As the house lights went up, the audience began to rise, applauding all the while.

Lizzie dashed a hand over her face and rose, too. The cast stood onstage, holding hands and bowing. One. Two. Three times.

Then the male lead stood out from the centre and bowed. People cheered. She saw Tom, who was holding hands with Imogen, say something to her and Imogen's face lit up and Lizzie saw, as if magnified, the extra squeeze she gave his hand.

Tom was happy, Lizzie knew it by looking at him. Domo had probably been trying to make her feel better by saying he was miserable. In all her time with him, Lizzie could never remember Tom looking so alive as he did at that moment, holding hands with the pretty girl who played opposite him. It was funny how she felt so detached about it. And yet, she thought in amazement, she was crying.

Without thinking, she started to push her way out. Luckily she was only three seats from the edge and at the very back. She excused herself and was soon out in the foyer, taking deep, calming breaths.

She had lost him, she realised, and not because he had let her go but because she had wandered so far away that she wasn't sure she could ever go back.

'You idiot,' John scolded as he drove Joe home. 'What on earth did you let him get to you for?'

Joe shrugged.

'You've walked into it now, you know. He's just the kind of man who'd have you for assault.'

'I've been accused of worse,' Joe muttered.

John obviously didn't believe him as he took no notice. 'I think you're barking up the wrong tree anyway. Cid would never do that.'

Joe rubbed his hands over his face. 'I can't think of anyone else who would.'

'Cid is a pain, I'll admit. But he loves the birds. You're way out of line, Joe.'

271

'So how do *you* think Prince lost his tag?'

John shrugged. 'I dunno. It's a mystery. Maybe some kids . . . I dunno.' His voice trailed off before he asked, 'And what's the story with the pigeons getting in Prince's way?'

Joe told him the story and finished to find John staring at him incredulously.

'It's true, I swear.'

John said nothing. Joe got the uneasy feeling that John thought he was imagining things.

Billy was at home when Lizzie arrived back. His mobile phone sat on the table beside him.

'Aileen's dad rang. She's coming to collect all her things next week,' he said glumly. 'And then she wants to discuss what to do with the house.'

Lizzie's heart sank even further. 'How does that make you feel?' She sat beside him and tried to peer into his face.

'If I could take back that look, I would,' Billy said. 'But I can't. And apparently she can't forget it.'

'But sure,' Lizzie spluttered, 'when she comes, just say that to her.'

He shrugged. 'Sometimes no reason is good enough for how much you hurt someone.'

A small chill wrapped itself around her. 'She'll come round, you'll see.'

Billy didn't reply.

41

ALONE. IN JOE'S house. He'd gone off about an hour earlier, apparently heading home.

'I thought you didn't like home,' Lizzie said, enjoying his discomfort.

Joe had dumped his coffee down the sink and stared out at the back garden. 'My mother is sick,' he'd said, 'so I figured . . .' He let the sentence hang.

She had feigned concern but he'd brushed it off. Instead he'd handed her the keys to the house and the lofts, accompanied by a list of instructions.

'You can get Anto to help you,' he said. 'He's not a bad little guy. And John and Noel are around if you run into problems. Noel will call to bring the birds on a training toss tomorrow.'

Lizzie had just fed the birds. Well, overfed the birds, and now here she was, standing in the centre of Joe's living room.

She gazed around and contempt for everything in it rose within her. It seeped right through her so she wasn't even aware that she was grinding her teeth and clenching her hands. She detested his crappy pale cream walls and scuffed floorboards. His CD collection and his DVDs. He seemed to like thrillers and comedies and his CDs were mostly singer-songwriters. She was so tempted to take them all out and grind them under her feet. But, knowing him, he'd have insurance and get the whole lot replaced with new stuff.

There were no photographs, no cards, nothing personal in the room. It was as if Joe was a blank canvas. A nowhere man.

She left the front room, giving the door a bit of a kick on the way out, and turned to climb the stairs, her hand gripping the banister. She knew what she was doing was wrong, but that only made it better. She was beyond caring what she did to Joe now, so long as she didn't get found out.

It wasn't a huge house. A narrow landing with three bedrooms and a bathroom leading off it. The first room she went into was small and totally empty, the floorboards dusty and neglected. Nothing in the built-in wardrobe.

She left and entered Joe's bedroom. She knew it was his because bits of him were all over the place. A pigeon racing magazine was thrown casually across his bed, which had been pushed up alongside the window. It sported a surprisingly clean blue and white duvet. The walls were painted a disgusting green and more books on pigeons were piled higgledy-piggledy on the floor at the end of the bed. A mirror and some aftershave took up space on a battered bedside locker. A small TV stood on a table in the corner. No lampshade covered the bulb. The room was functional, a place to sleep. Lizzie peered inside his wardrobe. Jeans and tracksuits. Nothing. She rifled along the shelves. Again, nothing.

Finally, after a fruitless search, she made her way to the bathroom. It, too, was clean. There was lino on the floor that was vaguely ugly and white tiles on the wall. Shampoos and a bottle of cleaning fluid were lined along the bath. Boring.

At length she entered the third bedroom. Small, like the first, there were a couple of sealed cardboard boxes on the floor. One of the boxes had split and books poked out through the tear. Lizzie very gently made the hole larger. More books spilled on to the floor. Bird books and fishing books. Nothing else.

Lizzie wasn't exactly sure what she'd hoped to achieve by poking around. Maybe just knowing that she'd invaded his privacy would be enough – just to hug the knowledge to herself while she broke his life. The thought made her jump. *Broke his life*. Lizzie winced. But what else was she doing? This man had murdered

274

her sister. Taken her on to a boat, hit her and then thrown her overboard. And now he was out. Free. Living his life. There was no way around it, no way she could see over it. She would only be happy when she'd broken his life.

So she hunkered down and pulled the sealing tape off the second box, knowing she could retape it. Inside, more books. Jesus, did this guy ever stop? There was surely only so much you could know about birds. There were a few videotapes, too, all about pigeons and pigeon breeders. It was no wonder he was still single, she thought. And then, right at the bottom of the box, she found some envelopes bound with elastic. Letters from Rossclare. It suddenly dawned on Lizzie that this was the stuff Joe had taken from prison with him. He'd boxed it and never looked at it since.

With shaking hands she pulled the first letter from its envelope.

Joseph, darling,

We miss you terribly and cry every night. You know we don't blame you for what happened, but we can't understand it either. Think, Joseph, please think. Try and remember the phone number of the text. Anything. Try, please, to give us some explanation for what happened that night. Is it possible you blanked out and don't recall? That can happen, you know. She was on your boat. With you. You have to know

Your father is devastated. He blames himself for your conviction. I'm only trying to help both of you. Please read this and reply.

Please say you'll let us visit.

Your mother, who loves you.

Dear Mr Jones,

Your application for appeal has been lodged.

Yours sincerely,

Messrs Frank O'Toole & Associates.

Dearest Joseph,

I know you do not wish us to contact you, but I feel you must be reading our letters as they are not being returned. I am sorry to hear that your appeal will not go ahead. It is not fair. I know how upset you must be and I wish I could visit you.

I also want to tell you what happened yesterday. I hope it will give you hope. I was in church, on my own, lighting a candle for you and praying for a miracle when, just as I turned to leave, in walked Megan Walsh's father. I forget his name. I got a terrible shock, Joseph, not because I believe you are guilty but because this man does. I didn't know what he would say or do.

Anyway, we looked at each other for a bit and then he held out his hand.

And I started to cry.

He patted me on the arm and said that he didn't blame me or your dad for any of this. I wanted to say to him that he shouldn't blame you either, Joseph, but I didn't. I wish I had but this man had lost his daughter and we still have you and so I just told him that I was sorry for his loss.

He thanked me and said we should always be able to pass each other and nod. That meant a lot because some people are not talking to us any more.

I know you are innocent, Joe. You are my child. I know what you're capable of. Anyone who knows you knows this. I will hold out for the miracle.

Lots of love,
Mammy.

Lizzie swallowed hard at the thought of her dad doing something like that. Part of her wanted to hug him for his gesture, and part of her hated him for being nice to these people who had sided with his daughter's murderer.

She opened another letter.

Joseph,

Your father is handing over the running of the paper to the subeditor. He can't work any more, he says. I think he's destroyed by what happened. He can't seem to eat or sleep. I'm making him go to the doctor tomorrow. Part of it is me being selfish, I want him out from under my feet.

I met Dessie on the street today and he said hello to me. I thought he might pass me by but he didn't. We had a bit of an awkward conversation and then I put my foot in it by asking him if he could recall sending Megan a text at all the day she died. He got a little angry with me then. 'I never texted Megan,' he said. 'The girl was nuts.' Then he said that he didn't appreciate you trying to stitch him up before he stormed off.

I can't sleep myself. The whole thing goes around and around inside my head. Please let me visit you. Until then, just hold on and don't lose faith.

Please write back,
Mammy.

Lizzie felt her hand curling involuntarily around these letters from Leah Jones. She must have written every week for years, Lizzie thought. Silly deluded woman. The letters in her hand made a sort of scrunching noise before she realised that she was twisting them. Jesus, she couldn't rip them up, Joe might notice. Instead, she flattened them back out.

There was another envelope, smaller than the rest, that she hadn't noticed. Unfolding the page inside, Lizzie realised that it was a newspaper clipping.

It was headlined GUILTY.

Joseph Jones, son of newspaper man Geoff Jones, was yesterday found guilty of murdering 19-year-old Megan Walsh in a case that has divided Co. Wexford. Joseph Jones now faces life in prison. The body of Ms Walsh was found washed up on a beach ten miles from her home town a year ago last August. She had been missing for

277

two days and the finger of suspicion fell on local man Joseph Jones when it was established that he was the last person to see her alive. Ms Walsh was wearing Joseph Jones' jumper when she was found on the beach. Coronary reports confirmed that she suffered a severe blow to the head in the hours before her death. A witness told how she had seen Megan Walsh climb on to Jones' father's boat and—

Lizzie felt her stomach heave and just made it to the bathroom before she vomited.

42

IT TOOK HIM exactly two and a half hours to get home as, mid-week, the traffic was light. He couldn't help the sweat that coated his hands and forehead as the roads became ever more familiar. And, finally, he was two hundred yards from home. As he neared the gateway his stomach heaved and he drove past, before pulling into a layby some distance away.

It was no use, he couldn't do it. He couldn't face them and pretend what they had done was all right. His parents had thrown him to the lions and watched as they savaged him. But his mother was sick. And his dad didn't look much better.

Joe closed his eyes and lay his head back on the headrest. What was he to do? He couldn't ever go back to the way he used to be with them – charming his mum and annoying the hell out of his dad with his passion for nature and birds instead of words and news. But he couldn't move on, either. He wasn't sure if he could build a relationship out of the ruins of the old one. And yet at the same time, seeing the familiar stone wall that surrounded the house had made his heart twist with something he thought he'd forgotten long ago. The comfort that only home can give.

To hell with it, he thought as he started his car up. Maybe he'd never move on, maybe they wouldn't, but surely he could just go this once and have a look and see how bad those ruins were.

He pulled his car on to the opposite side of the road, earning him a screech of brakes and two fingers from a driver he hadn't seen. Joe raised his hand in apology but it didn't stop the man rolling down his window and yelling something totally unintelligible at him.

Joe didn't care. Things like that never bothered him any more. He rarely overtook on roads or got annoyed waiting in queues. To him the whole idea of just being outside was wonderful. He drove as slowly as he could get away with and then, finally, with a huge intake of breath, he turned and drove up the driveway to his parents' house.

There was no car there.

A sense of anticlimax washed over him. He hadn't rung to say he was coming, just in case he did chicken out, and now he was on his own. He pulled the car up in front of the house and knew by the way all the windows were shut that it was empty. He'd hang around for a while, he decided. It'd be nice to wander around the back and walk through the garden. He'd loved the garden when he was a kid – it was big and open and green.

He pulled on his jacket and stepped out of the car. The freshness of the air hit him and on it came the scent of the sea. Slightly salty. Joe closed his eyes and took a deep breath and began to walk.

The back garden was just like he remembered. He stood looking at it for a second before becoming aware of birdsong and the flutter of wings in the trees. He shoved his hands into his pockets and began to walk.

'Oy!'

Joe jumped and turned. A man was peering at him from the garden of the house next door.

'Who are you?'

Joe recognised his old neighbour. Mr O'Connor. He couldn't remember the man's first name. They'd been really friendly with his mother and father.

'It's, eh, Joe,' he said, feeling ashamed having to admit it.

Mr O'Connor's face registered shock, then wariness. There was no welcome.

'Oh,' he said. He started to back away. 'Right. Well, your parents should be back soon. I think they've just gone into town for a bit.'

'Thanks,' Joe said despondently as the man hurried off, no doubt to inform his wife that the murderer was back.

He moved further along towards the back of the garden, where the trees and bushes were thickly planted. At least he could walk between them and not be observed. He didn't want to run into anyone else, even if it was highly unlikely.

It was about half an hour later that he heard a car pulling up. It sounded as if it was coming from the front of the house. He knew that his dad would recognise his son's car and be looking for him, so he left the protection of the trees and walked some way back towards the house. He didn't want to go right up to the door. He wasn't even sure if he wanted to go in. Instead, he stood almost in the centre of the garden as his parents came around the side of the house, obviously searching for him.

His father led his mother by the arm. Joe watched him talk to her as her eyes eagerly scanned the garden. And then she saw him. And he saw her. And they all stood looking at each other for what seemed like ages.

Joe couldn't move, even if he'd wanted to. His mother looked so frail: still beautiful, with her dark hair streaked very liberally with a brilliant white, but unsteady and unsure. His dad looked old, too. He didn't know what to say. He just remained standing, his legs apart and his hands shoved ever deeper into the pockets of his jacket. He met their steady gaze with a defiant gaze of his own.

'It's Joseph,' his dad said to his mother, breaking the silence. 'He's back.'

'Joseph?' She mouthed the name, framing it, saying it, tasting it like unfamiliar chocolate. 'My Joseph?'

'Our Joseph,' his dad nodded, his gaze going between his wife and his son. 'He must have come to visit.'

Joe watched as his mother walked swiftly towards him, her hands to her mouth. She came to a stop about two feet in front of him.

'Joe?' she said.

'Hi, Mum,' he said back. He wanted it to come out sounding normal. As if it hadn't been fourteen years since he'd seen her. Instead his voice shook a little and caught in his throat.

'You came back?'

He wasn't sure what this meant. 'I came for a . . .' He paused. 'A short visit. To say hi.'

His dad jangled his keys. 'Will you come in for a cuppa?'

His mother looked hopefully up at him.

'Yeah. Sure.'

'Good,' his mother nodded. She touched him briefly on the sleeve of his jacket. 'Great.'

Joe allowed himself a tiny smile.

The house looked fantastic. He had taken it for granted when he was a kid but now, having lived in a tiny cell and then in his bare house in Ranelagh, it was great to be sitting in a bright airy kitchen with a gleaming kettle bubbling away.

But he didn't slouch in the chair. He sat stiffly upright, uncomfortable in front of these two strangers who were looking at him with so much love. It made him feel claustrophobic.

'What made you come back now?' his mother asked as she got the tea ready.

His father shot him a sharp look.

'Eh, I dunno.' Joe looked at his hands. 'I just felt, well, that . . .' He paused, unable to frame a proper answer. He never would have come back if his mother hadn't been sick. At least he didn't think so. Why would he? He couldn't forget, no matter how hard he tried.

'Well, whatever the reason,' his mother said, 'I'm glad to see you.'

Joe nodded.

Silently his father put cups in front of them all and poured the tea. He placed a packet of biscuits on the table and sat down beside his wife. Joe put milk in his tea, then stared into it.

'So, how have things been?' his mother asked. 'You know, since,' she swallowed hard, 'since they let you out.'

'OK.' He fiddled with his teaspoon. 'My parole officer got me a job working with his brother in a sports centre. I teach swimming.'

'Oh.'

He nodded. 'And I have a loft of pigeons that I do well with.'

'So you're still into the pigeons,' his mother said. 'I'm glad about that.'

There was more silence.

'And do you go out and have a social life?' his mother asked. 'Are you happy?'

He shot her a look. 'I'm OK. I don't bother with going out.'

'Why?'

All this concern made him flinch. 'Got my fingers burned once. I won't be doing it again.'

'Oh, Joe.' She said it with sadness.

'Yeah well, I'd rather be at home on my own than stuck in a bloody prison cell.'

'You won't go to prison for going out and having a life,' she said.

'That's what I thought before.' He knew he sounded bitter, but damn it, he still felt angry and cheated and betrayed. He bit his lip and tried to get a grip on himself.

'So, how have you both been?'

A look passed between them and Joe saw his father nod.

'I'm not well, Joseph, I might as well tell you,' his mother said. She spoke firmly, without any emotion. 'I've been diagnosed with Alzheimer's.' She smiled a little. 'You picked a good day to come. Another day and I'd have been all over the place.'

His father laid a hand on her shoulder. 'She's being very good about it. She knows I'm always here, don't you, Leah?'

His mother nodded and caught her husband's hand. 'I'm so afraid I'll forget everyone,' she said. 'Not know who anyone is.'

'It'd take some disease to forget that I was in prison.' Joe managed a smile. 'That might be a good thing for you.'

'Never.' She shook her head. 'You never say that. You have made me proud, Joseph. I know with every part of me that you were innocent and I'm only sorry that I can't fight for you any more. But,' she took a breath, 'you don't stop fighting for yourself. You owe yourself a good life. You have fun. Do you hear me?'

283

He said nothing.

'We can't say anything but sorry,' his dad said. 'I didn't intentionally set out to be the star witness for the prosecution, Joe. They twisted everything.'

'You didn't have to say anything about the row.'

'I didn't think it meant much. They asked how well you had known the girl, that's all.'

'And what did you say? Well enough to have a row with?'

'I told the truth because I honestly believed you had nothing to fear. If I didn't believe in your innocence, would I have even let slip about the row?'

Joe gulped. He knew his dad was telling the truth and he wanted to let them in, but he knew that would involve pulling down a lot of his defences. He trusted very few people now. Forgetting and forgiving would leave him wide open all over again.

'I have to go now.' He stood up. 'Thanks for the tea.'

'Will you not stay a little longer?' His mother looked at him beseechingly. 'Please?'

'I can't.' He stared at them. 'Sorry.'

They didn't move as he stumbled towards the front door.

Some hours later he checked into the B&B he'd booked.

As he dumped his bag on the floor, he found it hard to remember what he'd done since leaving his parents' house. He'd driven around the county, revisiting old haunts and remembering. He'd walked the beach where Meg's body had been washed up, he'd walked along the harbour and seen big signs asking for Polly Walsh to be set free. Other signs telling people to protest about the harbour plan. His dad's boat was still there, the one he'd taken out all those years ago. It was more battered now, the name had peeled from the side. Joe knew that no one used it any more, probably hadn't in fourteen years. He'd walked by the newspaper offices, wondering if he'd catch a glimpse of Dessie, but he hadn't. Dessie hadn't contacted him since Joe had said that Meg was there to meet him that night. He'd been convinced that Joe was trying to frame him, but Joe hadn't been – that was what Meg had said. She had received a text . . .

Joe shook his head to clear it. There was no point in thinking about the past. He had to move on.

But he wished he knew where he was going.

43

Thursday, 26th August

Tomorrow, I am going to confront Dessie. I have made up my mind.

  I have been a week on holidays and the slimy toad hasn't even rung me. I hope it's because he's really busy. I mean, he's bound to be, isn't he, being in the office all on his own without me or Joe. But at the same time, I have rung him about forty-two times – once an hour. It just occurred to me when I went to ring him again that he has never given me his mobile number. I've asked for it and he keeps saying he can't remember it offhand and that he'd get it to me, but he never has. Maybe it was a hint all along, but if it was I'll find out tomorrow and, if he was using me, I'll have it out with him. I might not be the cleverest person on the planet but there is no way I'm going to be some easy woman for him to tell all his mates about and for Joe Jones to look smug and say that he told me so. No way. Dessie will learn that I am like that woman in England who they called the Iron Lady – I think it's the queen or someone. Anyway, he'll learn that he cannot mess me about like that.

Friday, 27th August

I told everyone in the house that I was meeting Dessie for lunch. Billy gave a bit of a cheer and said that maybe now I'd finally stop moping about the place and I said that I haven't been moping and Mammy, of course, had to get her oar in and say that if going around with a face like a dead cat wasn't moping she didn't know what was. I said that if she didn't know what a mopey face looked like, maybe she should look in a mirror.

Now she's not talking to me.

Anyway, I'm in my room, having cried my eyes out and made my headache worse by doing so. It did not go well. Not at all. Joe Jones was right. Dessie is just out for Dessie.

I dressed up to go see him. I wore a short green skirt, even though it was lushing rain and I was going to be freezing waiting for the bus. On top I wore my cute little white T-shirt with a picture of a Christmas tree saying, 'Christmas is for life not just December'. And I had a red short jacket and my red high heels. I looked great, I thought. And so did the bus driver because he let me on for free and gave me a wink.

Then I hopped off the bus in Rossclare town and stood outside the paper building for ages. I didn't really want to meet anyone and yet I had to go inside. So I went into the foyer, which was empty – the receptionist is hopeless actually. Then I scurried as fast as I could down to the ad office. Inside I could hear a phone ringing and I pushed open the door.

Things get a bit hazy here. It's weird, I can't quite remember what happened. I only know that Dessie's old girlfriend was perched on the desk and he was talking away to her. And she was messing his hair up. They looked happy. I said something like 'very cosy', and they both looked at me.

Then he went pale and asked really crossly what did I want and she looked from me to him in a sort of shocked way. Well, I thought to myself, no way is he going to treat me like just some ordinary person. So I said that last week I wanted him and that I was pretty sure that he'd wanted me as we'd done it in his car. Only I didn't say 'done it', I said 'fucked', which sounded a bit sluttish now I think about it. Anyway I probably didn't come across very well actually because I think I was shouting. Then Dessie's girlfriend hopped off the desk and demanded to know what the hell was happening. So I asked Dessie to explain and he turned to her and told her I was mad.

Me?

He said I'd been chasing him or some rubbish like that and I remember denying it and saying he chased me.

Then his girlfriend got cross and Dessie got cross and he called me a tart and told his girlfriend to look at the state of me. And he said, and this hurt, he said, 'Look, Megan, I sell ads. I bullshit. That's what happened with you and like all my customers you fell for it.'

Anger like I have never known before flooded right through me and, OK, I was going to cry too, so I knew I had to leave or I would throw something at him, which is what I should have done, or maybe I did I can't remember. Next thing I'm on the floor with the two of them bending over me, looking all shocked.

I'd fallen over the telephone cord as I'd made to run. Fallen over the cord and banged my head off the filing cabinet and the floor. How embarrassing. My head was full of stars and fireworks and my brain was muzzy. I had to get away, but I felt really sick so I had to put my head between my legs – how humiliating. Then it's a bit of a blur, they made me sit down and gave me water and I wouldn't drink it. It was all confused. I told them I was fine. I hardly remember what happened

288

after only that I somehow left and got the bus back and have been here since.

I hate him for what he's done and I hate Joe for being right.

OK, all that last bit can be scrapped because . . .

44

I T WAS AFTER eight and Lizzie had just locked up the lofts when Joe arrived back.

Anto had ruined her plans to stuff the birds with food. He'd been horrified to see corn and seeds in the bird feeders and had immediately emptied them out, looking at her accusingly and shaking his head and muttering stuff about Joe being a complete dickhead leaving her in charge.

As she pulled the side gate behind her, mentally cursing Anto, she almost banged into Joe, who didn't look particularly happy. When he saw her, however, his face broke into a grin.

'Hey, how's things? Those birds behaving themselves?'

She decided that she'd better come clean about the overfeeding or Anto would surely rat on her.

'I made a bit of a mistake with their food,' she said ruefully. 'Luckily Anto was on hand to put me right. I think I was over-feeding them.'

He looked a bit taken aback for a second but, with a wave of his hand, said, 'Aw, don't worry about it. Did Noel take them for the toss?'

'Yep. They were back within twenty minutes.'

'Not bad.'

She handed him his keys and he unlocked the front door.

'See you.' She turned to go.

'Hey!'

His shout stopped her. She turned back, heart hammering. Had he somehow noticed that she'd been poking around? She was certain there was nothing out of place. Well, there was nothing in his house to *be* out of place.

Joe was looking at her in a half embarrassed way, tossing his keys from hand to hand. 'Would you like to, eh, you know, go for a drink? My treat? To say thanks for minding the birds.'

'Go for a drink?' she stammered.

'Yeah.' He suddenly looked mortified. 'Well, only if you want. It's not a date or anything.'

Joe Jones drinking. He might let his guard down. She shrugged, trying to sound casual.

'Sure? When?'

'Tomorrow? I can meet you after work and we could grab a bite to eat? My shout?'

'OK. Great. Meet you at six-thirty outside Bewleys in Grafton Street.'

His mouth curved upward in the biggest smile Lizzie had seen in a long time. He was a bloody good-looking guy, she thought suddenly, hating him for it.

'See you then,' she called.

Lizzie was a few doors from home when Aileen's dad drove by her and pulled up outside the house. She watched, without going any closer, as he strode around to the passenger side of the car and opened the door for Aileen. Lizzie tried not to grin as he hauled his enormously pregnant daughter out of the car and held her as she swayed slightly. My God, Aileen was huge, she thought. She wondered why they were calling before realising that Aileen was probably coming to collect the remainder of her stuff. Obviously she'd brought her dad along for moral support. Poor Billy would be gutted, but if Aileen had her dad along, then Lizzie would be there for her brother.

'Hi,' Lizzie called, not sure if they'd spotted her.

They both turned and watched her approach. 'Hello, Lizzie,' Aileen's dad said pleasantly. 'How are you?'

'Good. You?'

'I'm very well, thank you.'

'You look, eh, great,' she said to Aileen, who managed a small smile.

'Yeah, great as in enormous. I'm as big as a house.' She giggled a little and Lizzie saw a touch of the old Aileen underneath the prickly mother-to-be.

'Only a duplex one, though,' Lizzie said and they smiled.

'Aileen has just, eh, you know, come to pick up some things,' her dad said, shuffling uncomfortably and unable to meet Lizzie's eye.

'There is no need to sound apologetic about it.' Aileen turned to her father, her smile vanishing. 'They are my things and this is half my house and Billy and I have to sort things out before the babies come.'

'I know, I was just saying—'

'Well don't just say!'

'Hormones,' Abe mouthed at Lizzie as they both followed Aileen up the path.

She strode with a speed that belied her size. At the door she fumbled with her house keys, but before she could insert her key into the lock, the door was wrenched open.

Billy stood glowering at them. He opened his mouth to speak but gulped audibly as he took in Aileen's changed shape. He had never seen her swollen belly, Lizzie realised, and she wanted to hug him as his scowl turned to wonder. He seemed incapable of saying anything and, without uttering a word, he opened the door wider to let them through.

'Billy,' Aileen said curtly as she passed him.

'Hi.' Billy attempted a small grin. 'You look . . .' He paused. 'Wow.'

Aileen glared at him. 'Pity you couldn't have said "wow" a few months ago.'

'Yeah, I know,' Billy agreed.

There was an edgy silence.

'Well, let's hope there's no confusion about who owns what,' Aileen said, recovering first.

292

'I'll need some space to sort through the things and I've some boxes in the car to pack stuff away in. Dad,' she looked at her father, 'would you get the boxes, please?' She spoke as if she was a matron in charge of a hospital.

'I've been thinking,' Billy blurted out, as Aileen's dad made a move, 'and, eh, Aileen, I'd really like you to hear what I've thought.'

'I don't think so, Billy,' Aileen said.

'Aw, come on, you haven't spoken to me since you left. That's not fair.'

'You didn't need any words to say what you meant that day in the hospital.'

'Jesus!' Billy threw his hands up in the air in exasperation. 'Do you want me to beg? Is that it?'

'No, I just want my stuff. It's the classy stuff.'

'Oh, yeah, I'm the Palestine.'

'It's philistine, actually.'

'Oh, get lost!' Billy rubbed a hand over his face and turned away from her. Lizzie went to comfort him but he shoved her off. He was near tears, she realised with a shock.

Aileen's dad must have realised it, too, because he said, 'Oh, Aileen will you give the lad a chance.' As Aileen tossed her head in a dismissive gesture, he continued softly, 'It's not like you to be so . . . so hard.'

'I'm hard because I have to be.'

'No one has to be hard.'

'Well, there is no way I'm going to be like you, Dad, that's for sure.'

'Pardon?'

'Taking Mam back every time she apologised. That's not for me, thanks.'

Her dad looked as if she'd struck him. Then, with a quiet fury, he said, 'Don't you talk to me like that. Don't you dare. I took your mother back for you. For you, every time. Because you loved her.'

'And so did you.'

'Yes,' Abe nodded. 'And I gave her a second chance. And a

third. I gave us every chance and, if you love Billy at all, you'll give him a chance to explain. I think, Aileen, it's time you faced facts. Now,' he started to count the facts on his fingers, 'you are pregnant with twins, you have left the house you bought with your boyfriend, you have left your boyfriend, and you will not give him a chance to explain or apologise. That is ridiculous. The lad has rung you night and day begging for a chance and you have blanked him. Well, I will not help you until you listen to what he has to say.'

'Eh, thanks, Abe,' Billy muttered, his voice suspiciously wobbly.

'Oh, I'm not doing it for you,' Abe said wearily. 'I'm doing it for my own sanity. She spends all her time giving out about you even though she says,' he made quote signs with his fingers, 'oh, I'm so over him.' He glared at his daughter, 'Now, you listen to him and then make up your mind.'

Aileen looked suddenly terrified. 'Dad!'

'And if you don't, I'm driving home right now and leaving you stranded here.'

'You can't do that!'

'Watch me!'

The two glared at each other.

Lizzie desperately wanted to leave, but if Abe was staying then so was she. The silence stretched on as father and daughter stared stonily at each other.

'Fine,' Aileen spat eventually, breaking the silence like scissors on a taut elastic band. She turned to Billy. 'Say what it is you have to say and then we can move on.'

Billy swallowed hard.

'Any chance of a cuppa, Lizzie?' Abe asked.

Thank God. It meant she wouldn't have to listen to what Billy had to say. 'Every chance, Abe.'

'No!' Billy's shout stopped them. 'I want everyone to hear this. I need you to back me up, Lizzie.' He indicated the sitting room. 'So can we go in here.'

Back him up? What was he on about? She watched as Billy led the way, with Aileen stomping in behind him. Abe shrugged and Lizzie rolled her eyes as they both followed Aileen, who had come to a standstill in the centre of the room, a look of horror on her face.

'Do you and Lizzie ever clean anything? Look at the dust on that fireplace.' She ran her finger along the ledge and Lizzie cringed. It had never occurred to her to dust that.

Aileen's eyes scanned the room. 'And you have stains on the table. I bought this table with my own money. Who put a hot mug on the table like that? Where are the coasters?'

'Aileen, can you give me a second here?' Billy said. He was rubbing his hand through his hair and making it stick up in spikes. It occurred to Lizzie that the sitting room wasn't the only thing that needed cleaning.

'Oh, believe me, that's all you're getting.' Aileen said. 'I can't believe you did this to my table.'

Billy looked desperately at Lizzie, who shrugged.

'Listen!' Abe snapped.

Everyone jumped.

'Will you sit down and listen?' Abe implored his daughter. He took her hand in his. 'Stop trying to distract yourself. Stop being so horrible. Stop being so scared of what Billy has to say.'

'I'm not scared,' Aileen said, a little too quickly.

'You are,' her dad said. 'You're scared you'll be like me. You're scared to listen to him in case he sweet-talks you like your mother did to me. But, Aileen, Billy isn't like your mother. He didn't leave you. You left him.'

Aileen paled. 'Whose side are you on?' she sniffed.

'Yours. Totally and firmly.' He wrapped an arm about her shoulder and led her gently to the sofa.

There was silence for a second. Billy coughed a little. 'Ready now?'

Aileen's dad nodded in her stead.

'It's, eh, hard to start,' Billy gulped out. 'Like, I had it all planned – what to say – and now . . .' He looked up at the ceiling and shoved his hands into the pockets of his trousers.

'Now, I want to find the right words to make it better and I'm scared I won't.' He swallowed hard. 'I don't want to blow it.'

'You've already blown it, Billy,' Aileen said, though she didn't sound angry, just sad. 'I don't trust you to stay with me now.'

'Billy would never leave you,' Lizzie said, indignant on Billy's behalf. 'Look at him, he's not like that!'

'Lizzie!' Billy snapped and then, more quietly, 'Just, just let me explain to her, OK?'

'Yeah, but she thinks—' Lizzie stopped at her brother's warning look. 'Sorry,' she muttered.

Billy turned back to his girlfriend. 'I was scared, Aileen,' he said, 'and I know it sounds crap but, well,' he winced, 'this is coming out all wrong. Look, you know the way you and I got together after, after . . . Well, after Megan died?'

Aileen didn't react, but Billy continued earnestly. 'I liked being with you because you were fun and all, but I liked it too because you were her best friend. And I felt close to her when you were with me and I know it was the same for you.'

Aileen's eyes glistened.

'She was my twin, closer to me than my own shadow, and when she died it wrecked our family.' He turned and asked Lizzie quietly, 'Didn't it, Liz?'

'Yep.' Lizzie wished he wouldn't talk about that. She studied the mark on the coffee table instead.

'We'd been happy before that,' she heard Billy say, 'only we never realised how happy, I guess. We were just a normal family. But when Megan died, it ripped the heart out of each of us. My dad refused to go out on the boat any more, he ended up selling it and farming instead. It doesn't make him happy. Mam got really cross and bitter and started fighting the whole world with protest after protest and Lizzie, well, she upped and left and refused to see anyone who reminded her of Meg, while I clung on to anything that reminded me of her like a life raft.' He paused and took a deep, shaky breath.

'So what has that to do with us?' Aileen asked quietly.

'Everything,' Billy answered earnestly. 'I was with you because you reminded me of the good times. I never wanted it to change. But things did change. We moved to Dublin, got the flat, took out the mortgage and God, Aileen, though I was happy, I was scared all the time, too. And then you got pregnant.'

'And?' Aileen's voice shook.

Billy crossed the room and sat down beside her. He held her gaze for a second before saying haltingly, 'Megan's death taught my family that life could change in a second and that nothing was guaranteed. And the closer you get to real happiness, the closer you are to complete devastation, too, Aileen. And I didn't want what happened to my folks to ever be us.'

Lizzie swallowed hard. She'd felt like that, too. That mark on the table wasn't so bad. Polish would remove it.

'I didn't want a family, I found it too scary. I didn't think I'd cope if anything happened. But I'm not coping now, Aileen, and I'd rather be scarily happy with you than like this.' He tried to catch her hand but she pulled away. 'Please give me another chance.'

Aileen didn't seem to know what to say.

'I just got scared, Aileen. People don't always know what they really want.'

'I did.' She suddenly looked small, despite her size. 'I wanted you and our little house and especially the babies.'

'I know,' he said back.

'I never had a proper family before, Billy. It's all I ever wanted. I loved your family. I loved you. You never said you were scared. If you had only said instead of humiliating me . . .' Her voice broke.

'How could I? I wanted you to be happy.'

'Oh, yeah,' she sniffed, a big tear running down her face and on to her chin, 'look at me, I'm sooo happy!'

'So come back and I swear I'll make you happy.'

'You used to be fun,' Aileen said through her tears.

'I know,' Billy said back. Then, on a half smile, 'You used to be thin.'

'Don't make me laugh,' Aileen said, sniffing as she laced a hand on her stomach.

'Why not? I love you and you look lovely.' He touched her face gently.

'I just can't forget that look you had that day.'

'If I could take back that look I would,' Billy said. 'Only I can't. And I know you're scared of taking a chance on me and I know I'm not perfect but I'll be the best I can be for you.'

'What if you get so scared that you do run off? Or what if something awful does happen?'

'Then I'll do what I'm doing now and try to fix it. I'm not going anywhere, Aileen.'

'I just wanted it to be perfect.'

'Oh, for God's sake,' Aileen's dad said, sounding as if he'd heard enough and he just wanted to be out of there. 'There is no such thing as perfection. We make our own perfection. People who think everything will be perfect all the time find it really hard when things go wrong. Like your mother. Like you, Aileen.'

'Pardon?'

'You ran off when Billy didn't give you perfection – that's what your mother did to me. You have to be scared to want to work at it, Aileen.'

'I thought you said you were on my side.'

'I am. Being on your side does not involve letting you throw your happiness out the window. Now, if you'll excuse me, Lizzie offered me some tea a while ago and I'm going to take it.' He looked at Lizzie. 'All right?'

Lizzie nodded.

She followed Abe out the door and was surprised when he hugged her.

'You poor girl. Here,' he handed her a handkerchief, 'they'd no right to make you cry like that.'

She was crying. Much the same way she'd been crying at Tom's play. Silently. Hardly aware she was doing it. It occurred to her that she was barely aware of anything she was doing these days. She sniffed hard and dashed a hand across her face and dabbed her eyes with the hankie. The only emotion she really seemed to truly feel any more was anger, and that was in Joe's presence.

'Sorry,' she sniffed as she followed him into the kitchen, where he put on the kettle and hunted for the coffee. 'I don't know why—'

'Because you had to listen to crap from the two of them, that's why!' Abe smiled at her.

Lizzie smiled shakily back though she knew, and he knew, that that wasn't the reason.

Then he gave her another hug and told her she could keep his hankie.

45

I T WAS A beautiful evening in the city. Lizzie left work slightly later than normal so that Joe would be at Bewleys before her. She didn't want to be first there and have him think she was actually eager to meet him.

She saw him as she approached, lounging against the wall of the café, one foot planted firmly against the brick of the wall. He checked his watch before pulling a cigarette pack from his jacket and lighting up. He inhaled and blew a long stream of smoke into the air.

'I'll have one of those,' Lizzie said from behind him.

'Hey,' he grinned in greeting as he held the packet out to her, 'take whatever you like, I'm trying to cut down.'

'Hate that.' She let him light the cigarette for her and the two of them stood, side by side, smoking contentedly.

'Yeah, my boss offered me a job managing a new sports centre in Meath today, so I reckon it's probably better if I don't smoke.'

'A promotion?' Lizzie couldn't believe it. How on earth could someone give an ex-con a job like that? Huh, he was probably going to be earning way more than her. Life really was not fair.

'Don't they know—' She stopped abruptly, horrified at what she had been about to say.

'Don't they know what?' Joe asked.

'That you're, eh, totally addicted to nicotine?' she gulped.

'Totally addicted might be pushing it a bit,' he said, his eyes sparkling. 'Mildly addicted.'

'You can't be mildly addicted to anything.' Lizzie couldn't help grinning, she felt so weak at the mess she'd narrowly avoided making. 'Chancer.'

He shrugged. 'Aw well, I've only smoked five so far today, so that's good. Now, where to? There's a great little place at the top of O'Connell Street, if you like.'

'Rocco's?'

He nodded. 'Yeah, that's the name I think.'

Lizzie was a bit stunned. That was her favourite restaurant in the whole of Dublin: gorgeous food, good wine list, reasonable prices and, even better than all that, a lovely warm smokers' lounge out the back.

'Good choice,' she nodded.

Joe looked relieved and pushed himself from the wall.

'Righto, let's head, so.' He looked at her footwear. 'Flat shoes. I like your style.'

She fell into step beside him. As they walked she couldn't fail to notice the admiring glances women tossed in his direction. Joe, however, seemed oblivious.

'So, how come you got a promotion?' Lizzie asked. 'Are you a real lick-arse?'

'Yeah. Basically.'

His answer made her laugh, despite herself.

Joe grinned. 'I just work hard and keep the head down,' he said. 'I was in trouble a few weeks ago for not turning up, but I did the humble worker thing and this is my reward.'

'And will you have to move to Meath?'

He shrugged. 'I dunno. I'll see what the commute is like. And to be honest, I'm not sure about moving the birds. I might stay for them.'

'I've heard of staying for kids and schools, but for birds?'

He looked a little surprised. 'Well, I'm responsible for my birds and I love them, so how could I upset them?'

Lizzie wanted to kick herself. Of course she should know that, her being a pretend pigeon-lover and all. Talk about stupid, it was her that seemed to be letting her guard down. 'Yeah, of course,' she said as she waved her cigarette about. 'Right.'

'And I'd miss the lads in the club. Well, most of them. I had a row with Cid the other night.'

'Did you? I can't imagine you rowing with anyone.' And, funnily enough, it was true. He just didn't seem the type. But he must be. Obviously.

Joe nodded ruefully and told her what had happened. She was horrified that he had started to blame Cid for her actions. That hadn't been in the plan at all. He was supposed to think he was going a bit nuts. Or that he had Alzheimer's, like his poor mother. Not start alienating his friends in the club. Though maybe that would be good, too – to leave him friendless. But still, bad as she was, she had to defend poor Cid. Hurting the pigeons and Joe was one thing, but someone being blamed unfairly for what she'd done was something even she couldn't live with.

'I can't see Cid doing something like that,' she stammered out. 'Like, he's a pain, but I doubt he'd ever hurt a bird.'

Joe just shrugged and flicked some ash on the ground.

'Are you sure Prince didn't just get his leg caught somewhere, and in order to help him someone cut the tag off?'

'I dunno. Maybe.' He blew out a long stream of smoke. 'I'm just uneasy about it, that's all.' Then he said softly, 'The lofts keep opening, too.'

'You forget to lock them, more like,' she teased, hoping to plant the thought in his head.

'Naw,' he shook his head, 'I always . . .' He paused. Took another drag of his cigarette before stamping it out.

Lizzie decided to change the subject. It was making her pretty uneasy talking about it now.

'So,' she said as they crossed over O'Connell Bridge, 'how'd the reunion go with your parents?'

He rolled his eyes. 'Don't ask.'

'That good, huh?'

'Do you get on with your folks?' he asked by way of reply.

Lizzie shrugged. 'Yeah, most of the time. Why?'

'No reason, just prefer to talk about you than me.'

'What do you want to know?'

Joe faced her and smiled. 'Everything.'

There was something in the way he said it, as if he really wanted to know every little thing about her. Did he fancy her or something? Would it help her if he did? Could she feign interest in him? The questions bounced about one after the other, alarming her. What if he wanted to kiss her? What then?

'Like?' she gulped.

'Anything you want to tell me.'

So she told him about her family. Omitted Megan and changed Billy's name to Alan. Told him about Aileen being pregnant and how Alan had begged her to come back.

'So now there's a sort of a truce. She's moving back in and they're having a trial period. It's all a bit stressful. I wish I could move out but I can't because he wants me to think up romantic things he can do for her. Tonight he's buying her all the Wham stuff he can get his hands on.'

Joe laughed. 'Must be nice to have a brother or sister,' he mused. 'I'm an only kid. I always hated it, all that pressure to be perfect.'

'Oh, I'm sure you were perfect.'

'No. No, I wasn't,' he said. 'Or at least not in their eyes.'

'How come?'

Joe didn't answer. He pushed open the door of the restaurant for her, where they were shown to a table and handed a menu each. When they had chosen what they wanted, Lizzie returned to the subject of Joe's parents.

'So, how come?'

'How come what?' He looked puzzled.

'How come you disappointed your folks?' She was gratified to see him wince.

Joe took a gulp of wine and looked across the table at her. 'I want you to like me,' he smiled lightly, 'so let's not go there.'

'I do like you,' Lizzie forced the words out and took a gulp of wine herself, 'but you play everything very close to your chest. You're hard to know.'

Joe flicked an uneasy glance at her. He rubbed his hand hard

303

over his face, fiddled with the cutlery, unfolded the napkin and drank some more wine. Finally he took a deep breath and said haltingly, 'I haven't dared to get too close to anyone in the last couple of years because of stuff that happened to me.'

'What stuff?' Her heart began a slow hammering. Was he going to tell her or not? How would he explain it?

'I like you, Lizzie,' Joe went on, with a sincerity that unnerved her. 'I've cleaned my house more times in the past few months than in the last few years put together.'

'Charming,' she offered, trying to break the mood.

He didn't return the smile. 'And I don't want to hurt you so . . .' He paused. 'Well, what I'm trying to figure out is, is it worth telling you stuff about me?' He poured some more wine into his glass. Jesus, he was going to be pissed. Which was good.

'Do you feel we could . . .' He gulped. 'You know, ever be . . .' He looked at her, her big gorgeous eyes and shiny multi-coloured cap of hair and asked himself if he was bonkers. 'Naw, forget it. Forget it.'

'Hey.' With a huge effort of will, Lizzie took his hand gently off the wine glass and squeezed it in hers. Her stomach rolled. 'I like you, Joe, we have fun with the birds and stuff, don't we?'

'Yep.' He smiled bleakly. Not what he was looking for.

'So, if you want to tell me something, that's fine. It'll go no further.'

Oh God, she hoped he wouldn't want to kiss her. The thought made her feel queasy. But if she said she liked him, she might get behind the barriers he'd created and find out the truth.

'I like you.' She swallowed hard. 'A lot.'

Joe's heart trembled. She liked him. A lot. He liked the feel of her hand in his. He liked her, full stop. But would she want to know him when he told her? Could he face the scorn in her eyes if she didn't? Would it be a sign of things to come? Was it worth the risk?

'Please tell me,' she said.

Oh shit. Oh shit. 'Promise you'll listen until I'm finished explaining and you won't get scared?'

304

'Sounds bad.'

Joe dipped his head. 'It is.'

'I promise.' Once again she squeezed his hand. His fingers were entwined with hers. He had good hands. Fisherman's hands.

Just then the waiter came and placed their main courses on the table with a big flourish, expecting a smile at least. Neither of them took any notice.

'Thanks,' he sniffed, stalking off.

Joe waited a second before saying softly, 'Can we eat up and then I'll tell you everything?'

'Sure.' She hoped he wouldn't lose his nerve. 'But you'd better let go of my hand, so.'

'Oh yeah, sorry.' He laughed a little and slowly let go of her fingers.

He watched as she took up her fork and began spooning pasta into her mouth. He didn't think he'd be able to eat a bloody thing. Damn, why did he have to say he'd tell her? Could he not have asked her out like any normal bloke and then maybe when things were going well, tell her then? Why now? He supposed he was trying in a stupid way to be honourable. Letting Lizzie know what she might be in for if she went out with him. He hoped she would consider a relationship, but he doubted it. She wouldn't go out with a convicted murderer. He liked Lizzie a lot. In fact, he couldn't stop thinking about her. She was the first girl he'd let himself be interested in since coming out of prison. Everything he'd ever wanted in a girl, she had. It was almost as if she'd known him in another life. He wondered where he could tell her. Here or at home? But before he broached it, a gang of people coming in the door caught her attention and she suddenly paled.

'Shit!'

Joe looked around and noticed that a guy in the group was staring at Lizzie the way she was staring at him. Then the guy came over to the table. He was handsome in an odd way. Lots of unattractive features that somehow made him attractive. Very weird clothes.

'Hiya,' the man said and Joe knew by his tone of voice that there was some sort of history there.

'Hi, Tom,' Lizzie said in a clipped voice. 'I see you're out with your friends.'

'Yeah.' Tom turned to Joe. 'And I see you're out with your *friend*.' He stressed the 'friend'. He sounded slightly aggressive.

'Joe, this is Tom. Tom, Joe.'

Joe nodded at Tom, who ignored him.

'So, there was no one else, was there not?' Tom said, as he lounged by the table. He flicked hurt, angry brown eyes at Lizzie. 'You didn't waste any time, though, did you?'

'It's not like that,' Lizzie said. 'We're only having dinner.'

'Hey, Tommy! Tommy, get over here!' Imogen called. Then she saw Lizzie and her eyes widened. 'Oh, hi, Lizzie. How are you?'

'Good.'

Imogen tottered over and came to stand beside Tom. She linked his arm possessively in hers.

'We're just celebrating getting an extended run, aren't we, Tommy?'

'Yeah.' His voice sounded curiously flat. 'Did you like it?' he asked Lizzie. 'The play? I heard you came one night.'

'Yeah,' she nodded, trying to keep her voice from wobbling, 'it was great. You were both great in it.'

Tom nodded his thanks then said, 'I thought you'd join us for a drink after but maybe you had other stuff on.' A quick glance at Joe.

'Come on, Tommy, let's order.' Imogen gently pulled him away. 'Good to see you, Lizzie,' she said pleasantly.

'You too,' Lizzie called after them. She watched as they both took their seats across the other side of the restaurant. A couple of people, obviously from the cast, threw curious glances in her direction as Imogen no doubt filled them in on who they'd been talking to.

'Friend of yours?' Joe asked.

'Ex,' Lizzie said, and despite her best efforts she sounded upset.

'He's the guy who you broke up with just a while ago?'

'What?'

'You know, you told me—'

'Yeah,' Lizzie suddenly remembered, 'that's him. It's the first time we've seen each other since.' She paused. 'He's a very good actor, you know. He's the best in his play.' As she said it, she felt a huge tug of sadness inside.

'You still like him, don't you?' As he asked, Joe felt like a thick for thinking that he even stood half a chance with Lizzie.

To his relief, she shrugged. 'I'm over it.'

Her smile was a little too bright, he thought. A little too quick. But she heaped her fork with pasta and said teasingly, 'Come on, eat up, I want to hear your deep dark secret.'

His heart lurched.

He brought her into his living room. It was the nicest room in the house and the tidiest. He asked her if she wanted tea and she shook her head. He asked if she wanted a beer and she said no. He said that he needed a beer and pulled one from the fridge, snapped the tab and cursed as it fizzed all over his jeans.

After wiping himself down he rejoined Lizzie in the front room and was startled to see her flicking through his DVDs.

'My favourite films,' he remarked.

'I guessed,' she nodded, putting them back and turning to him. 'So?'

'So,' he said back lamely.

'Are you going to tell me?'

'Do you want to sit down first?'

'That bad, ey?'

'Worse.' He couldn't look at her.

'Well?'

She was sitting down, looking expectantly up at him. She didn't seem too worried and that worried him. A lot.

'Well, you won't like it and please don't be frightened. The door is open,' he gestured to the living room door, 'you can leave any time you like.'

Lizzie wasn't about to go anywhere, not until he told the whole story. Not until the truth came out. It seemed too good to be true, the whole thing within her grasp like this. She felt terrified and excited in a way she couldn't even begin to explain. She didn't want to hear the story and yet she needed it like she needed to breathe. The pasta sat like lead in her stomach.

'I'm not going anywhere,' she said, her voice barely a whisper.

Joe clenched his can as tight as he could in his hand. This was it. He was launching himself into the unknown.

'Well, the reason my parents don't talk to me and stuff is that I was in . . .' He paused, knowing that what he would say next would change everything. 'Prison,' he finished up.

'Prison,' she repeated, and he was encouraged by the fact that she remained sitting.

'For twelve years. Originally it was life but there was an early release thing and stuff . . .' His voice trailed off.

'Life?'

'Uh-huh.' Would she realise the sort of people who got life?

She didn't, obviously. Still she remained sitting. There was an eagerness and a fear on her face that he couldn't get his head around. And then she asked it. Like he knew she would.

'What did you do?'

He stared up at the ceiling, down at the floor, trying to think of a good way to put it. But of course there was no other way of saying it except just saying it straight out. It was as if he was in free fall and could do nothing about it.

'I got sent away for . . .' He winced, screwing up his eyes. 'For murder.'

Lizzie still didn't move. Just stared at him. Her face paled a tiny bit.

'I swear, Lizzie, on my life, that I didn't do it.'

'You didn't do it?' she said slowly. 'So why—'

'Wrong place, wrong time. I dunno.'

'What happened?'

She sounded suddenly hard, for some reason. Maybe it was finally hitting her just who she was in the room with. He bit his lip.

308

'You're not running off, that's good,' he said despondently, trying for lightness.

She didn't smile back so he said haltingly, 'A girl I knew was found washed up on a beach, wearing my jumper. She had a head injury and the last person she'd been with was me.'

That much was true, she knew that. Lizzie considered the best way to frame her next question but before she had, Joe continued, 'I liked this girl. A lot, actually.' He stopped and took a drink. 'She was involved with a friend of mine who had treated her badly and this night, the night she died, I met her. She was waiting on the pier just right where my dad's boat was berthed. I was there, attempting to drink myself stupid as my granddad had died and, well, I guess I missed him. A week or so before I'd rowed with this girl and made an eejet of myself. Anyway, I went to talk to her to see if she'd speak to me again and we get talking and she tells me that she's waiting for my friend to show up. He sent her a text and told her to wait there for him. So we talked but he never showed up. That got her all upset. She was in a terrible state over it. She was this madcap girl so, like, seeing her cry was kinda, well,' he shrugged, 'scary, I guess. Especially when you're only nineteen and haven't a clue about making people stop crying.'

Lizzie gulped hard to quell the tears that threatened. She didn't want to think of Meg crying.

Joe kept going with his story, unable to stop now he'd started. 'Anyway, I gave her a can and we had a drink but she didn't drink hers because she was really pissed. Anyway—'

'She was—' Lizzie stopped herself. Megan had not been pissed. That was a bloody lie. 'She was what?' she asked, trying to make out she hadn't heard properly.

'Pissed. Drunk,' Joe said. 'She asked me to bring her out on the boat. And I said no 'cause I'd been drinking, but she kept asking me and, well, I liked her and so . . .' He shrugged. 'And we went out and I wasn't so drunk that I couldn't drive the boat, Lizzie. She didn't fall overboard or anything. We went out and the night was calm and she was laughing a little and had stopped crying, then she said she felt a little sick and she got sick over the side of the boat. I joked a bit about her being sorry in the morning. Then she started to cry again and she kept asking me where she was and stuff, and I told her to lie down and she said that was a good idea as she had a headache. So I decide to bring the boat in and get her home. I was worried she'd pass out. But she went mad, saying she didn't want to go home. But I brought the boat in anyway and I get off and tell her that I'll walk her back. And she shouts at me to get lost and I tell her that I'm bringing her home. And I grab her hand and she walloped me across the face.'

Lizzie watched as he touched his cheekbone, rubbing the skin that had been bruised in the days after Megan went missing.

'So I grabbed her hand and pulled her,' Joe swallowed hard, his voice shaking slightly, 'I pulled her on to the pier to try to get her to walk with me. She's staggering all over the place and she starts hitting me. So I have to let her go.'

Megan's wrist had been bruised. He hadn't just pulled her. Lizzie could feel her hands tremble so she sat on them.

'I think I hurt her wrist,' Joe said then. 'I didn't mean to but I wanted to bring her home. She was really bad, Lizzie. Anything could have happened to her.'

Anything did happen to her. She had died. 'And?'

Lizzie's voice was oddly cold. Joe flinched. She sounded like the judge the day he'd been sentenced.

'And she went missing that night. She never got home. I last saw her walking away from me up the pier.' He sank into a chair opposite Lizzie. Talking about this made him feel sick. 'Next thing is she's missing and they want to trace her steps that night, so I go to tell them she was on my boat only someone else has already told them that and before I can get to the station, they're knocking on my door. My granddad's door, as I was living there at the time. Of course they see my face with the big bruise on it and it didn't look good. I tell them my story. It turns out no one comes forward to say that she was seen getting off my boat. No one. So I'm the chief suspect but without a body they can't prove anything.'

Joe swallowed hard and shot a glance across at Lizzie. She was staring at him intensely, her eyes wide.

310

'You OK?' he asked.

She nodded. 'Go on.' She couldn't keep the anger from her voice. It came out hard and flat. This was the same crap he'd told in court. She wanted to shout at him to confess but she knew she couldn't.

Joe didn't seem to notice. Haltingly, he continued, 'Well, she was found a couple of days later, washed up on a beach, wearing my jumper, with bruises on her wrist where I must have pulled her. Everything crashed for me then. My story didn't stand up. Tests showed she hadn't been drunk and that she'd been killed by a blow to the head. I'm suddenly up on a charge for something I never did.'

'Who do you think did it then, if you didn't?'

Joe flinched at the tone of Lizzie's voice. Shock probably made her sound harsh.

'I dunno. I just know it wasn't me. She was drunk, I don't care what anyone else says. She was sick and staggering and drunk. And worse than that, the guy she said she was there to meet swore that he never sent her a text. No text is found on his phone. And her phone is in the sea somewhere, so they think I'm trying to frame my friend. We'd argued about this girl before. My dad then told the court that he'd walked in on a fight between me and this girl a week or so before she was . . . was killed. So there I am, living the ultimate nightmare, with no way of proving I'm telling the truth.' He blinked back tears. He'd never get used to talking about it. Never. 'No one saw her after she got on my boat. No one. And I'd already been in trouble with the police for skippering a boat when drunk so, all in all, I wasn't exactly a dazzling example of a good citizen.' He shook his can. All gone. 'I would have convicted me,' he said hopelessly. Then he added, 'But I'm not a murderer, Lizzie.'

To his surprise, she stood up. 'Is that the truth?' she asked, and he thought that she seemed about to cry.

'Hey.' He stood up but she took a step back from him. He flinched.

'There is no point in telling me all this stuff if it's not the truth.'

311

'Yeah, it's the truth.' He didn't even sound convincing, but he was beyond that. No one had believed him in court so why should she? 'I don't go about beating women up, Lizzie.'

'Well then how would you explain it?'

The question was fired at him, half in anger, half tearfully.

'I can't,' he said without looking at her. 'I wish I could.'

'You said she said there was a text. Did you see the text?'

'No.'

'Did you see her drinking?'

'No, she never even finished the can I gave her. But she was well on.'

'So why did they find out she wasn't drunk?' God, Lizzie thought in anguish, would he just not admit it? She just needed to know and she was so close to finding out and he was still lying. If he only admitted it then maybe she could start to get over it. To release the huge anger inside her that was slowly eating her away.

'I don't know.' Joe looked up at her. 'Do you not think I ask myself a million times why that was? I do, Lizzie. Please believe me.'

But she didn't. He could see it in her eyes. Why had he told her anything?

'You must know more,' she said. 'How could she be drunk when she wasn't?'

He shrugged. 'You don't believe me, do you?'

There was a silence.

Lizzie stared up into his face and knew that was it. He wasn't going to admit it. She was wasting her time. Disappointment and frustration washed through her. She stood, wondering if there was anything she could say. Just a word to get a confession. The silence went on.

Joe hardly dared to move. Lizzie was shaking and staring up at him. He desperately wanted her to believe him. It would give him hope that he could maybe live again. Then, as he watched, she turned from him and picked her coat from the sofa.

'Lizzie—'

But she was gone.

The hurt he felt was like being stabbed.

Lizzie walked up the road in a fury, hoping he wouldn't come after her. She didn't know what she'd do if he did. Hit him, probably. Or scream at him. She had spent months being nice to this guy, only to be told the same crap he'd said in court. She remembered sitting in court the day he was found guilty and seeing the look in his eyes and wanting to kill him. She felt like that now. This whole getting to know him was suddenly pointless. Everything she'd done to date had achieved nothing. All the guilt she'd quashed had been for this? She wanted to cry. She was crying, she realised. She wanted to lash out. Her mind was disorientated and confused and not a place she recognised. A black hole that was pulling her in with more force the closer she got to it.

He needed to be hurt the way they had been hurt.

46

JOE WONDERED IF he should try to contact Lizzie, but it suddenly occurred to him that he had no phone number or address for her. For someone who'd been so free with information about herself, he suddenly realised he had no way of finding her again. Unless he met her on the Luas or at the club, of course.

He was finding it hard to concentrate on his work today, thoughts of what had happened the night before filled his head. Had he frightened her off? There was nothing he could do if he had. That was his story and he couldn't change it. He wondered if she'd tell anyone else. He didn't want everyone in the club knowing, that would be a nightmare. But Lizzie didn't seem the sort to do that.

'Hey, Joe,' a girl called Sharon called, 'look!'

She swam a couple of strokes before stopping.

His face broke into a delighted smile. 'Brilliant. That's great. That's how you do it.'

'It's not that hard.'

'Nope.'

Joe watched her again. Wading cautiously out from the bar and ducking her head under. Then she started to swim and move away from the safety of the side. It was always a bittersweet moment when they learned to swim, as you knew that they didn't need you any more.

She ditched work that afternoon, telling Mark that she had a pain. She didn't wait for the inquisition – instead she caught the tram back to Billy's.

Both him and Aileen were at work. Things between them seemed to be slowly improving. The Wham stuff had gone down well, with George and Andrew singing about being 'Bad Boys' well into the night. Billy was quiet, though, almost afraid to say anything that would make Aileen take off again. The easy relationship they'd shared would take a lot of rebuilding.

Lizzie let herself into the house and sat for a few minutes, thinking about what she was going to do. She wished she could be a fly on the wall when she saw Joe's face but, damn it, he'd had the chance to confess to her and he hadn't – and despite all her sabotage, his pigeons continued to thrive. His life continued to improve.

A part of her mind that she had ignored this past while sneaked through and whispered that it wasn't his birds' fault he had done what he'd done. Lizzie winced but managed to push the thought away and it dissolved instantly.

Taking deep breaths, she reflected that Billy had been so accurate in pinpointing the damage Joe had caused to them all. None of them had been left the same. Her relationship with Tom had always been terrifying because of its very happiness – that was Joe's doing and she hated him for it. Twelve years in jail only to have a great life afterwards was *not* a punishment, she thought in despair. He deserved to really be taught a lesson. He had taken away their precious thing. She would take away his. An eye for an eye and all that.

'Here,' Anto handed Joe a present. 'Dat's for you.'

Joe took it in surprise. 'This? Why?'

Anto shrugged. 'Me ma thought you might like it. I think it's to say thanks for letting me help out. She bought something for Ellen, too, only Ellen's box is bigger.'

Joe suppressed a grin. 'Right. Thanks.'

'Open it,' Anto said. 'I actually picked it. She wanted to get you a poncy box of chocolates but I didn't think that was a good idea.' He hopped from foot to foot as Joe unwrapped the book on pigeons. 'My dad swore by that book,' he said finally, as Joe

315

flicked through the pages. 'He said there wasn't a thing about birds that wasn't in there.'

Joe swallowed. No one had given him a present in ages. He looked at Anto.

'That's brilliant,' he grinned. 'Thanks.'

'No worries,' Anto nodded. Then, awkwardly, he muttered, 'And doing this with you . . . it's stopped me being, you know, sad and shit.'

Joe nodded. The pigeons had saved him, too, he reckoned. 'Know what you mean,' he said. He handed Anto a bucket. 'Now for the fun part, let's clean them out.'

And though he had meant it as a joke, he knew that Anto did find it fun.

The following Thursday was the night she had decided to do it.

It's what she should have done at the start, only in the beginning part of her had been repelled by the idea of revenge. Looking back, it was probably why she had tried to get friendly with him, in the hope that he'd hang himself by confessing. But that hadn't worked. Doing things bit by bit, though, had made her decision easier. Like wading into cold water and getting used to the temperature. She'd numbed herself to the implications now and could stride all the way in.

She had decided that she would skip counselling that night – Anna would manage on her own, she was sure of that. Now that she had made her decision, the hard part was over. Succumbing to the temptation had been a relief. She was finally stepping into the abyss and she knew it was as far as she could go. That there was nothing else she could do or, a part of her mind whispered, no lower she could fall. His failure to confess would cost him.

At the thought of what she was about to do, she wasn't scared. Or happy. Or sad. There was just an overriding instinct to even things out.

47

'I'M GOING FOR a hospital appointment today.' Aileen tossed the comment at Billy as he was heading to work.

Billy froze in the act of opening the door. He half turned. 'Yeah?'

'Yeah.' Aileen spooned some flakes into her mouth.

Lizzie, who had just arrived down, prayed that he would say the right thing. Billy seemed to be trying to second guess Aileen all the time these days.

'Well, eh,' he smiled a little too brightly, 'what time?'

'One.' She wasn't looking at him any more and had turned her attention to a magazine.

'Eh,' Billy made a production of zipping up his jacket, 'd'you need any company, like?'

'Company?' She shot him a look.

'As in, can I go in with you?'

Aileen shrugged. 'I suppose. If you want.'

'I'd love to, actually.'

There was a pause. Aileen slowly brought her face up from her magazine.

'Good.' She smiled a little hesitantly.

'Will they do a scan, d'you think?' Billy asked shyly.

'I'd imagine so.'

'Great. Good.' He nodded a 'good morning' at Lizzie. 'See you at one, so.'

'Bye.'

Lizzie, who had been watching the exchange with some trepidation, felt that finally they were going to make it. She vowed to ring Billy up later to tell him to bring Aileen out somewhere nice afterwards.

She only felt a little guilty that it would suit her, too.

Joe hadn't slept since he'd told Lizzie. His dreams consisted of his mother crying and Megan calling for help and no matter how he tried, he couldn't help either of them and because he couldn't, Lizzie walked away and, by trying to catch hold of her, the other two women started to drown. He awoke at the point where Lizzie walked out of his house, slamming the door behind her.

He dragged himself from bed and, as he showered, he pondered whether to wait for Lizzie that night, as he'd recently started to do, or whether he should just avoid her. She hadn't contacted him at all, which could be a good sign or a bad sign. On one hand she didn't say that she wanted nothing to do with him, but on the other, by not contacting him, maybe it meant she wanted him out of her life completely. He wished he'd never met her, but it was too late now. She'd shown him normality for the first time in years, given him hope for a future.

To hell with it, he decided, he'd wait for her. And if she didn't want to talk to him, well, fine. At least he'd know.

Lizzie rang Anna at around five.

'Hey, could you manage without me tonight? I'm feeling sick.'

Anna's sympathetic reaction made her feel like a heel.

'Of course I can, what's the matter?'

'Just some kind of a bug,' Lizzie mumbled. 'I haven't been well all day so I'm going home early. Do you want me to see if I can get a stand-in?'

'No. You go home and get to bed, I'll manage.'

'Thanks, Anna, I owe you.'

She put the phone down and knew that she couldn't turn back now.

Eleven-ten. Joe left work early. Paperwork could wait, he decided. He was determined to see Lizzie, to have another go at explaining it to her. So, rather than waiting in Grafton Street as he normally did, he took up a position outside the Life offices. He would beg her to listen if necessary and, if that didn't work, he'd concede defeat. At least he'd have tried.

He glanced at his watch. Eleven-fifteen. She'd be out in quarter of an hour.

There was an older woman waiting by the building, too. She seemed as edgy as he was. Then she seemed edgy because it was just her and him. Joe smiled a little at her.

'It's OK,' he tried to reassure her, 'I'm harmless.'

The irony of him saying it almost made him laugh.

'I'm just waiting on my daughter,' the woman confided, sounding relieved. She thumbed to the LIFE sign. 'She works the night shift here on a Thursday.'

Joe winced. 'It's not Lizzie, is it?'

'No, her name is Anna. I've heard her speak of a Lizzie, though. They seem to be good friends.'

Joe shrugged, he didn't know. It struck him as slightly odd that Lizzie had never mentioned any friends.

'Are you waiting on Lizzie? Is she your girlfriend?' the woman asked. Now that she'd established that he wasn't out to mug her, she seemed eager to talk. Though it was in a nervy, babbling way.

'She's not my girlfriend,' Joe said, 'just a mate. I think she's angry at me so don't be surprised if she ignores me when she comes out.' He felt he had to say that, it'd save embarrassment if that's what happened.

To his surprise the woman laughed. 'Oh, a right pair they'll be, counselling tonight. I haven't talked to Anna in about eight weeks. I'm here to grovel and make peace. Kids, they don't know all you're doing is your best, even though you make a right mess of things sometimes.'

Joe smiled weakly.

Lizzie parked Billy's car two doors down from Joe's house. She would rather have waited until later but, with Aileen back home, there was no chance she could sneak out in the early hours without being heard.

Aileen was finding it hard to sleep with two babies growing inside her and Lizzie had been given a blow by blow on the various sleeping positions that hadn't worked for her. She'd also been given a blow-by-blow account by a newly-infatuated father on the state of Aileen's rapidly expanding uterus. The scan had been a roaring success and the two were now out having a meal before coming home. The newfound harmony only pointed up the frozen iciness in her own head.

Very gently she took her basket from the back seat of the car. This basket had come in handy, she thought objectively. She lifted it out and closed the car door as quietly as she could. A few people walked by but they didn't even glance in her direction. Joe's house was in darkness, as was his nosy neighbour's. Lizzie walked as confidently as she could up the street and stood opposite the two houses.

No one.

She swiftly crossed the street and, still scanning left and right, she walked into Joe's garden.

Nothing.

She slunk into the shadow at the side of his house, took some oil from her pocket and hastily lubricated the hinges on his side gate. Very gently she unlatched it and stepped into the darkness of the back garden.

A tall girl came out of Lizzie's building and she stopped dead at the sight of the woman Joe had been talking to. Joe watched a little awkwardly as they stared at each other.

'Hi, love.'

'Mammy.'

'I decided to come tonight in person to say that I've been wrong, but it was only because I loved you, darling. And because he hurt you so much.'

Joe shifted uncomfortably and moved a step away, scanning the door behind Anna as someone else slipped in. No one seemed to be exiting, though.

Anna was now hugging her mother and her mother was hugging her back. It all seemed terribly emotional and Joe had to turn away. Then he coughed slightly to remind them he was there so that they wouldn't say any more.

'Oh,' the woman said to Anna, 'this man here is looking for Lizzie.'

'Hi,' Joe said in as friendly a voice as he could, 'is she ready yet?'

Anna frowned. 'She's not on tonight.'

Joe felt his heart plummet. 'Is she not? I thought she always worked Thursdays.'

'Yeah, but she called in sick.'

He didn't even have the stomach to reply. Well, that was it then, he thought. His answer.

'Can I say who was looking for her?'

'Naw, it's OK. Thanks.'

'You sure?' Anna smiled at him, her arm still about her mother's waist.

'Yep.' His smile wasn't convincing so he turned away as quickly as he could.

He wished he'd never met Lizzie.

Again, like the first time she'd stolen into the loft, Lizzie waited to feel something. If guilt had hit her, she might have backed down. But there was nothing. As usual. Not even triumph that she was about to destroy Joe. There was just a hardness that was impossible for any emotion to break through.

She wondered if that's the way Joe had felt when he'd done what he'd done.

48

H E WAS HAVING the same dream again, only this time there
was more noise than just the slamming of a door. Someone
was screeching and wailing and then, suddenly, the screeching
became his pigeons. And his pigeons were flying around and Joe
was trying to catch them. Prince's leg had come right off.

'NO!' Joe shouted, waking himself up.

Outside, the noise of his dream continued. It was early morning;
dawn light was splashed across his bed. He very rarely drew the
curtains at night, preferring to look out at the sky. He rubbed his
eyes, sleep ebbing away, fragments of his nightmare scattering
until it registered in his still half dazed mind that the sounds he
was hearing were coming from his garden. His loft.

Jesus.

He flung off his covers, his feet getting tangled up in the sheet.
He fell out of bed, banging his head on the wooden floor. The
pain didn't even register. Taking the stairs two at a time, he raced
into the kitchen and, with clumsy hands, unlocked his back door
before running barefoot across the lawn to his loft.

Oh, Christ.

He froze for half a second before unlocking the loft door and
wrenching it open. He grabbed the shrieking cat by the scruff of
the neck and flung it out into his garden. It arched its back and
hissed before taking off over the wall.

Joe stood inside the door of his loft and swayed slightly before
grabbing on to the door frame. He couldn't take in how many
of his racers lay blood-soaked on the floor. How many of his
birds lay unharmed but shocked and shivering around the loft.

How many were dead already. The place was awash with blood and feathers.

Joe blinked. Once. Twice. He pinched himself, dazed, convinced he was dreaming. He turned around and vomited into the garden.

He blanked his mind to how it could have happened – he'd deal with that later. Instead he called the vet and, as he waited for him to arrive, he placed the injured birds gently into a basket and brought them indoors to keep them warm. He did the same with the birds he considered to be shell-shocked, talking softly to them all the time, letting them pick bits of grain and corn from his hands. Birds that were all right he placed into their boxes and left them there. And then he turned to survey the real carnage. Hero was dead. His one hope to replace Prince as a good racer. His body lay right at the front of the loft. His head had been torn from his little body. Nine other birds were dead, too. Some from shock, some from the cat. Over half his loft. Gone.

Joe dumped their bodies into a black sack that he'd got from the kitchen. As each corpse went in, he felt his heart twist. He'd spent years building up his loft and now the ground had been ripped from under his feet. How the hell had it happened? He was sure he'd locked up last night. And how had the cat got in? There was no way for a cat to sneak in. He felt numb inside, it was too big for him to take in just now. He had to concentrate on getting it back to normal.

The vet arrived within half an hour and Joe brought him into the house.

He groaned at the damage. 'When did the cat get in?' he asked, peering around at the shivering birds.

'Dunno,' Joe said dully. He watched the vet handle one of the birds. He gently pulled out a ragged wing.

'Broken.' He looked at Joe.

Joe winced.

'A cat wouldn't attack unless there was some movement, so it must have only begun once the birds started fluttering about.'

'Once there is light at all, they'll start to stir,' Joe said.

'Well, you've been lucky. It could have been worse. It was so early when you caught him.'

Lucky. Joe didn't feel lucky.

Another bird. Another broken wing. Joe could have told the vet that, only he hadn't the heart to go examining them himself.

'How did the cat get in?'

'Dunno. The loft was locked when I got to it.'

The vet raised his eyebrows. 'D'you think someone put it there?'

'I can't think of anything else,' Joe said.

'You should report it to the police.'

Joe flinched. He never wanted to get involved with the cops again. 'I might,' he said.

The vet handed Joe some sedatives for the birds. 'It'll calm them down.'

'Thanks.'

'Bloody brutal thing to do,' the vet said sympathetically.

Joe nodded and watched him leave.

Lizzie got up and showered. She knew she was going to be late for work, but she didn't want to run into Billy and Aileen. She couldn't relate to them. To the fact that while their lives were going on, hers seemed to have stopped. Their budding happiness was pulling them further and further away from her. What she had done last night, if she thought about it, was completely inhuman. Cruel. Disgusting. It marked her as different from everyone else, put her in a different place from everyone else. She wasn't going to think about it. It was easier to cope that way. In fact, in the past few months, Lizzie realised with a little jolt, she had stopped thinking about anything she had done – good and bad. If she was off guard and happy, she found that the horrible stuff seeped in like a bad smell under a door, poisoning the air. It was easier not to think, just to keep going. But it was hard trying to get through the day when inside she felt like a stranger to herself. Today, she knew it would be harder still. She let the water cascade over her for ages and scrubbed herself hard, hurting herself a little in the process, making her arms and legs bright red.

She was about an hour late for work.

She found she didn't really care that much.

John came round after Joe had rung him. He took one look at Joe's devastated face and made him sit down.

'You stay there, right? I'm going to clean the place up for you.'

'Naw, let me help, OK?'

John eyed him. 'If you're up to it. I know I'd never be able to face it if it was my loft.'

Joe didn't say anything else, but he watched John searching around for cleaning agents and straw and then, when he'd got everything, Joe stood up and walked outside with him. Together they stared on the horrible job of washing down the loft.

John took up the hopper. 'Hey, your malt is wet,' he exclaimed. 'You'd want to watch that, Joe.'

'Wet?' Joe examined it. Then shrugged hopelessly. 'The lofts are as dry as a bone, John.' He gulped. 'That always seems to be happening. I dunno, I think I'm going mad.'

'Either that or someone is out to get you.'

Joe shivered.

John looked at him questioningly. 'Have you done anything to anyone? You know, made any enemies?'

'Cid?'

John waved him away. 'Come on, Joe, you don't really believe that.'

'I don't know what to believe.'

He watched as John began to scrape feathers from the floor. Hero's feathers. Joe crouched down and picked one up and held it to his face. John leaned on the brush, watching him.

'You sure you haven't annoyed someone?'

Even in prison he hadn't offended anyone, Joe thought. He'd kept his head down, served his sentence and left. He looked at John, wondering if he should tell him. John was watching him, willing him to remember some little detail. Joe swallowed hard. Taking his silence as a negative, John started his sweeping again.

'I was in prison, John,' Joe blurted out.

John turned to face him. His expression was more curious than shocked. That'd soon change, Joe thought dismally. He barely cared. Right at that moment he felt as if everything had been taken away from him and it was only a matter of time before the rest was, too.

He stood up and faced his friend. 'I got convicted of murder.'

Now John's expression turned to incredulity.

'You?' he said.

Joe nodded.

'Self-defence?'

'Nope.' Joe shoved his hands in his pockets and sighed. 'I don't suppose you'll believe me, but I was innocent. They said I killed a girl.'

'You?' John said again. His face was unreadable.

'Me.'

The silence went on for ages. Joe wondered if John would walk out, the way Lizzie had done. He winced, trying not to think of her.

'You couldn't kill anyone,' John pronounced. 'Look at you now – your birds die and you're in bits.'

Joe couldn't speak for a second. There was a big lump in his throat.

'Thanks for saying that,' he gulped out.

'What happened, Joe?'

So Joe told him. Standing in his blood-soaked loft, he told him everything. When he finished, John stood staring at him.

'You poor fucker,' he said slowly. 'If I was you, I'd go and find out who did it. I'd make it my mission in life.'

Joe smiled glumly. 'I thought of that, too, once,' he said, 'but then, well, I figure that I'd only be wasting the rest of my life letting it dominate everything. I just wanted peace. The pigeons make me happy, so that's what I did.'

John nodded.

'And now—' Joe indicated the loft, his voice catching.

'We'll sort it out,' John promised. 'Honest.'

Joe swallowed hard. His best bird. Gone.

'Is it someone from prison, d'you think?'

'I dunno.'

'Who has been in here lately?'

'Just Anto and Lizzie.' He winced saying her name. 'Anto did say he'd check the loft for me last night, so I'll talk to him later.'

'And Lizzie?'

'Haven't seen her in a few days.'

'Oh.'

'I told her about – well, what I just told you.'

'And she didn't like it?'

Joe shrugged. 'I don't think she believed me. She hasn't rung or anything.'

John said nothing, just slapped him on the shoulder and got back to work.

'You're late,' Mark said as she arrived in. 'I'll have to dock your pay.'

Lizzie wasn't in the humour for him.

'Lizzie, I'd like to think we're mates '

'Well, we're not.'

It was the first time Mark recoiled from her. Then, as usual, he regained his composure. 'Well, regardless of what you think, I want you to know that coming to work late and leaving early is not acceptable.'

Lizzie kept her head down, pretending to examine her desk. She knew that it wasn't on. And she knew he was only saying it to her because he was annoyed.

'Now, I can accept it if you tell me why you're so damned weird these days.'

Lizzie glanced up at him. 'Takes one to know one.'

There was a silence.

'Is it Tom?'

'I am not going out with Tom any more.'

'Good. At least you're not in denial. I was in denial after my wife left me and—'

'Mark, I don't need to hear about you and your wife. Now,

there are three hundred and fifty people signed on for the para-chute jump. We need fifty more, which we will probably get, and—'

'I don't give a damn about the bloody jump,' Mark said edgily. 'What is wrong with you, Lizzie?'

'Nothing.' She knew she had snapped but she didn't apologise.

'Well,' Mark said, in a voice mixed with hurt and anger, 'if there is nothing wrong, then please be on time for work. Right?'

'Right.'

Mark seemed to wait for her to say more and when she didn't he left the office, banging the door behind him.

Lizzie flicked on her computer and her eye fell on a note in her inbox.

Lizzie – fab guy waiting outside for you last night!!! Who is he? Guys like that should NEVER be stood up! Also, Lori rang again. Wouldn't talk to me, says she wants you to talk to her. Wouldn't give me her number so I guess you'll be hearing from her soon.

And my mother turned up outside last night, too. She said she reckoned she had to do something totally unexpected to show me how much she cares and standing about in that lane at eleven at night was a bit of madness. She thought your hunk was out to rob her at some stage! Anyway, all good again.

Hope you're feeling better. Love, Anna.

Lizzie typed in a *Gld u will soon hve ur bbysttr back* and pressed 'send.' She didn't bother telling her who the guy was.

John stayed with Joe all day, sending out for lunch in the midst of cleaning up. Anto arrived after school and, jumping over the wall, he stopped dead at the sight of John.

'Cat got into the loft last night,' John said, carefully observing Anto's face for a reaction.

'No way!' Anto said in disbelief, striding toward the loft, 'Was there much damage?'

'Twelve birds so far,' Joe muttered.

'Twelve!' Anto looked as devastated as Joe. 'Dead?' At Joe's nod, he asked, 'How'd that happen?'

'Dunno,' Joe said. 'What time did you check them last night?'

'Nine-thirty, just before me ma collected me.'

'And did you notice anything? Was the loft open?'

'No, the loft was not open,' Anto said, as if Joe was a moron. 'D'ya think I'm stupid?'

'No,' Joe tried to reassure him, 'but, I dunno, maybe a cat sneaked in and you didn't see.'

'There was no cat in there when I checked.' He sounded hurt. 'D'you think it was me?'

'No, but just say —'

'You do,' Anto said. 'You do think it was me. Maybe it was you, maybe the cat sneaked in when you checked them after you came home from work.'

'I didn't check them,' Joe said dully. Normally he would have but last night he hadn't. The non appearance of Lizzie had upset him. And anyway, if a cat was quiet he mightn't have spotted it. 'So you were the last person to be in the loft.'

'I didn't let a cat in!' Anto shouted, his face red.

'I'm not saying you did—' Joe tried to say.

'The malt was wet, too,' John volunteered.

Anto looked from one to the other. His eyes rested on Joe.

'I thought you trusted me,' he said. 'You can keep your stupid birds.' Then he hopped back over the wall.

'Aw, Anto—'

But Anto was gone, back over the wall and into Ellen's. Joe groaned, he knew it was only a matter of time before she appeared to question him.

'You believe him?' John asked.

Joe nodded. 'Yeah. I'll talk to him later. If he said he checked . . .'

'Come on,' John said then, 'let's keep going.'

329

They worked on in silence for another while, before John asked quietly, 'How did you cope in prison, Joe?'

'Huh?' The question came out of the blue.

'In prison. How did you cope?'

Joe shrugged as he checked the walls for draughts. 'Just did. Told myself it'd be over one day and that when I got out I could do anything I wanted.'

'Fair play.'

Joe, despite himself, laughed. 'Eh – lots of people wouldn't agree with you.'

'Your life flipped and you dealt with it. That's great.'

'I had no choice.'

'You did, you could have cracked up.' John indicated his leg. 'See this?'

Joe nodded.

'I got that in a car crash when I was eighteen. Before that, I'd had dreams of playing professional football. In two seconds flat that disappeared. I had a new life without sport and a wife who kindly married me out of pity, then she realised her mistake and fecked off with my best friend.'

'No way. I thought she left because of the pigeons.'

'Nope. And I still hate her.' He grinned and rolled his eyes. 'I also had no job and a lot of time to drink. I was a mess. It took me ten years to figure out what you learned in prison. And even then, it was hard. You,' he nodded, 'did well, Joe.'

'I hang around with a bunch of old men – no offence, John – I steer clear of relationships, I have no contact with my folks . . .' He grinned a little. 'I'm doing great.'

'And you can smile about it,' John said firmly. 'You're doing better than great.'

Joe had never looked at it like that before.

49

'I'M SORRY. I thought I could but I can't.'

Mr Walsh shook his head firmly and crossed his arms as Lizzie looked at him in alarm.

'But Dad, Billy can't come as Aileen's dad has invited them over and you – you just decide not to come.'

'I didn't just decide,' her dad said, eyeballing her, 'I have been thinking of nothing else all week.'

'But why did you come up here if you'd already decided not to visit her?'

'First,' her father sighed, 'I'm finding it lonely without her at home. And second, I thought I could go through with it and I can't.' He sat back down at the kitchen table and looked up at Lizzie. 'I am sorry, Lizzie, but it's just seeing her in that place, surrounded by all those people, I just can't seem to handle it.'

'Yeah, I know it's horrible, Dad, but she really needs to see you, to keep her spirits up.'

'I don't want to keep her spirits up,' her father retorted. 'I want her home with me and if the only way to do that is to stay away, then I will. Keep her spirits up,' he snorted. 'That woman is breaking my heart.'

'Dad, please?'

'I can't, Lizzie. It's not good for either of us.'

'Please, Dad, I can't go on my own.' And she couldn't, she realised. Her mother being in jail was worse than she thought it would be. 'Please? Just today?'

Mr Walsh flinched. He didn't like to see Lizzie upset like this. He wondered what else was bothering her, she didn't seem to be as bubbly as usual. It was probably that actor fella she'd broken up with, he'd never liked him. Though at the time he couldn't help thinking how well suited he and Lizzie were, both of them with their weird dress sense, both of them loving that ridiculous film *Amelie* which he couldn't make head nor tail of. Both of them cheating at cards the only time Tom had come to visit. Really, the man was a bad influence on his daughter.

'Please, Dad? For me?'

He sighed deeply and, placing his hands on his knees, he hauled himself from the chair.

'Just today,' he warned. 'And I'll tell her that, too.'

Great, Lizzie thought glumly.

Her mother was sitting just inside the door, in the same place she'd been in the last couple of times they visited.

'Hi, Mammy.' Lizzie sat down. Her dad prowled behind her.

'Why don't you sit?' Mrs Walsh said to her husband, with a slight edge of irritation in her voice. 'There is a chair over there.' She pointed to the opposite wall.

'I'd prefer to stand, thanks.'

'Suit yourself.' She sniffed.

'Like you do, you mean.'

'And what is that supposed to mean?'

Mr Walsh leaned across the table to his wife and said in a cross voice, 'Will you ever go and apologise? You're making a holy show of yourself.'

'I am not! How dare you!'

'You are. What do you hope to achieve, ey? All this,' he waved expansively about the room, 'all this anger, what is it going to achieve?'

'It'll highlight the harbour plan.'

'Bollocks!'

Whether it was the fact that her dad shouted or the fact that for the first time in his life he cursed, Lizzie wasn't sure, but it shocked her.

'That is total rubbish,' he said.

'Everything OK?' a prison guard called over.

'OK, aside from the fact that my husband seems to be having some sort of a mental breakdown,' Polly said sarcastically.

'Well, we'll be company for each other then, won't we?'

The guard issued a gentle warning for them to keep it down.

'When did you become so angry?' Mr Walsh asked, his voice a mixture of sadness and defeat. 'I hardly know you any more, Polly.'

With that he straightened himself up and walked out of the room.

'Oh, that's charming.' Mrs Walsh shook her head as he left. 'Charming.' She turned to Lizzie. 'Well, I hope you'll do better than that.'

When *had* her mother got so angry? Lizzie wondered. It had been a sort of gradual thing. She'd been a worrier, a fretter, a comforter. But she never used to have that slash between her eyebrows and that permanent downturn to her mouth. The council could have built the Empire State building in her back garden and she probably wouldn't have gone to jail for it. But now it was like she was fighting the whole world.

'It's since Meg, isn't it?' Lizzie said, her voice catching at the mention of her sister's name.

'What?'

'You've been angry since Meg.'

'What are you talking about?'

'Mam,' Lizzie lowered her voice, tried to sound soothing the way you would counselling someone, 'Dad said he wasn't coming to see you any more. It upsets him to see you in here. Does that bother you?'

'Spineless. It bothers him because he hadn't the guts to join me.'

Her mother was completely delusional. 'No,' Lizzie shook her head, 'it bothers him because he sees his wife ruining her life. He sees his wife sitting in jail because she's angry at the whole world.'

Her mother had opened her mouth to protest but shut it again and glared balefully at her daughter.

333

'You can't change the fact that Megan isn't coming back by being angry,' Lizzie said gently.

'I can change the world that let her die,' Mrs Walsh said bitterly. 'I can make it better. I can—'

'You can't. You can't, Mam. You have to take what's left for you. Make the best of it. You've got Dad and me and Billy and we love you and want you home.'

Her mother said nothing, just curved her face away slightly.

'Please say sorry, Mammy.'

'I want to ask you to do something for me,' Mrs Walsh said instead, startling her.

'Mammy, are you listening?'

'Yes. But I need a favour.'

Lizzie sighed. 'What?'

'I want you to trace this mobile phone number.' She recited a number.

Lizzie looked blankly at her.

'Will you put it in your phone?' she snapped as Lizzie looked puzzled. 'They won't let me hand you anything.'

Lizzie took out her phone and keyed the number in.

'Is this to do with the harbour?'

'Just trace it, I'll tell you why later. I'll ring you during the week, OK?'

'Do you know how mad you sound?'

'Are you going to do this or not?'

'I will if you apologise.'

Her mother glared at her.

'Just say sorry, Mammy. That's all you have to do.' Lizzie leaned in towards her, 'You can't change anything by getting angry. It won't bring her back, you know.' And then her own words hit her. She paused with her mouth open and sank back down on to the seat, staring at her mother. She felt suddenly sick.

'Lizzie, do you know how mad you look?' her mother asked, quirking an eyebrow.

The rest of the visit went by in a blur.

When it ended and her mother had called after her again to

334

trace that number, Lizzie bolted right past her dad's car and told him that she didn't need a lift, that she needed a smoke. That she needed to think.

'A smoke? As in a cigarette?'

'Yes, Dad. I smoke. It's not the worst thing in the world.'

'Can I have one?'

Without saying a word, she handed him one. He stood beside her, smoking. Inhaling and exhaling with her until she'd calmed down.

'What happened?' he asked eventually.

She didn't answer and he didn't ask again. She wasn't even sure she knew herself.

Instead he wrapped an arm about her shoulder and led her back to the car.

It was true what she'd said to her mother: nothing could be changed by anger. Megan could never come back no matter how many roads or planning permissions her mother blocked. She'd never come back if Lizzie killed a million pigeons. She'd never come back if her mother never said sorry. She'd never come back if Lizzie never said sorry. Megan could never be avenged because there was nothing to replace her. Dead birds and altered roads were no substitute. They only fed the anger inside. Made it worse.

And her rage had grown the longer she'd been with Joe. And it hadn't changed anything except the way she felt about herself. Which wasn't good. What she had done was—. Lizzie couldn't even put a name on it. It danced before her, let out of the box in which she'd carefully stowed it away. 'Horrible' wasn't the right word. 'Justified' didn't seem to fit. What she had done was wrong, she realised. Wrong for her. Wrong because she'd managed to alter who she was. And wrong because it would never be right.

Her head was flooded with it. With the wrongness of it. By looking at the futility of her mother's battle, she had suddenly seen the senselessness of her own.

Lizzie pulled her duvet up around her shoulders and tried to get warm. It was as if in the past few months, she'd been on a drug. A drug that at first had made her feel sick but that eventually she'd become immune to. A drug that made her feel a false happiness and importance. A drug that had numbed her. But now she was cold turkey and she could see what it had done to her and she was sick. Too sick to cry. Too sick to think properly.

She picked up her mobile phone and dialled a number.

50

ANNA HAD HUGGED her and listened to her and made her cups of coffee. She'd told her that what she had done was understandable, horrible but totally understandable, which had given her a huge sense of release. But still, Lizzie knew what she had to do if she was to feel any better about herself. It didn't mean it was going to be easy – in fact, it was probably going to be the hardest thing she'd ever done. Well, the hardest apart from that first step she'd taken months ago, on to the road she was now determined to get off.

She had to apologise, or at least own up to what she'd done.

In person.

To a guy she detested.

He'd never apologised to her family, so at least in doing this she'd know she wasn't like him.

Joe normally spent Sundays at home so she hoped he'd be there when she arrived. Lizzie told Billy that she was going shopping and instead caught the Luas to Ranelagh. As it pulled into the station her legs were shaking so much she could hardly get off. She made herself take deep breaths before she began the ten-minute walk to Joe's home. It passed in a blur. She paused, two doors up from his house, and saw that his battered car was parked alongside the kerb. He was in.

Maybe if she just stopped, if she just disappeared and didn't bother him again, would that do? The thought flitted through her head and she quashed it. How would she live with herself? She'd be just like him then, not owning up to her misdeeds. Refusing to apologise for what she'd done. No, she was better than that, she decided. She was going to start over once the apology was done. Push it all away and start over.

With a thudding heart and clammy hands, her heavy black boots clunked up his driveway. She pressed the bell on the door and suddenly an odd calmness overcame her. She took more deep breaths. This was it. This. Was. It.

Her calm began to fray slightly when she heard noise from inside the house and saw Joe's tall silhouette through the glass. He pulled open the door and the smile he gave her made her feel worse than she already felt, if that was possible. It also made her resent him more, which she knew was impossible.

'Hey,' he said hesitantly, his large hazel eyes looking her up and down, 'thought I'd never see you again.'

She shrugged, her mouth suddenly dry.

His face fell when she didn't return his grin. He pulled the door wider and asked softly, 'D'you want to come in?'

Lizzie shook her head. She wondered if she'd be able to actually talk when the time came.

'Oh,' Joe nodded glumly, 'it's like that, ey?' He paused, his hand still on the door. It took a second before he spoke and then it was in a resigned sort of voice: 'Don't feel bad about it, I know I wouldn't be anyone's idea of a perfect partner.' He managed a rueful smile. 'But I didn't kill anyone, I swear.'

'That's not why I'm here,' she croaked out.

Joe looked startled. 'Have you had a cold?'

She shook her head. Her heart had started to pump so fast she was beginning to feel that she couldn't breathe. 'It's, it's about the . . . the birds.'

His eyes clouded. 'You heard, then,' he said flatly.

'Heard?'

'About the cat in the loft?'

'Eh—'

'Bastard got fourteen of my birds in the end.' He swallowed and looked away.

'Fourteen?' Lizzie winced. But surely—. 'I thought you checked the loft before you went to bed?'

338

'Not that night.' He pinned her with his gaze. 'I waited for you outside work and when you didn't show,' he shrugged, 'I forgot about the birds.'

Lizzie felt her stomach heave. Oh God. He'd go mad with her.

'Hey, are you OK? Come in.' Joe reached to touch her and she sprang back.

'No!'

He pulled his hand away as if he'd been burned. 'Sorry.'

She thought about running then. Just legging it up the road and out of his life. But she forced herself to stay still. She was here and she had to do this. Had to be better than him.

'It was me,' she blurted out.

'Huh?' he looked at her, uncomprehending.

'I— I put the cat in the loft.'

Joe looked as if he didn't understand. 'What?'

'I did it.' Lizzie gained courage from the admission. 'I did it.' As she watched the disbelief etch itself across his face, she went on, 'And I did everything else, too. I diluted their medicine, I put in the wild pigeon, and I took Prince.'

'What?' His brow was wrinkled. He seemed stunned, as if he'd been hit on the head or something.

'It was all me,' Lizzie said, not able to help the slight edge of malice that crept into her voice.

Joe looked at the pretty girl in front of him. Her vibrant scarf wrapped snugly about her neck even though it was heading into summer. Her long coat that he thought was cool on her. Her flyaway hair that he longed to run his hands through, if only she'd let him. He blinked, dazed. 'I don't understand,' he said. And he didn't. It was as if he'd been plunged into a surreal conversation.

'It was me.' She said the words slowly as if he was stupid. 'I did it. And, well, I just came to say that I won't be doing it any more.' She shrugged, her voice dipped. 'I'm sorry.'

She didn't sound that sorry, Joe thought. It just didn't make sense. Her? Lizzie? 'You took Prince?'

A nod.

'And, and, the cat—'

'Me.'

He knew he should be angry. He should shout, but he couldn't understand. Instead he just said, 'Why? Why would you do that?'

Lizzie seemed to take her time answering. Instead she searched his face as if she couldn't believe he wouldn't know. In the end she half whispered, 'Can't you guess?'

Guess? He shook his head.

How could it not dominate his every waking thought, the way it did hers? Lizzie thought angrily. How could he not guess?

'My name is Elizabeth Walsh.' Pause. 'I come from Rossclare.' Her voice rang clear and she stared him in the eye.

All the colour drained from his face. 'Walsh,' he repeated. And he suddenly knew. He'd known when he'd seen her first, only she'd disarmed him, so that he hadn't let the thought register.

'Megan's sister.' She felt her heart constrict again with the hate. And it was hate. 'That's why I did it.'

'Christ,' was all he could say. He flinched back from the look she gave him.

'How *dare* you have a good life?' she went on, her voice rising. 'How dare you! And she's dead.' Her voice broke and he did nothing, just looked at her. She swallowed hard. 'But what I did, well, I shouldn't have done it. It wasn't—' She hesitated. 'Right. And I don't know how I did it. It's, it's not me. Or it didn't used to be. You can report me to the police if you like.'

Joe didn't move. He seemed to look at her for a long time. When he spoke, his voice was soft.

'I already told you,' he said, 'I never laid a hand on Megan.'

'That is a lie!'

'No,' Joe shook his head. His voice rose now, too, only not as loud as hers. 'It's not. It's bloody well not!' He sounded angry. 'You can kill the rest of my birds if it makes you feel better.' He jammed his hands into the pocket of his jeans and pulled out his keys. 'Here.'

Lizzie took a step back.

'Take them,' he said, thrusting them towards her. Then he

paused. 'Oh, I guess you have your own.' He indicated the side gate. 'Go on in, kill them all if you want. But I am sick of being judged for stuff I did not do.'

'Look, I just came to say sorry.' She swallowed. 'It's more than you ever did.'

'I did twelve years for something I didn't do. I owe you *nothing*.'

Lizzie pulled her coat around her. 'Well, I felt I owed you an apology.'

'Did you? To make yourself feel better? Or because you felt bad?'

'Both.'

'Well, apology accepted,' Joe said. 'I wouldn't want you having a burden like that on your conscience.'

For some reason, she felt small. She turned to go.

Joe's eyes scanned the street. 'Did you not bring back-up with you?'

'Huh?' She turned back.

'In case I murdered you in a fit of rage.'

'Stop!'

He felt ashamed as her eyes filled up. But he didn't apologise. Instead, he closed the door in her face.

Why hadn't she thought to bring someone with her? Lizzie wondered. OK, she was deeply ashamed of what she'd done and didn't want people to know, but Billy would have come after first giving her an earful. It occurred to her suddenly that she hadn't felt the need for protection. She hadn't thought for one second Joe would do anything to her. And that made her head reel. Either she was very stupid or she didn't believe he would have hurt her.

And that made things worse.

Joe leaned his back against the front door and stayed there for a long time, letting the complete and utter devastation work its way through him like a slowly rising tide. His head still couldn't get around it. Lizzie was a cool sort of girl. The kind he liked. Lizzie was Megan's sister. Lizzie had done all that stuff to him. He supposed that he should be relieved that he wasn't going mad or losing his touch. But he wasn't. The only girl he'd actually liked in a long time had hated him. Maybe he'd got so used to being despised that he didn't notice when people didn't like him the way he would if he was normal.

Damn it – he *was* normal. Well, as normal as anyone would be if they'd just spent twelve years in jail for a murder they didn't commit.

He smiled ruefully. Bloody hell.

But there was something he'd said to Lizzie that he suddenly realised was true. He was sick of being blamed and silently judged for something he knew was not his fault. He was sick of hiding his past and hiding who he was and being afraid to go home. To hell with it, he was going, from right now, to throw off his victim role. He didn't care who knew what had happened him. He had nothing, nothing to be ashamed of. From right now . . .

Without giving himself time to think, he dialled John.

'Yo!'

'It's Joe.'

'How's things?'

'That stuff I told you the other day—'

'Won't go any further.'

'No, I'd appreciate it if you told a few guys. Billy and Alan and that. If you don't mind.'

There was a pause. 'Oh. OK. If that's what you want.'

'Yep. It is.' Joe didn't prolong the conversation. He put the phone down and decided that what he had to do now was to locate one very annoyed teenager.

Ellen had been very abrupt with him. No, Anto was not there. No, she wasn't sure where he was. Joe should know better than to falsely accuse someone. Really, she said, if anyone should know about doing that, it had to be Joseph. He'd been contrite, told Ellen that he knew Anto hadn't done anything and that the boy had taken him up wrong. Where was he now, please?

She had grudgingly supplied him with an address after telling him he should have gone and sorted it out with Anto the other night instead of leaving it until now, but Joe had left in the middle of her rant and was now at the top of Anto's road, thanking his lucky stars that all he drove was a crappy car. A decent car wouldn't have stood a chance in a place like this. The only thing close to Anto's estate was a war zone in the Middle East. The kerbs were ripped from the sides of the roads, litter was everywhere and gangs of teenagers were congregated on a green.

Joe hopped out of his car and studied the address he had written down.

The teenagers turned to look at he passed. A roar of laughter followed him up the street. Joe didn't turn. After what he'd been through, walking past a gang like that was child's play.

Anto's house was a lovely oasis on a street of bedlam. There were no flowers in the garden but the grass was neatly trimmed and the windows of the house looked all shiny and clean. It looked a lot better than his own place, Joe thought ruefully.

He rang the bell, wondering what sort of reception he'd get.

A woman who he recognised as Anto's mother answered the door. Her eyes widened in recognition as she took him in. Then they narrowed. 'What?' she barked out.

Joe flinched. 'Eh, I just came to, eh, thank you for the present you got me.'

She inclined her head. Then muttered, 'You didn't deserve it.'

Joe ignored that. 'And mainly I'm here to talk to Anto.'

'You going to accuse him of doing something else he didn't do now?'

God, he was sick of women hating him. Though at least she wasn't disguising her feelings. Joe sighed. 'I never accused him of anything, he just assumed that I had. I was just wondering why he hasn't been around the last couple of days.'

'That's not the version I got.'

He met her steely gaze, but she outstared him. 'Can I talk to him, please?'

Anto's mother was a lot tougher than she had appeared in the police station that day, Joe thought in grudging admiration. 'Look,' she said, 'you either trust Anto or you don't. Make up your mind. I'm not having him getting upset any more.'

'I trust him. He's great with the birds.'

'I didn't see a cat in the loft.' Anto surprised Joe as he spoke from behind his mother. He must have crept into the hall unnoticed.

His mother stood aside but didn't leave them alone.

'Yeah, I know.' Joe attempted a grin. 'I am sorry if you thought I didn't trust you.' He shrugged. 'Nine of the birds had been killed at that stage, Anto. I was in shock, you know.'

'When my dad died, I never said it was anyone's fault,' Anto said.

'I never said it was your fault.'

'You didn't have to.'

Joe wondered if he should say that he knew it was Lizzie, but decided not to. It might sound worse. 'Look,' he crouched down a bit to be on Anto's level, 'I know you're great. I know you'd see a cat a mile off. I know it wasn't your fault.'

'Good.' Anto folded his arms.

'Good.' His mother folded her arms.

Joe looked from one to the other. 'Will you be coming back to help me?' he asked.

Anto looked unsure. He glanced at his mother.

She gave a bark of a laugh. 'Help you? He'd rather cut his ears off, wouldn't you, Anto?'

'Eh—'

'I can pay you,' Joe said. 'For your help.'

'He doesn't need the money. Do you, Anto?'

'Eh—'

'Sure, have a think about it,' Joe said, looking at Anto's mother and trying not to grin at the desperate look on Anto's face. 'If he likes, I can even give him a pigeon of his own.' He paused then went on quietly, 'I am sorry, Anto. I know what it's like to have someone think you did something when you didn't and it's a horrible feeling. And I know I was hard on you at first because you broke into Ellen's, but you're not a bad lad.'

'He's a great lad!' his mother said.

'He is,' Joe nodded. 'And a great help and I need him, so if he'd like to come back minus his ears, I'll have him.'

The three stood looking at each other.

'Mam?' Anto said hesitantly.

His mother looked at him. Then looked at Joe. 'How much?'

'Sorry?'

'How much will you pay him?'

'Oh. A tenner an hour?'

'Wo—'

'Fifteen.' His mother elbowed her son to shut up.

'Twelve.'

'OK.'

Joe indicated his car up the road. 'D'you want to start now, Anto?'

Anto's smile almost made his day.

51

WHEN SHE GOT back, she had planned to go straight to her room. She knew people on the tram had been looking at her strangely. It was probably because she had been shaking violently all the way home. They probably thought she was on drugs or something.

It was the relief that made her tremble. The final letting go. The obsessive fixation that she'd had for the past few months was draining from her body and it was strange, but it was as if she could feel it loosening its hold on her heart and mind. She wondered how she would feel when it was gone. Would she feel again? Would she lose the anger inside that made her feel like snapping at everything, the way she'd snapped at Lori for taking her husband back? The way she'd snapped at Mark for caring enough to ask what was wrong?

Tears sprang into her eyes. She would focus on the parachute jump; focus on raising money for Life. Her life suddenly seemed simpler. Yes, the hole where Megan's loss was felt was still there, would be there for ever, but it was natural to feel like that. What she had been doing the past few months was not abnormal exactly, but it was unhealthy. Her shivering was helping her to detox, she thought wryly. And no matter how bad she'd feel for what she'd done, at least she'd be feeling something other than hate.

As she walked through the door, her father was talking urgently into the phone. He turned to face her and took a step back.

'What has happened to you?' he exclaimed.

Lizzie waved him away. 'I'll be fine.' Her voice broke a little.

'Can you excuse me a moment?' he said to the person at the

other end of the phone. Placing it down on the hall table he stared at his daughter. 'Lizzie?'

'Oh, Dad,' she suddenly needed him to hug her, to pat her on the back and smooth her hair with his fingers the way he used to do when she was a kid.

'I have to go,' he said into the phone as he slammed it back on to the cradle. Then he opened his arms and held his daughter while she cried.

After a bit, after she'd wiped her face, he continued to pat her on the back, eventually asking her what was wrong.

'It's just a bad day,' she sniffed. There was no point, it was over now, and he'd go ballistic with her and worry about her and he had enough to worry about. 'I'll be OK in a bit.'

He looked at her in concern. 'A bad day?' he asked sceptically. 'You look awful.'

Something suddenly dawned on him and he flushed a deep shade of red.

'What's wrong, Dad?'

He coughed a bit and didn't meet her eye. 'Eh, just wondering if there's something you'd like to tell me,' he stammered out.

'What?' She sounded alarmed. Did he know?

He nodded encouragingly. 'You can tell me, I know it's more a women's chat sort of thing but your mother isn't here so . . .' He flushed a deeper shade and his voice trailed off.

Lizzie was lost.

'Are you,' he nodded in the direction of her stomach, 'pregnant?' He could barely get the word out.

Lizzie found herself giggling. At him. At the very idea. 'No. No, no, no,' she shook her head, laughing. 'God, Dad!'

He looked relieved, though whether it was because she was laughing or because she wasn't pregnant, Lizzie didn't know. She hugged him impulsively.

He hugged her back.

'It's probably just hormones, though,' she said, smiling impishly.

'Will you go away outta that and don't be embarrassing me even more.' He flapped a hand at her.

Then he chucked her under the chin as he let her out of the circle of his arms. 'You OK now?'

'I'll be fine,' she said.

And she knew she would.

Eventually.

Joe handed Anto the keys to the loft and told him that he was going to make him responsible for the pigeons for that day and tomorrow.

'There is somewhere I have to go,' he said.

Anto looked thrilled. 'At twelve euro an hour, how much will I earn?' he asked.

Joe hadn't thought of that. It would be expensive. 'Eh – well, let's see, two hours today and maybe four on Monday. That's seventy-two. How does that sound?'

'Sweet!' Anto tossed the keys into the air and laughed.

His mother was right, Joe thought. He was a great kid.

'I think,' Mr Walsh said later at dinner as Billy dished up, 'that your mother is on the verge of apologising.'

Billy dropped a potato on the floor and, picking it up, placed it on Lizzie's plate.

'Oy! I don't want that.'

'Did you hear me?' Mr Walsh said crossly. 'Your mother is going to apologise.'

Billy looked at Lizzie. Aileen kept her head down.

'Eh, I wouldn't get your hopes up, Dad,' Billy tried to say tactfully. He took the spud from Lizzie's plate and reluctantly gave it to himself. 'You know Mammy.'

Mr Walsh nodded. 'I do. But I was on the phone today,' he said, 'and apparently she has asked to go before the court again. I was talking to her solicitor when Lizzie arrived home all upset.'

'You were upset?' Aileen asked. 'Why?'

'Eh, I'm trying to speak,' Mr Walsh said. He picked up a forkful of very overdone carrot and glanced at it suspiciously. 'Billy, how often does Aileen let you cook?'

348

'I thought you were trying to speak,' Billy prompted, evading the question.

'Oh yes, well, your mother is very upset. Probably because I walked out on her at the last visit and I think she's going to give in.'

Nobody said anything.

Lizzie shuddered. Her mother would not be happy having to give in. But maybe, behind it all, she knew it was the right thing to do. It was good to let go, she knew that.

'So,' Mr Walsh looked around at them all, 'I would appreciate it if, or rather when, she comes out, you would all ignore the fact that she has given way.'

'That might be a bit difficult, Dad,' Billy spluttered out.

'Take this seriously,' Mr Walsh snapped. He sighed then went on in a more composed voice, 'She'll be upset. And she'll feel she's let down—' he swallowed, 'well, herself and, and—' He couldn't say it.

'Megan,' Lizzie prompted softly.

Her dad nodded and caught her hand. 'Yes, Megan,' he said. 'But we know she hasn't, so let's make sure she knows that, ey?'

Billy and Aileen nodded.

Mr Walsh put his head down and scraped his carrots over to the side of his plate.

Joe arrived outside his parents' house after two solid hours of speeding. It was a wonder he hadn't been stopped. But he knew if he took his time he might turn back, and he desperately didn't want to.

He pulled up on the gravel outside his parents' front door with a screech. Then switched off the engine. The sudden silence unnerved him for the first time since his impulsive decision.

It had been a weird sort of day. He'd lost Lizzie – but he'd never had her in the first place, he knew that now. It hurt and he wanted to cry for the way she'd dashed his dreams into ashes. He wanted to yell at her for what she'd done, and yet, in a funny sort of way, he could understand it. And it would take more than losing Lizzie to ruin his life, he realised. You didn't spent twelve years in prison without appreciating every day of freedom. Lizzie was gone but his parents weren't. And he wasn't sure if he wanted to lose them. Despite everything, he had to try. Thrash it out with them. Try to see things from their perspective. He had all the stuff he needed to say in his head. Swallowing hard, he stood out of the car and slammed the door.

He hadn't even made it to the front door before it was opened. His mother and father stood there, a hesitant look of hope on both their faces.

All Joe's words disappeared. Everything he meant to say just seemed to dissolve. His eyes watered. He took a step towards them and then stopped.

They made to move, but didn't.

An eternity seemed to pass before Joe blurted out, 'Maybe I was wrong about stuff.'

And suddenly his dad was dragging him into the house. His mother had her hands up to her mouth.

He knew then that there'd be no need for any more words.

He had come home.

52

LIZZIE WALKED INTO Mark's office without knocking. He looked up from his desk and quirked his eyebrows.

'I am sorry for being late the other morning,' she mumbled.

Mark made a face and held his hand to his ear. 'Pardon? I didn't quite get that? Could you repeat it?'

'I said,' Lizzie smirked, 'that I am sorry for being late the other morning. I can assure you, as your humble employee, that it won't happen again.'

In response, Mark jumped from his seat and started to rotate his fists in a circular motion whilst chanting, 'Oh ye-ah, oh ye-ah!'

'I take it my apology has been accepted.'

He stopped and grinned. 'Oh ye-ah!'

Lizzie grinned back and, just as she was leaving, he called out, 'I take it that whatever was bothering you is over?'

Lizzie froze for a second before nodding, 'I guess. In a way. Anyway, I'm totally focused on the parachute jump now.'

'Good to have you back, only—'

'What?'

'Don't apologise in future, it freaks me out a little. It's not like you.'

'No problem, asshole.'

'That's my girl!'

Lizzie had landed him in it, and not just with Anto, Joe thought as he pulled up outside a ramshackle house in the middle of north county Dublin.

Fields lay in every direction, which was just as well as any sane person wouldn't want to live within five miles of the tumbledown heap. Joe could never understand why Cid came all the way to Ranelagh to race his birds when there was a club right beside him. Knowing Cid, however, he'd probably fallen out with everyone in that club and had been forced to go further afield. He hadn't even come back to the Ranelagh since the fight with Joe, which had made Joe even more suspicious of him and led the rest of the lads to believe he didn't do it and that he was mortally offended.

Joe resigned himself to being made to feel terrible as drove his car up the pot-holed driveway. Cid's front door was bright yellow and the paint peeling. Joe located a bell under some overgrown ivy and pressed it.

Cid opened the door within seconds. He stood back to look at Joe and smiled a little expectantly.

'Yes?' Then, before Joe could say anything, he asked, 'Where's the lunch box?'

'Lunch box?'

'Well, I presume you bought a big hunk of humble pie with you.'

'I ate it before I came,' Joe said back.

'Good. Tasty, was it?'

'Nope.'

Cid grinned and laughed softly.

Joe plunged, like a swimmer into cold water. 'I'm sorry I accused you over Prince, I should have known better.'

'Yeah,' Cid was serious now, 'you should have. I'd never do that. I heard from Noel that it was Lizzie. It's always the pretty ones you have to watch. You should report her.'

Joe shrugged.

'So,' Cid opened the door wider, 'you gonna stand here all day or you gonna come in and see my birds?' He paused and said, 'I've, eh, thought about gifting you an egg if you want, for your loft. It's from one of my best racers.'

Joe swallowed. 'Really?'

'Yeah.' Cid looked at him. 'Of course, if it does well, I'll want credit for it being my egg, you know.'

Joe nodded, touched. 'Thanks.'

'Well come on, so, don't be shy.' Cid pushed a bag full of rubbish out of the way and invited Joe inside.

Lizzie only remembered her mother's request to trace the mobile phone number later that day. And it only sprang to mind because she'd been enrolling for the Life parachute jump in an effort to atone for her sins. It would be the second most terrifying thing she'd ever done. As she keyed her own phone number into the online application form, she suddenly recalled that her mother was ringing her that evening to find out if she had managed to trace another mobile number. Shit!

Hastily, she flipped open her mobile and scrolled through the names until she found the one she had titled 'Find out'. Dialling it, she wondered what on earth she'd say to the person at the other end. It would have been handy if her mother had given her some clue as to why she needed the number traced.

'Hello,' a bright northern voice said.

'Eh, hi,' Lizzie stammered. 'Is that Laura?'

'No, wrong number, I'm afraid.'

'Oh.' Lizzie tried to sound as if she was puzzled. She'd grown good at lying over the last while, she realised uncomfortably. 'I've been told to ring this by my boss. I wonder if I've got your name wrong. I can't remember the name she told me. Sorry, what's your name?'

There was a tinkling laugh. 'Denise.'

'Denise Duggan,' Lizzie pronounced, as if she'd just unearthed the Golden Fleece.

'No, sorry. Denise McCabe.'

'OK, sorry about that. I must have the wrong number.'

'No bother. Hope you find who you're looking for.'

Lizzie hung up.

Joe left Cid's two hours later, having eaten the most revolting sandwich of his life. Cid had bustled about, examining the contents

353

of his fridge to see what was still edible before putting it between two inedible slices of bread.

'All that crap about you being a murderer,' Cid pronounced as Joe bit into the bread, 'I don't believe it for a second.'

'Thanks,' Joe said.

'Anyone who understands birds like you do wouldn't murder one.'

And then he laughed.

It wasn't the only thing that could be described as bad taste, Joe thought in semi-amusement.

'Did you trace that number for me?' was the first question her mother asked that night.

Lizzie was a little put out. 'I'm fine, Mammy, thanks. How are you?'

'Did you trace the number, Lizzie?'

'Well, I know whose phone it is.'

'Is it Dessie O'Sullivan's?'

The name startled her. 'Dessie?' she whispered, shocked. Then she asked, 'Mammy, what is this? What are you doing?'

Her mother took a deep breath. 'Is it Dessie's number?'

'No. It was a Denise McCabe.'

There was a pause from her mother's end of the line. 'Would that be Denise Owens, by any chance? Is she northern?'

'Yes. I think so.'

'His girlfriend,' Mrs Walsh said. 'We have to talk to her. You have to ring her again. Or I'll get the police to talk to her. Yes, that's it. I'm in the right place anyway, loads of police here.'

'Mammy, will you tell me what is going on?'

'Lizzie, I have something I want you to read. I'm going to post it to you. Read it as soon as you get it. Promise me.'

Her mother was going mad. She had to be. 'Mammy, are you—'

'Promise me.'

'OK, I promise.'

'And don't tell your father, not yet. Or Billy.'

This was ridiculous. What was wrong with her mother?

'Dad said you were going to apologise, is that true?' she asked sharply. She had to get her mother out of there.

There was a pause. Then Mrs Walsh said softly, 'Yes, it's true.'

Thank God. She heaved a silent sigh of relief. 'It's the right thing, Mammy.'

'I know that now, Lizzie. You were right what you said.'

Lizzie didn't reply.

Her mother went on gently, 'I'll bet you're a great counsellor.'

'I tend to be a lot better when it's someone I care about.'

Her mother swallowed hard. 'I never got on with her, you know,' she said shakily. 'We fought all the time. The day she disappeared, we weren't talking. But—but I loved her, Lizzie.' Her voice cracked.

'We all did, Mammy.'

'Hurry up, would ya? It's not *Oprah* yer on.' Someone at her mother's end of the phoneline said.

'I have to go, Lizzie. Look out for that package, OK?'

'I will.'

'And when you've read it, bring it to the police.'

The line went dead.

53

THE PACKAGE ARRIVED two days later. It was delivered to Lizzie at work and, as she tore it open, assuming it was work related, she unthinkingly pulled out the contents.

MEGAN'S DIARY: SUMMER was emblazoned across the front.

Lizzie dropped it with a clatter on to the desk. Was this a sick joke? Who could possibly know? An envelope fluttered to the ground. Opening it, her hands shaking, Lizzie recognised her mother's writing.

Lizzie, thought I'd send this to you in work so Billy won't be curious. Please read it as soon as you can and if you think it should be passed to the police, do so. I will be out within the month – all red tape, total rubbish – and I don't want to waste time. I found it under the floorboards in Megan's room when I was cleaning it this year. I read it just to feel close to her, not realising what it was.

Love you. xx

It took a second before Lizzie could open the diary of her older sister, who would for ever be nineteen years of age. It was bright and colourful, just like her. She'd written along the margins, drawn love hearts all through the text. *Megan loves Dessie. Aileen fancies Billy.*

It made her smile to see it.

Hoping Mark wouldn't notice, Lizzie took the phone off the hook and began to read.

Joe knocked on his boss's door and was beckoned into the office.

'About that job you offered me,' he said. 'Is it OK if I refuse it?'

'Refuse it?' his boss looked at him incredulously. 'Can I ask why?'

Joe shrugged. 'I teach people to swim, that's what I do. I was behind a desk once and I hated it.' He offered an apologetic smile. 'Life's too short to do what you hate. I've wasted too much of it already.'

Graham looked ever so slightly pissed off. 'So you're not interested?'

''Fraid not. You've made me like it too much here.'

'You might regret it.'

'Maybe.'

But he knew he wouldn't.

OK, all that last bit can be scrapped because I just got a text. It's him. Well, I guess it is.

It said: R U OK? D.

I texted back: Am I OK? Wot a stupid question. No.

He texted: Do U feel rele bad?

I texted yes.

He texted: Can we talk. D.

So I have arranged to meet him at the harbour at five. Enough time to get my red puffy eyes down. The others won't be back until at least ten.

I'll wear my really short skirt and do my hair. I've been sick twice since coming home, I knew I shouldn't have eaten that fish Dad caught yesterday. Mam cooked it and it was practically raw. She said, in front of Aileen, that I was so ungrateful. There are lots of people who would like fresh fish. I told her I'd prefer a fresh man, only I don't think she knew what I meant. Billy and Aileen did, though. Anyway, the fish has made me sick.

I also have the most massive headache. Probably from crying.

I am not going to tell anyone I'm meeting him just in case he makes a fool of me again. No one will know until I have him back again. And I will.

357

I will unleash the full power of the Megan Walsh charm.

Lizzie put the diary down, dazed, wondering what it all meant. It proved one thing though: Joe had been telling the truth about the texts. And the number, where had her mother got the number she'd asked Lizzie to dial? She scanned the diary and then she saw it, scrawled in the margin – *number for love – Dessie 045789326.* It was surrounded by a huge love heart.

Only it hadn't been Dessie who texted her at all, had it?

Lizzie felt suddenly sick with the realisation that since Joe had told the truth about the texts, he might have told the truth about everything else, too. Oh God, what if Joe hadn't done it? What if he was actually innocent? What if everything he'd said was true and he had only tried to help Megan? What if – and here her mind froze – what if he'd actually spent twelve years in jail for a death he hadn't been responsible for? *The poor guy.* Lizzie's stomach heaved. However bad she felt at what she'd done to him, she'd coped by telling herself that he was a murderer. And now . . . little flashes of Joe with his birds popped into her head. His gentleness, his soothing way of talking to them, his affectionate way of dealing with them. His thoughtfulness when he'd given her his granddad's book to read. She still had that book, she suddenly remembered.

If she hadn't been so filled with hate, maybe she might have seen what other people saw in him. What his neighbour saw, what his boss saw, what the lads in the pigeon club saw. But she'd been blinded.

And now, too late, her eyes had opened and what she saw was horrifying in its implications.

She picked up the phone and dialled the police.

54

THE TWO FAMILIES sat on opposite sides of the room. Joe, handsome in a grey suit and white shirt, kept his eyes pinned on the man who was about to speak. His face betrayed no emotion. On either side of him sat his parents. His dad looked slightly more apprehensive, his shoulders rigid, his lips set in a straight line. He wore an expensive suit and stared ahead of him, too, not acknowledging the family across from him. Joe's mother, slightly bewildered-looking, sat on his right. Her eyes darted here and there and finally came to rest on a tall, gangly girl, who sat alongside the family opposite. Leah Jones thought she recognised the girl, but then again, she knew that her memory wasn't as accurate as it used to be, so she turned away and studied her beautiful son. She'd always known that this day would come and tears sprang into her eyes as she slipped her hand into his. He wrapped it in his two hands and she marvelled at the strength of him. She would remember this moment, no matter what.

Mr and Mrs Walsh, too, looked anxious, but she in particular looked relieved. As if she'd finally found what she'd been looking for. Her face was softer, her eyes not as flat as they had been. Beside her sat Billy, his hand held firmly by Aileen, who was by far the most enormous person in the room. She wore a bright green long flowing blouse and black trousers. Her face was flushed and she looked uncomfortable. She hoped that the judge or whatever he was would get a move on. Lizzie sat, head bowed, unable to look up lest she catch Joe's eye or that of his parents.

The case had come up in court a lot quicker than anyone had anticipated. Lizzie had done well so far to avoid Joe and his parents – she wished she had never met him that time, never seen him on the street. Bad as she had felt when she thought he was guilty, she now felt worse. There had been no pretence about him, she realised. He was a good guy. A really nice fella. She couldn't, just couldn't, look at him.

She kept her head down as the man started to speak. As the photographers snapped and the journalists took notes. This would be front-page news tomorrow. As the man talked, she felt tears drip from her eyes, slide down her nose and on to her hands.

Joe's solicitor made a statement outside the court as the cameras snapped. Then the Walsh family's solicitor did the same. Then the two families unexpectedly came face to face. Lizzie hid behind Aileen. She couldn't bear for them to recognise her. The crowd quietened down.

Mr Walsh found himself in front of Joe. He opened his mouth to speak but realised that there was nothing he could say. Swallowing hard, he slowly extended his hand towards the boy he had been so fond of.

Joe gazed at it for a second before clasping it tightly in his. There was a moment of emotional silence when everything stopped. When even the cameras ceased clicking. Finally Joe said softly, 'I'm sorry you lost your daughter, Kev.'

'Thank you,' Mr Walsh gulped out, his voice barely audible as Polly wrapped her arms around him.

It was a 'sorry', but not the sorry Lizzie had imagined Joe would ever utter. This sorry meant more. Meant a lot to her dad, who had squeezed his eyes shut and was massaging them with his thumbs.

Lizzie watched in a daze as the two families exchanged handshakes. She stepped back, afraid Joe's parents would recognise her. Even though she'd had a haircut and coloured it red, she thought it would be unlikely they'd forget the girl who had come calling only a few months ago.

And yet she needed to see Joe. Had to.

She waited until he was slightly apart from his parents before crossing towards him. He saw her coming and waited. It was as if nothing else existed for him in that moment except seeing Lizzie again. It had to happen, but he was dreading it.

She looked up and her face flushed with shame.

'Hi, Lizzie,' he said quietly.

'There's nothing I can say to you that would excuse what I did.' Oh God, she was going to burst into tears.

'No,' he said softly, 'there probably isn't.'

Lizzie flinched and her voice wobbled. 'I am truly sorry, Joe. I'm sorry for believing you could do such a thing. I should have known.' She sniffed and said on a half sob, 'When I saw you with your birds, I should have known you weren't capable of it. I'm so sorry.'

There was a silence. When she looked up, she saw that Joe was studying her with solemn eyes.

'I'm not gonna lie, Lizzie, and say it was easy.' He spoke quietly. 'Twelve years for something I didn't do was . . . I dunno.' His eyes grew shiny and he blinked hard and didn't finish. Instead he added, 'But being in there and having nothing and coming out and having what I have, well, it has made me love my life now. I love life more than I ever would have otherwise.'

'Still—'

'Apology accepted, OK?' he interrupted, reaching out and touching her lightly on the sleeve. 'Don't beat yourself up over it. Let it go, ey?'

'Thank you.'

'No worries.' There was a pause, before he uttered, 'See you around.'

'Yeah,' she nodded. Then, as he turned to go, she said tentatively, 'Maybe I might see you walking up Grafton Street some evening after work?'

He hesitated for what seemed like the longest time. Then nodded. 'Yeah, maybe.' He gave an uncertain smile and quirked an eyebrow. 'You could give me my book back.'

'I will.' She felt tears brimming and one slipped out and down her cheek.

'Don't cry, ey? Life is good.'

With that he turned away and Lizzie knew that whatever it took, she'd make it up to him.

He'd dreaded meeting Lizzie more than anything else and it had hurt a lot when he'd seen her, but it was over now. He couldn't be angry at her, she'd set him free in a way. Thanks to her, he'd told the lads in the club about his past and, with one or two exceptions, they'd all declared that they didn't believe a word of it. It was good to know and now their faith in him had been proved right. Thanks to Lizzie, he'd decided to reclaim his life and not be blamed any more for something he was innocent of. Thanks to Lizzie, Cid had unexpectedly gifted him an egg that was looking incredibly promising. Thanks to—

'What on earth is that?' His dad broke into his thoughts as he pointed to a huge banner that was flapping in the breeze outside Joe's house.

'Christ,' Joe laughed loudly as he stared out the car window, 'where did that come from?'

CONGRATULATIONS ON YOUR INNOCENCE it said in three-foot-high writing.

Ellen bustled to meet him, her face red. Joe rolled down the window of the car.

'I couldn't stop them,' she said, casting her eyes heavenwards. 'I knew you'd hate it.'

In the doorway his friends from the club cheered and held aloft a bottle of champagne. Anto and his mother stood shyly to the side. His mates from work were there, too. Ellen made a hopeless gesture.

'Sorry,' she muttered.

A huge cheer went up as Joe emerged from the car.

His dad poked him in the back. 'You told us you hadn't got many friends,' he said, amused.

Joe didn't have time to answer because Cid had already legged it down the driveway. 'Hurry up, you're on telly, come on!'

And the party began.

55

HER MOTHER AND father were spending the night with Aileen's dad and Billy and Aileen had gone to bed, so Lizzie stretched out on the sofa and savoured the first bit of quiet she'd had all day.

It had been an unexpectedly good day, too, despite the sadness of finally finding out how her sister had died. After all these years and in light of Joe's original testimony, the pieces had slotted together and suddenly made sense. She felt sick when she thought of Joe spending twelve years in prison when he hadn't been to blame, felt sick when she thought of him and his family being gossiped about by their neighbours when all along he'd only tried to help. And then she had come into his life and done what she'd done and now he'd told her it was OK. His forgiveness was the greatest gift she'd ever received, which sounded a bit corny but which was absolutely true. She would make it up to him, she knew she would. She'd repay him for every pigeon he'd lost because of her. She would rebuild what she'd torn apart as best she could. She'd start by focusing on the parachute jump, which was taking place in two days' time. She'd try her best to help all the people who called her on a Thursday night. She'd keep her fingers crossed that Lori would ring again. She'd try to finish all those other stories for people she might never meet. No, she corrected herself, not finish. Begin. Help them to begin again, just like she was going to.

Just then the doorbell rang.

Standing up, Lizzie wondered if it was a neighbour coming by to give them their best. People had been calling all day, neighbours they didn't even know, to congratulate them and say how great it was for them to have closure. Lizzie thought Royal Lawns might be a good place to live, after all.

She opened the door and was shocked to see Tom standing there. He looked pretty good, dressed in a purple shirt and green jeans. Only Tom could wear something so horrendous and still have street cred.

'Tom, hi,' she said, her heart beginning to thump sickeningly. What was he doing here?

'Hi.' He smiled his devastating crooked-toothed smile and her heart went into free fall. 'You're probably wondering what I'm doing here.'

She could only nod.

'I'm here because I'm a bit annoyed with you, actually.' He was all casual nonchalance but she knew he was as nervous as she was.

'You are?' She tried to match his tone and failed.

'I always wanted to be the one on telly and you got there before me.'

She drank him in, not even able to smile at his feeble introductory joke. His eyes, his boxer's nose, his beautiful gorgeous sexy smile. It was months since she'd seen him that awful night in the restaurant, yet he still had the ability to make her want him.

'You looked sensational.'

She smiled a little. Not as sensational as him.

'The hair is great.'

She absently touched her violently red tresses. 'Thanks.'

His eyes became serious. 'I'm glad you finally got the truth.'

'Thanks.' Her voice wobbled.

He dug into his jeans and pulled out two tickets. 'So, in celebration, I got these for you. Freebies for a show next week. D'you want them? You can bring anyone you like.'

Oh, God.

'I'm free.' He smiled a little crookedly.

She couldn't pretend to be the person he thought she was. She was starting over and though it was tempting to forget what had gone on before, she wouldn't be able to live with herself. Or him. 'I don't know, Tom.'

'In case you haven't noticed, I'm willing to humiliate myself here.'

'There are things you don't know about me, Tom. You'd hate me if I told you.'

He paused and nodded before saying softly, 'I saw him on the telly, too, Liz, that guy in the restaurant. It doesn't matter.'

'It does.' Her heart flipped and she bowed her head. 'He was the reason I lied to you that night. I—I, well, I did awful things to him.'

Tom reached out and clasped her arm, squeezing it slightly. 'Well, good,' he declared. 'He was way better-looking than me. I don't mind telling you, he had me worried.'

She spluttered out a laugh but she still had to tell him. Let him know how horrible she'd been. If he still wanted her afterwards, well, that would be brilliant. If not . . . well, it was her own fault.

'D'you want to come in?' she asked. 'So I can explain?'

'You don't have to.'

'I do.' She held the door open wider and he stepped into the hall and looked around. 'Billy and Aileen are in bed. They don't know anything. Come in here.' She led the way into the front room, which was now really tidy since Aileen had moved back in. Tom stood in the centre of the room before sitting down. Lizzie suddenly understood how Joe must have felt when he was telling her about being in prison. How had he done it?

'I saw him on Grafton Street one night when I was coming out of Life,' she began. 'I recognised him and something inside me flipped, Tom. Just to see him living his life when Megan was dead, I couldn't take it.'

'Here,' Tom stood up and gently led her to the sofa, 'don't cry, for fuck's sake. It's only me.'

'Yeah, and I've treated you so badly. But Tom, I only got friendly with Joe to hurt him. Nothing ever happened. I wanted

366

to get at him the way he'd got at us. So I set out to sabotage his pigeons. That's what I did at the weekends. I stole his keys and messed about with his lofts.'

Tom said nothing.

'And when that didn't seem to work, I—I got a cat and I killed his birds.'

Tom flinched but he kept hold of her hand.

'I even went and stole his best bird.' Tears dripped off her chin and plopped on to Tom's hand as she relived how horrible she'd been.

'Yeah, well,' Tom placed his two hands around her face and with his thumbs he wiped her tears away, 'he stole mine.'

She sniffed.

'He did,' Tom said more seriously.

'I never fancied him.'

He grinned softly at her before asking solemnly, 'Why didn't you tell me?'

'You would have tried to stop me.'

'Maybe.'

'Plus I didn't want you to see how horrible I could be.' She said it quietly, her voice fading away at the end.

'Everyone can be horrible. I used to be horrible before I met you.'

'Did you?' He made it sound almost enticing.

'Well, I admit I wasn't a pigeon killer, but I lost a lot of mates.'

'You did?'

'Yep.' Now he looked ashamed. 'I was jealous and bitter. I hated that other people could get cast in a play and I couldn't. No one would work with me, I was such a temperamental bastard. The night I met you I'd been passed over for an ideal part and I was in shit form. Then you hauled me up over skipping that queue and in between feeling really annoyed I somehow copped on that you were the best thing ever to happen in my life. Bingo. The parts start flooding in. Why? Because I'm bloody happy.' He took her two hands in his. 'You bring out the best in me.'

'Do I?'

367

'Yeah. Do you not know that?'

She shook her head.

'I was nearly fired from *Angels Down* after we split. Poor Imogen had the job of keeping me on the straight and narrow. The night you came to see me in it, Imogen was hoping you'd come for a drink and get back with me. Only you didn't. I think she was more devastated than I was.'

'I saw you holding Imogen's hand onstage and looking really happy, that's why I didn't go.'

'I looked happy 'cause I thought I'd see you. I thought maybe we could patch things up.'

'Oh.'

'You fool,' he said tenderly as he brought his forehead to meet hers.

'I get scared,' she said, 'when I'm really happy. I sometimes wonder if Joe's pigeons weren't the only thing I sabotaged.'

He pushed her hair back from her face. She could taste his breath. Feel his lips move.

'Life is like a bungee jump,' he said.

'What?'

'You can either be scared and close your eyes, or just let go and enjoy the ride.'

'Are you offering me a ride?'

He laughed loudly, then his brown eyes suddenly grew serious. 'I have missed you so much.'

'AAAAGGGGHHHHHHHHHH!'

The yell came from upstairs and Tom and Lizzie jumped away from each other as if scalded.

'The babies are coming!' Billy shouted. 'Lizzie, are you awake?'

'Down here!' She raced into the hall, Tom in her wake.

Billy appeared at the top of the stairs. 'Get her case, would you? Ring Mam and Dad. I'm driving her in.' He was about to go back and get Aileen when he spied Tom. 'Hi, Tom. You back on the scene?'

'AAAAGGGGHHHHHHHHH!'

'Jesus!' He ran back into the bedroom as Lizzie searched

frantically for Aileen's case. She'd packed it over a month ago and Lizzie finally located it under the hall table. Lizzie and Tom watched as Billy led Aileen carefully down the stairs. She was dressed in a stripy nightdress and looked to Tom like a marquee.

'Are you sure the babies are on their way?' Billy asked her as he got her down the final step.

'Sure? Am I sure! AAAGGGHHHHHH!' Aileen clenched her stomach and glared at Billy. 'Does that answer your question?' She suddenly spied Tom. 'Oh, Tom, are you talking to Lizzie again? Oh, great. I think it's so important to talk out any troubles you have.'

'My arse, you do,' Billy snorted. 'It took you ages to talk to me. Don't mind her, Tom, she's full of shit.'

'I'm ringing Mam and Dad and your dad now,' Lizzie said as she gave Aileen a brief hug. 'Good luck.'

'Thanks.' Aileen hugged her back. 'Oh, this is so scary.'

'It'll be great,' Billy kissed her cheek, 'and I'm going to be with you all the way.'

'You better mean that,' Aileen said, smiling at him.

Lizzie's niece and nephew were born in record time and, despite being all scrunched up and wrinkly, were the most beautiful people she had ever seen. So pure and innocent and they smelled all cuddly OK, bits of dried blood clung to their scalps, but everyone ignored that as they passed them around for a look.

'It's like a new start,' Mrs Walsh said, her face glowing as she kissed her little granddaughter.

Lizzie thought how calm her mother suddenly looked now. New life, new hope.

Mr Walsh put his arm about his wife. 'It's been some day, ey?'

She put her arm about him, too. 'It has. A good day.' Then she glanced at Lizzie. 'Are you back with . . .' she indicated Tom with a nod of her head, 'him?'

Lizzie smiled across the ward at Tom, who was hanging back now that her parents had arrived. 'I think I am.'

'Did he get dressed in the dark?'

'No, they're his normal clothes.' She blew him a kiss, he bowed extravagantly and blew her one back.

Her mother snorted but said, 'It's great to see you smile like that.'

One of the babies started to cry suddenly.

'Oh, I think it needs to be fed,' Billy announced as he took his new son and passed him to Aileen. She unbuttoned her pyjama top and latched the baby to her breast. He was soon feeding away.

'Look at that,' Billy said in admiration.

'Right.' Mr Walsh, totally mortified but trying not to show it, clapped his hands together. 'I think we'd better get out of your way.'

'I think so, too,' Abe said. He laid his new granddaughter into the bed beside Aileen. 'Take care, love.'

One by one they said their goodbyes and Billy walked them to the hospital exit.

'So,' Lizzie hugged her brother as she left, 'how does it feel, Daddy? Are you still scared?'

'Terrified,' he admitted. 'And d'you know what?'

'What?'

'When Aileen held them, she told me she knew what I meant now. She said she doesn't know how Mammy and Daddy coped.'

Lizzie looked at her parents as they argued about where her dad had parked his car and shrugged. 'I don't know how any of us coped,' she said. 'I think we all went a little crazy.'

Billy nodded.

'You take care of your little family, OK?' she said.

'I will.'

She turned away and left him talking to Aileen's father, who was congratulating him.

Tom slung an arm about her shoulder before glancing uneasily at her. 'May I?'

She pulled Tom to her. 'Can we go back to your place and finish what we started a few months ago?'

'That's a question you don't have to ask,' Tom replied, his voice husky. He stopped walking and enfolded her in his arms. She inhaled the scent of him and it was like coming home.

'Oh, by the way,' Tom said nonchalantly, 'I'm doing your parachute jump.'

'Me too,' Lizzie said back, just as nonchalantly. 'I mean, I can't expect people to jump when I won't do it myself.'

He grinned delightedly at her. 'Yeah?'

'Yeah. I said to myself,' she attempted to mimic Tom's gorgeous voice, "great, a new experience".'

He laughed loudly. 'You gonna keep your eyes open?'

'What's the point otherwise?' she smiled.

And then she closed her eyes as he kissed her.

Epilogue

CONVICTION OVERTURNED IN DRAMATIC NEW TWIST

Joseph Jones (34), who was convicted of the murder of Megan Walsh fourteen years ago and who subsequently served twelve years in prison, yesterday had his conviction overturned as dramatic new evidence came to light.

Megan Walsh went missing from her home in Rossclare, Co. Wexford, and two days later her body was washed up on Grange Strand. She had bruising to the wrist and had suffered a severe head injury before her death. The last person to see her alive was Joseph Jones. It emerged during the trial that Ms Walsh spent the last night of her life on Mr Jones' boat. Joseph Jones denied that the girl had fallen overboard or that he had pushed her. He maintained throughout his trial that he had attempted to bring Ms Walsh home because she was drunk, an argument had broken out and that the last sighting he had of her was as she walked away from him.

Mr Jones was convicted on two key pieces of evidence: no alcohol was found in the young woman's bloodstream despite Mr Jones' assertion that she was drunk; and no text message was ever traced back to her boyfriend's mobile phone asking Ms Walsh to meet him at the pier. It was stated by the prosecution at the time that Joe Jones was annoyed with Ms Walsh as she had rejected his advances in favour of his friend, Mr Dessie O'Sullivan. Joe Jones' father stated that he had witnessed Ms Walsh slapping his son during a row at his father-in-law's house.

It has since emerged, through a diary kept by the victim, that Megan Walsh suffered a head injury at her place of work earlier that day. An altercation had broken out when she had found her boyfriend and co-worker, Mr O'Sullivan, in the office with his ex girlfriend Denise Owens, now Denise McCabe. According to both witnesses, and the diary, when Ms Walsh attempted to leave, she tripped over a phone cable and hit her head. She was unconscious, according to Mrs McCabe, for 'about ten minutes'. When she recovered consciousness, 'she seemed fine, if a bit confused' and left without wanting to see a doctor. Mrs McCabe had later acquired Ms Walsh's mobile number from her boyfriend's phone and text messaged her to see if she was all right. Mrs McCabe never told her then boyfriend that she had sent a text to Ms Walsh as she feared he'd 'go mad'. Mrs McCabe did not meet Ms Walsh on the night in question as she had seen her chatting to Mr Jones at the pier and assumed that she was fine. She was 'horrified' to find out that her texts had been confused by Megan Walsh as coming from her former boyfriend. 'At the time, I thought Joe was just lying to stitch Dessie up. He had liked Megan too and was angry at Dessie for stealing her.'

It was also established that Ms Walsh's apparently drunken behaviour on Mr Jones' boat could be directly attributed to the head injury she sustained in the office. The court judged it most likely that Megan Walsh simply fell into the water of Rossclare harbour while slipping into unconsciousness as the injury to her head was severe. Mr O'Sullivan and Mrs McCabe are being charged with withholding evidence that might have helped Mr Jones at his former trial. They maintain that at the time they didn't believe Ms Walsh's fall was relevant to the murder and that, if they had mentioned it, it might have cast unnecessary suspicion on Mr O'Sullivan, whom Mr Jones seemed to want to implicate.

Mr O'Sullivan and his former girlfriend spent the night of the murder in a nightclub and had been ruled out of the inquiry at an early stage.

Outside the court, the two families shook hands and Joseph Jones said that while he regrets the time he spent in prison, he is now looking forward to getting on with his life.

'I've been given a chance to start again,' he said, 'and I'm going to grab it with both hands.'

Author's note

While I realise that fourteen years ago mobile phones and texting were not in common use, I have included them as part of the plot. This, I think, ensures that the book will not date as quickly.